NW

*Jane Marcus*

N          YS ON VIRGINIA WOOLF

A WOOLF: A Feminist Slant

THE YOUNG REBECCA: Writings of Rebecca West,
1911–1917

# VIRGINIA WOOLF AND BLOOMSBURY

*A Centenary Celebration*

*Edited by*

## Jane Marcus

MACMILLAN
PRESS

First published 1987

Published by
THE MACMILLAN PRESS LTD
Houndmills, Basingstoke, Hampshire RG21 2XS
and London
Companies and representatives
throughout the world

Printed in Hong Kong

British Library Cataloguing in Publication Data
Virginia Woolf and Bloomsbury: a centenary celebration.
1. Woolf, Virginia – Criticism and interpretation
I. Marcus, Jane
823'.912    PR6045.072Z/
ISBN 0–333–39397–X (hc)
ISBN 0–333–39398–8 (pbk)

*For Jason*

# Contents

# Acknowledgements

The editor and contributors are grateful to Quentin Bell for permission to quote from published and unpublished materials, to Nigel Nicolson and Joanne Trautmann, editors of Woolf's letters, and to Anne Olivier Bell, editor of her diaries.

This book began as a series of Virginia Woolf Centenary Lectures at the University of Texas in autumn 1982. I should like to thank the University of Texas, in particular Robert King, Dean of the College of Liberal Arts, for generous support of the lectures, the University Research Council for a grant for the preparation of the typescript of this book, and Susanne Fawcett for help in typing. The Women's Studies Program and the English Department also sponsored the lectures, as well as the Humanities Research Center, home of an enormously rich collection of Bloomsbury manuscripts, letters and papers. Ellen Dunlap and Sally Leach opened the resources of the Humanities Research Center to students and visiting scholars; Kurth Sprague and his British Studies Seminar were excellent hosts; my colleagues and students in the seminar contributed to the lively debate sparked by the lectures. Standish Meacham, Kay Avery, Elizabeth Cullingford, Alan Friedman, Beverly Stoeltje, and B. J. Fernea worked to make the visiting lecturers and their seminars comfortable and successful.

To Melissa Hield I owe the warmest and most sincere thanks, for it was entirely owing to her unflagging energy and cheerful and efficient work that the semester-long conference was so well organised and well received. And finally I should like to thank my husband and sons for their patient and humorous toleration of yet another year when Virginia Woolf was a daily figure in family life, an invisible presence, like a brilliant and absurd great aunt dominating the dinner table.

The essays by Noel Annan, Nigel Nicolson, Michael Holroyd, Louise DeSalvo, Carol MacKay and Angela Ingram were written for and delivered at the University of Texas Virginia Woolf Centenary Celebration; Sandra Shattuck was a student in that seminar. Sandra Gilbert's and Catherine Smith's papers were presented at the Virginia Woolf Society Seminar at the Modern Language Association meeting in Los Angeles in December 1982. Mine was read at the Brown University Symposium on Virginia Woolf and Sexual Difference, organised by Elizabeth Weed and Roger Henkle. Kathleen Dobie's paper was written for Louise DeSalvo in an undergraduate class at Hunter College. Laura Moss Gottlieb's paper was read at the Woolf sessions organised by Beth Riegel Daugherty at the National Women's Studies Meeting in Columbus, Ohio, in June 1983. Elizabeth Abel's essay is part of her forthcoming book on Woolf and Freud, and Judith Johnston's will also appear in her book on women writers and fascism.

It is perhaps not impertinent to suggest that Virginia Woolf would have enjoyed the solemn and hilarious, the scholarly and polemical, the frivolous and forthright tone of this posthumous birthday party, and that it was celebrated so well in Austin, Texas, not in Cambridge or London. There are moments she would have relished – the dismantling of the security system of the Humanities Research Center to smuggle out a copy of *Orlando* in which Nigel Nicolson inscribed his notes regarding obscure references to Vita Sackville-West, her family and dogs, and the unwavering smile with which he took a student's paperback copy, stamped USED in large yellow letters, to annotate as a memento of the occasion.

The moment I treasure most was the appearance at one seminar of an angular, stern and very beautiful old woman in a picture hat, looking in profile exactly like the woman whose work we were celebrating. She sat very still and listened intently, vanishing completely at the end of the talk. She looked like a poet and a 'bag lady', like Sara Pargiter in *The Years*, ferocious, eccentric, wickedly judgemental and capable of shameless glee. It is that elusive creature whose birth we celebrate in this volume, on a January day in 1882 when she burst from the amniotic bliss of her mother's womb. Like no other writer before her, Virginia Woolf captured that universal desire to merge with mother in *To the Lighthouse*. Yet there was no more unremitting critic of the patriarchal family. Family life and friendship as she described them and lived them hardly exist any longer. In remembering Virginia Woolf, we remember the social institutions which she attacked and whose demise she celebrated, not the least of which was the university. The University of Texas cannot claim to be the new, free university Woolf demanded in *Three Guineas*. But it is, in a sense, far more democratic than the universities which shadowed her life, and I like to think she would have enjoyed being fêted in such an atmosphere.

*Austin, Texas*                                                    *Jane Marcus*

# Source Abbreviations

The following abbreviations are used throughout in references.

## WRITINGS OF VIRGINIA WOOLF

Almost all the works and collections listed below are published by the Hogarth Press in London and by Harcourt Brace Jovanovich (predecessors Harcourt, Brace and Co., Harcourt, Brace and World) in New York. Unless otherwise stated, the editions used by the contributors are published by Harcourt Brace, dates as indicated.

| | |
|---|---|
| *AROO* | *A Room of One's Own* (1929) |
| *BA* | *Between the Acts* (1941) |
| *BA*, 1969 | *Between the Acts*, Harvest paperback (1969) |
| *BP* | *Books and Portraits*, ed. Mary Lyon (London: Hogarth Press, 1977) |
| *CDB* | *'The Captain's Death Bed' and Other Essays* (1950) |
| *CE* | *Collected Essays*, ed. Leonard Woolf (1967) |
| *D* | *The Diary of Virginia Woolf* |
| | I: *1915–1919*, ed. Anne Oliver Bell, intro. Quentin Bell (1977) |
| | II: *1920–1924*, ed. Anne Oliver Bell and Andrew McNeillie (1978) |
| | III: *1925–1930*, ed. Bell and McNeillie (1980) |
| | IV: *1931–1935*, ed. Bell and McNeillie (1982) |
| *DM* | *'The Death of the Moth' and Other Essays* (1942) |
| *JR* | *Jacob's Room* (1922) |
| *L* | *The Letters of Virginia Woolf*, ed. Nigel Nicolson and Joanne Trautmann |
| | I: *1888–1912* (1975) |
| | II: *1912–1922* (1976) |
| | III: *1923–1928* (1977) |
| | IV: *1929–1931* (1978) |

|      |                                                                                 |
| ---- | ------------------------------------------------------------------------------- |
|      | V: *1932–1935* (1979)                                                            |
|      | VI: *1936–1941* (1980)                                                           |
| M    | *'Melymbrosia': Early Version of 'The Voyage Out'*, ed. Louise A. DeSalvo (New York: New York Public Library, 1982) |
| MB   | *Moments of Being: Unpublished Autobiographical Writings*, ed. Jeanne Schulkind (Brighton: Sussex University Press, 1976) |
| MD   | *Mrs Dalloway* (1925)                                                            |
| ND   | *Night and Day* (1919)                                                           |
| O    | *Orlando* (1928)                                                                 |
| P    | *'The Pargiters': The Novel–Essay Portion of 'The Years'*, ed. Mitchell A. Leaska (1977) |
| PH   | *'Pointz Hall': The Earlier and Later Typescripts of 'Between the Acts'*, ed. Mitchell A. Leaska (New York: University Publications, 1983) |
| RF   | *Roger Fry: A Biography* (1940)                                                  |
| TG   | *Three Guineas* (1938)                                                           |
| TL   | *To the Lighthouse* (1927)                                                       |
| VO   | *The Voyage Out* (1915)                                                          |
| W    | *The Waves* (1931)                                                               |
| WD   | *A Writer's Diary*, ed. Leonard Woolf (London: Hogarth Press, 1953)             |
| Y    | *The Years* (1937)                                                               |

## JOURNALS

|       |                                                |
| ----- | ---------------------------------------------- |
| BNYPL | *Bulletin of the New York Public Library*      |
| PMLA  | *Publications of the Modern Language Association* |
| TLS   | *The Times Literary Supplement*                |

## MANUSCRIPT SOURCES

|      |                                                                                 |
| ---- | ------------------------------------------------------------------------------- |
| Berg | Henry W. and Albert A. Berg Collection, New York Public Library, Astor, Lennox and Tilden Foundations |
| BL   | British Library                                                                 |
| CUL  | Cambridge University Library                                                    |

# Notes on the Contributors

**Elizabeth Abel,** Assistant Professor of English at the University of California at Berkeley, edited *The Voyage In* and *Writing and Sexual Difference*. She is completing a book on Woolf and Freud.

**Noel Annan** (Lord Annan), Victorian scholar and public administrator, has just published a revised and updated version of his classic intellectual biography of Leslie Stephen.

**John W. Bicknell,** Emeritus Professor of English at Drew University, is preparing an edition of the letters of Leslie Stephen to his wife and others.

**Louise A. DeSalvo,** Associate Professor at Hunter College, is the author of *Virginia Woolf's First Voyage* and editor of *Melymbrosia, Between Women* and *Vita Sackville West's Letters to Virginia Woolf*, as well as the author of numerous essays. She has just finished a book on Hawthorne.

**Kathleen Dobie** was a student at Hunter College in New York when this essay was written. She is now a reporter for the *Brooklyn Phoenix*.

**Sandra M. Gilbert,** Professor of English at Princeton University, is co-editor with Susan Gubar of the *Norton Anthology of Women's Literature*. Together they wrote the classic of feminist criticism, *The Madwoman in the Attic*, and they are completing a sequel. Professor Gilbert is also a poet. Her latest volume is called *Emily's Bread*.

**Laura Moss Gottlieb** is the co-editor of *Virginia Woolf Centennial Essays* and publishes an annual bibliography of Woolf criticism in *Virginia Woolf Miscellany*.

**Michael Holroyd** is the biographer of Lytton Strachey and Augustus John, and is writing the authorised biography of Bernard Shaw.

**Angela Ingram,** Assistant Professor of English at Southwest Texas State University, has recently published *In the Posture of a Whore: Changing Attitudes to 'Bad' Women in Elizabethan and Jacobean Drama.* Her current research is on censorship and women's writing in the 1920s.

**Judith L. Johnston,** who has taught at Columbia University, is an independent scholar working on a book called *Years that Ask Questions: Women Novelists' Responses to Fascism, 1936–1946.*

**Carol Hanbery MacKay,** Associate Professor of English at the University of Texas, has written articles on Dickens, Carlyle, Thackeray and Hawthorne. She has completed a study of soliloquy in nineteenth-century fiction and is preparing a critical introduction to Anne Thackeray Ritchie's prefaces to her father's canon.

**Jane Marcus,** Associate Professor of English at the University of Texas, has edited two volumes of Woolf criticism, and *The Young Rebecca West. Virginia Woolf and the Languages of Patriarchy* and *Art and Anger* were recently published.

**Nigel Nicolson** edited his father's papers as well as the six volumes of Virginia Woolf's *Letters* and is the author of *Portrait of a Marriage* as well as other books.

**Sandra D. Shattuck** is a graduate student at the University of Texas, currently in Germany on a Fulbright research grant.

**Catherine F. Smith,** Associate Professor of English and Director of the Writing Program at Bucknell University, is the author of essays on the English mystic Jane Lead and Virginia Woolf. She is currently working on a book on the mystical tradition in women's writing.

# Introduction:
# Umbrellas and Bluebonnets

JANE MARCUS

I used to think that the notion that there was a Virginia Woolf Cult was a fabrication of conservative critics to discredit both Virginia Woolf and her readers. But, shortly before its demise as the arbiter of American middlebrow taste, the *Saturday Review* published a coy article on the subject, attributing the revival of Woolf's reputation to her own feminism and the interest of feminist critics. There is obviously some truth to this, as *A Room of One's Own* is required reading in many Women's Studies courses. On what authority I do not know, the writer in the *Saturday Review* named me as the leader of the Woolf Cult, a fact I learned with some dismay as a pile of letters (mostly from women in small Southern American towns) arrived, asking to join. No one would use the word 'cult' to describe the drinking of green beer on Bloomsday or the myriad readings, conferences, plays, speeches and newspaper articles which celebrated the Joyce centenary. Yet Joyce fans do seem to be more prone to ritual observance and religious enthusiasm than Woolf fans are. (I do remember at a conference years ago an all-night collective reading of *The Waves*, but it is the only incident which could even vaguely confer cult status on readers of Virginia Woolf.) Shortly afterwards, Peter Watson quoted the *Saturday Review* article for readers of the London *Times*, mocking the vulgarity of American readers and critics for the tastelessness of an interest in Virginia Woolf which he compared to the Marilyn Monroe following – all based on madness, suicide, odd marriages and feminism. Again I was singled out, for the folly of responding to Quentin Bell's character-isation of American feminists as 'lupine critics' by declaring that we ought to wear the label proudly as long as we can't escape it. I once compared us to a tall, hardy variety of lupine which flourishes in the Wind Rivers in Wyoming. But now that I am in Texas, there is a natural parallel in the state flower, a lupine called

1

Bluebonnet, native to Texas and planted by Lady Bird Johnson in abundance along the highways.

As Nigel Nicolson explains in his essay (Ch. 1), Bernard Levin's 'Cry, Woolf, but I Won't Be Listening' (*The Times*, 8 May 1980) is a fair example of the attitude of some British readers toward Virginia Woolf and Bloomsbury. In Noel Annan's essay on Bloomsbury and the Leavises (Ch. 2), one may find an answer to their contempt for Woolf in that there appears to be no professor of literature at a major university untainted by the Leavis hatred of all they thought she stood for, who could come to her defence or organise a conference in her honour. Nigel Nicolson is correct in pointing out that there were no British celebrations on Woolf's centenary except, I have since been informed, a conference organised by a librarian at King's College, Cambridge. Even *The Times Literary Supplement*, a journal for which she faithfully wrote for a lifetime, made no mention of the event, though Joyce was duly fêted both in the universities and in the journals (see *TLS*, 25 Feb 1982).

But it is not only the Leavises' poisonous pronouncements which produce British diffidence and distaste. In an interview in the *Guardian* (21 Mar 1982) Quentin and Olivier Bell were quoted as saying, 'she wasn't a feminist and she wasn't political'. They 'kept their heads down', hoping that Woolf's centenary would not be celebrated, were 'relieved' that it was not celebrated in her mother country and sorry that Americans see her as Joan of Arc. 'The shunning of the anniversary in Britain has not caused pain to the Bells.' In the next column Frank Tuohy reviewed volume V of the diary 'of a notoriously touchy lady', admitting that he found Woolf's novels 'nearly unreadable'. He said that her images are 'meaningless as a hiccup', complaining of 'woozy pretentiousness' in her fiction. Bernard Levin went even further and declared that he would never read anything about Woolf or Bloomsbury again as long as he lives. He boasted that he hadn't read her fiction ('in my opinion all Virginia Woolf's novels are unreadable, and none of them would be worth reading even if they weren't').

In Mr Levin's opinion, all of Bloomsbury, with the exception of Forster, deserves no more than a footnote. But that footnote has spawned:

> forty shelvesful of books, ranging from three . . . volume studies of her use of the semi-colon to the memoirs of her chiropodist,

from massive biographies of the manager of the shop where she used to get her coffee (by post) to examinations of the parallels between her work and that of Damon Runyon, from books designed to prove that the early essays attributed to her were in fact written by George the Fifth to books designed to disprove the theory that Radclyffe Hall was one of her pseudonyms. (It was as a matter of fact.)

Levin claimed that he was being persecuted by Bloomsbury and said that he would shortly turn around and hit it with his umbrella. One may see this book as a loaded umbrella with which to do battle with the likes of Mr Levin, though I sincerely regret that we have no essay on Woolf's use of the comma. My hope is that it is now being written in the wilds of North Dakota, and will turn up in the next Bloomsbury book. What I find most amusing about Levin's essay is his complete ignorance of the fact that his anti-academic stance of 'common reader' against the professors of literature, his comic intimacy with his reader, even his umbrella-brandishing, derive directly from Virginia Woolf's own review-ing-style! It was she who gave him the language and form for his essay. It was, after all, Virginia Woolf who wrote, 'It is always well to re-read the classics. It is always wholesome to make sure that they still earn their pedestals and do not merely cast their shadows over heads bent superstitiously from custom' (*TLS*, 7 Feb 1918). I envy Mr Levin his first reading of *To the Lighthouse* on some clear day when the clouds of the Leavises' spirits have stopped raining on the literature departments of British universities.

Lest the reader have the impression that umbrella bashing is exclusively a British sport, let me call attention to a syndicated column by the conservative American George F. Will which appeared on 9 January 1983. He attacked the Equal Rights Amendment, using *A Room of One's Own* as his club (or umbrella), misreading a great democratic document as a 'flight of chilling whimsy', arguing for the education of only an intellectual elite of women. This is a direct reversal of the message of the text. Where did Mr Will get the notion that Virginia Woolf was an elitist? Not, I assure you, from any writings of hers, but from those books about Bloomsbury which maintain this myth. Whose interest, we may ask, does the maintenance of this myth serve?

It is the purpose of this book to show the wealth and diversity of Woolf criticism on both sides of the Atlantic. Her novels and essays appeal to common and to uncommon readers, to students, non-professionals, academics, historians. Our British contributors, Lord Annan, Michael Holroyd and Nigel Nicolson, place her firmly in the historical context of her culture. The American contributors have read her texts closely and bring a fresh vision and the most contemporary critical approaches to her novels. The views of British men of letters and American textual scholars, students and distinguished critics contribute to this composite of old and new attitudes toward Virginia Woolf which suggest directions in which postcentenary criticism of Woolf may go.

In America the celebrants of Woolf's centenary have been as enthusiastic as Mrs Dalloway about their parties. In Austin, Morgantown, Minneapolis, New Brunswick and Providence (and many other places besides), candles were lit and papers were read; Dominick Argento's song cycle was played, and the songs of Dame Ethel Smyth were sung. *Freshwater* was acted in a particularly amusing and deliberately amateur production at the West Virginia Centennial Conference, organised with great panache and skill by Elaine Ginsberg. With her student Laura Moss Gottlieb (who delivered a brilliant paper while in an advanced stage of pregnancy), she has edited the proceedings of this conference (Troy, NY: Whitston Press, 1983), with papers by Rosenbaum, Marcus, Stemerick, Lyon, Haring-Smith, Libertin, Faris, Herman, Sypher, Klein, Haller, Gottlieb, Daugherty and Lewis, and an introduction by Joanne Trautmann. As we met in Morgantown in full view of the coal mines, in rooms encircling an enormous basketball coliseum, listening to papers punctuated by the occasional plop, plop of a basketball being dribbled round the arena, we celebrated Woolf in a style one thinks she would have liked. Tillie Olsen, as the keynote speaker, eloquently extended the arguments of *Three Guineas* to the present danger of nuclear war, remarking on Woolf's pacifism, feminism and socialism and their relevance today. In honour of Woolf's common reader, Olsen's talk was televised and she spoke to common readers in public libraries throughout the state. Virginia Woolf's novels are not thought unreadable in West Virginia. One morning our breakfast was served by the talented student contralto who had sung Ethel Smyth's songs the night before. Joanne Trautmann brought a message from Quentin Bell and Nigel Nicolson suggesting that American feminist critics ought to be more respectful to the British guardians of Woolf's reputation, and the feminist critics listened. This book might be seen as a truce between the two sides.

At the College of St Catherine in Minneapolis, Susan Bowers organised 'Virginia Woolf and the Life of a Woman: A Conference for Common Readers and Scholars', which emphasised Woolf's relevance to ordinary women. I was delighted by the enthusiastic response of nuns to my notion of 'the erotics of chastity' in my talk on the influence of her Quaker aunt Caroline Stephen. Highlights were Beth Daugherty's paper on *To the Lighthouse*, 'Killing Reverence'; Evelyn Haller's discussion of E. M. Forster's revision of Egyptian history to exclude the goddess Isis, who is a central figure in Woolf's work; and a rabble-rousing political speech by writer Carol Bly, 'Virginia Woolf and Public Morals', a good match to Tillie Olsen's speech at West Virginia.

Our University of Texas Woolf Centenary brought widely diverse points of view to an eager audience. Nigel Nicolson's revelation of the fallibility of memory is important, as is his analysis of Bloomsbury friendships (Ch. 1). Noel Annan then takes up a subject dear to my heart, the Leavises' opposition to Bloomsbury, from the point of view of an intellectual historian (Ch. 2). As the author of a well-known study of Leslie Stephen and Victorian thought newly re-issued and a ground-breaking paper on the 'intellectual aristocracy' in England, Lord Annan has contributed brilliantly to our understanding of the period and its institutions. Michael Holroyd compares Bloomsbury and the Fabians (Ch. 3). His famous biography of Lytton Strachey and years of work on his present project, a biography of Shaw, eminently suited him for this project.

John Bicknell, who has just finished editing *Dearest Julia*, Leslie Stephen's letters to Virginia Woolf's mother, comes to Stephen's defence in 'Mr Ramsay Was Young Once' (Ch. 4). My colleague Carol MacKay, who is working on a larger project on Anne Thackeray Ritchie, traces her influence on Woolf in 'The Thackeray Connection' (Ch. 5). In 'As "Miss Jan Says"' (Ch. 6) Louise DeSalvo, editor of *Melymbrosia* and author of *Virginia Woolf's First Voyage*, shares her work on Woolf's unpublished early diaries, traces her enormous appetite for reading and her invention of another self, whom she called 'Miss Jan' to bear the burden of her adolescent anxiety. Angela Ingram dissects Woolf's obsession with King's College, Cambridge, in a paper (Ch. 7) which seems to be a continuation of Woolf's own paper 'Professions for Women'.

In ' "Taking the Bull by the Udders' " (Ch. 8), I am concerned with the way Woolf established herself as 'her sister's voice', and with the narrative strategy of *A Room of One's Own*. Elizabeth Abel's ' "Cam the Wicked' " (Ch. 9) is a close reading of part of *To the Lighthouse* from a feminist psychoanalytical perspective. Kathleen Dobie's paper on *Jacob's Room* (Ch. 10), an analysis of the treatment of class and sex in the novel, was written for a class with Louise DeSalvo at Hunter College. Sandra Gilbert, the author, with Susan Gubar, of the brilliant and controversial study of Victorian women writers *The Madwoman in the Attic*, contributes a study of the 'linguistic fantasies' of Woolf and Joyce (Ch. 11). She and her co-author are at work on a study of twentieth-century women writers.

Catherine F. Smith sees *Three Guineas* as Woolf's prophecy, in the tradition of Jane Lead and the early English women mystics (Ch. 12). Laura Moss Gottlieb compares *Three Guineas* to Leonard Woolf's anti-war book, much to Leonard's disadvantage, in 'The War between the Woolfs' (Ch. 13). Judith L. Johnston reads *Between the Acts* as a 'revisioning of cultural history' and compares the novel to other women's anti-fascist works (Ch. 14), while Sandra Shattuck's essay (Ch. 15) demonstrates the essential influence of Jane Harrison's work on ritual and festival in *Between the Acts*.

Here are fifteen birthday presents for Virginia Woolf. They come in all sizes and shapes, some personal, some political, some bunches of bluebonnets, some umbrellas; the point of all of them is to bring new readers to Virginia Woolf's writing and to suggest to those who find her 'unreadable' the joy and intellectual excitement we have found in her work.

She had her own say about centenaries in an essay on Christina Rossetti written in Rossetti's voice:

> Yes (she seems to say), I am a poet. You who pretend to know my centenary are no better than the idle prophet at Mrs Tabb's tea-party. Here you are rambling among unimportant trifles, rattling my writing-table drawers, making fun of the Mummies and Maria and my love affairs when all I care for you to know is here. Behold this green volume. It is a copy of my collected works. It costs four shillings and sixpence. Read that.

Our excuse for rattling Woolf's writing-table drawers, is that by doing this we may bring more readers to her collected works.

# 1 Bloomsbury: the Myth and the Reality

NIGEL NICOLSON

My first visit to your university causes me both pleasure and distress – pleasure because I have known of it almost since childhood and delighted in the unique way in which you identify yourselves geographically, the words 'at Austin' dangling like a label from an elegant piece of luggage; and distress because it seems to me sad that I should need to come to Texas in order to celebrate the centenary of the birth of Virginia Woolf, since in my own country, which was also hers, there has been no comparable celebration. Last January the memory of her was not just overshadowed, but virtually obliterated, by the memory of James Joyce, who was born only a week later. There were no memorial articles about Virginia in our literary journals as there were in yours, no broadcasts, no gatherings of the faithful outside the many rooms which she could call her own, no society named in her honour as you have, no equivalent to your MLA sessions on the Bloomsbury writers or the symposium you held this summer in West Virginia. In fact, as far as I observed, there was only one reference to her in the British press, and that was a fiendish attack on Bloomsbury in *The Times*, not, as you might imagine, for their opinions and influence, their books or their paintings, but because, in the author's view, Bloomsbury consisted in a set of crashing bores.

This article was not written by some hack temporarily short of copy. It was by Bernard Levin, the most respected, humane and witty of our journalists, a man devoted to literature, music, friendship, art, good living and the charms of a metropolitan society – all things in which Bloomsbury itself delighted. But here he was, swearing a public oath that never, never would he read another line written by or about them, nor subject even his basest enemy to so unpleasant an ordeal. Nobody except myself protested, and my letter was rejected by *The Times*. I argued that, if

7

I had written an article to expose Shakespeare as a bore, or Wagner as a bore, there would have been an outcry, not least from Levin. But everyone was as delighted by his exposure of Bloomsbury as was the crowd when the child remarked that the Emperor was stark naked. Bloomsbury is regarded in England as fair game for abuse. It can be called boring with impunity, although of all the epithets of disapproval which might be applied to it, that is the least appropriate. Why, I wondered, should this be so?

I have a nasty feeling that we have here an example of the most unattractive of our national characteristics, the dislike of the intellectual. We are mentally a lazy people. If Levin says that we needn't read *The Waves* because it is incomprehensible and dull, and that he has no intention of trying to read it himself (which gives away the fact that he has no basis for his judgement), we heave a sigh of gratitude and relief, as if we were told by a bishop that as non-believers we needn't go to church. If, further, Bloomsbury can be stigmatised as having got it all wrong, whatever 'it' may be, an aesthetic theory, God, sex or the country's economy, we British will hug ourselves with joy, just as we did some twenty-five years ago when the skull of Piltdown Man, reputedly the oldest inhabitant of our islands, was exposed as the skull of a contemporary ape painted brown. The whole nation hooted with delight, as if we had collectively scored off not only the professors of anthropology but the entire educational establishment. It is much the same with Bloomsbury. Bloomsbury, as the saying goes, was too clever by half, by which we mean that they lacked common sense, were unlovable, too pleased with themselves and despised people like us. They were in fact snobs and, what was far worse in British eyes, intellectual snobs. Those of us who tried to correct this widespread but erroneous doctrine only succeeded in propagating it further. The more information we supplied, the deeper the hostility we aroused. All those letters, diaries, memoirs and biographies of the Bloomsbury Group and their descendants, all those exhibitions to be visited, houses to be saved, auctions to bid at, lectures to attend, made too great a demand upon the public's patience and appetite for culture. It was like an avalanche of unsolicited mail. People grew to hate the source of all this propaganda, and Bloomsbury-hating became a national sport. Of course, indirectly it was a tribute to them. The degree of hatred a person arouses is a measure of his influence, and

I think it remarkable that so small a group of men and women who flourished in the early part of this century, and who are now almost without exception dead, should today cause such annoyance to millions of their countrymen who scarcely know who they were. Ask the average Briton what he knows about Virginia Woolf, and he will give you Albee. I truly believe that, if T. S. Eliot had been more closely associated with the group, he would not have become the cult symbol which he now is. But of course Eliot had little to do with Bloomsbury, and he was an American, which excuses much, even the fact that he was a supremely gifted poet.

So I come to the United States to find kindred spirits who believe with me that Bloomsbury did contribute something of which we are all beneficiaries, and that they were exciting people well worth studying today. Far more attention is given to Bloomsbury in your universities than in ours. At Cambridge, until a couple of years ago, Virginia Woolf was virtually ignored by the English Literature school. At Oxford it is a little better: she is slowly escaping the stigma of second-rateness which the Leavises managed to attach to her for two generations, but she is regarded there more as a theorist and practitioner of the novel than as a central figure in Bloomsbury or a standard-bearer for the feminist movement. But even at Oxford there is nothing faintly comparable to the interest which she arouses in America. There is much more serious work done on her here, more courses, more enthusiasm, but almost too much veneration, I suggest, for Virginia Woolf was only one member of the group, and she should not be allowed to eclipse others who are equally important in the history of ideas – Lytton Strachey, for example, Roger Fry, Vanessa Bell and Leonard Woolf.

The interest in America, it seems to me, operates on three levels.

There is first the scholarly interest, with which I have complete sympathy, the joy of finding unpublished material, the academic sparring, with footnotes as the favoured weapon, the pleasure of turning a multi-faceted glass ball this way and that in order to catch and distribute the light from a slightly new direction, and the feeling that Bloomsbury is still only two-thirds discovered, like an archaeological site in the fourth year of excavation, when its shape and outline history are known, but the potsherds and tesserae seem inexhaustible and the interpretations tantalisingly open to new conjectures. Bloomsbury, like the Old Testament, is

exceptionally fertile ground for commentary and expertise, and
the fun is that, unlike an archaeological site, each new generation
can start all over again.

At the second level of interest is the relevance of Bloomsbury to
questions which still concern us today – pacifism, feminism,
socialism. While for you Bloomsbury bulks large in the development of these ideas, it is not the same in Britain. We look for our
pioneers to the Fabians, the Webbs, Wells, Shaw, Marie Stopes,
Ethel Smyth, Millicent Fawcett, Mrs Pankhurst, contemporaries
of Bloomsbury but not by any conceivable definition part of
Bloomsbury. I shall have more to say later about their political
attitudes. For the moment, I simply call attention to the danger
that you may be overestimating, and we underestimating, the
contribution which Bloomsbury made to social and political
change. You may inadvertently be moulding these characters into
your preconceived notions of them, and put into their mouths
things that you wish they had said or meant, but which they didn't
actually say or mean, while we may be dismissing the important
things that they did say as plagiarisms or platitudes. American
and British scholarship could grow apart, the British resenting
that 'our' Bloomsbury has been collared by America, that 'our'
Virginia has become your Woolf (for it often happens that what
one least cherishes one is most reluctant to give away), and
America resenting that we are diminishing her, or at least
honouring her for the wrong reasons, fixing her like a fly-in-amber
as something curious, or labelling her as mad, bad and dangerous
to know. At the moment there is some trans-Atlantic suspicion of
each other's motives, to which Joanne Trautmann drew attention
at your West Virginia consortium. She hoped, as I do, that this
unreal controversy will soon settle down to a mid-Atlantic
position on which we can all agree. Neither of our nations should
try to force Bloomsbury into straitjackets of our own design. The
British should not regard it as a historical incident which has little
relevance to us today; America must not regard it as a phenomenon of universal significance, much as we regard the small
group of men who centred around Jefferson at a time when you
were right and we were wrong. You may think it strange, but the
first Philadelphia Congress of 1774 means more to a pro-
Bloomsbury Englishman such as I than Bloomsbury will ever
mean.

At the third level, there's the fascination which these people still

exert on us as individuals and in their combined lives. The
discovery of their intimacies, the cat's cradle of their correspondence, the vicarious excitement which they generate in us, are
pleasures familiar to all of us who have done a course in
Bloomsbury. We are privileged to know more about them than
any one of them knew about the others. We can catch their
portraits not just in one mirror, but in a dozen mirrors set at
slightly different angles. For American students, there is an extra
perspective, for Bloomsbury men and women existed half a
century ago at their prime and 5000 miles from Austin, so that
they must appear to you like characters in a Trollope novel, half in
your world and half out, recognisably human, moving in predict-
able ways, yet as different as Canadians are from Texans, but not
so different as Texans are from, say, Japanese. Many of the social
devices which we take for granted today were first practised by
Bloomsbury, such as the techniques of starting or breaking off a
love affair, praising a friend's book which we have much disliked
without actually lying, or maintaining a triangular relationship
without pain to any of the three persons involved. Bloomsbury can
still teach us how to live, how to be happy, how to allocate our
time. I do not regard as foolish the study of them as social beings,
particularly as we are unlikely ever to know so much about an
equivalent group of friends. If there is a neo-Bloomsbury Group
now forming at Austin, as there may well be, I am prepared to bet
that you are not documenting its origins as thoroughly as
Bloomsbury did theirs.

Let us pause for a moment to examine the overflowing written
and oral testimony that Bloomsbury has left behind. Is it wholly
trustworthy? If we are tempted to make of them something which
they were not, were they not guilty of deceiving us? Did
Bloomsbury invent Bloomsbury? Just because they were so
articulate, they were not entirely truthful. I do not simply mean
that they told white lies, such as writing to Lady Ottoline Morrell
that you loved your weekend at Garsington and were furious at
being suddenly summoned home, when out of sheer boredom you
had sent the telegram to yourself from the village post office.
Bloomsbury were masters of the social fib. No, I mean that they
were so anxious to amuse each other that they exaggerated their
friends' failings and misfortunes, magnified their own small
adventures, and gilded every lily so richly that there was little of
the original flower left visible. One early distinction made

between the Cambridge and Gordon Square phases of Bloomsbury was that at Cambridge you never said anything witty unless
it was also profound, and in Bloomsbury you never said anything
profound unless it was also witty. They liked to dress up their
compliments as insults, their ideas as mental frolics, incidents as
major dramas. In their letters they would assume attitudes
familiar to their correspondents but puzzling or shocking to
outsiders, use words such as 'fascinating' or 'deplorable' with
certain values peculiar to the group. Within the Bloomsbury
language there were a variety of dialects. Thus the Virginia–
Leonard baby talk would have astonished Vanessa if she could
have read their letters to each other, and Carrington when talking
or writing to Lytton Strachey was quite a different person from
when she was with Gerald Brenan. We must be cautious before
accepting it all at face value.

Bloomsbury was not exactly malicious. They simply enjoyed
epistolatory repartee. Let us remember that there was much more
leisure then, even for active people. There were servants to cook
and clean for then, no television, not many cars or telephones,
little moral pressure to be constantly at work. So they had the time
and inclination to write letters. It was an accepted social art. The
postal services were then very rapid – a letter mailed in London
before 10 a.m. would reach its address in Sussex that very evening
– and so the letter was the perfect vehicle for the polished insult. It
could be replied to before the writer's lips had had time to uncurl.
It was like playing a game of chess by telegram. But we who are
privileged to read these letters fifty years later cannot, as the
recipient could, visualise the affectionate smile that accompanied
the written jibe, nor hear in the witticisms a remembered and
much loved tone of voice. What to them was kittenish teasing
seems to us feline bitchiness; what was expressed with apparent
indifference (like her family's joking references to Virginia's
terrible bouts of lunacy) was a cover-up for intense concern.
Bloomsbury seldom wrote intimately. If one of them wished to
express undying devotion, it was suggested, rarely declared. If a
letter of sympathy was required, the method was to refer to the
disaster in a sentence, and then bury it under the latest gossip, as
when visiting a friend in hospital you must toss the flowers on the
bed and then quickly tell stories of the world outside. On their
work, their writing or their art, they rarely corresponded. A
Bloomsbury probationer would soon learn that the one thing you

must never do to an artist is ask him what he is writing, painting, composing or acting now.

So the letters, fun to read, may give us quite a false impression of their society, which was fundamentally a serious one. They may lead us to think them frivolous and cold. Surely the diaries will rectify this? No, not entirely. For what is a diary – yours, mine, Virginia Woolf's – but a wineglass to exaggerate the sparkle of our pleasure and a sump for our despair? After keeping a diary for a few months, Byron gave it up, saying that he found that he lied to himself even more than he did to other people. Although we may assert that we write our diaries for no other eye than our own in old age, surely we would not impose this daily task upon ourselves unless we had half an eye cocked upon posterity, and we don't wish posterity to think as ill of us as we periodically think of ourselves. So we write, 'The Secretary of State was amused when I told him . . .,' remembering all too vividly how the Secretary was glancing over our shoulder in search of more congenial company. Bloomsbury was quite capable of such self-deceit. We have to guess which of two versions of a conversation or incident is more likely to be true, from our knowledge of the diarists' characters, but it is a chancy business when you are dealing with such chancy people.

Even more misleading are the essays written for Bloomsbury's Memoir Club. Never has there been such self-satisfaction posing as self-criticism. I do not believe that any such club would be conceivable today. I ask you to imagine that your present special group of friends will reunite monthly for the next forty years to read to each other recollections of your time at this university, and that your children, when even they are middle-aged, will still enjoy listening to their dotard parents rambling on about the 1980s, and confessing, indeed wallowing in, the indiscretions of their youth. You wouldn't do it. But Bloomsbury did. That was how the group was kept alive for so long, and one reason why we know so much about them. But the memorialists were not on oath. They were talking to intimates who would know what was exaggerated, invented or grossly unfair, and, although they were far more honest about themselves than most of us, there is a limit. As Mark Twain once remarked, when refusing to write his autobiography, 'Confession may be good for my soul, but it sure plays hell with my reputation.'

But, if we dismiss as suspect the letters, the diaries, the Memoir

Club, surely we can trust the memories of people who knew Bloomsbury at first hand? Certainly not. Beware the eye-witness, and even more the ear-witness. Because they have so often said that such-and-such happened, they are determined that it must have happened, and anyone who challenges their version is met with the crushing rejoinder, 'But I was there and you weren't even born.' We have all been guilty of making our favourite anecdotes a little brighter with each telling, and gradually establish as truth in our own minds what we once knew was an invention. For years I have told a story about a visit I paid to Monk's House in 1933 when I was sixteen (pause for some elementary mathematics). I was taken by my mother to have supper with Virginia and Leonard Woolf, and the only other people there were Maynard Keynes and his wife, the ballerina Lydia Lopokova. We sat around the fire, all except Virginia, who stood beside it, her elbow resting on the high mantelpiece in the classic pose which flatters the slender figure, and as she talked she stroked her long dark hair. The conversation rose and fell much like the flames of the logs burning in the grate. I forget its subject. But what I remember quite distinctly is that for the first time in my life I discovered in Virginia the distinction between a beautiful woman and a pretty woman, and in the easy association between the four other people something that was almost sublime. There came a moment when Virginia grew excited by the argument, began to speak a bit wildly and wave her hands about, and Leonard, observing her, rose from his chair, walked across to where she was standing, and put one hand upon her shoulder, at which, without a word of inquiry or protest, she immediately left the room with him and went upstairs. They returned some ten minutes later, and nobody asked what had happened, for all except myself knew exactly what had happened. Leonard had recognised the danger signals, and knew that, if Virginia were to continue talking so excitedly, she might trigger off another attack of madness. Later that evening, she took me up to her room, asked kindly after my life at school and gave me a copy of *Flush*, which she had just published.

Well, on occasions, if the audience looked innocent enough, I would add to this story enticing detail, but I firmly believed that, apart from these embellishments, it was a true story. Then I thought that I should check it before retelling it to you today. I went to Monk's House. The mantelpiece was far too high for any elbow to rest upon it. From a photograph, it is clear that Virginia at that period wore her hair closely shingled, and she could not have stroked it in the way that I'd described. Moreover, from her diary (which confirms that Vita brought her younger son with her), I learnt that the other people were not Keynes and Lopokova, but Duncan Grant and Vanessa Bell. At least it was true about *Flush*, for I still have the copy which she inscribed for me that evening.

I got many of the facts wrong, but I do think that I got the atmosphere right, and the relationship between these people. This is something which the eye-witness can supply and documentation cannot. We can know all there is to know about Abraham Lincoln except what it was like to be in the same room with him. That is why I can answer with some confidence those who maintain that Virginia and Leonard did not get on, that he undermined her confidence in herself, and was indirectly responsible for her suicide. Anybody who ever saw them together will know that this is a travesty of the truth. That single gesture, when he touched her on the shoulder, was almost biblical in its tenderness. The pleasure which they all took that evening in each other's company is something which I could never have invented. I had a sudden glimpse of a society that was different from any other.

But Bloomsbury would deny it. Bloomsbury itself was responsible for the legend that Bloomsbury had never existed, that it was the invention of its enemies. The two people who were most vocal in denying its reality, Virginia and Leonard, were the same two who gave the expression widest currency. Virginia would say to an outsider such as Ethel Smyth, 'Why do you call me Bloomsbury? I don't call you Chelsea,' but in writing on the very same day to her nephew Julian Bell in China she speaks of Bloomsbury as a shorthand expression which needs no explanation. It was not simply a convenient term to identify a group of friends who happened to live in the same part of London; to her, it denoted a special type of mind, shared characteristics, experiences and beliefs. How can we explain why they rejected publicly a term which they constantly employed privately? I think it was because they were annoyed, as we should all be, to be labelled as belonging to a single set, like a class at school, when they all had friends and careers outside that set, and often disagreed profoundly with those within it. Also, Bloomsbury was used by its enemies in a pejorative sense, and it took some time before Bloomsbury adopted it in self-defence, much as the Conservatives in my country began to call themselves Tories, a name originally used for Irish rogues and marauders and then applied to the Conservatives by their opponents. But Bloomsbury came into general use mainly among the Woolfs and Bells. Fry, Strachey, Forster and MacCarthy rarely employed it, probably thinking it silly and self-approving. And, who, in any case, composed the group? All had different versions. For instance, Roger Fry, writing to Vanessa in 1917, gave his list but omitted Leonard Woolf and E. M. Forster, whom others would consider to be among its stars.

I need not retell the familiar story of how it all started in 1904, when a group of young men who had been friends at Cambridge moved to London and formed, with the two sisters of one of them, Thoby Stephen, the habit of meeting every Thursday evening to discuss art, literature and philosophy. In retrospect, this early period of Bloomsbury seemed its heyday, when its members shook off the habits and prejudices of their parents, and life was just one long festival of youth. The fact that the two young women, Vanessa and Virginia Stephen, were more beautiful than any girl has a right to be, and the young men plainer than any youth has the right to be, didn't matter. They were all in love, man with girl, man with man, girl with man, girl with girl, and January was permanently June. Such, at least, was the legend. But when you come to read the contemporary record, it wasn't like that at all. In 1905, Virginia thus described for Violet Dickinson a Bloomsbury party in Cornwall:

> They sit silent, absolutely silent, all the time; occasionally they escape to a corner and chuckle over a Latin joke. Perhaps they are falling in love with Nessa. Who knows? It would be a silent and very learned process. However, I don't think they are robust enough to feel very much. Oh women are my line, not these inanimate creatures.

And four years later, in 1909, she writes to Vanessa, again from Cornwall, about another disastrous holiday:

> Then there came Lytton, James Strachey and Frankie Birrell, Duncan Grant, Keynes, Norton, and Horace Cole [let me interpolate that this was probably the most scintillating group of young people you could assemble in one room at that time].

They sat around mostly silent, and I wished for any woman –
and you would have been a miracle. I talked to Frankie and
Keynes most of the time. It was desperate work, like climbing a
wall perpetually.

Of course, she was exaggerating. If parties are as awful as this, you
do not repeat them every week for years. They must have been
more convivial, particularly if Clive Bell was present, for so
infectious was his delight that it was impossible not to be happy in
his company, and as they grew older they all lost the gravity of
their student days. But it is true that at the start the women were
stronger characters than the men.

I can just remember what it was like, because once I crept into a
Bloomsbury party under my mother's skirts. The room was large,
smoky and warmed more by excitement than by any artificial
means. There were divans and carpets and gaudily painted walls,
like a seraglio, gramophone records on trays and books every-
where. There were people sitting on the floor at other people's feet
in no special order of precedence, and there was a lot of noise and
laughter, high-pitched and faintly neighing, which ceased suddenly on the arrival of new people such as we. It was extremely
alarming, not in the least like Monk's House. Vita Sackville-West
was not entirely accepted by Bloomsbury, but she was allowed in
as Virginia's friend, and we found a corner where we could sit
more or less unobserved. I was given a tomato sandwich. People
were jumping up all the time, reaching for a book, peering into a
picture, and there was an undercurrent of competitiveness, as if
everyone there had to justify their presence each time afresh. If
you were under fifteen, as I was, you were left alone. But, if you
were even marginally adult, you had to look after yourself, as in a
medieval mêlée. It has been recorded that on one such occasion
when Virginia told a particularly malicious and funny story, and
the laughter had died down, she turned to a girl of eighteen and
said, 'Now you tell us a story.'

Of course it wasn't kind. It wasn't intended to be. Bloomsbury
demanded that people should be able to catch the ball when it was
suddenly thrown in their direction, and if you missed you weren't
asked again, and probably didn't want to be.

In this way they acquired a not undeserved reputation for
exclusivity. They seemed to draw a circle around themselves.
They were not only alarming, but could be gratuitously offensive.

Stories began to circulate in Kensington and Chelsea, such as the reply of a Bloomsbury conscientious objector in the First World War to the question why he didn't want to fight with other young men in the defence of civilisation, 'Because I am the civilisation they are fighting to defend.' When an eminent composer introduced himself to Lytton Strachey with the words, 'I think we met once before, Mr Strachey, about four years ago', Strachey replied, 'A very good interval', and walked on. This attitude is not one which I should commend to you as the best way to make friends and influence people. Bloomsbury would defend itself by saying that honesty is always the best policy, that it did bores good to know that they were bores, and if you have high intellectual standards you should never compromise with philistines. They were equally plain-spoken about each other. If Forster thought *Night and Day* a bad book, he told Virginia so. If she thought Fry's latest portrait of Vanessa poorly painted, she said so, to his face. Let those who accuse Bloomsbury of being a mutual-admiration society look again at the evidence, which proves the opposite.

Nor were they especially immoral or unconventional. They were thought to be, but they accepted 90 per cent of the precepts which Lord Chesterfield had enunciated as virtues a century and a half before, such as sobriety, industry, truthfulness and tolerance. In public they would have passed not just as citizens, but as decent citizens. If in their private lives they were unfaithful to their spouses, their infidelities tended to be permanent. If some of their children were illegitimate, they waited till they were sixteen before they told them so. Virginia Woolf tolerated but couldn't conceal her distaste for the homosexual mannerisms of some of her male friends. And let us remember two other things about their society. First, they were professional people who in their different ways were trying to do the most difficult thing a person can attempt, to give an art a new form which will convince their contemporaries and remain a permanent influence upon their successors, and nearly all suceeded. They were ambitious, hard-working people. Secondly, Bloomsbury was a slowly weakening magnet in their lives. As its grip began to loosen, roughly at the outbreak of the First World War, their friendships and activities widened so rapidly that by the late 1920s it could almost be said that Bloomsbury only existed as an alumni club to which one would pay occasional sentimental visits. To take a rough but no unfair measure, in the year 1930 Virginia Woolf wrote 180 letters that have survived. There were twelve to her sister Vanessa, four to Clive Bell, one each to Forster, Desmond MacCarthy, Saxon Sydney-Turner and David Garnett, and none at all to Fry, Strachey or Duncan Grant. In contrast, she wrote during this year thirty-four letters to Vita and fifty-seven to Ethel Smyth, neither of whom was in any true sense 'Bloomsbury' and both of whom she was seeing the whole time. What does this prove? I think it proves that Bloomsbury was too busy to be constantly intercommunicative and that by this time they took their friendship for granted. For all their love of gossip, they remained surprisingly ignorant of what we can all now know, such as the amorous adventures of Forster, the financial troubles of the MacCarthys, the extraordinary relationship of Arthur Waley with a New Zealand girl, which lasted thirty-seven years and remained secret from nearly all his friends. Bloomsbury was jealous of its privacy. They might have taken as their theme the lines of Kahlil Gibran:

> Love one another, but make not a bond of love.
> Fill each other's cup but drink not from one cup.
> Let there be spaces in your togetherness.

If it can be said that a group exists, that it has an identity, surely it must hold certain ideas in common and wish to propagate them. Although I am convinced that Bloomsbury did exist, I find it very hard to define what those ideas were, beyond saying, in the loosest sense, that the members of the group were more liberated than their predecessors, expressed themselves more frankly, treated women as equals to men and had a general respect for intellectual excellence. But that does not amount to a doctrine. Michael Holroyd has pointed out that it is quite untrue that they shared a system of aesthetics or philosophy, and that those who claim they did, 'understand next to nothing of the isolated way in which a work of art is evolved'. Forster's novels owe nothing to Virginia's, Strachey's theory of civilisation little to Clive Bell's. Or take Leonard's thinking on international affairs, or Keynes's on economics: in no way could it be said that either was a Bloomsbury way of thinking. There was a little more community of taste in art and music, and in a negative way they were linked by their indifference to science and religion, as well as by their pacifism in the First World War.

Ah, you might say, but what about their socialism and their feminism? I reply that it would be a bold person who described Bloomsbury as socialist in any sense that we would mean today. In *Civilisation* Bell said that to be completely civilised a human being must be liberated from material cares, like the non-slave Greeks. Therefore, there must be servants and capital and freehold property. Bloomsbury's attitude to servants was that they were necessary and their status almost unalterable. If they resigned or complained, they were exercising their undoubted rights, but it was thought disloyal and a nuisance. Women spent more time scolding and soothing their servants than if they had done the household chores themselves, and they never seemed to resent the loss of privacy which living-in servants entailed. Nor was Bloomsbury really sympathetic to the working classes. With only a slight sense of guilt, they accepted and enjoyed the economic system as they had inherited it. Bloomsbury was quite well off, and a few of them, such as Keynes and the Woolfs, made a lot of money by their own efforts. They thought the class gap unbridgeable. Virginia made a few gallant efforts, as when she lectured at Morley College and organised at Hogarth House meetings of the Women's Co-operative Guild, but her innermost feeling about the working class was that they were curiously dull. She wrote to Margaret Llewelyn Davies in October 1930, 'What depresses me is that the workers seem to have taken on all the middle class respectabilities which we have faced and thrown out', and she gave examples, such as they were shocked by a woman smoking a pipe, or reading a detective novel, or admitting that she was fat though it was no fault of her own, or using the word 'impure'. When she voted Labour at an election, she did so without any deep commitment, for, although she approved in general of Labour's political aims, she disliked intensely the political process. She seems to have agreed with Henry Adams that 'politics is the systematic organization of hatred', that oratory is the meanest of the arts, that committees and conferences never achieve anything, and that a statesman was merely a dead politician. I cannot remember a single passage in her writings, public or private, where she expresses admiration for the skills of political persuasion, even on behalf of causes in which she believed, even with Leonard beside her as an example. I hesitate to restate an opinion which has already got me into trouble, but I think I must. Virginia Woolf held strong political views, but did not possess a political mind.

We can all agree that she felt deeply about the position of women. She was not the only person in Bloomsbury to do so, but she was the most articulate. If we look into the lives and letters of other Bloomsbury women, Vanessa, Molly MacCarthy, Mary Hutchinson, Carrington, the Strachey sisters, and the Frys, we miss the note of indignation and challenge that we find in *A Room of One's Own* and *Three Guineas*. Why should this be? It was partly because Virginia was so splendid a standard-bearer that she needed no lieutenants. And partly because Bloomsbury took the women's case as self-evident. All Bloomsbury men were in favour of votes for women, all were in favour of opening the universities and professions to them, and most were husbands or intimate friends of women who had seized their opportunities and made the most of them. Keynes and Leonard Woolf did not disagree with the feminist argument in *Three Guineas*, but they thought it unnecessarily strident, an accusation which Virginia herself brought against Ethel Smyth. Bloomsbury's true claim to a medal in the battle for women's rights lies not in their polemics, apart from those of Virginia herself, but in the way they treated women among themselves. People are people of different types, they thought, and two of the types are male and female, not except biologically a distinction of great importance. This was a rare assumption at the time.

But Virginia Woolf's championship of women did not extend very far down the social scale. She certainly wanted women of the cultured classes to become doctors, lawyers, teachers, writers, but she did not argue, as we would today, that mill girls should have the chance to become factory charge hands or secretaries directors of the firms in which they work. Nor did she make much protest that it was the lot of most women to remain at home and cook their husband's dinners. In fact, she believed that, if working women moved socially upwards, they might lose some of their robustness, humour, independence and pride, qualities which she praised in her Introduction to *Life as We Have Known It*. To expose them to what she calls there 'the contamination of wealth and comfort' might do them an actual disservice, or so she said sometimes. But it is what she did that counts more than what she said or wrote, the example she set, her affirmation that she was a match for men and proving it. She rejected absolutely Lear's praise for Cordelia: 'Her voice was ever soft, / Gentle and low, an excellent thing in women', and reacted against her own mother, who was no weakling but found it impossible, almost indecent, to dispute with men or enter a crowded room alone. The traditionally feminine virtues of patience and reticence have confined women's lives most terribly, and, if both men and women recognise that today, it is thanks to the example of such women as Virginia Woolf and, I should like to add, Jane Marcus.

This, then, is my answer to the question I implicitly posed in the title to this lecture. Bloomsbury was a reality. It did exist. It is identifiable with named individuals about whom we can now know a great deal. Separately they achieved much in different fields, and collectively they expressed an attitude to life of which each of us is unconsciously an inheritor. But do not let us exaggerate that inheritance. We must leave ourselves other moulds to break. The best of their legacies is their concept of friendship. Nothing – not age, nor success, nor rivalry in art or love, nor different careers and different friends, nor separation for long periods by war, travel or occupation – ever parted these people who had first come together as young men and women. How surprised they would be if they could know that a man would be lecturing about them in Austin, Texas, nearly eighty years later, but not I think, wholly displeased that he should emphasise, above all other achievements, their gift for friendship.

# 2 Bloomsbury and the Leavises

NOEL ANNAN

No one can make sense of the dispute between Bloomsbury and their bitter critics the Leavises if he does not recognise that Bloomsbury wrote in the service of the artistic revolution in whose shadow we all still live – of atonalist music; the painting of Picasso and Matisse; the post-Symbolist poets; and the experimental novel; perhaps, above all, a new scepticism about authority and tradition. English revolutionaries are tame cats compared with those on the continent of Europe, and nothing could have been less Wagnerian than the chamber music of Bloomsbury. But, however many light years Strachey was from being a revolutionary, the work which made its author and Bloomsbury first famous, was in fact a polemic. Strachey's *Eminent Victorians* is neither history nor biography. It is a polemic against the Victorian establishment and its culture – that culture which Bloomsbury believed had begot the terrible slaughter of the First World War. The essay on Gordon was an attack on imperialism and power politics. It was also an attack on Messianic Christianity, and, lest anyone think that more sophisticated versions of Christianity were not as dangerous, Strachey satirised Cardinal Manning, the worldly-wise, scheming prelate of the Church of Rome, and the – to him – ludicrous agonising over points of doctrine which edged him towards conversion to Catholicism. Next, he chose Dr Arnold as an arch-public-school headmaster, where the cult of compulsory games stultified boys' intellects, and where Arnold's recipe for building character produced boys with what E. M. Forster described as well-developed bodies, fairly developed minds and underdeveloped hearts. Finally, Strachey struck at the one great movement that had salved the conscience of Victorian England – he struck at humanitarianism. He did not deny that Florence Nightingale's work was magnificent. He simply removed the picture of the lady with the lamp, and drew in its place the portrait of a commanding, ruthless bird of prey destroying anybody, her friends or her foes, who stood in her path, and whose nature had been misunderstood even by her family. 'It was not a swan that they had hatched', he wrote, 'It was an eagle'.[1]

Respect for the integrity and happiness of other people was the first Bloomsbury commandment. Generals, headmasters, archbishops, even heroines, were corrupted by their determination to succeed in their profession. Worldly success was regarded by Bloomsbury as an evil. That typical Edwardian friend of Churchill, Freddy Birkenhead, the brilliant lawyer, politician, Lord Chancellor and drunkard, had advised schoolboys on speech days to seize life's 'glittering prizes'. Not Bloomsbury. Bloomsbury thought they were not prizes but poison; we ought to be guided in our relations with others by letting good sense and reason play upon problems as they arose. We should not judge others by an inflexible code of conduct such as Victorian religion imposed, still less should we take our values from the religion of worldly success. 'Human beings', wrote Strachey, 'are too important to be treated as mere symptoms of the past. They have a value which is independent of any temporal processes which is eternal, and must be felt for its own sake.'[2] And it was impossible to create informality, affection and intimacy, if, like the Victorians, you were always portentously weighing this person or that in the scales of judgement. That was why Bloomsbury rejected the great apostle and critic of Victorian culture, Matthew Arnold.

Arnold, you will of course remember, laid down three principles concerning culture. First, the state of the nation's culture lay in the hands of an intellectual elite whose duty was to train their sensibility through the act of criticism. Second, the function of the elite was to spread sweetness and light among the three classes in society: the aristocratic barbarians, the middle-class philistines, and the lower-class populace. Third, the elite could fulfil their duties only if they realised that the purpose of criticism was to discriminate and commit themselves in the culture war.

There was much in Arnold that Bloomsbury might have admired. Bloomsbury, like Arnold, enjoyed shocking their elders. Like Arnold, they were only too willing to see themselves as an elite. Like Arnold, they believed that sweetness and light should be spread as widely as possible. Keynes's brainchild the Arts Council, which in Britain disburses public money to opera, ballet and the theatre, was only one of a number of institutions and exhibitions and events which Bloomsbury had a hand in conceiving and which put Arnold's ideal into practice. But they rejected Arnold's theory of literary criticism.

They had special grounds for doing so. Arnold's own criteria of what made for fine literature were hopelessly inadequate for understanding the artists of Modernism, let alone for judging them. Even more crass were the judgements upon the new generation of writers and artists made by reviewers or the professors of literature at British universities. These critics made fools of themselves because they kept setting modern works of art against a rigid standard derived from works of art in the past whose intention was quite different. Criticism consisted, in their view, in seeing what was the essence of a work, what made the author tick, what distinguished it from other works and gave it singularity. Judgement entered in only so far as the critic might be expected to set the work in question against his own urbanely rationalist sensibility. If Bloomsbury can be said to have had a theory of criticism, it was deference to the artist, coupled with an amused appreciation of the infinite peculiarities of human behaviour which defied the attempts of moralists to tape it and square it and tie it neatly into bundles with bows and labels.

Of course, Bloomsbury did make judgements – very severe judgements – on human beings, on events, on art. But they delivered such judgements in a style that bore no relation to the Victorian style of pontification. The Bloomsbury style was to make assertions within a flow of apparently rational cool discourse and to make no attempt to justify them except by raising the eyebrows. The only way to dissent from a Bloomsbury judgement was to make a counter-assertion and raise your eyebrows even higher. You raised your eyebrows to indicate that a statement was incongruous when set beside the opinions that any enlightened man would hold. Judgement was an act of disdain.

It was not surprising that Bloomsbury held such a theory of criticism – if it can be so called. It sprang directly from the manifestos of the artistic revolution. The manifestos asserted loudly the importance of freedom from rules and conventions, from conservatories or salons or academies, and of outraging bourgeois taste and institutions. It sprang also from the rejection of the Victorian obsession with beauty – that beauty which cascaded like treacle over every object in the home and emerged in the shape of stucco moulding, buttons, beading, Berlin wool, lincrusta, papier mâché, buttresses, cherubs, scroll work and foliage.[3]

Finally, Bloomsbury rejected the idea popularised by Diderot and developed by Ruskin and Arnold that beauty is indissolubly connected with overt morality. In making this connection, Ruskin had seemed to them to imply that art arises not from delight in the visible world but from a kind of social anxiety or ostentation. After the First World War, Bloomsbury's disciples eagerly watched for new art forms, for the new young genius or for the new trend or experiment. No set of rules could be permitted to hamper experiment, no code of morality or laws of obscenity or censorship should be allowed to strangle the artist. The artist laboured under only one obligation – the duty to express himself. The sole duty of the critic was to elucidate that expression and defend it against philistinism or the dead hand of academics.

Bloomsbury had no love for academies. Strachey often insinuated that the worst enemies of literature were the so-called scholars of literature at the universities, men who spent years of work trying to prove Racine inferior to Shakespeare or, more likely, avoiding any discussion of their poetry as such and taking refuge in philology or, like Cazamian, in historical exegesis. Bloomsbury's object was to rescue culture from the *bien-pensants*.

After the First World War, Bloomsbury became famous. They spoke to the young in those destructive, deflationary days of the twenties. The young admired their version of the folly of the war and the even more astonishing folly of the peace. They admired their style of life, their championing of post-impressionism and Virginia Woolf's exploration of the experimental novel. By the end of the 1920s, they were surrounded by imitators, and the literary columns of the *Nation* and the *New Statesman*, under Desmond MacCarthy and Raymond Mortimer, were at their command. But two shadows fell across them. D. H. Lawrence, whose so-called 'obscene' work *The Rainbow* they defended, broke with them, and their friend T. S. Eliot was converted to Anglicanism, and distanced himself gently but decisively from Bloomsbury as a whole. Yet, more significant than these defections was the rise of a movement which unwittingly they themselves had provoked. That movement was Cambridge literary criticism.

The departments of English set up at British universities before the twenties studied the history of the English language and literature. For instance, W. P. Ker and R. W. Chambers at

London called criticism 'literary chatter' and believed in teaching philology and the acquisition of concrete knowledge. But, in the 1920s the new department at Cambridge established a syllabus which did not compel students to learn Anglo-Saxon. It ranged over the whole of English literature to the present day, and related it to the literature of Greece and Rome and to the English moralists. It enables a student to consider the theory of criticism from Artistotle to Eliot.

The staff were determined, from the first, to meet the gibes of Bloomsbury that the last thing professors of literature ever asked themselves was why poetry and novels touch the heart. Some of the younger members of the new department, such as F. L. Lucas and George Rylands, were second generation Bloomsberries. But in 1920 *The Sacred Wood* had appeared. Two years later, I. A. Richards published at Cambridge the first of his works on the theory of criticism. From then on, almost every year during the 1920s, a pronouncement on criticism appeared from either Eliot in London or Richards in Cambridge. Practical criticism was born and crossed the Atlantic, where it was called the 'New Criticism'. For, although I. A. Richards wanted to know why his class of students gave such bizarre answers when he asked them the author, date and meaning of the poem he handed to them, he also asked why they thought one poem better than another. Once you asked that question, you had to ask, as they did, what criteria you had for saying so – why a war poet who called himself 'Woodbine Willie' was better than Christina Rossetti: it was inevitable that someone would set up a new hierarchy among the poets as, indeed, Eliot was doing. One of the younger dons at Cambridge and his wife began to do so. They were the Leavises.

Some people marry their opposites, others their mirror images. The latter damage themselves more – for in an incestuous marriage the virtues never seem to be strengthened as intensely as the vices. As a young man, F. R. Leavis was a loner scarred psychologically by his experiences in the First World War, but he found friends in Cambridge who got him work as a teaching-assistant. Then he met a graduate student, Queenie Roth, who made up her formidable mind to marry him. *She* certainly had some cause to feel rejected: her strict Orthodox Jewish parents disowned her for marrying into the *goyim*. Queenie turned Leavis in upon himself. Whereas his friends, the Bennetts, were beginning to convince him that life was not a conspiracy directed against him, she did her best to create one. She made him break with his friends and with virtually all his colleagues, who, so they told their students openly, were intellectually contemptible. But, for the Leavises, there were bigger conspiracies than those which existed inside Cambridge. The worst conspiracy was within the world of letters, where a corrupt clique had captured the intellectual establishment. That clique was Bloomsbury, whose tentacles, so they said, stretched over all the important organs of British intellectual life. Through their influences in London, they were able, in effect, to control the organs of opinion which ought to have been in opposition to worldly upper-class morality, such as the BBC and the leading periodicals of the Left. And through the British Council they offered to foreign countries an image of British culture that was fashioned by Bloomsbury. The Arts Council subsidised *their* taste and ignored minority views such as the Leavises' own. How was it possible, Queenie Leavis asked, that the high seriousness of great Victorian intellectuals at Cambridge such as Sidgwick, Leslie Stephen and Maitland had disappeared to be replaced by admiration for Russell's brittle intellect, or E. M. Forster's feeble Hellenism or Lytton Strachey's sneer?[4]

The only two members of Bloomsbury the Leavises admitted to have distinction of mind were Forster and Keynes. Queenie Leavis did the main hatchet job on Virginia Woolf. Her review of *Three Guineas* on Virginia Woolf's feminism, a singularly unscrupulous attack, stands high as an example of modern invective. She characteristically left it to a disciple to dismiss *The Waves* and *The Years*. She did it by 'placing' Virginia Woolf, as the Leavises liked to call it. She habitually referred to her as 'the clever daughter of Sir Leslie Stephen'. Leavis wrote, in 1938, a genuinely appreciative essay in *Scrutiny* on Forster, though he managed to infer that he thought him inferior to L. H. Myers: after the war, when Forster lived at King's College, he revised his view and denigrated him. Keynes, he could hardly deny, had distinction of mind, but shortly after his death the publication of Keynes's memoir 'My Early Beliefs' gave Leavis the opening he needed. In that memoir, Keynes examined why it was that Lawrence had once exploded with rage to David Garnett, telling him how repulsive he found the conversation of Keynes and Frankie Birrell. With remarkable candour, Keynes admitted that Lawrence's criticism of himself and his friends had some justice. 'It can see us as water-spiders,' he wrote, 'gracefully skimming, as light and reasonable as air, the surface of the stream without any contact at all with the eddies and currents underneath . . . [We practised] a thin rationalism, ignoring both the reality and the value of the vulgar passions joined to libertinism and comprehensive irreverence.'[5] This act of repentance brought no absolution from Leavis. Is it repentance to ignore one's real depravity? Leavis indicted Bloomsbury's morality in a memorable sentence.

Articulateness and unreality cultivated together: callowness disguising itself in articulateness; conceit casing itself safely in a confined sense of high sophistication; the uncertainty as to whether one is serious or not taking itself for ironic pose; who has not at some time observed the process?[6]

Did the Leavises succeed in discrediting Bloomsbury?

Between the end of the Second World War and the 1960s they certainly did. The tradition of *belles lettres* in America as well as in Britain was being displaced among the intelligentsia by one of the most hard-working and confident of critical movements, in university departments of English in America even more than in Britain. Leavis was a technical critic of the first rank. His insights, dedication and intense seriousness won him praise, particularly in America. His opponents denounced him for admitting only a handful of poets and novelists to his pantheon, but such elegant sneers at Leavis's puritanism and style seemed superficial when set beside the very tortuousness, the strenuousness of his writing – a style which became known as 'The Mind at Work'. Leavis spent years in fashioning his rhetoric into a deadly weapon of attack and defence. It borrowed from Arnold his tone of high irony, from Lawrence his fury and hatred of the modern world, and, above all, from Henry James his celebrated, convoluted way of conveying what was *not* in order to hint at what was.

Leavis showed his contempt for the apparatus of scholarship – footnotes, references, acknowledgements. Consider his treatment of Dickens. In his revaluation of the English novel in *The Great Tradition*, he declared that Dickens' 'genius was that of a great entertainer, and he had for the most part no profounder responsibility as a creative artist than this description suggests . . . challenge to an unusual and sustained seriousness'.[7] In that book, published in 1948, he relegated consideration of Dickens to an

appendix of *Hard Times*. Exactly the same line about Dickens had
been taken by Queenie Leavis in 1934. But in 1970 the Leavises
published a rapturous criticism of Dickens, bubbling over with
superlatives. There was no acknowledgement of a change of heart:
only a note in the Preface to say that *if* the omission of Dickens
from *The Great Tradition* 'looked odd, it was meant as an avowal . . .
of a deferred commitment to making the default good'.[8] As
Professor George H. Ford of the University of Rochester, smarting
under Queenie Leavis's designation of America as a vulgar
country, said, 'There is a vulgar term for this kind of report: it is
called weaseling.'[9]

The Leavises employed another tactic. Anyone who had
previously written important criticism about Dickens – Hum-
phrey House, Orwell, and especially Edmund Wilson – was
vilified. They knew that most readers do not go to the library to see
what, for instance, Wilson had in fact said. Yet, if they had, they
would have found that Leavis had appropriated seven of Edmund
Wilson's most notable judgements.

In making such personal attacks, Leavis implicitly denied that
there could by any difference between the man himself and what
he wrote. You were judged by your written word whether that
word was an *ex cathedra* conclusion in a learned article, or a
throw-away line in an interview with a reporter who probably
quoted it out of context. Similarly, a poet or a novelist had no
individual life of his own – except when Leavis found a quotation
from his letters or journals which enabled him to make his point:
he existed only through his works. In this, he resembled a Parisian
or a New York intellectual who expresses dissent in hard and
sometimes bitter personal dissociation. In these cities, intellectuals are expected to commit themselves to a view on every
contentious moral issue of the day. It is held against a man or a
woman that he or she took such a stand at such a time. You are
inseparable from your views. Britain *per contra* is a country of high
civility. Intellectual consistency is not particularly valued. Nor do
we care particularly if someone whom we find agreeable or
charming holds dangerous or idiotic views. Our long parliamentary tradition accustoms men of strikingly different views to work
and live together, as in a club, not only in Parliament but in other
institutions; and this blurs the edges of intellectual life. Leavis
rejected this tradition. Colleagues were, for him, the betrayers of
the very activity they purported to be engaged in – the criticism of

literature – and therefore he could have no commerce with them. In the 1950s, a number of intellectuals thought that the British intelligentsia were far too cosy and complacent and they praised Leavis for dissociating himself from the British world of indefinable circles in which people do not express their opinions too forcibly because they are so strongly aware of social relationships and the necessary existence of different orders of intelligence and response.

Leavis's most frequent accusation was that Bloomsbury had established a coterie; and I must say frankly that I consider that observation to be just. Although Clive, and later his son Quentin, Bell both protested that the members of Old Bloomsbury criticised each other unsparingly, they closed ranks against the rest of the world, and would appeal to each other's wisdom and regarded a question in, say, politics as settled if Leonard or Maynard had spoken. The Leavises determined not to lay themselves open to the same charge. They had an eagle eye for anyone, such as George Steiner, who attempted to jump on their bandwagon, and, if some wretched adherent praised Leavis in a review, he would at once reply and point out how lamentably the fellow had missed the achievement he ought to have praised. But, if they permitted no coterie to form, the Leavises did something as damaging. They founded a sect. The sect was very strict and excommunicated all other critics as an act of ritual. The chief tenet of the sect was that criticism is the only discipline which can expose and save the nation's culture.

However great a technical critic Leavis might be, his attack upon Bloomsbury would never have carried weight had it not purported to explain British culture. Leavis's theory of culture is an amalgam of Ruskin, William Morris and Lawrence and of such minor figures as Eric Gill and Sturt. According to this theory, society became corrupted by industrialism and urban polish and insincerity. Once there was a rural world in which speech was natural and vigorous, in which life was deeply felt and morality simple and unalloyed. But this had been overcome by machine civilisation, surburban falsities and the glitter of polished upper-class civilities. The native vigour had been sapped by Bloomsbury cosmopolitanism, the natural robust response to language had been gelded by advertising. In the process, high culture had become divorced from folk culture. No 'organic relationship' any longer existed between the two. As a result, high culture had become coterie culture. Bloomsbury set a vulgar elegance above sincerity. They established a court of cosy self-flatterers. They adopted as their own the limited, if disinterested, philosophy of G. E. Moore and turned his austere method into the dialectic of a coterie. This dialectic, the product of their immature undergraduate days, they then used complacently for the rest of their lives. They claimed to be unworldly, but they were, in fact, merely setters of fashion. It was no excuse to argue that the money Keynes amassed by speculation was spent on learning and the arts; he was corrupted by the act of amassing it. Bloomsbury substituted social–personal values for real values. That was why its adherents would praise extravagantly the latest fashionable product, such as science fiction, and create a network of on-the-make dons, literary editors who controlled government agencies and chic journals and who joined with the vulgarians and showmen in ignoring the awkward spiky geniuses of our time, such as Lawrence.

To a historian, Leavis's theory of culture is ridiculous; but the historian of ideas will recognise it as a perennial plant. It has its roots in Rousseau and the eighteenth century, it burgeons in passages in Herder. In our own times, it can be found flourishing in the neo-Marxist flowerbeds of the Frankfurt school, in Marcuse and Habermas, and in numerous preservationist, conservationist and other groups concerned with the natural environment. But the vitality of the doctrine should not divert our attention from another element in Leavis's thought. If we are to isolate the most important element in Leavis's make-up, we must use the referent in British society which provides so many clues to British behaviour. We must observe class differences.

The members of Old Bloomsbury belonged to the English upper middle class – indeed, many of them belonged to a particular stratum in that class: the intellectual aristocracy. Bloomsbury assumed that the elite would have been born into these circles, and no one was quicker to observe that Virginia Woolf if one of their protégés came from a somewhat lower order in society. (One of her best essays is called, 'Am I a Snob?') And, if that person did, Bloomsbury assumed that he or she would be anxious to assimilate to their way of life and culture. They were intrigued to be taken up in their youth by the eccentric Lady Ottoline Morrell, though they were irritated by her presumptions and tyrannies; and did not Keynes say, after being exposed to the charm of Lord Salisbury, 'I never could resist a Cecil?' Considered in strict relation to their age, they were not snobs. But they were – Leonard Woolf and E. M. Forster excepted – thoroughly gratified by the manners of their own class.

Bloomsbury addressed themselves to the English clerisy, to the elite who had been educated at public schools and at Oxbridge, together with any who had climbed the educational and social ladder and had assimilated to the upper middle class. The eclecticism of their approach to literature and their hatred of insularity made them assume that any educated person spoke and read French and also probably German, and was thoroughly acquainted with Russian literature in translation. That he had read the Greek and Latin classics in the original went without saying. As for *English* literature and letters, they were part of the heritage of the nursery and schoolroom. It was only through the widest reading and by travel that men learnt to understand the complexity of human nature. Bloomsbury's audience was the new class of *revoltés* in post-1910 England, the intelligent and rebellious public-school boy who was consciously emancipating himself from his philistine schoolfellows when he set sail on the vast sea of European literature.

Leavis, on the other hand, was the son of a piano-dealer in Cambridge who was a vigorous rationalist and republican. He came, therefore, from lower-middle-class non-conformist stock, and went to the local grammar school. It was to pupils who came from the same educational background that he was to appeal. His denunciation of the metropolitan culture purveyed by Bloomsbury's disciples won an immediate response from the grammar-school boy or girl coming from the provinces to the university, often from a home where books were a rarity. Such people were apt to be scared or depressed by the vast area of reading that seemed to be expected of them before they were thought fit to utter a word about the literature of their own country. Now they felt able to turn their backs on foreign literature, on the grounds that the critic cannot profitably deal with a work unless he can unravel every strand of the texture of its language.

Leavis gave such students a new kind of self-respect. He taught his pupils that they could belong to the elite: not to the false, fashionable elite that Bloomsbury had sponsored, but to an embattled elite fighting for intellectual standards against fearful odds. He told them that they were the true descendants of Arnold, a trained body of readers who could set the tone for the whole of society by rigidly denouncing anything that was worthless and trivial, while praising only those authors that a true critic must perceive were of lasting importance. He differed from anyone before him in asserting that the elite had to be trained in literary criticism at the university, which was the only discipline which defined culture and defined it in terms of morality. He went further. He asserted that the activity of criticism was the most important of all the activities in the humanities, indeed that an English faculty ought to be at the centre of every university curriculum. He went further still. He declared that only when students were taught to discriminate and place authors in relation to each other could there emerge a climate of opinion in a country which would benefit creative artists and awaken them to what is valuable or what is childish or trivial in their own experience. Thus, he gave to students what the most influential teachers always in some way or other impart – the sense of belonging to a dedicated minority, a minority that would, in the end, triumph and convert suceeding generations, a minority which held the key to establishing truth and defining goodness. It was, after all, such a sense that Bloomsbury had imparted to their disciples.

And just as Bloomsbury drew their disciples from the disillusioned young after the First World War, so Leavis spoke to the condition of a very different generation of young after the Second World War. His pupils were not then writing for the newspapers and periodicals. Despising research, he sent them into the schools, into the state, not the public, schools to pass on the lessons of their master that much of what was most deplorable in British culture had been engendered by Bloomsbury. Thanks to the Education Act of 1944, the reputation and influence of the grammar schools rose, and that of the public schools correspondingly declined, and therefore Leavis's influence grew. Later pupils of his began to write regularly for the periodicals. Karl Miller was one of his pupils and became successively Literary Editor of the *Spectator, New Statesman, Listener,* and today of the *London Review of Books.* The columns of the *Guardian* became the preserve of Leavisite criticism. The present Director of the Royal Shakespeare Company, Trevor Nunn, was his pupil. Miller and Nunn retained the seriousness of their master, while emancipating themselves from his narrowness. But in the 1960s several departments of English in new universities taught the pure Leavisite doctrine.

Yet, in fact, so far from Bloomsbury being permanently

discredited, the disposition of mind which they admired began to win acceptance: a gentle hedonism; a commitment to reason as the civilised way of dealing with a social problem or of conducting politics; a contempt for pomp, ritual and authority; high esteem for unexplosive spontaneity; the rejection of moral codes; the appreciation of personal relations and of physical pleasure – especially sexual pleasure. In the 1960s, Parliament abolished the absurdities, as Bloomsbury and certainly I saw them, of theatre censorship, and relaxed the stringent obscenity laws under which publishers could be prosecuted; and among civilians in England and Wales homosexual practices *per se* ceased to be a crime. After the humiliation of Suez, the Conservative Party could hardly wait to get rid of Britain's imperialist past. Both the Conservative and the Labour Party embraced Keynesianism and full employment. Even the turbulent younger generations in the 1960s and 1970s were astonished to find, as Bloomsbury biographies, diaries and letters were published, that sixty years ago another group of young men and women had mocked authority and organised the Dreadnought Hoax; that Vanessa had moved without fuss from her husband to Roger Fry and then to the homosexual Duncan Grant, by whom she had a daughter; that Keynes, before his marriage to Lopokova, had for long been homosexual; that Forster, after a deep passion in Alexandria for an Egyptian tram-conductor during the First World War had had a homosexual relationship with a London policeman which lasted to his death; that Virginia Woolf had had an affair with the openly lesbian Vita Sackville-West; and that, when Strachey died, Carrington, married to one of his loves, had killed herself rather than live without him. And the publication of Virginia Woolf's papers, diaries and letters established beyond question what the Leavises had denied: her claim to be one of the greatest writers of her age.

There is, indeed, something paradoxical and disturbing when we consider the reaction of Leavis to Old Bloomsbury. He probably hated Strachey most, yet were not Leavis's methods in depicting individuals at least as unscrupulous as those of Strachey? If Strachey, as he said he intended to do in his Preface to *Eminent Victorians*, pulled fish out of the ocean of history and treated them as curious specimens, did not Leavis use similar methods to Strachey – a mixture of inference and assertion, of hints and asides, of guilt by association? Bloomsbury's art lay in enveloping an opponent with ridicule: Leavis preferred misrepresentation of his opponent by unscrupulous use of quotation. Contempt for an artist or critic was the inevitable outcome of Leavis's method, because, like Strachey, he considered people as specimens for the moralist's dissecting-table; but, unlike Strachey, there could never be for him the slightest discrepancy between the artist and the man. What the artist wrote *was* the man. A great artist must *a fortiori* be a good man, a bad artist must by definition be despicable. Such a belief shows an astonishing lack of knowledge of the world. Is it more penetrating than Strachey's habit of setting poets, soldiers, priests, statesmen and scholars all against his own rationalist theory of behaviour instead of against the standards appropriate to their age and their profession? What Leavis objected to in Bloomsbury was its ethos, and I have already quoted his famous denunciation, 'Articulateness and unreality cultivated together; callowness disguised from itself in articulateness. . . .' Perhaps one could rewrite that sentence and apply it to Leavis: 'Portentousness issuing from inflexible self-righteousness; self-righteousness masked by unctuous humility; the hypertrophy of conscience which excludes half of what is human and poisons the mind of the critic in the act of judgement.'

Both Bloomsbury and Leavis took a *simpliste* view of the relation of culture to society. With the exception of Forster, they were nineteenth-century positivists. Society was a collection of individuals; it progressed or improved because men became more rational and enlightened; anything which impeded this process of enlightenment was to be deplored. Society consisted of an enlightened, rational elite of intellectuals, a worldly middlebrow or philistine upper and middle class, and the boorish masses. Is this all that far distance from Queenie Leavis's division of the reading public, in the book with which she made her name, except that the elite is very much smaller? Leavis's understanding of society was equally simple-minded. His contention that a once-flourishing organic culture had become corrupted by the machine age is linked to a conspiracy theory. Conspiracy theorists, as we know, believe that a group of men belonging to a particular class, if they are Marxist, or to a race, if they are Fascists, or to bureaucracies, if they follow Burnham, or to followers of Bloomsbury and Bentham, if they are the Leavises, have somehow got hold of the strings of power and are playing with the puppets; and the puppets are the vast majority of their fellow citizens.

But, if one compares Bloomsbury with the Leavises, one comes to not merely a paradoxical but a disturbing conclusion. The more one muses upon the acceptability of moral judgement, the more it appears to a historian to rest only partly on the coherence of the intellectual justification the moralist offers. The personality of the critic and the strength of character that comes through his prose are of equal force in persuading his readers to accept what must, inevitably, be assertions. And, the more powerful the assertions, the more likely the risk of distortion. Perhaps such distortion is inevitable – and is this thought not disturbing? For a Keynes to propound his general theory, the fruits of years of struggle and failure in juggling with the intractable material of economics, or for Leavis to develop a critical method, the product of reading and rereading and communing and meditating, or, for an artist such as Virginia Woolf to establish herself in the first rank by enduring the suffering and disappointment that is the almost-inevitable lot of the creator – for such men and women to impose their will upon reality and upon their contemporaries, they must practise either what a scholar would call distortion or display what a moralist would call arrogance. Scholars should perform another function. To establish truth, they have to sift the material on which others may have expressed rash opinions, they have to be aware of the defect of every merit, they have to preserve what Keats called 'negative sensibility' in order to come to a just conclusion. But scholars know, in their hearts, where greatness lies. It lies in those who did something more than elucidate obscurity. It lies in those who create a new framework, who transform truth for their contemporaries. It lies in the wilful, inaccurate, rebels.

Does this mean that scholarship is a vain pursuit, fit only for inferior beings? We scholars should comfort ourselves by recalling a passage in the *Iliad*. When Achilles continues to refuse to fight on the plains of Troy because Agamemnon has insulted him, Odysseus and Ajax call on him to change his mind; and his old tutor, Phoenix, pleads with him also. Phoenix tells Achilles to pray to the gods, for

Prayers, too, are the daughters of Zeus, though they are lame and wrinkled and blear-eyed. They go behind ruinous infatuation, always dogging her. But infatuation is strong and fleet-footed; she easily outruns them all, and arrived before them all over the earth, doing men harm. Then prayers come behind to cure the hurt. If a man refuses them and stubbornly rejects them, they pray to Zeus that infatuation may go with him, so that he be harmed and pay the penalty. But do you, Achilles, give the daughters of Zeus their honour.[10]

Agamemnon and Archilles rejected the suppliants who prayed, and their infatuation caused terrible misery. But in the end Achilles listened, and gave Hector's body back to his father who knelt before him.

Scholars, too, are the daughters of Zeus, slow and plodding though they are. In the end, they establish truth and heal the hurt that the heroes made.

## NOTES

1. Lytton Strachey, 'Florence Nightingale', in *Eminent Victorians* (London, 1928 edn) p.120.

2. Preface, ibid., p. viii.

3. Cf. Quentin Bell, *Victorian Artists* (London, 1967) p.6.

4. See Q.D. Leavis, 'Leslie Stephen – Cambridge Critic', *Scrutiny*, VII (Mar 1939).

5. J. M. Keynes, *Two Memoirs* (London, 1949) p.103.

6. F. R. Leavis, *The Common Pursuit* (London, 1952) p.257.

7. F. R. Leavis, *The Great Tradition* (London, 1948) p.19.

8. F. R. and Q. D. Leavis, *Dickens* (London, 1970) p.xi.

9. George H. Ford, 'Leavises, Levi and some Dickensian Priorities', *Nineteenth-Century Fiction* (June 1971) p.99

10. J.T. Sheppard, *The Pattern of 'The Iliad'* (London, 1922) p.210; Homer IX. 502 ff.

# 3    Bloomsbury and the Fabians

MICHAEL HOLROYD

For the purposes of this paper I shall be taking Lytton Strachey
and Bernard Shaw, respectively, as representatives of the Bloomsbury Group and the Fabian Society.

Fifty years after his death, Strachey is still one of the most
controversial writers in the history of biography. This is not
simply my opinion. At a symposium on international biography
held last year in (of all places) Hawaii, Strachey's books were
voted among the most influential of the genre, almost rivalling the
team of Johnson and Boswell. That he is still controversial is to
say, of course, that his work is not wholly popular. Robert
Gittings, for example, in his recent book *The Nature of Biography*,
calls him a 'self-contradictory' figure, a description which reflects
perhaps the mixed feelings many have experienced when studying
his work. He was, so Mr Gittings in some exasperation complains,
'the classic example of doing the right things for the wrong
reason'. In correcting, as he so effectively did, one kind of falsity,
was he now perpetrating another: replacing Victorian piety with a
1920s giggle? And was he not, in doing this, a true representative
of Bloomsbury? After all, it has been argued, post-war cynicism
was merely the obverse of nineteenth-century sentimentality. For
all his persuasiveness, his psychological innuendo, where were
Strachey's first-hand sources, where (within quotation marks) the
necessary ellipses? Where, for God's sake, were the footnotes and
reference notes?

Strachey was not, it must be conceded, an academic scholar.
But then of course (and this is very shocking) nor was Dr Johnson.
Nor, when you consider Plutarch, was Shakespeare, come to that.
And nor was Shaw. Literature as an almost exclusive university
activity is comparatively modern. On the other hand, in his own
fashion, Strachey was almost as disreputable a character as
Boswell. 'Discretion', he once said, 'is not the better part of
biography.' And this is true. Biography, as opposed to history, has
always been somewhat bohemian. For all his reading, Strachey

was a fallen man – that is to say, a man of letters. For the men of
letters have fallen as the men of numbers (the monetarists) have
risen in our time. Strachey did not inflict his work upon students.
Like Shaw, he earned his living from that disappearing species,
the general reader. These general readers are still (as it were) his
students. So he *had* to be readable – there was no captive audience.
He didn't teach and he hadn't the voice for lecturing. Once, when
he attempted to give a talk on radio, his voice cracked and rose so
high, it is reputed, that only animals heard it. Nor did he
command a platoon of research workers. After Cambridge (and
again like Shaw) he used what was then called the Reading Room
of the British Museum as his university, and he wrote at home.
And then he went to his friends' houses and, in those pre-television
times, read (or let them read) what he had written.

Perhaps the most celebrated instance of this Bloomsbury
tradition was at Charleston, the Sussex home of Virginia Woolf's
sister, Vanessa Bell, who shared it with her husband Clive Bell
and her fellow painter Duncan Grant. It was here, on his first visit
in the late summer of 1917, that Strachey read out the first two
essays of *Eminent Victorians* – the ones on Cardinal Manning and
Florence Nightingale. Those who feel convinced that the Bloomsbury Group was an exclusive club for reciprocal civilities should
look at the varied response of his friends to this performance.
Duncan Grant (rather in the manner of William Archer with
Bernard Shaw – affectionate, that is, but despairing) fell asleep –
which is a form of criticism. Vanessa Bell was critical not of
Strachey's attitude to his subjects but of his prose style, its
informality and colloquialisms. Clive Bell was more appreciative,
but only the novelist David Garnett among the Charleston
audience that week was really impressed, realising, so he later
wrote, that 'Lytton's essays were designed to undermine the
foundations on which the age that brought war about had been
built'.

The places where a writer works, the conditions under which he
or she writes, the whole manner in which his or her books are
nursed into being, affects – or should affect – the content and
especially the tone of those books. In this respect at least Strachey
was not self-contradictory. After his Cambridge dissertation on
Warren Hastings, his essays and biographies are never part of a
*curriculum vitae;* they are an extension of his personal life, as
Virginia Woolf's novels are an extension of her life. Both displaced

their experiences into literature, transforming what was personal into something universal. As I said, Strachey's essays were written at home and their first audiences, as at Charleston, were his friends. And this, as I shall try to show, was part of their purpose: the purpose of replacing, in the minds of his readers, the ambitions of public life with the civilised values of private life. It is this that still makes him controversial in our age of publicity and is central to our understanding of the Bloomsbury Group.

Lurking in the minds of some biographers has been the suspicion that the genre itself might have emerged with more public respect from the pompous shadow of history if only its past luminaries – poor wandering Izaak Walton, that old goose John Aubrey, that atrocious gossip Boswell and such an *enfant terrible* as Strachey himself – could have been more (there is no avoiding the word) *eminent*. What a crew they were! In short: if only the art of biography in the twentieth century could have been revived by someone other than Lytton Strachey – that to some extent seems to have been the secret wish of Robert Gittings and other critics. And yet it was Strachey, Mr Gittings generously concludes, who 'brought back to biography what it had lost since Boswell . . . . After Strachey no good biographer has dared to be less than an artist. Biography designed as literature derives mainly from him.'

Strachey had rescued biography from the nineteen-century blight of earnestness – of solemnity masquerading as seriousness. But Mr Gittings' tone of reluctance, no less than his favourable judgement, is an accurate measurement of Strachey's reputation. For, if fame, as Dr Johnson once suggested, is a shuttlecock that needs determined play from the other side of the net to keep it in lively contention, then the polemic of *Eminent Victorians*, followed by the perfectly constructed romanticism of *Queen Victoria* and the experiment in pyschological melodrama of *Elizabeth and Essex* have proved a fine combination to keep the rally going. Strachey had revitalised the art of biography and in doing so had influenced the culture in which we live.

He has not lacked formidable opponents. Indeed, it is to them he largely owes his controversial prestige. He has been satirised by Wyndham Lewis and ticked off by Lewis's sergeant-at-arms Geoffrey Grigson; he was repeatedly dismissed by Dr Leavis and his *Scrutiny* gang (see above, Ch. 2); and he had been loudly ignored by a succession of historians that have included, in America, Douglas Southall Freeman and, in Britain, no less than

Hugh Trevor-Roper, now Lord Dacre. To be called 'the man who brilliantly ruined the art of biography', someone 'incapable of creation in life or in literature', who produced works that were a substitute for both: these are back-handers of a heavy order of which anyone given defensively to paradox might justifiably feel proud. Objections to Strachey's work have centred on his inexactness of language and of fact, and on the false moral basis from which this sentimental inexactness arose. So formidably did these critics press home their attack in the decades following his death that Strachey's reputation appeared to have been exploded. Yet there are particular dangers, I would suggest, in attacking a master of irony, and a number of unforced errors were made of the sort we had been taught to define as Stracheyesque: that is, of setting up a caricature puppet of your adversary and, having knocked it down, declaring the adversary dead.

Strachey's defence was modestly but properly kept afloat by Max Beerbohm and by Lord David Cecil, with spirited surges from a miscellany of distinguished writers from Cyril Connolly to Nigel Dennis, and came to rest on an interesting revaluation by Noel Annan. Plotting the ways of Bloomsbury against the socialist movement, the Fabians, he conducted an analysis of Strachey's cultural as well as his literary influence, of which he concluded, 'it is certainly not as a historian that Strachey will continue to exist, but as a biographer'. The two, it should be emphasised, are distinct. History surveys mankind; biography looks at man and woman. History gives the overall view, biography the eye-level view. Annan had argued that the First World War seemed to have severed the 1920s from the past. He wrote,

> The profound emotional impact of the horror and slaughter convinced many that the values which held good before the war must now, by definition, be wrong – if indeed they were not responsible for causing the war. A society which permitted such a catastrophe to occur must be destroyed, because the presuppositions of that comfortable pre-war England were manifestly false. Searching for a new way in which to regard conduct, the twenties came to see it through the eyes of either Mrs Webb or Mrs Woolf.
>
> (*Listener*, 8 Feb 1951, p.211)

Beatrice Webb or Virginia Woolf – they didn't take to each other.

'I can't think how two small old people like that manage to destroy everything one likes and believes in', wrote Virginia Woolf about Sidney and Beatrice Webb. But Beatrice Webb, was like Virginia, an authentic writer – a novelist *manqué*. Her diaries can stand on the same shelf without dishonour. But she didn't like Virginia Woolf's novels, because the characters, she complained, had no predominant aims, nor powerful reactions from the mental environment, and because their states of mind followed one another without any particular reason. Here was the objective versus the subjective view of life. And it is possible to cast the same scenario with Mr Shaw versus Mr Strachey: GBS or GLS.

To begin with, the distinction between Bloomsbury and the Fabians is one of chronology. Shaw, for example, was a Victorian; Strachey the son of a Victorian. Beatrice Webb too was Victorian in a way that Virginia Woolf was not. The quarter of a century between their births helps to explain a difference in tone as well as in the purpose of their work. Shaw, who was alive when Darwin's *Origin of Species* first appeared and felt a lifelong need of some religious structure with which to replace, up there, the Old Gent with a beard, laboured to make scientific discoveries part of our religious equipment. Strachey, who announced that the religious motive had slipped quietly out of modern life, attacked (in the persons of Cardinal Manning and General Gordon, for example) a wordly religion of success that sprang from the self-deception of attributing our own wishes to the deity. It was this that David Garnett had recognised at Charleston. However, in the business of replacing deception with truth, it was Shaw who, as an anonymous contributor to the *Pall Mall Gazette*, called for the revolution in biography (reflecting a revolution in life) that Strachey was actually to lead more than thirty years later. 'The truth is that queens, like other people, can be too good for the sympathies of their finite fellow-creatures', Shaw wrote in 1886.

A few faults are indispensable to a really popular monarch. . . . And if the Royal Jubilee is to be a success, the sooner some competent cynic writes a book about Her Majesty's shortcomings the better. With her merits we are familiar, and may expect to be more so before the last Jubilee bookmaker has given the throne a final coat of whitewash. We know that she has been of all wives the best, of all mother the fondest, of all widows the most faithful. We have often seen her, despite her lofty station, moved by famines, colliery explosions, shipwrecks, and railway accidents; thereby teaching us that a heart beats in her Royal breast as in the humblest of her subjects. She has proved that she can, when she chooses, put off her state and play the pianoforte, write books, and illustrate them like any common lady novelist. We all remember how she repealed the corn laws, invented the steam locomotive, and introduced railways; devised the penny post, developed telegraphy, and laid the Atlantic cable; how she captured Coomassie and Alexandria, regenerated art by the Pre-Raphaelite movement, speculated in Suez Canal stock, extended the franchise, founded the Primrose League, became Empress of India, and, in short, went through such a programme as no previous potentate ever dreamed of. What we need now is a book entitled 'Queen Victoria: by a Personal Acquaintance who dislikes her'.

And yet, Shaw continues, such a book could not find a publisher in the 1880s because of the thick atmosphere of superstitious loyalty that engulfed the country:

That the Queen, if no longer actually hedged with divinity, is yet more than merely human in the eyes of many of us, is made plain by the sacredness which trivial things assume when touched by a Royal hand. What is more banal than a pair of boots? What more uninteresting than an umbrella? But the Queen's boots! are they banal? the Queen's umbrella! what would you not give for the reversion of it? When a tornado devastates an American province it is chronicled in a quarter of a column. Yet were a gust of wind to blow off our Sovereign's head-gear tomorrow, 'The Queen's Bonnet' would crowd Bulgaria out of the papers.

                         (*Pall Mall Gazette*, 7 January 1886, p. 6)

But by the time Strachey published his *Queen Victoria* in 1921, Shaw in his sixties had himself become an old gent with a beard, a Grand Old Man waggishly reminding us that 'when you read a biography remember that the truth is never fit for publication'. The pessimism implied by such an observation may obliquely reflect his sense of failure in permeating British society with the socialist religion of Fabianism. The two strongest influences in the twentieth century have been Karl Marx and Sigmund Freud. One referred everything to external, the other to internal causes. Shaw was attracted (via the American economist Henry George) to Marx. Strachey, who had been so carried away by G. E. Moore's *Principia Ethica* as to date 'the beginning of the Age of Reason' from its publication in 1903, later moved (via Dostoyevsky) to Freud who became the chief influence behind his *Elizabeth and Essex*. This book was published in 1928 and may be regarded as the equivalent, among Virginia Woolf's publications, of *Orlando*. *Elizabeth and Essex* was dedicated to James and Alix Strachey, Lytton's brother and sister-in-law, who had actually spent their honeymoon in Vienna being psychoanalysed by Freud – to emerge a little later as his English-language translators, whose publishers were Leonard and Virginia's Hogarth Press.

Freud had been comically dismissed by Shaw as 'an author utterly without delicacy'. For to the Fabians this Moore–Freud axis appeared disastrous: 'that way madness lies' warned Beatrice Webb, who claimed to find nothing in Moore's *Principia Ethica* 'except a metaphysical justification for doing what you like'. It was in fact a method of raising personal relationships into a philosophy and making respectable what to the Victorians had been so unrespectable, indeed unspeakable. What the Fabians distrusted was the sexual emancipation pioneered by the Apostles at Cambridge and taken up by the Bloomsbury Group during the early years of this century. Strachey, for instance, had turned the nineteenth-century aesthetic cult of homosexuality into a modern twentieth-century weapon of revolt – a parallel for which may be found in Virginia Woolf's relationship with Vita Sackville-West. But the Fabians believed that it was the political, not sexual, mores of Victorianism from which we needed to cut loose. Sex, in their view, was primarily a matter of economics. That is to say: money kept the class structure in place; and people did not marry across class frontiers. Shaw, who associated *Heartbreak House* with Virginia Woolf because, he remembered, 'I conceived it in that house somewhere in Sussex where I first met you', employed a molecular Bloomsbury structure in that play to depict a morally bankrupt society drifting towards war. Politically nothing had changed: 'The same nice people, the same utter futility'. In his judgement, Bloomsbury's failure lay in not helping by political means to dismantle the British class system. But, as the attempted portrait of Strachey in his play *Village Wooing* confirms, Shaw knew little of the individual members of Bloomsbury. In fact 'Mr A' in that play is Shaw in Strachey's clothing and demonstrates the futility not only of the literary life but of words themselves as triggers for action in modern society. In *Heartbreak House*, Shaw portrays a society that has perhaps more in common with the Oxford Souls than with a circle with its provenance in Cambridge. Though E. M. Forster posed the riddle of friendship versus country, it was the Oxford Union, not Cambridge, that went on to vote against fighting in a Second World War.

Personal relationships plus aesthetic sensibility equals the good life: that was the Bloomsbury formula derived from G. E. Moore. Beatrice Webb feared that the intellect and character of the younger Fabians such as Rupert Brooke might be perverted by such free and easy ways; but Shaw decided that most Fabians were wonderfully immune from permeation (which, translated into Bloomsbury terms, means seduction) because of their philistinism. The arts and the cult of personal relationships withered in the impersonal Fabian atmosphere of cold showers, knickerbockered bicycle-rides and early-morning Swedish drill. Shavian socialism had a different formula: equality of income (*not* incidentally equality of opportunity) plus abolition of private property – that would lead to the good life. This socialism had little to do with the politics of the Labour Party, which, Shaw argued, had become a trade-union party slogging out a new version of the old capitalist class war with the employers' party, the Conservatives. Shaw's philosophy was wholly remote from the literary members of Bloomsbury such as Strachey and Virginia Woolf, who thought, like Shelley, that poets were the unacknow-ledged legislators of the world and that Shaw, though publicly acknowledged to an unnerving degree as a literary figure, was no poet.

But was he a prophet? Leonard Woolf (who was also by this standard no poet) reckoned Shaw's impact on ordinary people to have been tremendous and he criticised Virginia's attitude as narrow. The second generation of Bloomsbury, some of whom found (as had Leonard Woolf) their poetry in politics, were themselves influenced by Shaw. 'I only wish they didn't both . . . think Bernard Shaw greater than Shakespeare', Virginia Woolf complained of her nephews Julian and Quentin in 1927. This phase did not last long and was followed, I think, by quite a firm reaction. The choice proposed by Noel Annan between Virginia Woolf and Beatrice Webb, Strachey and Shaw, Bloomsbury and Fabianism, appeared to have been settled largely in favour of

Bloomsbury. It was primarily a sexual not an economic revolution that Britain enjoyed in the 1920s.

But there followed a curious twist. In his Courtauld lecture 'From Bloomsbury to Marxism' Anthony Blunt dated the arrival of Marxism in Cambridge and within the Cambridge Apostles at 1933, the year of Strachey's posthumous *Characters and Commentaries*. The Fabian programme of permeation had had little effect on orthodox politics partly because Fabians such as Sidney Webb possessed such a meagre political instinct, and partly because their methods, though given wit and sophistication by Shaw, were so crushingly unappealing. I have often thought that, if Beatrice Webb had only served more food and some wine at her political lunches, the whole course of British politics might have been changed. But politicians went away from these occasions intoxicated only by an intellectual feast. The atmosphere at the Webbs' house, or Shaw's at Ayot St Lawrence, was utterly un-Bloomsburgian. The result was that almost the only people reasonably sympathetic to the Fabian programme seemed to be those who (again like Leonard Woolf) were almost as ascetic as the Webbs themselves. The thesis and antithesis of Mrs Webb and Mrs Woolf, of Mr Shaw and Mr Strachey, had by the 1930s produced the synthesis of the double agent: a species of man turned inside out between the internal and external influences of Freud and Marx. What Shaw's Fabians and Strachey's Bloomsbury Group had shared was a compelling interest in power without the capacity for action. Both Shaw and Strachey tried to alter the future by rewriting the past and setting contemporary history on different routes. But in an age of growing political illiteracy they appealed for the most part only to other intellectuals who found a way of combining private with public life, sexual with political radicalism, collectivism with individuality not through indoctrinating political men-of-action but by entering politics themselves under cover. It was less a classical synthesis between two disciplines of life than the romantic living of a double life. This solution, though it might have appealed to their sense of irony, would (I feel confident) have satisfied neither Shaw nor Strachey. But it seems true that for the writer, the intellectual, there was no other obvious way of sustaining at least the illusion of some political influence.

In all the speculation and analysis of the Blunt espionage affair, though there was strangely no mention of Shaw and the Webbs as the leading apostles in Britain of Soviet Russia, much was regretfully attributed to the Cambridge Apostles, to Strachey and Maynard Keynes (who in fact deplored the religion of communism among the young). This was largely because, like Anthony Blunt, they were homosexual. A simple argument. Yet it had been the replacement of sexual by economic politics that had exhaled this curious intellectual atmosphere of the 1930s. The process had been caused by an infiltration of those naturally sympathetic to Bloomsbury by the Fabian ethic. Here was the revenge by men of literary and artistic imagination against a closed system of party politics that had branded them all as politically redundant. As can be seen from presidents no less than prime ministers, there is a price to pay for this illiteracy. You exclude the writer at some peril, for there is still some magic in the written word and some lingering respect for its practitioners. Think, for example, of Mr Nixon. A number of you I am certain will remember him. There was a matter of some tapes. Why did these tapes unthrone him? Not for any revelations they contained – all the facts were generally known or sufficiently suspected. But, like Monsieur Jourdain, Mr Nixon was talking prose. As Cinna the poet was killed for his bad verses so Mr Nixon was sacked for his lousy prose.

The frustration of Shaw, who had tried on innumerable committees over many years to work our democratic machinery effectively, was translated into a dangerous respect for strong men, such as Stalin, who got things done. Strachey's involvement with power, which like Shaw's was an assertion of literary style, is less obvious because it took the form of an assault on ambitious men and women already dead, and (as with several of the Bloomsbury Group) of conscientious objection in the First World War; and because this assault lost some impetus once his own literary ambitions began to be fulfilled. In *Eminent Victorians* he had attacked imperialism and pulled down the powerful from their high places; but ten years later, in *Portraits in Miniature*, he raised up the victims of life – pedagogues and antiquaries pushed by circumstances into dreadful shapes – and treated them with humorous tenderness.

And it is here, I think as a miniaturist, that Strachey is supreme. Like Virginia Woolf, he is a fine essayist. *Eminent Victorians* after all is a quartet of essays; the construction of *Queen Victoria* too is that of a series of interrelated essays. The reputation of *Elizabeth and Essex*, the only full-length work in which Strachey forsook the essay for an experiment in biography as theatrical drama, has been less secure.

The centenary of Strachey's birth fell in 1980. Centenaries, though highly artificial occasions, provide a useful opportunity for measuring the enduring value of a writer's work. We are, of course, still immersed in those of Virginia Woolf, Wyndham Lewis, James Joyce and Eric Gill, and it is too soon to survey them. Strachey's centenary festivities ranged from an exhibition of photographs at the National Portrait Gallery in London to the publication in France of a magisterial and comprehensive critical and biographical study by Gabriel Merle, and the appearance here in America of an excellent bibliography by Michael Edmonds. Oxford University Press brought out a new selection of his essays entitled *The Shorter Strachey,* and there were lectures, articles, reviews by the leader of the Labour Party, Michael Foot, by John Lehmann, by Angus Wilson, and by a number of historians and biographers, including Piers Brendon, Peter Clarke and Stephen Koss: all of which showed that admirers of Strachey are as heterogeneous a lot as his detractors. Their opinions too varied widely. Nigel Dennis, echoing Virginia Woolf's opinion, wrote that Strachey had 'created' Queen Victoria as Boswell had 'created' Johnson or Macaulay 'created' Clive. But he wrote,

> The fate of this wonderful book has been extremely sad. It appeared when kings and queens were on the way out among historians, yielding sovereignty to economics and social studies. As Strachey's overwhelming interest was in the characters of Victoria and Albert, his book was regarded as frivolous – a stigma that it has kept to this very day.
>
> (*Sunday Telegraph,* 2 March 1980)

Other critics approached Strachey from a different angle. The wit and iconoclasm of *Eminent Victorians* made it a finer book, some of them suggested, than the rather muted *Queen Victoria.* It had caught the mood of the time marvellously and anticipated the modern disarmament plea: 'Make love, not war.' Indeed, with his pacifism, homosexuality and that split between his classical mind and romantic imagination, Strachey might have become a conventional folk hero of the 1960s. That he did not was attributed by Piers Brendon to the influence among students of Dr Leavis, who 'had actually told his Cambridge pupils that Strachey had been responsible, through his influence on Maynard Keynes, for the outbreak of the Second World War' (*NOW!*, 29 February – 6 March 1980, p.77). Powerful stuff!

There was also a centenary radio broadcast in which Noel Annan claimed for Strachey, despite his lack of a university, the role of educator – for example, as an indirect political influence on E. M. Forster's *A Passage to India* and Keynes's *Economic Consequences of the Peace*. He pointed also to his influence on subsequent sexual law reforms in Britain. Strachey's work and that of his friends was, in that wider sense, certainly political. For many, Strachey's greatest attribute was his humour, his marvellous capacity for seeing human beings in terms of being ridiculous. In the public arena humour was his weapon; in his personal life it was a gift, a quality that endeared him to his friends. Even his silences were funny. And it was particularly in the quieter private realm that the programme's power to move the listener lay – in the almost intolerably poignant evocation of his life with Carrington. 'He was', she wrote, 'the only person to whom I never needed to lie.' That, when you think about it, is a very remarkable tribute that reinforces Quentin Bell's verdict on Strachey as 'a life-enchancing person. He made one happy and one was devoted to him because he did dispense delight so much. That was my immediate feeling. This is a good person – a delectable person.'

It was the quality of this life, of Virginia Woolf's life given over to her novels, diaries, letters and essays, of Vanessa Bell's and Duncan Grant's lives given to their painting and decoration, of all their lives given to the arts, that those members of Bloomsbury who entered more directly the world of politics, in particular Maynard Keynes and Leonard Woolf, sought to protect from the indiscriminate economic and political revolution of the twentieth century. 'Everything one likes and believes in' as Virginia Woolf had put it, should not be destroyed.

Shaw and the Webbs did not have that concern. Beatrice, as a brave act of independence, had switched off her emotions, or at least tried to eliminate romance, by rejecting a subservient marriage to the autocratic but sexually attractive figure of Chamberlain. Romance in Sidney Webb's life was minimal – even while desperately in love with Beatrice he had dreamed of her between the files and dispatch boxes of his Civil Servant's office. Shaw, despite his genuine love of music and feeling for literature (he claimed he was an intellectual voluptuary, never denying himself a Beethoven symphony), could not bear to expose his feelings to the shocks and accidents of life, and eventually came to accept, almost to welcome, the destruction of libraries and pictures and – why not? – human beings too. After all, they were hardly a lovable species and seldom treated themselves with consideration. There is a lot of Beckett hidden in Shaw.

Bloomsbury was more careful. Its members were reformers rather than revolutionaries. In painting Roger Fry was opposed by the avant-garde Wyndham Lewis as well as by the academic Henry Tonks, Professor of the Slade School of Fine Arts with its bohemian star Augustus John. Virginia Woolf turned up her nose a little at James Joyce, but also turned her back on the solid traditional novels of Arnold Bennett. All Bloomsbury supported D. H. Lawrence, but tepidly. Though they might intellectually approve of him, they were socially and temperamentally averse to him – and kept their distance. To their enemies (such as Lawrence) they were ugly and superficial, 'spiders and water-beetles'. They seemed an elitist closed circle, pacifist in wartime, attacking their rivals between the wars and exercising too much exclusive power on the literary journals of the period – *The Times Literary Supplement*, the back half of the *New Statesman* (the political front half of which was Fabian) and Desmond MacCarthy's *Life and Letters*. They were seen by their enemies as a cul-de-sac of a movement, tidily kept but leading nowhere. To their friends, however, they stood for tolerance, intelligence and the Voltairean virtue of cultivating your own garden: and (as with the Sitwells) their enemy was philistinism in art and in life.

In his book *Civilisation*, Clive Bell argues for the benefits of an economically independent life, with servants to help release one's energies for writing, painting, thinking. Put another way, it is Virginia Woolf's private income and a room of one's own. Like all artists they wanted money to buy time to work. Money was freedom of action. Unlike the Fabians, they did not set out to redistribute income by a socialist programme of levelling-up, but to shore up the good life of personal relationships and aesthetic enjoyment for those who were able to enjoy it. They wanted to develop their own emotions and talent first, and to influence society indirectly, by example more than precept. It was a renewal of eighteenth-century culture in place of Victorian values.

# 4   Mr Ramsay was Young Once

## JOHN W. BICKNELL

In her diary for 6 May 1935, under the heading 'Ideas that struck me', Virginia Woolf observes,

> That the more complex a vision the less it lends itself to satire: the more it understands the less is it able to sum up & make linear. For examples Shre [Shakespeare] & Dostoevsky neither of them satirize. The Age of Understanding: the Age of Destroying & so on.   (*D*, IV, 309)

The aptness of Woolf's terms to the history of *To the Lighthouse* criticism is apparent now that we seem to have passed through the Age of Destroying, in which Mr Ramsay is said to be the butt of malicious satire and Mrs Ramsay a saintly lady with a lamp, into the Age of Understanding, in which we are less able to sum up and make linear: Mrs Ramsay has become a Madonna with feet of clay and Mr Ramsay a tormented, ornery, but ultimately lovable and noble creature. Likewise, judgements on the character of Leslie Stephen are beginning to move from outright condemnation of him as an old wretch to some attempt to understand him, while the sanctification of Julia Stephen is now yielding to more sceptical appraisals. Careful scholarship is also beginning to cast a cool eye on the portraits Virginia Woolf drew of her father, portraits that seem to have been accepted as the whole truth by a number of Woolf scholars and readers. Yet those who read everything Woolf said about her father see that she is constantly revising and retouching those portraits in her letters and her diaries and most notably in the recently discovered portion of 'A Sketch of the Past'. We see her conducting a recurring struggle to bring into some kind of synthesis the impulse to destroy and the impulse to understand, the claims of anger and the claims of compassionate irony, the compulsion to expose and the need to admire and love. No doubt it is comforting to some to picture Stephen after the model of Bernard Shaw's Roebuck Ramsden. We all remember Ramsden's horror when Violet is discovered to be pregnant. Well, Shaw's Ramsden is linear, a caricature, too simple to guide us to the character of Stephen. True, he was shocked when Anny Thackeray fell in love with her young cousin Richmond Ritchie, but years later, when Vanessa and Jack Hills were thinking of marriage, it was George Duckworth who, like Matthew Arnold, was upset at the possibility of marriage with his deceased wife's sister, and it was Leslie who said Vanessa should do as she pleased.

As is obvious, the point of my title is to provoke some clarification of the relation of Mr Ramsay to Leslie Stephen. To what extent can we infer Stephen's life and work from the fictional portrait? We may decide, for example, that Stephen, like Ramsay, was primarily a frustrated philosopher who could not get beyond Q. Now, if we take R or Z to represent some metaphysical ultimate, some answer to the ontological question, and then extrapolate this concern to Stephen, we shall be quite wrong, for he considered ontology a futile enterprise. As an agnostic, he could hardly think anything else. All one has to do is to read the essays in his *Agnostic's Apology* (1893) or his essay on Arthur Balfour's *Foundations of Belief*.[1] Certainly Stephen asked epistemological questions and illustrated them; Andrew's 'Think of a kitchen table then' could well have its source in Stephen's lecture 'What is Materialism?'; but, unlike Mr Ramsay's, Stephen's books are not about 'subject and object and the nature of reality'.[2] For him a philosophy was 'a poetry stated in terms of logic', a word such as 'atoms' was a useful convenience but not a statement about the *Ding an sich*; in fact, he felt strongly that to use such a concept as the *Ding an sich* was to beg the question. By what right, he asked, do we assume there is such a thing? No, the people who claim to have reached Z suffer from pretentious vanity: 'The grave humorists, indeed, who call themselves historians of philosophy seem to be at times under the impression that the development of the world has been affected by the last new feat of some great man in the art of hair-splitting.' Moreover, he would assert that 'every ultimate problem is wrapped in the profoundest mystery' and movingly evoke the long history of human error in the search for truth. The search has produced, not Truth, but 'certain reliable truths. They don't take us very far, and the condition of discovering them has been distrust of *a priori* guesses, and the systematic interrogation of experience.'[3] Leslie Stephen reading Mr Ramsay's anxieties over reaching Z would have advised him to spend his time more usefully.

We might also imagine Leslie Stephen reading that in a forthcoming lecture Mr Ramsay 'would find some way of snubbing the arts. He would argue that the world exists for the average human being; that the arts are merely a decoration imposed on the top of human life; they do not express it'.[4] One can imagine Leslie's splutters of indignation, for, though he believed that literature and art emerged from human existence and experience rather than descending from some transcendental realm, he certainly believed they were expressive of life and not mere decorations, that books could be life-enhancing as well as life-demanding, and that the greatest works of literary art were those which expressed the human predicament in a particular time and place with greatest power and eloquence.

Suppose, too, that we infer Stephen's opinion of Julia's intelligence from the scene in which Mr and Mrs Ramsay are reading together and in which Mr R is represented as liking to think that his wife is not clever or book-learned: 'He wondered if she understood what she was reading.' Such an inference would lead us quite astray, for, while it is true that Julia Stephen declared she was totally uneducated, it is quite clear from the letters they exchanged in 1877 that Leslie respected Julia's intelligence; they read and discussed Arnold's *Empedocles*, the works of George Sand, John Morley on Voltaire, among other works of note; moreover, they discussed Leslie's own writings and it is clear that he respected her opinions. I see no signs that he underestimated her intelligence.

These few examples suggest that it is impossible to use Mr Ramsay as a guide to the complex character and work of Leslie Stephen. Just as there are several Mr Ramsays there are several Leslie Stephens. There is Leslie the father of Virginia and Sir Leslie the public man of letters. Each of these, however, is subject to binary or even multiple fission. Leslie as father is the old wretch and the benign repairer of toy boats; a tyrant and a liberator. Certainly for Woolf scholars the father Virginia experienced is of great significance and interest. But Virginia's Leslie is not *our* Leslie, whose character and work impinge upon us in their own right. He is, or should be, part of our heritage as scholars, as critics and biographers, as people who think about philosophical issues, theories of history, or literary history, or even as human beings confronting the social and intellectual issues of our own time. The fact is, however, that too many of us are not conscious of Leslie Stephen as part of our heritage, for the simple reason that, despite his high rank among Victorian men-of-letters, he has not been represented in anthologies of Victorian literature in any way that suggests the scope and power of his work. We were all taught to genuflect before Arnold, Carlyle, Newman, Ruskin and even Pater, but even in most graduate courses we were not exposed to the challenge the non-Christian humanists laid down before their more or less Christian counterparts. We read Newman, but not 'The Scepticism of Believers', *Literature and Dogma* but not 'Mr Matthew Arnold and the Church of England', not to mention Stephen's major works in the history of ideas. The reader will be relieved to hear that I do not intend to provide what education has neglected, but I do hope to suggest that the young Mr Ramsay is of some interest and not easy to sum up or make linear.

I begin with a passage from a letter to 'Mrs Ramsay' written in March 1887 as 'Mr Ramsay' rode a slow train from Edinburgh to St Andrew's where he was to deliver his lecture 'The Study of English Literature':

> The chief interest to me was a place called Burntisland where I spent a month in the summer of 1848 in my most sickly time. I saw a place where I used to lie on the grass & look at the gulls & the seals & where I once caught an eel but I spent most of my time in bed sometimes with leeches on & my bones still shiver when I think of it.[5]

In 1848 'Mr Ramsay' was sixteen. He had been removed from Eton two years before for poor health and had been studying with tutors; his eldest brother had died in Dresden; the family had moved to Wimbledon; he had spent a first term at King's College, London, and in the summer the family had gone to the Lakes, where he came down with what was called asthma; it was feared he might become lame. He was delicate from childhood.

Moreover, his mother tells us, he was the most sensitive child she ever saw. He would not look at pictures of the Crucifixion and wanted a happy ending provided for Goethe's 'Erl King'; he refused to ride a donkey to church for he didn't think a donkey should work on Sunday. He was also volatile; 'He is very impetuous indeed . . . very turbulent and self-willed and rather passionate, but in a moment changes to kindness and affection. . . . He cannot bear a word or look of reproof.' His mother adds,

> It is beautiful to see him with his sister. He has a remarkable love for lovely things, especially for views of Switzerland. He has a passion for flowers. He is always drawing . . . has long conversations with the beasts of Noah's ark . . . [and didn't like books] that went *wiggling* from one subject to another; . . . he liked to have a great deal on one subject and in regular order.[6]

This child is certainly fathering the Leslie Stephen we know. Soon, however, he was to disturb his mother and his doctor by an agitated addiction to poetry, the reciting of which sent the blood to his head and his pulse racing. We turn again to Lady Stephen's journal:

> [Dr Ferguson] said there was a danger of his becoming effeminate, and that the danger to his body would be that of becoming deformed. I told him we had just made up our minds to keep him at home for two years. He said 'Then the mischief would be irremediable.' Advises to send to public school for dull routine.

And a month later (Leslie was eight years old):

> the blood circulation about his head was so much too rapid that his veins worked like those of a man of fifty. He (the doctor) said that the blood which should nourish his limbs & frame was diverted entirely to his head & that his limbs wd become too weak to bear the weight & that deformity might ensue.[7]

Poetry was forbidden, but vigorous exercise was prescribed and light study of only humdrum subjects. Eton was to be the remedy, which included a flogging 'so unjust that I am even now [1901] stung by the thought of it'.[8] Flogging was perhaps only one of the reasons why the remedy failed. He was withdrawn and turned over to tutors before entering King's College, where he prepared himself to enter Cambridge.

Thus, two years after his summer with the leeches, 'he found himself', in Maitland's anticipation of a famous title, 'the master of a set of rooms' at Trinity Hall, Cambridge. There he became a mathematician, an enthusiastic crewman and walker, and spoke nine times at the Union, supporting the ballot, parliamentary reform, and the admission of dissenters to the universities. Graduating in 1854, he was offered a fellowship which required him to take orders as a clergyman in the Church of England. If we are to believe his sister's account given to Maitland in 1905, his decision to take orders was to a large extent determined by pressure from his father, who, longing to have one son in the Church, consistently argued to show Leslie that he was not qualified by health or by temperament for any other profession. His sister Milly thought it a mistake, for she felt Leslie had no sense of clerical vocation, but he put her objections aside, no doubt to please his father.[9] However, 'the whirligigs of time bring in their revenges': ten years later, Leslie had left Cambridge; he could no longer believe in the Thirty-Nine Articles.

After he left Cambridge he often deplored and resented much of the time spent there, but I suspect that the resentment came after the religious issues became pressing. While he tutored passmen and harangued the crews on the river and could talk with Henry Fawcett, life seemed pretty exciting. Writing Fawcett's life in the 1880s, he could remember that he 'never heard such excellent talk as [he] heard in Cambridge in those days'. And what was the talk of? Politics, reform, Mill's *On Liberty*, the American Civil War, Mill's *Logic*, and everything that flowed from it. By the early 1860s one of the major topics was the state of official Christianity challenged by the higher criticism, Darwinism, and by the behaviour of the orthodox in the face of *Essays and Reviews* (1860). There were, as well, the moral objections raised against the conception of a deity who would arbitrarily condemn a large number of his creatures to everlasting damnation. As Leslie tells it in *Some Early Impressions,* he went through no soul crisis; he merely discovered that he had never really been a believer and was hence shedding an awkward burden – a nice linear version of what other testimony suggests was a complex and painful process.

There are, for example, hints in a letter quoted by Maitland[10] in which Sir Robert Romer recalls that Stephen's pain of severance was acute; there is also Leslie's own cryptic remark in the

*Mausoleum Book* about 'some struggles through which I had to pass',[11] the knowledge of which he will take to his grave; finally, there is Virginia's report that Maitland hinted to her that her father suffered enough anguish to think of suicide.[12] The basis for Maitland's hint can be found in a letter to him written by Sedley Taylor (1834–1920), a contemporary of Leslie's at Cambridge. Having just read Leslie's account of his deconversion cited above, Taylor felt a great discrepancy between it and what Henry Fawcett had once told him about Leslie's state of mind during the process: 'Fawcett said that he was with Stephen late one night discussing the position and that when he quitted him Stephen's state of mind was such that Fawcett entertained serious fears he might cut his throat during the night.'[13]

Well, that is dramatic indeed, but we still have to inquire as to the accuracy of Fawcett's reading of his friend's state of mind and of the literalness of his language (if he really thought Leslie was going to cut this throat, it was irresponsible to leave him alone). We have also to inquire if the anguish was caused more by the religious question or by the wrench he knew he would give his mother, or at the giving up of a vocation as Fellow, or if there was not an ingredient of anger at his father for having pressed him into a situation from which he must now extricate himself – at the years wasted down a cul-de-sac. Whatever we may conclude, it is clear that he did some pargetting when he wrote the *Mausoleum Book* and *Some Early Impressions*; in fact he was quite frank about it. Commenting on the latter text to Charles Eliot Norton in America he wrote, 'No, I have no indiscreet reminiscences pressing for publication. I do remember some things unfit, but so very unfit that they don't press.'[14] Assuming that Fawcett's story was one of the 'unfit', posterity as usual defeated the effort to preserve respectability.

His departure from Cambridge brought Leslie to London and journalism; it also brought him back to the house of his mother and sister and introduced him to a social circle including the daughters of the late William Makepeace Thackeray. Leslie and Minny (Harriet Marion), the younger of the two, took to each other and in late 1866 they were engaged – after a bit of backing and filling. As usual, he returned to Trinity Hall for the Christmas 'exceedings', as the annual feastings and topings were called. Writing to Minny in satirical vein, he describes the enormous menu and a walk with Fawcett, which includes a macabre landscape: 'the country . . . looked as it could soon be all over blue mould . . . just the place for a gallows. I shall propose to the Jamaica Committee to hire the windmill to be used in this capacity for Governor Eyre.' Later in the day he and Wolstenholme goaded Robert Romer into attacks on 'Wellington, Prince Albert & various swells & praising Fenianism'. Reporting the dinner-table conversation, he tells Minny of a long 'discussion about wine; which seems to me to be the kind of talk in which prize pigs would indulge if prize pigs drank claret'. A few days later he had to sit at another dinner:

> However, I enjoyed myself very well with certain friends, including Paley, a Papist, but as little of a fool as a papist can be – and after dinner Huxley joined our smoking party & we had a good talk, denouncing Governor Eyre & the British aristocracy by the hour. It would have done you good to hear us.[15]

What these vignettes of high table iconoclasm reveal is the rambunctious side of the more serious attacks that Stephen and a vociferous group of middle-class radical intellectuals were conducting against various bastions of the mid-Victorian establishment, an establishment that supported the slave states in the American Civil War and stubbornly resisted proposals for parliamentary reform, for national education, for Church disestablishment, for the rights of trade unions, the emancipation of women, and independence for Ireland. The Age of Equipoise was passing. A number of academic radicals were cheerfully disturbing a fragile equilibrium. John Morley, Frederic Harrison, E. S. Beesly, Stephen and others, theoretical spokesmen of various insurgent groupings in British society, both middle and working class, vigorously sought to make Britain more democratic, reduce the political power of the aristocracy, and modernise a society creaking with obsolete institutions and ideas. Thus one found a number of young men and women, most of them disciples of J. S. Mill, clustered around the *Westminster Review* (G. H. Lewes, Marian Evans, Herbert Spencer), or around the *Fortnightly*, the most radical of the academic party (Morley, Harrison, Huxley, and so on), and, further to the left, the *National Reformer*, more representative of the Midlands and the North, jointly edited by Charles Bradlaugh and Annie Besant.

Where did Leslie stand in all this? First, in 1863, disgusted with the fashionable support for the South, he took himself to America and arrived just after Gettysburg, travelled as far west as St Louis, saw Lincoln in Washington, returned to Boston and then home in October to produce that stinging pamphlet *The Times and the American War* (1865), a remarkable piece of destructive analysis comparable to some recent *exposés* of biased reporting in Vietnam or El Salvador. In the same period he turned his sniper fire on the universities in *The Poll Degree* (1863) and in his humorous *Sketches of Cambridge by a Don* (first published in the *Pall Mall Gazette*, 1865). The 'Don' who creates these *Sketches* is a fat, dilettante classicist, whose college is clearly *not* Trinity Hall. The tutors, he intones, are not as they once were: 'Respectability has spread its leaden mantle over the whole country, the old eccentric characters have died out from our walls, and the man wins the race who worships that great goddess with the most undivided attention'; as for the whole enterprise, he drily remarks, 'Our plan is not to teach anyone anything, but to offer heavy prizes for competitions in certain well-defined intellectual contests.'[16] (Later, in the seventies, he went after the public schools in a couple of *Cornhill* essays 'By an Outsider' – a *nom de plume* his daughter picked up.)

The universities and their restrictions, however, were just one wall of the Establishment against which Stephen and his colleagues trained their guns. Not only were the working classes demonstrating in the North and marching in Hyde Park to support an enlarged franchise; not only was there devastating poverty in the East End (as Stephen noted in his weekly letters to the New York *Nation*); but the climate of opinion became unsettled. The salubrious sunshine of the Great Exhibition was dissipating in storms of controversy. Calm confidence in the verities of orthodox religion, heretofore only eroded by the steady wind of rationalist scepticism, was shaken by great gusts of Darwinism and the cold blast of higher criticism. Thus one of the major targets of the *Fortnightly* radicals was the Church of England, 'the praying section of the Tory party' as one wag put it. As John Morley proclaimed in 1873,

[The Anglican Church is] not the Church of a nation but the Church of a class; not the benign counsellor and helpful protector of the poor, but a mean serving maid of the rich. She is as inveterate a foe to new social hope as we know her to be to a new scientific truth.[17]

It was the Church, Leslie contended, that preached indifference to social ills, while it is

> the atheists, infidels, and rationalists, as they are kindly called who have taught us to take a fresh interest in our poor fellow denizens of the world, and not to despise them because almighty benevolence could not be expected to admit them to heaven . . . .[18]

It is in this context, so briefly sketched, that we must observe Stephen between his thirtieth and fiftieth years. As an activist, his career was short-lived. In the early 1860s he managed Henry Fawcett's Brighton campaign for Parliament and got properly sloshed when the news of defeat came in. He joined John Mill's committee for the prosecution of Governor Eyre for conducting the Jamaica Massacre. In 1867 he contributed to *Essays on Reform,* the political counterpart of *Essays and Reviews* (1860), and in the following year wrote an optimistic account of the political situation for the *North American Review,* asserting that 'we are witnessing the beginning of a peaceful revolution in England'. But by the time of Gladstone's collapse in 1874 Stephen was disappointed and disillusioned, much less sanguine about the future and less involved in politics, for which he was temperamentally unsuited anyway. His analysis of the Condition of Britain, however, was no less radical.

Probably his most radical position is to be found in an essay on Ruskin, written in 1874. There are passages in this essay in which the voice of Ruskin and the voice of the author seem indistinguishable. This is one of them:

> The world is out of joint. The songs of triumph over peace and progress which were so popular a few years ago have been quenched in gloomy silence. . . . Peace has not come down on the world, and there is more demand for swords than for ploughshares. The nations are glaring at each other distrustfully, muttering ominous threats, and arming themselves to the teeth. Their mechanical skill is absorbed in devising more efficient means of mutual destruction, and the growth of material wealth is scarcely able to support the burden of warlike preparations. . . . Everywhere the division between classes widens instead of narrowing. . . .[19]

Likewise, in the next year, turning to Hare's scheme of prop-
ortional representation, he reveals the temper of one who does not
believe that tinkering with this or that scheme of voting ('cheese-
paring' he would have called it) will really affect the power
relationships in Britain. 'Society is an organism', he writes; thus 'a
change in machinery that really reflects a change in the distribu-
tion of power is realistic.' But what is the situation in Britain? The
upper classes

> are strong because rank is still worshipped by large classes; they
> are strong because they form a tacit league, wielding all the
> powers of rank and wealth and ancient prestige, and of a social
> organisation of which they are the traditional chiefs, and in the
> presence of classes numerous, it is true, but ignorant, helpless,
> disunited, and dependent at every turn upon the smooth
> working of the existing machinery; they are strong, not only
> from the positive hold which they may have upon the prejudices
> or principles of their countrymen, but also because there is no
> consistent scheme of a new order to take the place of the old
> which has any hold upon the imaginations of the masses.[20]

Therefore, he concludes, Hare's scheme will not really change the
situation; it will affect 'rather the mode in which power is
exercised than its reality'. Though his prescription for change
tended to be Fabian, his analysis remained radical. Despite his
disgust with Gladstone and virtual withdrawal from active
politics, his vision of the way society worked remained constant.

It remained constant even after the sudden, shocking death of
Minny on his birthday, 28 November 1875, knocked the pins out
from under him. We hear nothing now of high jinks at Cambridge
or anywhere else; he resigned from the clubs where he used to
discuss politics with his fellow radicals. He finished his *magnum
opus, English Thought in the Eighteenth Century,* and wrote in the same
year (1876) that most moving and eloquent essay, 'An Agnostic's
Apology'. Soon after, he found Julia and they began to create a
new family. He continued to edit the *Cornhill,* wrote *The Science of
Ethics,* and then took up the arduous, killing task of editing the
*Dictionary of National Biography.* Occasionally, however, he returned to the firing-line. In 1880, when the atheist Charles
Bradlaugh was elected to Parliament for Northampton, he was
denied his seat because he wished to affirm rather than take his

oath of office on the Bible. Leslie was appalled, took the old gun down off the rack, cleaned the barrel, and let drive.[21] Three years later, when the secularist George Foote was prosecuted for blasphemy, Leslie joined the ranks of those who appealed for the remission of the harsh sentence. It was, in fact, this example of late-Victorian ideological oppression that stimulated his remarkable two-part essay 'The Suppression of Poisonous Opinions', first published in the *Nineteenth Century* (Mar–Apr 1883). Admirers of Mill's *On Liberty* might well find this a profound rethinking of the argument for freedom of expression – perhaps, as Noel Annan suggests, 'an even more cogent argument' than Mill's.[22]

Perhaps now we can begin to see why members of his own and the immediately succeeding generations considered him, as Maitland put it, 'one of our liberators'. According to Harold Laski, Professor Alexander of Manchester echoed Maitland's sentiments and asserted that 'when he was a young don at Oxford, things like the "Agnostic's Apology" seemed like beacons of light in a world which the theologian seemed to possess lock, stock, and barrel'.[23] And Frankie Birrell on the evening of 25 February 1926 told Virginia that her father dominated the twentieth century, 'He made it possible for me to have a decent life', Birrell went on; 'he pulled down the whole edifice & never knew what he was doing' (*D*,III,61). No doubt Frankie Birrell's gratitude to Leslie is excessive and no doubt the testimony I have given hardly turns the young 'Mr Ramsay' into a flaming radical, but perhaps I have said enough to suggest that the difference between Mr Ramsay and his living prototype are as important as the similarities. It would be, in fact, a nice exercise to work out the differences in full detail.[24] I hope also to have suggested that, in addition to the social father that Virginia says she never knew, there is the man who lived and wrote for many years before Virginia was born. It would also be a nice exercise to take all the statements Virginia made about her father and check them against what we know about his life and behaviour and intellectual ability and work. Despite her insight, not only does she sometimes contradict herself; in my opinion, she is occasionally quite wrong. Children are not infallible witnesses to their parents – no more than parents are to their children. More than once, for example, she claims that he had no imagination. One wonders if she had ever read 'The Alps in Winter' or 'The Ascent of the Schreckhorn'. She also writes that her father probably justified his bad behaviour because he adhered to the 'genius theory' – that genius was allowed a certain licence to behave badly. In the same passage she mentions his essay on Coleridge; had she read that essay carefully, she could not have missed Leslie's vigorous condemnation of precisely that notion. Her contention that he was narrow she supports by saying he never went to Italy or stayed in Paris, but always headed for the Alps.[25] Well, he did go to Italy on his honeymoon and had visited Paris as well as Germany; true, he did rather look down his nose at foreigners, but the charge comes rather awkwardly from someone who refused to cross the Atlantic for what appear to be snobbish reasons; her father crossed it thrice. Then, too, we can set beside those ambivalent passages in 'A Sketch of the Past' that lyrical passage in her diary for 22 December 1940, written when the clouds of depression were forming again, a passage in which she bathes her parents in the glow of an astonishing vision of serenity:

> How beautiful they were, those old people – I mean father and mother – how simple, how clear, how untroubled. I have been dipping into old letters and father's memoirs. He loved her; oh and was so candid and reasonable and transparent. How serene and gay even, their life reads to me; no mud; no whirlpools. And so human – with the little hum and song of the nursery.    (*WD*, p.360)

Simple? Untroubled? No whirlpools? The answers are obvious and tell us that the doctrine of Virginian infallibility won't do. What *will* do and what we must do is to emulate her constant attempt to 'get it right' and obey her axiom with which this paper began.

It is precisely in the interest of making it difficult for us 'to sum up and make linear' that I have, using documents less easily available than his major works, tried to stress the personal and political aspects of Stephen's life and work. I hope, too, that I have been able to suggest that the agenda for one generation is not the agenda for another; that, while a mover of one agenda may not fully satisfy the movers of a later agenda, his or her moving retains its validity for its own time. The more we know of that history the less liable we are to fall into the fallacy of lumping (i.e. of treating similarities as identities). Thus the young 'Mr Ramsay' was part and parcel of a patriarchal society and shared some, if not all, of its assumptions. He did not believe that women and blacks had been proved to be the equals of men and of whites, but he did insist that everyone should have the untrammelled right to full self-development. This meant getting rid of slavery and of any legal obstructions to the exercise of that right. Again, by and large, Stephen accepted the basic principles of Victorian political economy as set forth by Mill; he was no William Morris (in fact, they got into an argument the only time they met), but near the end of his life he was ready to assert that

> Socialism, in one form, at least, also raises individualism to its highest power [and in human history] the economic factor is a most essential factor, and if Marx emphasised it too exclusively, he was certainly calling attention to a point of real importance. History written without reference to economic conditions, to the physical welfare of society, and to the relations between the classes . . . must be hopelessly superficial.[26]

This statement may surprise some, but no one who has read the first volume of his *English Utilitarians* (1900) or even the Preface to *English Thought in the Eighteenth Century* (1876) will be surprised at his view of history; what may surprise all is the endorsement of some form of socialism. But, then, Leslie is often full of surprises, as when in his eulogy of Henry Sidgwick he remarked that Sidgwick was so high minded that he 'could not really have a conscience – much as he professed to esteem that quality – because I could not see that his conscience would ever have anything to do'.[27]

That touch brings me back where I began, with the personal. It reminds us that, no matter how hard the young Leslie tried to make himself into an athlete, mental and physical, a 'masculinist' if you like, he never really succeeded. His love of poetry, his sensitivity, his love for Julia and his family and friends, male and female, his tenderness and need for affection kept pushing through the crust of Cambridge rationalism. Cruelty appalled him. Jingoistic patriotism was 'a vulgar brag'. If he praised the 'manly' he kept himself distant from the rough brutality of his brother Fitzjames, whom John Morley once characterised as 'Bill Sikes converted by Jeremy Bentham'. And, if he abhorred the effeminate (Coventry Patmore was his prime example), he believed that 'every man ought to be feminine, i.e., to have quick and delicate feelings'.[28] He defined chivalry – a word now a bit out of fashion – as 'a refinement of the sense of justice – an instinctive capacity for sympathizing with everyone who is the victim of oppression in any of its forms.'[29] There are worse definitions.

## NOTES

1. Leslie Stephen, 'The Vanity of Philosophising', *Social Rights and Duties*, II, 192, 201, 222–3.
2. 'What is Materialism?' in *An Agnostic's Apology* (London: Smith, Elder, 1903) pp. 127–68. See esp. p. 137. The essay was first composed as a lecture delivered in South Place Chapel to the London Ethical Society in 1886, and printed in the 1st edn of *An Agnostic's Apology* in 1893.
3. Ibid., pp. 296, 40.
4. BL Add. MS. 61973. It has been announced that this document will be included in the new edn of *Moments of Being* being prepared by Jeanne Schulkind.
5. Leslie to Julia Stephen, 25 Mar 1887, quoted with the permission of the Henry W. and Albert A. Berg Collection, the New York Public Library Astor, Lennox and Tilden Foundations, and of Quentin Bell.
6. F. W. Maitland, *The Life and Letters of Leslie Stephen* (London: Duckworth, 1906) p. 24.
7. Maitland Papers, CUL Add. MS. 5944, notations for 30 Sep and 12 Oct 1840, respectively. Quotations from the Maitland Papers with the permission of the Cambridge University Library.
8. Leslie Stephen, 'In Praise of Walking', *Studies of a Biographer* (London: Duckworth, 1902) III, 258; first published in the *Monthly Review*, IV (1901) 33–48.
9. Caroline Emilia Stephen to F. W. Maitland, Maitland Papers, CUL Add. MS 7008.305. Milly's view of the matter is paralleled by that of Leslie's cousin, Edward Dicey, as expressed in his letter to Maitland dated 1 Sep 1904 and his 'Notes on Leslie Stephen's Youth' (CUL Add. MS 7001.24).
10. Maitland, *Life and Letters of Leslie Stephen*, p.146.
11. Leslie Stephen, *Mausoleum Book* (Oxford: Clarendon Press, 1977) p.4.
12. BL Add. MS. 61973.
13. Maitland Papers, CUL Add. MS. 7007.296. I am grateful to Bernie Lightman for finding this passage.
14. Leslie Stephen to Charles Eliot Norton, 25 July 1903, quoted with the permission of the Houghton Library and of Quentin Bell.
15. Leslie Stephen to Harriet Marion Thackeray, 24, 25, 30 Dec 1866, quoted with the permission of the Manuscript Department of William R. Perkins Library, Duke University, and of Quentin Bell.

16. Leslie Stephen, *Sketches from Cambridge by a Don*, with a Foreword by G. M. Trevelyan (London: Oxford University Press, 1932) pp. 82,89.

17. *Fortnightly Review*, XIV (Sep 1873) 314.

18. Leslie Stephen, *Freethinking and Plainspeaking* (London: Smith, Elder, 1907) p. 400 (1st edn 1873).

19. Leslie Stephen, 'Mr Ruskin's Recent Writings', *Fraser's Magazine*, IX (June 1874) 688.

20. Leslie Stephen, 'The Value of Political Machinery', *Fortnightly Review*, XXIV (Dec 1875) 840.

21. Leslie Stephen, 'Mr Bradlaugh and his Opponents', *Fortnightly Review*, XXXIV (Aug 1880) 176–87.

22. This essay was republished, much revised and retitled 'Poisonous Opinions' in *An Agnostic's Apology* (1893), then revised even more and again retitled 'Toleration' in the 1903 edn.

23. *The Letters of Harold Laski to O.W. Holmes, Jr*, ed. M. DeWitt Howe (Cambridge, Mass.: Harvard University Press, 1952) II, 1408.

24. In case any doubters remain, let them read the postscript to Virginia Woolf's letter to Jacques-Emile Blanche (20 Aug 1937): 'I did not mean to paint an exact portrait of my father in Mr Ramsay. A book makes everything into itself, and the portrait became changed to fit as I wrote' (*L*, VI, 517).

25. BL Add. MS. 61793.

26. Leslie Stephen, 'The Ascendancy of the Future', *Nineteenth Century*, LI (1902) 807.

27. Leslie Stephen, 'Henry Sidgwick', *Mind*, XXXVII (Jan 1901) 14.

28. Maitland, *Life and Letters of Leslie Stephen*, p. 314.

29. Leslie Stephen, *The Life of Henry Fawcett* (London: Smith, Elder, 1886) p. 180.

# 5 The Thackeray Connection: Virginia Woolf's Aunt Anny[1]

## CAROL HANBERY MACKAY

In *A Room of One's Own,* Virginia Woolf describes her thwarted attempt to examine the manuscripts of John Milton's 'Lycidas' and William Makepeace Thackeray's *The History of Henry Esmond, Esq.* in 'that famous library' at Oxbridge:

> 'like a guardian angel barring the way with a flutter of black gown instead of white wings, a deprecating, silvery, kindly gentleman . . . regretted in a low voice as he waved me back that ladies are only admitted to the library if accompanied by a Fellow of the College or furnished with a letter of introduction. (*AROO*, pp. 7–8)

Woolf's curiosity about Thackeray's manuscript was piqued by *Henry Esmond*'s reputation as his 'most perfect novel', despite its affectation of imitating eighteenth-century style. She wondered if that style were natural to Thackeray, a question she thought might be answered by studying the revisions. Had she examined the manuscript, she would have discovered the absence of significant revision – a fact that her father, Leslie Stephen, had known when he donated the manuscript to Trinity College but which continued to be ignored by the popular tradition that this was the most carefully reworked of Thackeray's novels.[2] Had she been allowed to see the manuscript, she would also have noted that it was written in several hands, for the successful author of *Vanity Fair* could afford to hire an amanuensis, Eyre Crowe, as well as solicit the willing aid of his daughter, Anne Isabella Thackeray, later Mrs Richmond Ritchie.[3] So, if Virginia had indeed been permitted to examine the manuscript of *Henry Esmond*, she would have seen her own aunt's handwriting, which had recorded Anne's famous father's improvisatory method of literary creation.

Anne Thackeray Ritchie (1837–1919) was Leslie Stephen's

sister-in-law by his first marriage to Harriet Marion ('Minny') Thackeray, who died in 1875, leaving him with a five-year-old daughter, Laura. Despite his subsequent marriage to Julia Jackson Duckworth in 1878, the introduction of the three Duckworth children, and the birth of four more Stephen children – including Virginia in 1882 – Leslie remained close to 'Anny', albeit in his usual fashion of maintaining a rather tempestuous relationship with the women in his life. Aunt Anny was thus a frequent visitor to the Stephen household and a mainstay during Leslie's bereavement for Julia and his own deathbed days. But she served a special role to the young Virginia, the Stephen child who became a writer and who, more than any other of the children in the family, had to contend with the ghost of her father. Aunt Anny was a model for Virginia of 'the daughter of an educated man' who became an author in her own right. Through her Aunt Anny, Virginia discovered the power of speaking in her own voice and exercising her sense of humour in her writing.[4]

## 1 'DAUGHTERS OF EDUCATED MEN'

In *Three Guineas* Virginia Woolf describes 'daughters of educated men' as a class apart. Their fathers having attended public school and university, these young women rely upon their fathers for support and for the reading-lists that will constitute their education. In contrast, their brothers can expect to be sent to the best schools, whether or not they evidence much interest in learning. Even their mothers join in the conspiracy, as did Julia Stephen – like Thackeray's Mrs Pendennis saving toward 'Arthur's Education Fund'.[5] This is the double bind that Virginia found herself trapped in: on the one hand, she valued her father's attention and direction; on the other, she felt left out of the circle of learning that was available to her brothers without their asking. We all know how she overcame her apparent handicap – what a voracious reader she became, how she sought out and developed the intellectual community called Bloomsbury – but the sense of loss remained. A year before her death, Woolf could still write to Benedict Nicolson, 'Now my own education (alone among my books) was a very bad one.'[6]

Aunt Anny did not experience such a sense of loss, however, and by delighting in her self-education she helped Virginia and other young women writers to recognise some of the advantages of choosing one's own lines of literary confluence. Thackeray acted the part of first mentor in this respect. 'I had written several novels and a tragedy by the age of fifteen,' Anne Ritchie replied to publisher George Smith in response to his query about when she began to write, 'but then my father forbade me to waste my time [with] any more scribbling, and desired me to read *other* people's books'.[7] Although her father was the one to announce her readiness to take up the pen again in 1860 – and even to select her first topic for publication, 'Little Scholars', published in the *Cornhill Magazine* under his editorship – the young Miss Thackeray had in the meantime acquired a confidence in her own voice. The years of reading and writing following her father's death in 1863 testify to this self-confidence: she read and memorialised not only the works of her father's contemporaries but also those of the generation to follow her own, and she produced some eight novels as well as biographical introductions to her father's entire canon. Anne Ritchie's advice to budding authors often starts with a quotation from her father, but it is likely to end on a personal reaction – coupled with a note of genuine encouragement and an offer to help in that crucial first step to publication.[8]

For both Anny and Virginia, authorship began in the privacy of keeping a diary and the relative privacy of letter-writing. Woolf could see in her aunt a specific example of how the free play of words in diaries and letters can fuel novel-writing and provide a testing-ground for stylistic experimentation. Five years after Lady Ritchie's death, her daughter Hester published a selection of her letters and journals. It was this source that supplied Virginia with Anny's 'happy' simile, 'The sky was like a divine parrot's breast, just now, with a deep, deep, flapping sea', which she cited in her own tribute to her aunt; it was this occasion that caused Virginia to observe of Anny's style, 'Her most typical, and, indeed inimitable sentences rope together a handful of swiftly gathered opposites.'[9] One letter from Blois, dated 'Yesterday', particularly captures Anny's self-conscious impressionism:

All the old women have got their white caps on; the east wind has made every weather-cock shine. I can't think how to tell you what a lovely old place it is, sunny-streaked up and down, stones flung into *now* from St Louis's days, others rising into carved staircases and gabions and gargoyles. This isn't a description – I wish it were – it isn't white or crisp enough, or high enough.[10]

On the one hand Anny could record in her journal, 'I try to write a diary but it all seems sham', and on the other she could turn diary-keeping to fictional self-accounting in *Miss Williamson's Divagations*.[11] These same contradictory options were also available to Virginia, part of her self-critical yet self-generating repertoire.

Both Anny and Virginia knew what it was like to be subjected to Leslie Stephen's wrath and critical judgement, but her aunt was a survivor – and Virginia knew it. Ironically enough, one of Leslie's most vociferous criticisms of Anny reflected her situation as 'the daughter of an educated man': 'Anny, for example, is about the most uneducated person I ever knew', he wrote to his prospective wife in 1877.[12] Still, Anny stood up to Leslie, in life and the continued production of her art. She piqued him into begrudging admiration for her 'genius': 'I must say that Anny's audacity in sewing together a lot of descriptions of scenery and calling it a story rather amuses me. But she certainly has or had a "gift" as they call it', he wrote to Julia when Virginia was five.[13] His attitude toward fiction could be not unlike that of Carlyle – he was entertained by it but not always willing to admit that it deserved serious consideration. He may have managed to preserve the manuscript of *Henry Esmond* in the Trinity library, yet he failed to persevere in setting the record straight about its composition. Although Thackeray was one of Leslie's favourite authors, he may have been slightly embarrassed by Thackeray's improvisatory method of creation – something Anny knew about first-hand and Virginia intuitively sought to confirm.

As Thackeray's sometime amanuensis, Anny was often his first reader. She learned from him how the creative process operates – that it comes and goes in starts and fits, that sometimes one steeps oneself in facts and figures, and that at other times the words just seem to flow as if dictated by an inner voice. Writing came naturally to her, and as a teenager she could already envision herself taking on multiple careers in the arts: 'At one moment I'm mad to be an artist, the next I languish for an author's fame, the third, I would be mistress of German, and the fourth practise five hours a day at the pianoforte.'[14] Anny's own impressionistic style suggests that she shared with Thackeray the gift for 'spontaneous rhapsody' that could also be said to characterise Virginia's genius.[15] Even if Virginia achieved that impression of spontaneity through constant reworking and polishing, she valued the same final effect and the strong sense of personal voice that it entailed. In fact, it was Anny's early fiction, novels such as *The Village on the Cliff* and *Old Kensington*, which drew most heavily on impressions of childhood experiences, that Virginia especially admired. When Jonathan Cape expressed an interest in republishing some of these novels and approached Woolf about writing an introduction to one of them, she was eager to co-operate – and, when the project fell through, it was only because she intended to write a longer, more general response to Anny's fiction.[16]

What Virginia could detect in Anny's written style, she had always recognised in her personality: Anny was a free spirit, an iconoclast concurrently accepted by three generations, a genuine individual. As a child of ten, Virginia described her aunt's reaction to learning that Leslie had become President of the London Library: 'Mrs Ritchie the daughter of Thackeray who came to luncheon the next day expressed her delight by jumping from her chair and clapping her hands in a childish manner but none the less sincerely.'[17] In this early description, we can see traces of Virginia's ambivalence toward Anny's spontaneity, yet as always Aunt Anny wins her over. Miss Thackeray had shocked her friends and family by marrying a man seventeen years her junior, and she continued to unsettle them with her eccentric ways. But Woolf declares her final allegiance to her aunt when she takes such pleasure in citing Anny's childhood adventure of breaking 'the enormous respectability of Bloomsbury' by escaping from her nurse and dancing in the street to the music of an organ:

> For the rest of her long life, through war and peace, calamity and prosperity, Miss Thackeray, or Mrs Richmond Ritchie, or Lady Ritchie, was always escaping from the Victorian gloom and dancing to the strains of her own enchanted organ. . . . And the music to which she dances, frail and fantastic, but true and distinct, will sound on outside our formidable residences when all the brass bands of literature have (let us hope) blared themselves to perdition.[18]

The bond that Lady Ritchie and Woolf thus shared in life and

art can be summed up in terms of playful irreverence and the spirit
of individualism, and it manifests itself through their sense of
humour in particular. It is a sense of humour that delights in
provocation by exaggeration. Desmond MacCarthy recalls
Anny's remark to Samuel Butler about Shakespeare's sonnets, 'O,
Mr Butler, I hope you think they were written by Anne Hathaway
to Shakespeare?' Butler was not amused – but, as MacCarthy
notes, he may have conveniently forgotten that his own last book
was entitled *The Authoress of the Odyssey*.[19] Virginia herself relates
an instance of how Leslie's sobriety seemed to provoke her aunt's
'tissue of exaggerations':

> 'There are 40,000,000 unmarried women in London alone!'
> Lady Ritchie once informed him. 'Oh, Annie, Annie!' my father
> exclaimed in tones of horrified but affectionate rebuke. But
> Lady Ritchie, as if she enjoyed being rebuked, would pile it up
> even higher next time she came.[20]

Virginia, too, could provoke the sobriety of an equally humourless
age. Whether gleefully participating in the great Dreadnought
Hoax or playfully tackling *Orlando* and *Flush* – her 'holiday books'
– Virginia carried on her aunt's tradition. Sometimes, in fact, it
has taken us decades to get the joke, for Virginia delighted in
lacing her novels with private references and innuendo.[21]

## II  *NIGHT AND DAY*

One of those novels, of course, was *Night and Day*, in which the
character of Mrs Hilbery is an acknowledged portrait of Lady
Ritchie. Published in 1919, the year of Anny's death, *Night and Day*
indulges in playful irony reminiscent of Jane Austen, and Jane
Marcus has recently argued that we can profitably read it as comic
opera.[22] Katharine Hilbery may be the heroine of the piece, but
behind and around her, linking the generations and finding
solutions where others see only problems, is Mrs Hilbery – 'Aunt
Anny on a really liberal scale'.[23] Inspired by her aunt's scatter-
brained escapades that somehow 'come out all right', Woolf
creates in Mrs Hilbery her contribution to the female version of
the archetype of the wise fool. Anny may have sent her novel *Miss
Angel* to Australia 'with her feet foremost, and the proofs all wrong

and the end *first*!!!' – but it was not her undoing as a novelist. And, when she arrived to visit Charles Darwin a week before he had expected her, she had somehow grasped the urgency of seeing him then – a week later he was dying. Citing both these examples in 'The Enchanted Organ', Virginia concludes, 'To embrace oddities and produce a charming, laughing harmony from incongruities was her genius in life and letters.'[24] And so it was for Virginia through Mrs Hilbery.

Mrs Hilbery devotes her life to the writing of her father's biography, but as a life-long process it seems more true to the spirit of the biographer than to whatever facts could be said to constitute the poet's life. The task seems unending, unlikely ever to reach completion. 'She could not decide how far the public was to be told the truth about the poet's separation from his wife', for instance, notes Katharine. 'She drafted passages to suit either case, and then liked each so well that she could not decide upon the rejection of either.'[25] In this, Mrs Hilbery represents Anny's own adherence to the conditions Thackeray set to publication of his biography – although Anny did have it both ways by writing the piecemeal biographical introductions to her father's complete works. And Mrs Hilbery also reflects Anny's and Virginia's views about the difficulty of knowing the truth, possibly best reached through fictions or apparent contradictions: 'Lies will flow from my lips, but there may perhaps be some truth mixed up with them', writes Woolf in *A Room of One's Own*; 'it is for you to seek out this truth and to decide whether any part of it is worth keeping'.[26]

Virginia, like Mrs Hilbery, had been expected to worship at the shrine of her ancestors. Leslie Stephen, whose grand project in life was *The Dictionary of National Biography*, had groomed her to follow in his footsteps as a biographer and historian, but Virginia's greatest fear, recorded in her diary almost twenty-five years after her father's death, was that if Leslie had lived longer 'his life would have entirely ended mine. What would have happened? No writing, no books; – inconceivable.'[27] Luckily, since she was only twenty-two at his death, Virginia was able to turn his training to her own account – to make it serve her version of the personal essay, one that let her write in her own voice and yet not impose her ego on her subject; to write the innovative novels that grew out of intimate knowledge of traditional forms. Given the intense ambivalence that underlay her feelings about her father, it is no wonder that she limited her public portrait of him to the single, rather innocuous biographical essay that appeared in *The Times* to mark the centenary of his birth.[28] The stronger feelings remained buried in her psyche for years, working themselves out in the privacy of her diary and the symbolic privacy of her novels. Within a year of her suicide, Woolf was still 'obsessed' with the relationship: 'Until I wrote it out, I would find my lips moving; I would be arguing with him, raging against him, saying to myself all the things that I never said to him.'[29]

Anne Thackeray's felicitous relationship with her own father did not reflect a similar ambivalence, however, and through Mrs Hilbery's impressionistic manner of composing we can detect the link that shows Virginia recognising and perhaps benefiting from the model that such a reciprocal relationship provides. Working closely with Thackeray – taking his dictation, writing his letters, winning his praise for her literary skills, later editing his canon – Anny learned to write freely, without fear of censorship and the bogy of crippling self-criticism, and she so steeped herself in his style that she gained the advantage of any author who builds on stylistic reverberations with another voice. Mrs Hilbery 'had no difficulty in writing, and covered a page every morning as instinctively as a thrush sings'[30] – and the same could be said of Anny. In fact, the conscious choice of a digressive style, as emphasised by Anny's own title *Miss Williamson's Divagations,* became a topic for Virginia in 'The Journal of Mistress Joan Martyn' thirteen years before she epitomised it in Mrs Hilbery's 'spells of inspiration'.[31] Furthermore, although Woolf could not so easily dispel the external and internal voices of criticism that drove her to constant revision and the verge of madness, she did know the ultimate creative power of copying and reading the words of other writers in the midst of her own incapacity to write.

In Thackeray's *Roundabout Papers,* his last *Cornhill* series, we can find the typical Thackerayan improvisatory method and his frequent theme of regretting the passage of time. Anny turned both his method and theme to her own purposes, serving herself as a link between past generations and the ones to follow. And, in her turn, Virginia re-created her aunt in Mrs Hilbery, the one character who could grasp the past in the present and hence communicate it to the new generation: 'Mrs Hilbery had in her own head as bright a vision of that time as now remained to the living, and could give those flashes and thrills to the old words which gave them almost the substance of flesh.'[32] We tend to think of Virginia Woolf as satirising or rejecting the past and embracing the new order – especially when we consider her attacks on the Victorian Age in works such as *Freshwater* and *The Years*. But Mrs Hilbery and her source in Lady Ritchie also remind us of the Virginia who could capture 'moments of being' – the past as eternally present. Mrs Hilbery is the key figure in *Night and Day* because she cuts through petty incompatibilities and misunderstandings to reveal the important realities that lie beneath them: it is she who unites the opposites of night and day. Like Anny, she can 'embrace oddities and produce a charming, laughing harmony from incongruities'. In this, only her second novel, Virginia already displays her indebtedness to her aunt as a progenitor for subject, style and tone.

## III  'THE TIES THAT BIND'

Let us return to the family ties for a moment – to retrace the interconnections and to understand better why Virginia should have been so alert to Anny's example in the first place. The issues raised by the father–daughter relationship are central to this consideration. In Aunt Anny, Virginia found someone who could join in friendly combat with her own father, Leslie Stephen. Unlike the young Virginia, who had to remain silent in the face of Leslie's temperamental outbursts or who reacted to them through her own apparently motiveless raging, Anny elected a balanced response – one that let her quietly challenge Leslie through her own brand of humour. The man who had written in 1869, 'What are we to do with this army of spinsters whose enforced celibacy is an evil to themselves and society?'[33] harboured preconceptions about women that Anny laughingly exploded by her extravagant accounting of '40,000,000 unmarried women in London alone!' Anne Thackeray lived with Leslie and Minny after their marriage in 1867 and maintained the household with him for the two years following Minny's death until her own marriage in 1877. These were her training-years, when she learned how to hold her own against Leslie and assert her optimism. Over the years, she gradually broke down some of Leslie's reserve and resistance, until he finally could turn her self-mocking humour against himself by comparing their correspondence to 'a dove talking to a gorilla'. During his last illness, Anny once broke the gloom that had become so oppressive to Virginia and the other Stephen children by initiating their conversation with the words, 'Well Leslie – Damn – Damn – *Damn!*'[34]

Anny's strength in dealing with Leslie and other authority figures derived from a much more healthy relationship with Thackeray than Virginia had known with her own father. Isabella Thackeray's mental incapacity left her husband with two young daughters to raise. Despite his rather Bohemian lifestyle and the years when the girls lived with the grandparents in Paris, Thackeray developed a close relationship with his daughters, always favouring Anny over Minny as herself a budding 'man of genius'. Anny was his secretary, his confidante, his pride. Although he could selfishly wish to retain her as his companion, he did so in protective terms – 'O may she never fall in love absurdly and marry an ass!' – and he compensated for such thoughts by asserting to both his daughters 'what immense happiness you enjoy I daresay with the right man'.[35] Anny responded by delighting in his companionship and instruction yet developing her unique talents as a writer. And, in one sense, Thackeray could never impose on his daughter the onerous weight felt by Virginia as the 'daughter of an educated man', because he sidestepped his university career – like his semi-autobiographical character Arthur Pendennis, Thackeray left Cambridge (Pen's hybrid 'Oxbridge') after two years.

Aunt Anny also provided Virginia with a model of courage in handling the fears of family insanity. Anne Thackeray's mother, Isabella, had first shown signs of mental breakdown when her daughter was a child of three, and Anny witnessed her father's anguish as he repeatedly raised his hopes that she might recover only to see his worst fears realised again and again. Throughout Isabella's life (she outlived Thackeray by thirty years, dying within a year of Julia Stephen), her daughter visited her regularly, becoming more like a mother to her own mother, whose form of schizophrenia kept her in childlike innocence. Perhaps it was this intimate acquaintance with her mother that led Anny to recognise similar symptoms in the young Laura Stephen. Again, Anny was accepting and understanding, not judgemental, as her dedication to *Old Kensington* indicates: 'And meanwhile Laura measures the present with her soft little fingers as she beats time upon her mother's hand to her own vague music.'[36]

Virginia herself did not learn to talk until she was three, and her violent tantrums caused no small degree of alarm in a family worried about inherited instability (her brother Thoby, too, exhibited fits of insanity, but they were adjudged merely 'temporary').[37] We have uncovered no record of what Aunt Anny might have done directly for Virginia during her bouts of madness, but her letters to Vanessa Bell and Leonard Woolf repeatedly reveal her 'hidden agenda' of concern about 'Gennie'. From 'Nessa' Aunt Anny tries to coax 'a few signs on paper' about 'how Ginia is' or she reiterates, 'It made me very happy seeing Ginia again.'[38] Correspondence with Leonard is more round-about and playful, but equally loving and persistent. The following letter, signed, 'Yours auntfully Anne Ritchie', shows her circuitous insistence on receiving a reply as well as her perpetual sparring with Leslie:

> I wonder if you would do me a kindness – one gets little fads as one grows old – I find one of mine is to read myself to sleep over certain books wh. send me off peacefully. I despatched one of these to dear Ginia – Leslies life + works thinking it might have the same sophorific [*sic*] effect upon her – ! – would you – if she does not want it – send it back to me + forgive my boring you – I find that I miss it + I cant get another copy myself.
>
> But what I want still more is a good account for her + news of her . . . .[39]

Furthermore, by joining the family contingent of females who visited Laura after she was sent away to a home, Anne Ritchie continued to confront and accept where Leslie had merely avoided. And there is no question what Anny would have thought of a supposed cure that denied Virginia her outlets of reading and writing.

Despite her optimism and strength of will, Anny did experience her own bouts of depression and suffered from a variety of physical ailments. The point here is that she overcame them. And, although Virginia was almost overwhelmed by pain and depression throughout her life, she too persisted – until the thought of another attack finally became unbearable. Both Anny and Virginia had known what it was like to live with temperamental fathers, but somehow the association between temperament and genius seemed to explain and perhaps excuse the manic-depressive cycles. Time has in fact conferred the label 'genius' on three of the four figures in our father–daughter parallelogram. Leonard Woolf was only one of many to make the connection between Anny and her father by acknowledging, 'Aunt Anny was a rare instance of the child of a man of genius inheriting some of that genius', but it was Virginia herself who dismissed her father from the canon by his own admission:

> I think he said unconsciously as he worked himself up into one of those violent outbursts, 'This is a sign of my genius', and he called in Carlyle to confirm him, and let himself fly. . . . But was he a genius? No; that was not alas quite the case. 'Only a good second class mind', he once told me. . . .[40]

Yet Woolf, an unquestioned genius to our age, kept this admission and her own dismissal buried from public view in her unpublished 'Sketch of the Past'. She was still maintaining her ambivalence toward her father – an ambivalence that remained too highly charged for her to be able to resolve it as Aunt Anny had, through playful contention. Nevertheless, I think we can see that Anny's solution provided Virginia with considerable gratification – and perhaps made her yearn toward emulation.

## IV  COMMON CHORDS

Now we are prepared to sum up Anny's influence on Virginia by reviewing their written records – by determining their common literary forms, shared impressionistic style, similar subject matter, and basic feminism. Additional documentation comes from Woolf's assessments of her aunt's life and work – the character of Mrs Hilbery in *Night and Day*, Woolf's diary entry upon that novel's completion, her obituary notice about Lady Ritchie, and the review-essay called 'The Enchanted Organ' – even though all of them were published early in Virginia's novel-writing career, and none of them acknowledges an overt line of influence from Anny to Virginia.[41] If we read between the lines (Woolf herself reports, 'I suppose my feeling for her is half moonshine; or rather half reflected from other feelings'), we can recognise likely influence through the affinities – affinities which were strengthened by family ties and similar backgrounds.[42] These ties include the common ancestor, Thackeray, who represented a literary tradition that both women as novelists needed to come to terms with. The result for both of them was a complex attitude toward the past, which informed their sensibility to time and to representing consciousness. As for their similar backgrounds as the 'daughters of educated men', both Anny and Virginia reacted by transforming biography into a more lyrical mode and by drawing more attention to women writers. In this latter respect, their common chord as women shapes the contours of influence, highlighting mutual interests and techniques for survival.

Virginia grew up in a household that was conversant with Thackeray's novels, and she enjoyed reading and rereading his fiction – 'It takes me back to the days of my childhood', she reports to Emma Vaughan.[43] But Woolf also viewed him through critical eyes, generally treating him as a touchstone for the Victorian Age (*Vanity Fair* fell short of *Wuthering Heights*, however), and occasionally even comparing him favourably with one of the Moderns. Recalling her conversation with T. S. Eliot about *Ulysses*, she expresses disappointment with the novel's 'psychology': 'It doesn't tell as much as some casual glance from outside often tells. I said I had found *Pendennis* more illuminating in this way.'[44] Retaining her critical edge, Virginia was hardly sentimental about the family 'relics' either. She was anxious to sell the Samuel Laurence portrait of Thackeray – 'We have had this drawing knocking about for years, and at last wish to be rid of it' – and she was grateful that the sale of one page of the manuscript of *Vanity Fair* to Pierpont Morgan enabled her and Leonard to buy a press.[45] Aunt Anny might have shuddered in her grave at the tone of voice describing her father's portrait, but I suspect she would have rejoiced in the exchange of a scrap of Thackeray's writing for a means to publish her niece's own writing.[46] Virginia never wrote a single piece devoted to Thackeray, just as she never published an essay about Shakespeare or tackled the extended article on Anny that she always intended to write, but in a more important sense she could be said to have incorporated their influences into her entire outlook.[47] Both Anny and Virginia had come to terms with Thackeray and his tradition.

There was yet another tradition that Anny and Virginia embraced and made their own – that of the elegy. In order 'to capture the uniqueness of Woolf's form in *A Room of One's Own*', Jane Marcus recommends that we see it as 'an elegy written in a college courtyard for the lost traditions of women's culture',[48] an elegy that transforms mourning the loss of a hypothetical Judith Shakespeare into celebrating the potential of her rebirth. Denied access to the manuscripts of 'Lycidas', the quintessential elegy, and *Henry Esmond*, Thackeray's digressive elegiac novel, Woolf rejects their formality while casting their lyricism in a new mould. Marcus further notes that much of Virginia's fiction begins as 'elegies for her own dead': 'The ghosts of her loved ones haunted her imagination, and she played god, the writer, resurrecting them into fictional life.'[49] In this respect, she shares the tradition of the female elegy with Anny, who memorialised the generations she outlived not only in her novels but also in her *mémoires*, which broke down the rigidity of traditional biographies.

In the recent and long overdue biography of Anne Thackeray Ritchie, Winifred Gérin characterises her impressionistic method: 'The value of [Anny's] approach lay in its essentially personal quality, but it is not that she seeks to put herself in the picture, rather that without her presence the picture would not exist.'[50] Anne Ritchie's memorials to Thackeray's contemporaries – Alfred Tennyson, John Ruskin, the Brownings, the Carlyles, all of whom she had come to know in her own light – become elegaic evocations of a past that continues to live in their author's present. She reaches that past through remembered impressions which reveal how intensely she experienced primary sensations. The 'record' of Elizabeth Barrett Browning centers on the following sense of time and place:

> Perhaps all the more vivid is the recollection of the peaceful home, of the fireside where the logs are burning, while the lady of that kind hearth is established in her safe corner, with her little boy curled up by her side, the door opening and shutting meanwhile to the quick step of the master of the house, to the life of the world without as it came to find her quiet nook. The hours seemed to my sister and to me warmer, more full of interest and peace, in her sitting-room than elsewhere. Whether at Florence, at Rome, at Paris, or in London once more, she seemed to carry her own atmosphere always, something serious, motherly, absolutely artless, and yet impassioned, noble, and sincere.[51]

This, too, is Anne Ritchie's method as she prepares to tell the story of her father's work – to approach it through setting and mood, to revive the conditions of authorship and the living memories of active collaboration.[52]

'It is so curious how all one's life remains – things don't go, we fade not they. It is all there.' So Anny at sixty reports to her son on learning of Mrs Oliphant's fatal illness and recollecting her own father's happiness at seeing her first review at twenty-three in *Blackwood's*, granted to her by Mrs Oliphant.[53] Anny and Virginia may have differed in their viewpoints on the Victorian and Edwardians, but they were alike in their habit of evoking the past and treating it as their subject. They both counted on memory and the inner voice that can still engage in dialogue with those long gone. And as avid journal-keepers and letter-writers, they were accustomed to trying to record actual conversations, so that the imaginary ones they 're-created' had the ring of truth.[54] In fact, Miss Thackeray's use of letters in her fiction encouraged her to develop an array of authentic internal voices. Whereas Anny served as a link between generations, Virginia acted as their critic – yet each recognised a personal obligation (and then revelled in it) to be faithful to the experience she chose to depict.

Writing of Lady Ritchie a week after her death, Virginia observes,

> unlike most old aunts, she had the wits to feel how sharply we differed on current questions; & this, perhaps, gave her a sense, hardly existing with her usual circle, of age, obsoleteness, extinction. For myself, though, she need have had no anxieties on this head, since I admired her sincerely; but still the generations certainly look very different ways.[55]

So the differences surface, get set aside, and return again. We might be inclined to feel them most strongly when we read *Freshwater*, Woolf's sharply satiric comedy about the Victorian Age.[56] Set at the private resort on the Isle of Wight where Anne Thackeray retreated after her father's death and later spent her last days, this play pokes fun at Victorian mores in general and the idolising of Tennyson in particular (he is always droning on in the background, reciting *Maud*). But, even if Virginia is debunking one of Anny's heroes in *Freshwater*, it is hard to imagine that Aunt Anny's self-mocking brand of humour would not have taken considerable delight in the play. Furthermore, if we examine Miss Thackeray's youthful accounts of her days at Freshwater, we might well suspect Woolf found a source in them: 'Everybody is either a genius or a poet or a painter or peculiar in some way; poor Miss Stephen says is there *nobody* common-place?'[57]

A review of Anny's and Virginia's publications in fact reveals more similarities than differences, and the chief common element is their attention to women writers. Both Anny and Virginia devoted individual essays or introductions to specific texts to Mme de Sévigné (in this case, Anny's contribution was an entire book), Jane Austen, Mrs Gaskell, Miss Mitford, Elizabeth Barrett Browning, George Eliot and Julia Margaret Cameron (also the main personage in *Freshwater*). In addition, they both took up many of the same women writers in review-essays – Anny in 'Heroines and Grandmothers' and 'A Discourse on Modern Sibyls' (the 1913 Presidential Address of the English Association),[58] Virginia in 'Professions for Women' and 'Women Novelists'. But there are two pairs of works that deserve particularly close comparisons – the essays 'Toilers and Spinsters' and *A Room of One's Own*, and the novels *Old Kensington* and *Night and Day*.

In *Bloomsbury Heritage: Their Mothers and their Aunts*, Elizabeth French Boyd points out that Miss Thackeray's essay 'Toilers and Spinsters' anticipates *A Room of One's Own*, and the case is not hard to make.[59] 'May not spinsters, as well as bachelors,' asks Anne Thackeray, 'give their opinions on every subject, no matter how ignorant they may be; travel about anywhere, in any costume, however convenient; climb up craters, publish their experiences, tame horses, wear pork-pie hats, write articles in the *Saturday Review*?'[60] The significant factor, she answers, is money, not husbands. Woolf offers a similar argument in *A Room of One's Own*, where the narrator acknowledges the greater value of her inheritance over the right to vote, for it is the money that will buy her that 'room of one's own' in which to write undisturbed. In these two key feminist essays, Anny and Virginia are in a sense responding to and refuting Leslie's article 'The Redundancy of Women', published in an 1869 issue of the *Saturday Review*.[61] 'We have an uncomfortable suspicion that a great deal of satire will have to be expended before women cease to be extravagant', he writes – and we already know how Anny turned her extravagant statistics about unmarried women to satire at Leslie's expense. But it is his remarks about spinsters as undoubtedly preferring to be married that provoke his daughter to develop an extended example of the opposite case. Later, in *Three Guineas*, she would reply more sarcastically, yet still protecting his anonymity: 'But biography shows how natural it was, even in the present century, for the most enlightened of men to conceive all women as spinsters, all desiring marriage.'[62]

*Old Kensington* and *Night and Day*, written when their authors were in their mid thirties, show both Anny and Virginia returning to the days of their young womanhood in the same Kensington district. Beyond the autobiographical parallels is the shared fascination with consciousness – with trying to penetrate yet preserve the mystery of the mind through setting and sensation. Building on a more narrow discussion of inner life in a previous chapter, Anne Thackeray recasts the questions of identity and self-awareness for her heroine, Dolly Vanborough:

> 'Inner life', thinks Dolly. 'What is inner life? George says he knows. John Morgan makes it all into the day's work and being tired. Aunt Sarah says it is repentance. Robert won't even listen to me when I speak of it. Have I got it? What am I?' . . . This is what she is at the instant – so she thinks at least: Some whitewashed walls, a light through a big window; John Morgan's voice echoing in an odd melancholy way, and her own two hands lying on the cushion before her. Nothing more . . . a bird's shadow . . . the branch of a tree. . . .[63]

This technique surely foreshadows some of Woolf's later stream-of-consciousness, and in comparison with *Night and Day* Miss Thackeray's style here seems almost avant-garde, for *Night and Day*'s more traditional approach draws heavily on the soliloquy convention to portray the mind at work. Yet the common setting and attention to the movement of mind make these two novels more alike than different. It is no wonder that Virginia cast her Aunt Anny in the world of *Night and Day*.

From the outset of her novel-writing career, Anne Thackeray looked ahead to Modernist modes of narrating consciousness. Both *The Story of Elizabeth* (1863) and *The Village on the Cliff* (1867) show her experimenting with interior monologue and free indirect speech. Observe, for example, how the narration recounts and surrounds the thoughts of Catherine George, one of the two heroines, in *The Village on the Cliff*:

She understood, though no one had ever told her, all that was passing before her. She listened to the music: it seemed warning, beseeching, prophesying, by turns. There is one magnificent song without words in the adagio, in which it seems as if one person alone is uttering and telling a story, passionate, pathetic, unutterably touching. Catherine thought it was Beamish telling his own story in those beautiful passionate notes to Catherine [Butler], as she sat there in her great cloud dress, with her golden hair shining in the sunset. Was she listening? Did she understand him? Ah, yes! she must! Did everybody listen to a story like this once in their lives? Catherine George wondered. People said so. But, ah! Was it true?[64]

'If experience consists of impressions, it may be said that impressions *are* experience', argued Henry James (he was making this point with respect to a good friend, 'an English novelist, a woman of genius' – namely Anne Thackeray Ritchie – and the growth of her novel *The Story of Elizabeth* from a 'direct personal impression').[65] Both Anny and her niece took this awareness about life and applied it to their art, re-creating and linking up a series of recognisable yet unique 'moments' in their novels. For both of them, these moments epitomise the meaning of life and art. As the author of *Miss Angel*, Miss Thackeray addresses that meaning openly, in terms of both the threat and power of the passage of time:

It may be our blessing as well as our punishment that the *now* is not all with us as we hold it, nor the moment all over that is past. It is never quite too late to remember, never quite too late to love; although the heart no longer throbs that we might have warmed, the arms are laid low that would have opened to us. But who shall say that time and place are to be a limit to the intangible spirit of love and reconciliation, and that new-found trust and long-delayed gratitude may not mean more than we imagine in our lonely and silenced regret?[66]

All of Virginia's 'heroines', like her aunt's, reflect a similar awareness of 'moments of being'.

When Woolf wrote her aunt's obituary notice for *The Times*, she emphasised the same linking role she had depicted for Mrs

Hilbery in *Night and Day*: '[Lady Ritchie] will be the unacknowledged source of much that remains in men's minds about the Victorian age. She will be the transparent medium through which we behold the dead. We shall see them lit up by her tender and radiant glow.'[67] A few years later, the 'Diary Column' of *The Times* would fail to note the fact of Anny's relation to Virginia, much less her interrelating role for the two generations: the writer observes instead that, since Minny Stephen was not Virginia's mother, 'the literary succession is indirect so far as Thackeray is concerned'.[68] But the literary influence of Thackeray and its filtered examples through Anny's life and art constituted much more than an indirect succession for Virginia. Anne Thackeray Ritchie experienced her own self-doubts about writing and witnessed how her father had turned self-criticism upon himself. At twenty, young Miss Thackeray records these fears and tensions in her journal:

> things seem to pierce through and through my brain somehow, to get inside my head and remain there jangling. I wonder if it is having nothing to do all day pottering about with no particular object? It is no use writing novels, they are so stupid, it's no use drawing little pictures, what's the good of them?

It is thus not surprising to find that she also shared Virginia's understanding that suicide might be 'better than long years of mental suffering'. Writing to her childhood friend Edith Story in 1907, Anny expresses her sorrow that 'we have again in our family had the same cruel catastrophe – the death of a young man 'by his own hand in some sudden excitement in an over-wrought brain'.[69] That 'same cruel catastrophe' would strike in her family again – but not until Virginia had fulfilled her aunt's literary promise.

## NOTES

1. I wish to thank Martine Stemerick, Louise DeSalvo and John Bicknell for their assistance and their model of scholarship. I am also grateful for permission to quote from their holdings to Dr Lola L. Szladits, Curator of the Berg Collection at the New York Public Library, Astor, Lennox and Tilden Foundations; Frank Walker, Curator of the Fales Library, New York University Library; Mary Robertson, Curator of Manuscripts, the Henry E. Huntington Library; Ellen Dunlap, Research Librarian at the Humanities Research Centre, The University

of Texas at Austin; Quentin Bell; Belinda Norman Butler; Gordon N. Ray; the University of Sussex (Monk's House Papers); and the British Library. Finally, I am indebted to Jane Marcus, who encouraged me to undertake this project – who helped me to see Anny Thackeray Ritchie in her own light, not just in her father's shadow.

2. In his edition of W. M. Thackeray's *The History of Henry Esmond, Esq.* (London: Oxford University Press, 1908) pp. xxvii, George Saintsbury reproduces Leslie Stephen's letter to the College Librarian, which accompanied Anne Thackeray Ritchie's gift of the manuscript. The letter comments on the three handwritings and the relative absence of alteration. General agreement that *Henry Esmond* was not revised but instead 'is genetically no different from the novels published from month to month in numbers' did not arrive until J. A. Sutherland clarified the controversy in *Thackeray at Work* (London: Athlone Press, 1974) pp. 56–8.

3. Eyre Crowe discusses his role as part-time amanuensis for *Henry Esmond* in *With Thackeray in America* (New York: Charles Scribner's Sons, 1894) pp. 3–5. He dedicates his book to Mrs Richmond Ritchie 'as a tribute of admiration for her inherited literary gifts and for the sake of a life-long friendship'.

4. Aunt Caroline Stephen provided Virginia with yet another model – that of 'female power derived from chastity'. Aunt Caroline also dealt with family insanity and served as her own father's amanuensis, but she valued 'association with educated men' over training outside the home. See Jane Marcus, 'The Niece of a Nun: Virginia Woolf, Caroline Stephen and the Cloistered Imagination', in *Virginia Woolf: A Feminist Slant*, ed. Marcus (Lincoln, Nebr.: Nebraska University Press, 1984) pp. 7–36. For another study by Marcus that argues Virginia's reciprocal relationship as a writer with her female relatives and friends, see 'Thinking Back through our Mothers', in *New Feminist Essays on Virginia Woolf*, ed. Marcus (London: Macmillan; Lincoln, Nebr.: University of Nebraska Press, 1981) pp. 1–30.

5. Virginia introduces the term 'daughters of educated men' in *TG*, p. 4, in the context of her discussion of 'Arthur's Education Fund', derived from Thackeray's *History of Pendennis: His Fortunes and Misfortunes, his Friend and his Greatest Enemy* (1848–50). She also derives her 'invention' of 'Oxbridge' from *Pendennis*.

6. In two unpublished drafts, 13 Aug 1940, Monk's House Papers, University of Sussex; cited by Martine Kaela Stemerick in 'From Stephen to Woolf: The Victorian Family and Modern Rebellion' (Diss., University of Texas, 1982) p. 28.

7. Dated 1900, in *Thackeray and his Daughter* (British title: *Letters of Anne Thackeray Ritchie*), ed. Hester Thackeray Ritchie (New York: Harper, 1924) p. 124; hereafter cited as *ATR Letters*. Both Anny and Virginia felt strongly about the privacy of letters, yet each has had her letters (and diaries) held up to considerable public scrutiny. Lady Ritchie need not

have worried about her gentle jibes being made public, but Woolf's case can be summed up by the subtitle of her last volume of letters: *Leave the Letters till we're Dead.*

8. See esp. her letters to Mrs Legard and Mary Cholmondeley, dated 1883, in *ATR Letters*, pp. 201–22.

9. Virginia's tribute to Anny, 'The Enchanted Organ' (*CE*, IV, 73–5) was written as a review of her published letters. The parrot simile comes from a letter to Anny's husband, Richmond Ritchie, 10 Jan [1899], in *ATR Letters*, p. 268.

10. To Richmond Ritchie (three years before their marriage), in *ATR Letters*, pp. 167–8.

11. See her journal entry for 2 Jan 1868, in *ATR Letters*, p. 145, and *'Madame de Sévigné'; 'From a Stage Box': 'Miss Williamson's Divagations'* (Leipzig: Bernhard Tauchnitz, 1881) esp. pp. 204–5. At eighteen, Anne Thackeray had enthusiastically recorded in her journal, 'I found Madame D'Arblay in my father's room yesterday, and that has excited me to go on with my own journal and I am seriously thinking of sending a Pepysina of my own to Messrs. Bradbury and Evans.' See her entry for 21 Sep 1855, in *ATR Letters*, pp.76–7.

12. Coniston, 18 July 1877, Berg. I am grateful to John Bicknell for calling this letter to my attention.

13. 4 Oct 1887, Berg.

14. Journal entry for 21 Sep 1855, in *ATR Letters*, p. 77.

15. Elizabeth French Boyd speaks of Anny's and Virginia's shared 'literary gift of spontaneous rhapsody' in her chapter on Anny in *Bloomsbury Heritage: Their Mothers and their Aunts* (New York: Taplinger, 1976) p.88. And, thanks to Brenda Silver, we now know more about Virginia's writing-habits – that the kernels of her critical essays lie in the 'spontaneous impressions' that she first recorded as reading-notes. See Silver, *Virginia Woolf's Reading Notebooks* (Princeton, NJ: Princeton University Press, 1983).

16. See her correspondence with Cape between 12 Apr 1931 and 9 May 1931, in *L*, IV, 310–12, 326, 328. Woolf never fulfilled her intention 'to write a longer and more general article upon [Miss Thackeray's] books'.

17. Written for the *Hyde Park News*, II, no. 45 (21 Nov 1892), a weekly publication started the previous year with Thoby and Vanessa and continued until 1895 largely through Virginia's efforts; repr. in George Spater and Ian Parsons, *A Marriage of True Minds: An Intimate Portrait of Leonard and Virginia Woolf* (London: Jonathan Cape and the Hogarth Press, 1977) p. 10. Ironically, Leslie Stephen's position with the London Library was turned against his daughter in later years. Marcus notes of Virginia, 'She developed what her husband called her "London Library complex" when she expected E. M. Forster to invite her to be the token woman on its board. But his effort failed, he said. They wanted no

women, and cited as precedent Leslie Stephen's annoyance with the previous woman, Mrs [J.R.] Green, the novelist' – 'Liberty, Sorority, Misogyny', in *The Representation of Women in Fiction*, ed. Carolyn G. Heilbrun and Margaret R. Higonnet, Selected Papers from the English Institute, 1981, n.s., no. 7 (Baltimore: Johns Hopkins University Press, 1983) p. 85. It now appears that Forster may have confused Leslie's reaction with that of another board member. See Leslie's letter to Julia, 7 Sep 1894, Berg.

18. 'The Enchanted Organ', *CE*, IV, 73 and 75.

19. See his Foreword in Hester Thackeray Fuller and Violet Hammersley, *Thackeray's Daughter: Some Recollections of Anne Thackeray Ritchie* (Dublin: Euphorion, 1951) p. 7. Virginia incorporates some of Anny's playful reverence for Shakespeare into Mrs Hilbery's character in *Night and Day*.

20. Virginia Woolf, 'Leslie Stephen', *The Times*, 28 Nov 1932; repr. in *CDB*, and in *CE*, IV, 77.

21. *Orlando* (1928) is a good example. In a 1982 seminar discussion at the University of Texas at Austin, celebrating the Virginia Woolf centenary, Nigel Nicolson explained one of those jokes: the 365 rooms in Vita Sackville-West's home, Knole, were transformed by Virginia into 365 bedrooms for Orlando's residence.

22. See Jane Marcus, 'Enchanted Organs, Magic Bells: *Night and Day* as Comic Opera', in *Virginia Woolf: Revaluation and Continuity*, ed. Ralph Freedman (Berkeley, Calif., and Los Angeles: University of California Press, 1980) pp. 97–122. For other pertinent studies, see Joanne P. Zuckerman, 'Anne Thackeray Ritchie as the Model for Mrs Hilbery in Virginia Woolf's *Night and Day*', *Virginia Woolf Quarterly*, I, no. 3 (Spring 1973) 32–46, and Margaret Comstock, ' "The Current Answers Don't Do": The Comic Form of *Night and Day*', *Women's Studies*, IV (1977) 153–72.

23. Entry for 5 Mar 1919 (a week after Lady Ritchie's death), in *D*, I, 247–8.

24. The first book edn of *Miss Angel* (1875), based on the life of the painter Angelica Kauffmann, was dedicated to Julia Duckworth six months before Minny Stephen's death: 'Will you take what is mine to dedicate to you in this little book, of which so much is yours already.' Leslie discusses the jumbled order of the Australian edn in his *Mausoleum Book*, ed. Alan Bell (Oxford: Clarendon Press, 1977) p. 14. See Anny's letter to Mrs Douglas Freshfield [1875], and her journal for 1882, in *ATR Letters*, pp. 180 and 199–200.

25. *ND*, p. 41.

26. *AROO*, p. 4. See also her discussion of truth and personality as being like granite and rainbow in 'The New Biography', *CE*, IV, 229 (first appeared in the *New York Herald Tribune*, 30 Oct 1927), as well as the practical twist in her speech before the London National Society for

Women's Service, 21 Jan 1931; edited and published as 'Professions for Women'(*The Moment*, 1942): 'if one has five hundred a year there is no need to tell lies and it is much more amusing to tell the truth' (TS. transcribed in *P*, p. xxxi).

27. Entry for 28 Nov 1928 (Leslie's birthday – 'he would have been 96'), in *D*, III, 280. For two differing interpretations of Leslie's training of Virginia, see Katherine C. Hill, 'Virginia Woolf and Leslie Stephen: History and Literary Revolution', *PMLA*, XCVI (1981) 351–62; and Louise DeSalvo, '1897: Virginia Woolf at Fifteen', in *Virginia Woolf: A Feminist Slant*, pp. 78–108.

28. See n. 20. For her more penetrating private portrait, see the autobiographical TS. 'A Sketch of the Past I', British Library Add. MS. 61973 – Woolf's revision of the second MS. portion (Monk's House Papers, AA5d) of memoirs published as *Moments of Being*. Since the policy for the *Dictionary of National Biography* had been largely to emphasise the biographies of powerful men, it is no wonder that Anny's entry became an appendage to her husband's contributions to the Indian Office – might Virginia have also intended to avenge this slight? (NB. Anny became Lady Ritchie in 1907 only because Richmond was knighted for service to his nation.)

29. Unpublished diary entry, 19 June 1940; cited in Stemerick, 'From Stephen to Woolf', pp. 6–7. For another example of saying those things that one could never say to one's father, see Franz Kafka, 'Dearest Father', abridged and repr. in *The Essential Prose*, ed. Dorothy Van Ghent and Willard Maas (Indianapolis: Bobbs-Merrill, 1966) pp. 95–105. Stemerick also cites Virginia's first reading of Freud and her discovery 'that this violently disturbing conflict of love and hate [regarding our relation as father and daughter] is a common feeling; and is called ambivalence' ('From Stephen to Woolf', p. 95); see BL Add. MS. 61973, p. 2.

30. *ND*, p. 40.

31. See 'Virginia Woolf's "The Journal of Mistress Joan Martyn" ', ed. and intro. Susan M. Squier and Louise DeSalvo, *Twentieth Century Literature*, XXV, nos 3–4 (Autumn–Winter 1979) 241, and DeSalvo, 'Shakespeare's *Other Sister*', in *New Feminist Essays*, pp. 61–81.

32. *ND*, p. 40. Woolf was quick to point out that Lady Ritchie 'was no visionary', however: her insight derived from her intimate acquaintance with 'the homelier objects which she preferred. . . . Her happiness was a domestic flame, tried by many sorrows' ('The Enchanted Organ', *CE*, IV, 75).

33. Leslie Stephen, 'The Redundancy of Women', *Saturday Review*, 24 Apr 1869, p. 546; cited and discussed in Stemerick, 'From Stephen to Woolf', pp. 140–1.

34. Letter from Leslie to Anny, 22 Nov 1897, and recounted anecdote, in Fuller and Hammersley, *Thackeray's Daughter*, pp. 159 and 156. Over

the years, Leslie had come to appreciate Anny's genuine good will.

35. Letters to Jane Shawe, July 1846; Mrs [Jane] Brookfield, 17–21 July 1851; and Anny and Minny ('My loaves'), 8 Mar 1857 – in *The Letters and Private Papers of William Makepeace Thackeray*, ed. Gordon N. Ray (Cambridge Mass.: Harvard University Press, 1946) II, 240 and 796, and IV, 32.

36. Anne Thackeray, *Old Kensington* (Leipzig: Bernhard Tauchnitz, 1873) p. 6.

37. See the letter of G. T. Worsley, Master at Evelyn's, to Julia Stephen, 6 Mar 1894, in the Collection of Quentin Bell; cited and discussed in Stemerick, 'From Stephen to Woolf', pp. 251–16.

38. 19 June and 'Thursday' [1915–18]. Another letter to Vanessa from this period, simply dated 'Sep 3 at night', reflects Anny's strong tie to her nieces: 'I have been writing no letters – but I woke up just now thinking tho that I *had* answered you in my thoughts . . . .' In the author's private collection.

39. 1 June [1914], Berg. A follow-up letter to Leonard, 10 June 1914, urges that he and 'Ginia' stay at her Freshwater cottage, 'The Porch', for a few weeks. This 'Porch' is not to be confused, as Winifred Gérin has done, with the Cambridge retreat of the same name that Virginia sought under her Aunt Caroline's protection in 1904. See Gérin, *Anne Thackeray Ritchie: A Biography* (Oxford: Oxford University Press, 1981) p. 259. For a discussion of Caroline's inner sanctuary, see Marcus, 'The Niece of a Nun', in *Virginia Woolf: A Feminist Slant*, p. 34, n. 12.

40. See Leonard Sidney Woolf, *Beginning Again: An Autobiography of the Years 1911–1918* (London: Hogarth Press, 1964) pp. 70–1; and Virginia Woolf, 'A Sketch of the Past I', pp. 4–5; cited in Stemerick, 'From Stephen to Woolf', p. 197. This description of Leslie also recalls Mr Ramsay's limitations in *To the Lighthouse*.

41. The case of Anny's literary influence on Virginia would of course be bolstered by correspondence and diary entries on either side which offered or acknowledged direct advice or encouragement, but unfortunately that kind of evidence either does not exist or has not yet come to light. When Hester was compiling the collection of her mother's letters, she did write to Virginia, who at that time had none to provide (letter to Vanessa Bell [mid-September 1921], in *L*, II, 483); but, a year before Lady Ritchie's death, Virginia had forwarded one of her letters to Vanessa, asking that it be returned (2 Jan 1918, *L*, II, 207). Leonard quotes from several of Aunt Anny's letters in order to illustrate her empathy, style and characteristic manner. See *Beginning Again*, pp. 71–2, which includes excerpts from a letter to Virginia that acknowledges 'Dr Morley on yr Father + G. Meredith, he your Father loved.' See undated letter (c. 1916), Berg. Aunt Anny's only other letter to Virginia that I have seen is a playful thank-you note, containing a sketch of Billy Ritchie 'with a warrior crown of wire + Feathers'. See letter to 'My dearest

Gennie' [1889–94], Fales Collection, New York University Library.

42. Entry for 5 Mar 1919, *D*, I, 247. Barbara J. Dunlap notes, 'Perhaps in 1919 Mrs Woolf was unable either to recognize or admit to these affinities, especially in an obituary article which appeared without her signature; but as far as is now known, she never did come to terms with the influence of Anne Thackeray on her own work' – see 'Anne Thackeray Ritchie', in *Victorian Novelists after 1885*, ed. Ira B. Nadel and William E. Fredeman, *Dictionary of Literary Biography*, XVIII (Detroit: Gale Research, 1983) 256.

43. 19 Apr 1900, in *L*, I, 31 – at the ripe old age of eighteen! Compare Anne Thackeray at eighteen, as documented by nn.11 and 18.

44. See letter to Gerald Brenan, 1 Dec 23, citing an earlier, unfinished letter in which Woolf had 'observed that Vanity Fair is inferior as a work of art to Wuthering Heights' (*L*, III, 79); and diary entry for 26 Sep 1922 (*D*, II, 203).

45. For Virginia's plans to sell the Thackeray portrait, see her letter to Hugh Walpole, 15 Apr [1930], in *L*, IV, 157); for her hopes about the sale of the *Vanity Fair* page, see her letter to Vanessa, [3? Dec 1916] in *L*, II, 128. Actually, it was Thoby who made the most profit from the sale of a Thackeray 'relic' – George Duckworth sold Thackeray's manuscript of *Lord Bateman* to Pierpont Morgan for £1000 on Thoby's behalf. Virginia reports to Vanessa, 'So all Bar expenses and Greek expenses are more than paid for. I wish my manuscripts would sell for more than their meaning!' (*L*, I, 232).

46. Over the years, Anne Thackeray Ritchie parted with quite a few Thackeray 'scraps' herself – both as gifts to his readers and as items for profit. She retained a considerable storehouse, however, and parted reluctantly with much that she eventually sold. For a record of some of those dealings, see her correspondence with J. Pearson, 1899–1907, and C.E. Shepheard, 1890–1907, in the Berg and Pierpont Morgan Library.

47. For another argument along similar lines, see Perry Meisel, *The Absent Father: Virginia Woolf and Walter Pater* (New Haven, Conn.: Yale University Press, 1980). Meisel makes a case for Pater's influence on Woolf largely on the grounds of her relative silence about him. Virginia did review Lewis Melville's book *The Thackeray Country* (letter to Violet Dickinson [mid-Feb 1905], *L*, I, 178), but she refused a summary article on Thackeray (see her diary entry for 17 Aug 1920, *D*, III, 58). And she did briefly review at least three Shakespeare productions: review of *A Midsommer Night's Dreame*, *Nation and Athenaeum*, 23 Aug 1924, pp. 645–6; review of *A Lover's Complaint*, *Nation and Athenaeum*, 17 Nov 1928, p. 255; and 'Twelfth Night at the Old Vic', *New Statesman and Nation*, 30 Sep 1933, pp. 385–6. I am grateful to Louise DeSalvo for pointing out these examples of Woolf's interest in Shakespeare.

48. Marcus, 'Liberty, Sorority, Misogyny', in *The Representation of Women in Fiction*, p. 65.

49. Marcus, 'The Niece of a Nun', in *Virginia Woolf: A Feminist Slant*, p. 12. The primary example, of course, is Virginia's depiction of her mother as Mrs Ramsay in *To the Lighthouse*, but we should beware of easy equations. Her mother, and Caroline, and Anny all emerge through multiple portraits, and each single fictional character is herself a composite.

50. Gérin, *Anne Thackeray Ritchie*, p. 219.

51. Anne Ritchie, *Records of Tennyson, Ruskin, and Robert and Elizabeth Browning* (London and New York: Macmillan, 1892). Much of this accounting first appeared in Anne Ritchie's 1885 article for *The Dictionary of National Biography*, commissioned by Leslie, who begrudged her propensity for 'sentimental reflection'; see Fuller and Hammersley, *Thackeray's Daughter*, p. 157. Of course, Virginia turned such propensity upside down in her tale of Mrs Browning's cocker spaniel, *Flush: A Biography* (New York: Harcourt, Brace and World, 1933).

52. See, for example, Ritchie's introduction to *Philip* in the Centenary Biographical Edition (London: Smith, Elder, 1910–11) XVIII. AMS Press has in progress a single-volume reprint of all the introductions, with historical and bibliographical introductions by Carol MacKay and Peter Shillingsburg.

53. See VW's attack on Mrs Oliphant in *TG*. See also *ATR Letters*, p. 261.

54. 'As I had not read Madame D'Arblay then, I don't remember much of [Mr Frederick Tennyson's and Mr Solomon Hart's] conversation', reports Anne Thackeray in 1855, but her later journals are filled with remembered dialogue (see *ATR Letters*, pp. 77 and 166–7, for example). Virginia experiences both the frustrations and achievement of trying to 'write talk down' (see her apparent resignation and subsequent refutation in the example of her reported conversation with T. S. Eliot: entry for 26 Sep 1922, in *D*, II, 202–3).

55. Entry for 5 Mar 1919, in *D*, I, 247.

56. Virginia Woolf, *Freshwater: A Comedy*, ed. and intro. Lucio P. Ruotolo (New York: Harcourt Brace Jovanovich, 1976). The play was first written in 1923 and revised for private performance in 1935.

57. To Walter Senior [Easter 1865], in *ATR Letters*, p. 138. The Miss Stephen is Aunt Caroline. Another Freshwater source for Woolf's fiction may well lie in Miss Thackeray's novella 'From an Island', which bears comparison with *To the Lighthouse*. Note, for example, the centrality of the 'beacon' in Anne's tale: 'It stood there stiff and black upon its knoll, an old weather-beaten stick with a creaking coop for a crown, the pivot round which most of this little story turns. For when these holiday people travelled away out of its reach, they also passed out of my ken' – '*The Village on the Cliff' with Other Stories and Sketches* (Boston: Fields, Osgood, 1869) p. 162.

58. Because of Richmond's recent death on 12 Oct 1912, the address

was read by Ernest G. von Glehn at the Annual General Meeting (10 Jan 1913). Spater and Parsons suggest that Virginia is probably having fun with her aunt's title as well as playing with the name of Sybil Colefax when she introduces the following line in *Orlando*: 'The hostess is our modern Sybil' (*A Marriage of True Minds*, p. 17). Anny also published *A Book of Sibyls* (London: Smith, Elder, 1883), containing her essays on Mrs Barbauld, Miss Edgeworth, Mrs Opie and Miss Austen.

59. Boyd, *Bloomsbury Heritage*, p. 87.

60. Anne Thackeray, 'Toilers and Spinsters', in *'The Village on the Cliff' with Other Stories and Sketches*, p. 215. The essay was started in 1860 and appeared in its final form in 1874 in *'Toilers and Spinsters' and Other Essays*. See also *Miss Williamson's Divagations* for the narration of a self-reflexive spinster governess, who suggests comparison with Thackeray's Charles Batchelor in *Lovel the Widower* (1860).

61. See n. 33. It is hard not to read Anny's remark about writing articles in the *Saturday Review* as a reference to Leslie. To be fair to Leslie, however, it must be admitted that his apparent intention in writing this article was to focus attention on the great waste and misuse of women. Incidentally, it was Virginia's other aunt – Leslie's sister, Caroline Stephen – who provided her with the legacy that was the model for the one in *A Room of One's Own* and that actually helped her buy the time and space in which to write.

62. Virginia Woolf, *Three Guineas*, p. 157. Aunt Anny provides Virginia with an interesting precedent in another request for three guineas – this time to one recipient, Arthur Joseph Munby, whose educational schemes included a course in autodidactism and separate schooling for males. Miss Thackeray offers to pay a 'guinea a year for three years' but then adds her own opinion in favour of co-education: 'I think I *do* think on the whole it a good thing that men + women should live + learn together in the world into which they were all together created' – see letter of 3 May [1874], in the Henry E. Huntington Library. See also Aunt Anny's playful reference to Virginia as 'Guinea' in her letter to Leonard Woolf, 10 June 1914, in the Berg Collection.

63. Anne Thackeray, *Old Kensington*, I, ch. 19, pp. 194–5. Boyd, too, notes Anny's foreshadowing, and I am indebted to her creative editing of this passage for some of its dramatic effect (*Bloomsbury Heritage*, pp. 88–9).

64. Anne Thackeray, *The Village on the Cliff*, ch. 3, p. 31. I discuss Anny's use of free indirect speech, as well as Virginia Woolf's rhetorical fluidity in narrating consciousness, in my forthcoming book, *Soliloquy in Nineteenth-Century Fiction* (London: Macmillan, 1986).

65. Henry James, 'The Art of Fiction' (1884); repr. in *Theory of Fiction: Henry James*, ed. and intro. James E. Miller, Jr (Lincoln, Nebr.: Univ. of Nebraska Press, 1972) p. 35.

66. Anne Thackeray, *Miss Angel*, ch. 19, pp. 158–9.

67. *TLS*, 6 Mar 1919; repr. in Gérin, *Anne Thackeray Ritchie*, pp. 279–84. This notice appeared the day after Virginia's extended diary entry on Aunt Anny.

68. 'Literary Descent', *The Times Weekly Edition*, 16 Aug 1922; cited in *D*, II, 194, n.17.

69. Journal entry for 25 June 1856, in *ATR Letters*, pp. 103–4. See Anny's unpublished letter to Edith [Story] de Peruzzi de Medici, 30 July [1907], in the Humanities Research Center, University of Texas at Austin.

# 6   As 'Miss Jan Says': Virginia Woolf's Early Journals

LOUISE A. DESALVO

On Sunday, 3 January 1897, just before her fifteenth birthday, Virginia Woolf (then Virginia Stephen), an angular, ungainly adolescent, if ever there was one, picked up her favourite pen (and she was passionate about pens), the one with the thin sharp nib that bit into the paper as it crossed over it, but without leaving ink trails – a trait that was unforgivable in nibs. She picked up her diary, a tiny brown leather one, trimmed with gilt, which had a lock and a key, a diary a little larger than the palm of your hand,[1] and she headed for an empty corner of the teeming Stephen family house in Hyde Park Gate in London, where she could have some solitude away from the peering, penetrating, evaluating eyes of servants, half-brothers, a half-sister, her father, and her three energetic siblings, all of whom were always on the lookout for some sign of deviance, some sign of anxiety in this strange creature called Virginia who inhabited this household of theirs. And she wrote a diary entry in which she described how she and her sister Vanessa and her brother Adrian had started to record the happenings of their days in diaries.

In this diary entry, in a reference to how she was riding her new bicycle for the first time, and how uncomfortable it was for her, we see, for the first time, how the adolescent Virginia Stephen created a fictional persona called Miss Jan, whom she used to be her mouthpiece during this difficult year which she called 'the first really *lived* year of my life'.[2] In her entry, rather than saying that she herself is riding the bicycle, she describes how uncomfortable the bicycle is for Miss Jan.

During this year, it was far easier for Virginia Stephen to record what Miss Jan said, as Miss Jan said it, than it was for her to deal with the feelings that she herself was having. Indeed, during this year, if Virginia had something very difficult to say, particularly about her feelings, she very often said it in the voice of Miss Jan.

96

And I shall suggest, later in this essay, that the voice of Miss Jan allowed the adolescent Virginia Stephen to explore thoughts and ideas of a theological nature that were, in the household of her father, the agnostic Sir Leslie Stephen, tantamount to heresy.

Through Miss Jan, and perhaps even because of Miss Jan, Virginia Stephen was able to explore thoughts and ideas that were radically different from those of her father, and she was able, as well, for the first time in her life,[3] to keep a record for the better part of a whole year – a record which now provides for us a portrait of the artist as a very young woman.

As I have spent the last few years working with the seven unpublished diaries and journals of Virginia Woolf (the one that I have just quoted from, which she began when she was fourteen, and which she kept throughout her fifteenth year; one that she kept while on a summer holiday at Warboys, when she was seventeen, in 1899; and those that she kept through the year 1909,[4] when she was twenty-seven, and a woman in the throes of writing the third or fourth draft of her first novel, which she was calling *Melymbrosia*[5] at the time, and already a respected critic, writing for publications like *The Times Literary Supplement*, with well over ninety-four published reviews and essays to her credit[6]), I have been forced again and again to wonder why they have not been published before.[7] I myself have found them to be immensely important documents, documents that will force us to revise much of what we have already written about Virginia Woolf as a person and as a writer in embryo, documents that have allowed those of us who have worked with them already to begin this exciting task.[8]

But, no matter how often I ponder this issue of why these documents have not yet been published, I think of the way the journals would have been treated prior to this time if they had been written by James Joyce – or indeed, by any male writer of sufficient critical reputation – and not by a woman, not by Virginia Woolf. I am forced to conclude that there is something about this woman in the process of learning her craft as a writer – there is something about a portrait of the artist as a young woman[9] – that makes us extremely uneasy, willing to forget the fact that these documents exist.

It must be this, for I should like us to consider for a minute how the literary and scholarly world might respond to the fact that seven volumes of journals of James Joyce, written from his fourteenth year to his twenty-seventh year, which provided, among other things, a day-by-day record of a period of his adolescence during which a mother surrogate died, and which documented his reading of fifty or so books that he alluded to in his maturity, in addition to thirty unpublished essays, written when he was in his twenties, existed, and had not been published.

Well, I think that it is fair to say that if such journals existed, and if they were James Joyce's, they would be considered important – no, they would be considered *essential* to our understanding of James Joyce's intellectual and artistic development. But we do not seem to be willing to see a woman artist in the process of her growth, because it would entail witnessing her struggle against the prevailing current, which requires that a woman be silent. We seem to shrink from the portrait of the artist as a young woman – even as we celebrate the portrait of the young man as he shapes himself into an artist – largely because any portrait of the young woman as an artist must in fact be an indictment of the society in which she struggles to find her own voice.

The early journals of women who transform themselves into writers are, in and of themselves, radical documents. They must, by their very nature, be radical documents. For women, as everyone knows, are not supposed to have voices of their own. We are content to let them speak through the megaphones and the mouthpieces of those men who represent them to the world biographically and economically and politically. Should they want voices of their own, in addition to wanting rooms of their own, the journals which document the process by which a woman wrests herself free from the shackles of silence must, perforce, be uncomfortable documents for us to read, much less publish. Thus, we almost insist that there be a conspiracy of silence surrounding the early moments of a woman's writing life. It is a struggle that is too hard for us to bear, especially for those of us who have been fortunate enough, owing to sex, class or circumstance, to have found our own voice.


First, I should like to provide a catalogue of what these early diaries contain, and suggest very briefly how they might deepen our insight into the development of Virginia Woolf as a writer, as a thinker, and as a human being. I shall suggest, later, how valuable these diaries are by demonstrating, by a close analysis of just one entry, how these diaries shed light on Virginia Stephen's psychological development during her adolescence. I shall also indicate how they might be used by researchers other than literary critics by arguing that they provide additional documentation for the important theory of female development articulated by Carol Gilligan in *In a Different Voice*.[10] I shall end with an analysis of how Virginia Stephen used the persona of 'Miss Jan' to help her begin the process which psychoanalysts refer to as individuation, her development of an identity as a thinker which was radically different from that of other members of her family, although I do not suggest here that she completed that process during the time span which I am examining.

The seven unpublished journals of Virginia Stephen contain a treasure trove of material. The first volume, her 1897 diary, provides a day-by-day account of a critical year in Woolf's life, a year in which she records, among other things, the marriage, and untimely death in a childbirth-related illness, of her surrogate mother, Stella Duckworth, and her own eye-witness account of Queen Victoria's Diamond Jubilee procession; a catalogue and commentary on the more than fifty books that she read during that year; descriptions of the lessons that she was allowed to have, and the restrictions upon her behaviour as well. I have written in detail elsewhere, about how the contents of this diary force us to revise some judgements that have been made about Woolf's adolescence.[11] The diary helps us see that Woolf was struggling valiantly in this year to carve out an identity for herself within a family that preferred to see her as incipiently insane rather than do the difficult work that was required in order to help her recover from the emotional stress of the death of her mother. I have also argued that in the Stephen household the incestuous advances that Woolf and her sister were forced to endure from her half-brothers, George and Gerald Duckworth, probably scarred both of them for life and that insufficient attention has been paid to how their father perhaps unconsciously allowed these young men to act out his own incestuous fantasies towards his daughters, which he expressed, more overtly, towards Stella Duckworth, and how the fact of his not protecting his daughters from those advances, even perhaps unconsciously colluding with the Duckworth brothers in allowing these advances to occur, all contributed to the recurrence, in Woolf's adulthood, of mental illness.[12]

Another journal, kept in 1899, while the family spent the summer at Warboys, is significant because it demonstrates the process whereby Woolf developed herself as a writer by imagining an audience. According to many theorists of the composing process, this is a necessary step for a writer if he or she is to ever achieve a mature voice.[13]

It is unfortunate that Quentin Bell's published description of this diary has led at least one feminist critic, who had not examined it, to argue that the diary depicts Woolf in the throes of insanity. In her essay 'Unmaking and Making in *To the Lighthouse*', Gayatri C. Spivak argues that the novel's section 'Time Passes' 'narrates the production of a discourse of madness within this autobiographical roman à clef'.[14] She uses as evidence to support her reading – that the autobiographical nature of the novel is rooted in Woolf's madness – the following description of the 1899 Warboys journal provided by Quentin Bell in his biography of his aunt. Spivak writes, quoting Bell, who, in turn, quotes Woolf,

> One is invited to interpret the curious surface of writing of Virginia Stephen's 1899 diary as a desecration of the right use of reason. It was written 'in a minute, spidery, often virtually illegible hand, which she made more difficult to read by gluing her pages on to or between Dr Isaac Watt's *Logick / or / the right use of Reason / with a variety of rules to guard against error in the affairs of religion and human life as well as in the sciences . . . .* Virginia bought this in St Ives for its binding and its format: "Any other book, almost, would have been too sacred to undergo the desecration that I planned.". . .'[15]

But the Warboys journal is not mad at all. It is an extremely lucid series of essays and writing exercises that Woolf felt impelled, at the end of the summer, to paste into Dr Watt's book that she purchased because she liked the binding – she did not even know what the title was when she bought the book. What eludes both the biographer and the critic is that the eighteen-year-old Virginia Stephen did not write this diary for the eye of either her biographer or her critic, so that to use as evidence for madness the fact that the diary is difficult to read is to miss the point completely and to misunderstand, as well, why the adolescent Virginia glued up her diary with the pages of Dr Watt's book: *she did not want anyone in her family to be able to read her diary; it was for her eyes only; it was private; it was her own property.* To use, as evidence for insanity, an illegible hand and a craving for privacy is seriously to misrepresent normal, healthy adolescent behaviour as evidence of insanity.

What *does* require exploration is why Virginia Stephen at eighteen had to go to such lengths to hide her completely innocuous writing-exercises, which are largely descriptions of nature, of sunset, of places that she had seen. Why did the household afford her no privacy? But what I find particularly distressing is that, without seeking out the evidence of the documents themselves, critics such as Spivak will simply use second-hand descriptions of Woolf's words. For, if Spivak had had a transcription of Woolf's Warboys diary available to her, she never would have made those claims. Instead, she probably would have seen how the Warboys journal provides evidence of how Woolf developed her voice as a writer. Here, now, is Virginia Stephen, in her own voice, in the Warboys journal:

> . . . the edge of this . . . [cloud] glistened with fire – vivid & glowing in the east like some sword of judgement or vengeance – & yet the intensity of its light melted & faded as it touched the gray sky behind so that there was no clearly defined outline. This one observation that I have made from my observation of many sunsets – that no shape of cloud has one line that is the least sharp or hard – nowhere can you draw a straight line with your pencil & say 'this line goes so'. Everything is done by different shades and degrees of light – melting & mixing infinitely – Well may an Artist despair![16]

Evidence of Woolf's insanity? Hardly. At the end of another entry, one for 12 August 1899, Woolf explores the notion that all art is imitation of a greater truth that exists in the universe. This entry is a sophisticated exploration of a Platonic conception of art, and a discourse on the limits of language. It is important to note that as early as 1899 Woolf was exploring a mimetic definition of literature that she was to repeat in her maturity, and that was fundamentally different from, say, that of Clive Bell. In that 12 August entry, in discoursing on the function of art, Woolf capitalises the word 'Heaven', which some literary scholars might use as evidence for Woolf's pantheistic or even religious conception of nature. In any event, whatever the Warboys journal is, it is most clearly not an invitation to 'interpret the curious surface of writing . . . as a desecration of the right use of reason', as Spivak asserts.

According to the Woolf scholar Madeline Moore, the act of writing 'completed autonomy for Woolf – and the emotional quality of this autonomy was mystical'.[17] Many years later, when Virginia Woolf was writing *The Waves*, in the holograph of that novel, she distinguished the children from one another by the way in which they went about the act of writing:

> They sat in rows, yawning or writing very laboriously, for already, though that might have seemed impossible, they had their minds, their characters. There was, for instance, one most solemn child. He never dipped his pen without deliberation; often hesitating half an hour perhaps. But when he wrote the letters were firm & clear. Compare him with that moody fitful little girl. She swayed at her task, as if she despaired of ever getting it done; & then suddenly made a dart & wrote something very fast; & then there was a boy who gaped at the page; & rolled in his seat & rumpled his hair. And the eel like boy; so fastidious so agile. One after another they dipped their pens . . . .[18]

Indeed, in the holographs of *The Waves*, Woolf calls writing 'the great conspiracy of civilized people; which is to communicate impressions of life'.[19] Writing, in the holograph of *The Waves*, becomes the way in which the youngsters define themselves; it is also the way in which they construct a reality outside of themselves which they communicate to each other, so that each of them first creates his or her perceptions of what the world is like, then objectifies those perceptions in the act of writing them down, and then tests those perceptions through sharing the writing with other human beings. Although writing begins as an intensely private act, it ends as a public one – as a 'great conspiracy of civilized people'.

The entries in Woolf's Warboys journal verify Moore's perception that the act of writing 'completed autonomy for Woolf'. In addition, the act of writing performed the function, for Woolf, of connecting her with reality, very much as for the children in the holograph of *The Waves*. In entry after entry, Woolf indicates that writing, for her, established a sense of connection with her own experience, a connection that she apparently did not feel as intensely unless she wrote down her thoughts. On Sunday, 6 August 1899, for example, she wrote that it was necessary to write down her impressions of the moment because they would pass quickly. We see this early, therefore, Woolf's preoccupation with recording moments of being. And in one of the very last entries which Woolf made into her diary before she died, she wrote that she would need to put down her writing to cook dinner: 'Haddock and sausage meat. I think it is true that one gains a certain hold on sausage and haddock by writing them down.'[20]

And she loved to write for the sheer joy of passing pen across paper, so that if anything happened to one of her pens, it was almost as if something happened to herself, and, conversely, when she herself was feeling unwell, she often describes how her pen is not well. On 7 August 1899, for example, she describes how her joy in writing is lost when her pen does not perform as it should, but, rather than describing herself as unable to perform the act of writing, she described her pen as if it is, in fact, unwell.

At a significant point in the diary, she supposes a reader, which forces her to write for an audience other than herself, and she describes that process as an act which is similar to putting on fancy clothes, of dressing up, as it were.[21] Often, in the diaries, she is delighted with herself, and with her intellect; she is self-conscious, as so many young people are, about having discovered that she can think, and she describes the fact that mental activity is so important to her, that it is the activity that keeps her going. The image that she uses to describe her thinking process is fascinating: she compares it to the function of the paddle of a steamship. Thinking is the thing that makes her go on, just as the steamship paddle is the thing that enables the ship to move through the water.[22]

What the Warboys journal *does* contain that would be of enormous interest to a biographer is an extract based upon an incident which, apparently, did happen to Woolf. It is entitled 'Extract from the Huntingdonshire Gazette. TERRIBLE TRAGEDY IN A DUCKPOND'.[23] The extract describes how a boat had capsized in the water while three young people (including Virginia) were taking a moonlight ride. The extract, written from the point of view of a newspaper reporter, is extremely significant, for it details feelings of abandonment, a certain knowledge that in a time of terrible tragedy, no one, including her father, Sir Leslie Stephen, will come to her aid. The extract details the fact that the only people capable of hearing the cries for help were in the kitchen; and the reporter describes her incapacity to detail the scene in which the angry pond swallowed up its victims. The entry includes, as well, a fascinating fictional creation of what it must feel like to drown, and how absolutely alone and uncared for one is in the process of drowning. Rather than recording Woolf's madness, the Warboys journal offers the reader a very significant insight into Woolf's feeling of abandonment. In this diary entry, Woolf equates the act of drowning with having been utterly and absolutely abandoned, and because she herself chose death by drowning as her own particular method of committing suicide, this journal entry is especially significant, for it suggests that Woolf's continuing feelings of despair and worthlessness through-out her life were linked to her feelings of having been abandoned, and that she chose suicide by drowning both as a result of, and a re-enactment of those feelings of utter loneliness and desolation at having been uncared for.

In the context of the Warboys journal, therefore, the 'Time Passes' section of *To the Lighthouse* does not record the psycho-pathology of a mad woman; rather, it details an acute sense of hopelessness which results, quite naturally, from having been unparented.[24]

Other journals provide equally important information for the critic and scholar. In another journal there is a record of a voyage to Greece that was the living analogue for the journey motif and the classical references at the core of her first novel *The Voyage Out*, which she was writing at the time. This trip, and her descriptions of Greece, were also called upon when she wrote *Jacob's Room*, her third novel. One of the fascinations of this travel journal is that one can see how Woolf used the people that she met on her journey for the material of her art. On one of her trips, Woolf met a young woman who probably contributed to her fictional creation Rachel Vinrace, the heroine of her first novel. She met a young Greek woman who, like Rachel, loved music 'for itself and its own sake'. She typified the kind of young woman – Greek or English – who travels to find a more suitable husband than the restrictions of her class will allow her to find at home.[25]

Many of these journals – for example, the one that she kept

April 1906 to 1–14 August 1908, during trips to Giggleswick, Blo'
Norton Hall, the New Forest and Manorbier, among other places,
and the one that she kept in 1905 during a trip to Cornwall, to her
childhood summer home – have detailed and sensitive nature
descriptions that served to prepare her later in her career to write
such passages as those in *Jacob's Room* in which Cornwall and
Scarborough are described so exquisitely, and the scenes in *To the
Lighthouse* describing the beach on which the children play.[26] She
was able to capture the essence of such scenes so well because of
her early and continuous practice in the art of nature description,
and critics of her literary style will find much in these journals to
relate to her published texts.

There is also a journal recording Woolf's day-by-day effort to
deal with the lingering effects of her father's death, and detailing
the effort she put into the note she wrote for inclusion in Frederic
Maitland's biography of her father,[27] her first public published
statement about him. The journal documents how she assisted
Maitland in other ways, by helping to choose and organise letters
of her father and mother that were significant. In the context of
this journal, the subject of Woolf's second novel, *Night and Day*,
which discusses the preoccupation of Katherine Hilbery with her
illustrious ancestor Richard Alardyce, and how living with his
spectre put 'the insignificant present moment . . . to shame', takes
on a very important autobiographical meaning.[28] The journal,
which Woolf kept from Christmas 1904 to 31 May 1905,
documents the fact that Woolf was closely involved with Maitland
during his writing of her father's biography. Thus, her fictional
portraits of her father in *The Voyage Out* (as Willoughby Vinrace),
in *Night and Day* (as Mr Hilbery), in *To the Lighthouse* (as Mr
Ramsay) and in *The Years* (as Colonel Abel Pargiter)[29] were based
upon her knowledge of her father's most private documents – his
love letters to her mother, for example.

Thus, Woolf had an extremely intimate knowledge of her
father's past, and when she created her fictional portraits of him in
her maturity, they were portaits that came from a knowledge of
him that was deepened, and no doubt complicated, by her study of
these documents. And, in all likelihood, she became even more
aware of the connection between her own emotional make-up and
her father's, that they were very similar as human beings.

In 1905, for example, when she was working on the note for
Maitland, Woolf bought herself a very special walking-stick, one

with a silver head, and had it specially engraved. This walking-stick was a way for her to identify with Sir Leslie, a great walker, who took his own walking-stick and his daughter on so many, many walks through Hyde Park and through the English countryside. Thus, for Woolf the significance of the past was very different from that for those of us who know our parents only through the lenses of our own perceptions.

In Woolf's case, she got to know her father in a way that a historian might, in a way that a biographer would, and she had to wed that knowledge of him to the memories that she had from living with him as his daughter. Her tendency to see her parents in the context of historical processes, to see them as emblems of a certain kind of maternity and paternity, came, I believe, from her participating in Maitland's attempts to place her father in the context of his times. This journal indicates that Woolf could not see her father as an individual man; he became representative, to her, of the archetypal Victorian father, with all of the difficulties inherent in that historical type. The 1905 entries provide invaluable insights into Woolf in the process of changing her perception of Sir Leslie Stephen from private father to public personage.[30]

And then there is a notebook, which Virginia Woolf kept from 30 June to 1 October 1903, which contains thirty completed unpublished essays and writing exercises – the earliest ones (except for juvenile works) for which we have evidence. The essays are charming pieces of work, on topics as varied as her trip to Stonehenge, in which she muses about the Druids, and a recollection of her Greek teacher, Miss Janet Case, in which she details precisely what her lessons in Greek were like. In this essay on Miss Case, Woolf describes her as a 'valiant, strong-minded woman', 'tall, classical looking, masterful'. Critics such as William Herman are revising our knowledge of exactly how much Greek Woolf knew, and this essay supplies important evidence.

The sketches in this volume are significant for other reasons. They detail the process by which Woolf practised scene-setting, a process that it is, of course, necessary for the novelist to control, and the Woolf critic Susan Squier has called upon this volume in her analysis of the politics of city space in Woolf's novels.[31] A description of a dance in Queens Gate, for example, indicates that Woolf's party scenes in *Mrs Dalloway* were the descendants of a number of earlier attempts to capture people in social settings.

I should now like to discuss just one entry in Virginia Woolf's 1897 diary, to illustrate how this diary (and Woolf's other adolescent and young adult diaries) might be used by students of Woolf and by theoreticians of female adolescent development. On 1 February 1897, a few days after her fifteenth birthday, Woolf made an entry in which she described how her sister Vanessa had gone to a drawing lesson; how she and her father Sir Leslie had gone out for one of their customary walks; how her half-sister and she had gone to the doctor for some new medicines, but had forgotten to ask the doctor if Virginia could continue her studies. The entry continues:

> A terrible idea started that Stella and I should take lodgings at Eastbourne or some such place, where Jack is going next week – Impossible to be alone with those two creatures, yet if I do not go, Stella will not, and Jack particularly wishes her to – The question is, whether Nessa will be allowed to come too – If so it would be better – but goodness knows how we shall come out of this *quandary* as Vanessa calls it.[32]

Later on the page, she records that she has been in a temper all day, and that she has been making life difficult for Stella and Vanessa, but that she could not protest '*too* strongly against going' although she was protesting, or else Stella would have to give up her trip, and Jack Hills, her financé, would be miserable. But she cannot imagine going.

In this diary entry she records plans that were being made for a trip that she *did not want* to make to Bognor Regis with her half-sister and mother surrogate Stella Duckworth, and Stella's husband-to-be, Jack Waller Hills. A close reading of this diary entry will indicate why it was necessary for her to create this alter ego of hers, this Miss Jan.

Carol Gilligan, in her widely acclaimed book *In a Different Voice: Psychological Theory and Women's Development*, has brilliantly argued that 'the secrets of the female adolescent pertain to the silencing of her own voice, a silencing enforced by the wish not to hurt others but also by the fear that, in speaking, her voice will not be heard'. Woolf's diary entry reaffirms Gilligan's description of a young woman's adolescence. It offers a moment-by-moment record of the process whereby a young woman, who would, in fact, one day find her own voice, silences herself in the interest of others. It is a major piece of evidence in support of Gilligan's theory (although it suggests some important ways in which Gilligan's theory might be emended to take into account the realities of a young girl's existence in a patriarchal society in which her powerlessness is based upon her gender and not upon her capacity for accomplishment), for it demonstrates how a young woman, *precisely because* she knows that her voice will not be heard and heeded, subverts her own wishes and desires, and converts them, instead, into a desire to please others – what Gilligan refers to as an 'ethic of care'.[33]

On the one hand, in this diary entry, we can see how the fifteen-year-old Virginia recognises her own mind and her own feelings: she knew that she *did not want to* go to Bognor because it was 'Impossible to be alone with those two creatures.' Yet, on the other hand, as soon as she articulates her insight into what her reactions will be if she does go, she puts her own feelings aside and she switches, immediately, to the consequences, for Stella, of her not going: she understands her own feelings, but she puts them aside, ostensibly in the interest of someone else: 'yet if I do not go, Stella will not'. At fifteen, we see Woolf developing what Gilligan refers to as 'an awareness of the connection between people' which 'gives rise to a recognition of responsibility for one another, a perception of the need for response'.[34]

What is significant, in Woolf's case, and I suspect in the case of many girls, is that this 'awareness of the connection between people' seems to develop as a defensive strategy rather than as an authentic caring response. She states that she will act on the basis of caring about how Stella feels, and do what she does not want to do, only because no one will act on the basis of how *she* feels, and they will not allow *her* to act on the basis of how she feels. In this context, one must question whether, in fact, girls really act from 'a recognition of responsibility for one another' or whether they use the language of empathy to mask the fact that they have been coerced into putting aside self-interest as an appropriate motive for action.

But as soon as Woolf articulates that she is putting aside her own wishes so that *Stella's* wishes will be satisfied, she utters the recognition that Stella, because she *too* is a woman, is doing exactly what she is doing – putting aside her own wishes in the interest of someone else: 'yet if I do not go, Stella will not, and Jack particularly wishes her to –'. Stella, because she is a woman, is not necessarily doing what *she* wants to do; she is doing what 'Jack particularly wishes her to'. And so, Stella will be no ally, for Stella is also powerless and is also bound to put someone else's interests (a man's) ahead of her own.

Although Woolf knows that she is really powerless to choose what she wants to do, she acts as if it were her concern for someone else's wishes, for Stella's wishes, that prompts her to reconsider whether or not she will go to Bognor. Thus reading Woolf's entry illustrates how 'empathy' is 'built into their [girls'] primary definition of self'.[35] In the case of Woolf, and I suspect in the case of virtually all young women, it seems as if this empathy is not so much 'built into' the young girl's definition of self so much as coerced into it.

The next move Woolf's psyche makes is to cast about for something that will assuage the feelings that well up as a result of her knowledge of her own powerlessness. She casts about for something that will relieve her sense of pain and hopelessness at having to go even if she doesn't want to: 'The question is,' she writes, 'whether Nessa will be allowed to come too – If so it would be better . . . .' We see her already trying to make the best of it, already helping herself get over her despair at the fact that she will have to go to Bognor by thinking that, at least, she will be able to look forward to the compassion and companionship of her sister.

Whether or not Woolf would have to go to Bognor with Stella and Jack was not such a trivial issue as it might at first appear, but an issue of major importance, with damaging long-term consequences for the development of Woolf's psyche, which I have written about at length elsewhere.[36] It seems as if the family (or more precisely, Sir Leslie Stephen, Woolf's father) was using Woolf as a chaperone for Stella just before her marriage to Jack Hills, and we can be sure that Woolf did not want to be held responsible for their conduct. As naïve as the existing portraits of her at the time make her appear, her diary indicates that she was not at all naïve. Rather, she had powerful insights into how the family might make her the scapegoat if anything went wrong at Bognor, and she also knew what might go wrong at Bognor. And so her protests against going were not simply the protests of a spoiled adolescent or the protests of an irrational young woman, but, instead, the protests of a young woman who was extraordinarily aware that she could only lose if she was forced to be responsible for Stella and Jack.

According to Gilligan, 'the qualities deemed necessary for adulthood' – 'the capacity for autonomous thinking, clear decision-making, and responsible action – are those associated with masculinity and considered undesirable attributes of the feminine self'.[37] What becomes abundantly clear as one reads through Woolf's 1897 diary is how this young woman (and many other young women) have the traits deemed necessary for adulthood trained out of them. In Woolf's case, it is not that she could not think clearly and make decisions and act responsibly; she was forced into acting *against* the independent assessment that she herself had made about what it was good for her to do for herself; she was thus forced into doing something that she herself knew would damage her.

Knowing that she would, in all likelihood, be forced to go, she probably knew from the start that her voice would not be heard. Knowing that she was completely powerless to effect change, she converted her feeling of powerlessness into something that she could live with as she could not live with the hopelessness of her own powerlessness – she converted her having to go into a virtue, into a wish to go to please some other person. She will go because Stella won't be able to go unless she comes along. But this feeling, she probably knew, was not authentic, but feigned. It is both illuminating and horrifying to watch how the young Woolf – and all young women – are forced to feign selflessness in order to mask the utterly disabling feeling of powerlessness.

Woolf, knowing that *her* feelings will not be heeded in the matter, that *her* voice will not be heard, reacts, appropriately, with anger: 'I have been in a dreadful temper all day long. . . .' But, as soon as she describes her rage, she dissociates herself from her feelings – 'I have been in a dreadful temper all day long, poor creature . . . .' She stops being Virginia Stephen when she has these feelings; she does not allow Virginia Stephen to have these feelings; she becomes a poor creature when she has these feelings. Rather than 'owning' her own feelings, she has learned, by the time that she is fifteen, to stand outside herself, to disconnect herself from those feelings, and the pity that she expresses is not for herself, but for some poor creature. She learns to disconnect herself from her feelings, as most young women do. She learns, therefore, to do the exact opposite of what is commonly defined as a criterion of mental health – a connection with and knowledge of what one is feeling at any given moment.

But it is also fascinating to see that she cannot utter or does not utter 'poor me' or 'poor Virginia' but, instead, 'poor creature'. She is denying herself, as the world denies her, permission to feel legitimately sorry for herself because she is going to be forced to do something she doesn't want to do. But she is also trying not to be a sympathy–monger; she is trying to be brave and not show how poor a creature she is to the world.

She is also indicating that she has internalised that anger is not appropriate in a woman. It is not Virginia Stephen who has been in a dreadful temper all day; rather, it is the creaturely part of herself, the base part of herself that has been in a temper all day, and, soon, she will take her cue from how the world expects women to behave, and she will quell that anger and behave as a young lady is expected to behave; she will put the feelings and the wishes of others, particularly men, before her own wishes: 'Can not protest *too* strongly against going (though I do) or else Stella will have to give it up, and her poor young man would be miserable . . . .'

And so Jack, a man, will get his way, after all. And we see how Woolf converts her knowledge of her own powerlessness into a choice that she is making to control herself to please someone else. But she cannot continue with this self-delusion for very long, and her real feelings well up and must be expressed:' – but think of going!' And then she begins to accustom herself to the fact of the impending journey by describing it as a mere possibility: 'If we go we should start next Monday, and stay away till Saturday.' And then, at the end of the entry, we hear from her fictional self: 'Poor Miss Jan is bewildered' as well she might be, as any sane person would be who was forced to suppress a deep unwillingness to do something, to repress anger at being forced to do something, to convert a feeling of powerlessness into a concern for someone else's happiness. But it is necessary for her to express her legitimate feeling of bewilderment in the voice of her fictional, rather than her actual, self.

Virginia Woolf's adolescent diary, therefore, is evidence for how a young woman is forced to participate in the culture's insistence that she learn at a very early age to silence herself and subvert herself, that she learn to put aside her own wishes, her own feelings, her own desires, that she convert her own knowledge of what she wants into 'an ethic of care'. Looking at Virginia Woolf's diary entry through the lenses of Gilligan's schema is particularly illuminating, for the diary, Woolf's 'secret' of female adolescence, demonstrates on page after page how Woolf learned not to hurt others, learned that her voice would not be heard, learned to silence her own voice.

But not entirely. For throughout this diary, throughout this intimate look at this coming into womanhood of one of this century's most gifted writers, Woolf maintains, through the persona of Miss Jan, a private self whom she allows to express her feelings. It is an unfortunate necessity, but an accommodation, none the less, to the way that women are socialised to silence their own voices. This diary also records how a young woman, even as she concedes to society's insistence that she develop in this way, manages to keep a small part of herself for herself, a fictionalised self, a 'Miss Jan' whom she will not permit anyone to know about, a 'Miss Jan' whom she will lock up within the covers of a brown gilt diary, even as she is forced to lock up her feelings and wishes and desires.

Virginia Stephen used the cover of Miss Jan to express emotions that, in the Stephen household, it might have been difficult for her to express overtly – disapproval of the behaviour of other people – for example, of her brother Adrian's buying a luggage carrier for his bicycle which she has Miss Jan describe as extravagant behaviour. But she also used the voice of Miss Jan to chastise herself, to express, for example, self-deprecation about how she liked the pantomime Aladdin because it was more accessible to her than a play written for adults; or embarrassment (in an entry where she describes losing her composure when she dropped an umbrella, and how she talked nonsense). She uses Miss Jan to express simple discomfort (how the seat of her new bicycle was uncomfortable); boredom (how she had a horrible time at a tea at which dances were discussed, in which Miss Jan did not take much interest); self-censorship (Miss Jan cannot bring herself to enter the remarks of a group of schoolboys she saw); even extreme joy (how Miss Jan was jubilant).[38]

But one simply cannot make the case that the young Virginia Stephen couldn't express her emotions without the mask of Miss Jan; in fact, Jan disappears entirely from these pages after 2 May 1897 before her step-sister, Stella Duckworth Hills died, and many of the complex emotions dredged up as a result of Stella's death Woolf describes in her own voice.

What does seem clear, however, is that the voice of Miss Jan, and, indeed, the whole process of writing, helped Woolf begin to carve out an identity separate from the rest of the family, although it can, of course, be argued that Woolf continued to struggle with this process throughout her life. And there is extremely important evidence for the fact that the creation of Miss Jan helped Woolf achieve whatever individuation she was capable of achieving. On Friday, 5 February 1897, Virginia Stephen entered in her diary the fact that she was writing the Eternal Miss Jan. On Wednesday, 28 April, she wrote, in response to a family crisis, that everything was as dismal as it could be, and how difficult it was to live in this world, which she referred to as a Miss Janism. And on Monday, 9 August, while she was away after the death of Stella, she wrote that she had very little time for writing in her diary, but that her great work [probably 'The Eternal Miss Jan'] was proceeding, and that it had received her sister Vanessa's approval.

In December 1929, when she was in the process of writing *The Waves*, Woolf made a diary entry which clarifies what 'The Eternal Miss Jan', the 'great work' which preoccupied her for much of 1897, was about:

It was the Elizabethan prose writers I loved first & most wildly, stirred by Hakluyt, which father lugged home for me – I think of it with some sentiment – father tramping over the Library with his little girl sitting at H[yde] P[ark] G[ate] in mind. He must have been 65; I 15 or 16, then; & why I dont know, but I became enraptured, though not exactly interested, but the sight of the large yellow page entranced me. I used to read it & dream of those obscure adventurers, & no doubt practised their style in my copy books. *I was then writing a long picturesque essay upon the Christian religion, I think; called Religio Laici, I believe, proving that man has need of a God; but the God was described in process of change*; & I also wrote a history of Women; & a history of my own family – all very longwinded & El[izabe]than in style.[39]

'Religio Laici' and 'The Eternal Miss Jan' might very well have been the same work. Woolf's writing 'a long picturesque essay upon the Christian religion . . . proving that man has need of a God' was an immensely significant act in 1897, precisely because it was a work in which she described views that were the exact opposite of those of her father, Sir Leslie Stephen, whose famous work '*An Agnostic's Apology' and Other Essays* (1893) criticised those, like his daughter, who attempt to describe the nature of God. In 1897, Woolf was doing exactly that – describing the nature of a God, and man's (or her own) need for a God. Her writing this discourse about the existence of God was an act of independent thinking in the household of a man who believed 'that the ancient secret is secret still; that man knows nothing of the Infinite and Absolute; and that, knowing nothing, he had better not be dogmatic about his ignorance'.[40]

In 'The Eternal Miss Jan' or 'Religio Laici', therefore, the young Virginia Stephen claimed, for herself, a mystical function for language – and in claiming this mystical function for language, in using language to assert that man has need of a God, in using language to describe the nature of a God, Woolf was, very privately, and very quietly, challenging her father's system of belief and erecting a value system that she apparently needed at the time. This would certainly have been frowned upon, especially in the household of a man who had made his reputation publicly as an agnostic, of a man who believed, unlike his daughter, 'Firstly, dogmatic religious systems are unreal; secondly, evidence does not support belief in God's existence; thirdly, religion demoralises society'.[41]

Believing in a mystical view of the world was, of course, for the daughter of the author of *An Agnostic's Apology*, a defiant act, an act, in 1897, of individuation, of establishing an identity as profoundly different from her father's as she could. Stephen's staunch rationalism in the face of the death of his wife is described by Noel Annan:

> Shortly after the death of his first wife and with a heart laden with sorrow, he wrote, 'Standing by an open grave, and moved by all the most solemn sentiments of our nature, we all, I think – I can only speak for myself with certainty – must feel that the Psalmist takes his sorrow like a man, and as we, with whatever difference of dialect, should wish to take our own sorrows; while the Apostle is desperately trying to shirk the inevitable and at best resembles the weak comforters who try to cover up the terrible reality under a veil of well-meant fiction. I would rather face the inevitable with open eyes.'[42]

'I would rather face the inevitable with open eyes': this was Sir Leslie Stephen's public account of his response to his wife's death and his avowed belief in the fact that it is effeminate to use religion to support oneself in a time of crisis. His *private* response was quite different, however.[43] We know from his own testimony, and from that of his daughter, that he insisted upon the sympathy of his children and his wife's children, that he acted out his own grief and his sorrow and his loss, even as he seems to have abandoned them in their grief, or even insisted that they be stoic in the face of their loss. As Woolf herself put it:

> But no words of mine can convey what he felt, or even the energy of the visible expression of it, which took place in one scene after another all through that dreadful summer . . . and there were dreadful meal-times when, unable to hear what we said, or disdaining its comfort, he gave himself up to the passion which seemed to burn within him, and groaned aloud or protested again and again his wish to die. . . . For exhausted and unstrung as he was he came to torment himself piteously . . . .[44]

His children, therefore, were denied the solace that religion might have offered them, even as they were denied the right to grieve which their own father permitted himself. More importantly, they completely lost him to his grief, so they had no adult presence to help them deal with their profound loss. Because of this prior history of Sir Leslie's behaviour and Woolf's experience after the death of her mother, it is easy to see why Woolf, at age fifteen, should write an essay about man's need for a God, which countervailed her own father's system of belief. During the following year, Woolf had yet again to live through the death of a mother figure. And, while her father wrote, for the public's eye, about how the rationalist, about how the agnostic, should take his grief like a man, without the solace that religion might offer, in private, he again allowed himself to act out his own despair, even as he again offered his children no solace for their own enormous loss.

That Woolf *herself* should feel the need for a God during this year is not surprising, given the reality of her experience of living with an agnostic and a rationalist who insisted upon standards of behaviour for his children which he did not insist upon for himself.[45]

There are glimpses in the diary of this private self, this Miss Jan, who believed in God, who had need of a God, who was composing a theological essay about the existence of God. On Sunday, 2 May, for example, we learn from Woolf's diary that her father was lecturing on Pascal at the Kensington Town Hall, and Virginia was in the audience. She criticises his performance by saying that the lecture was too deep, not only for the audience, but also that it was too logical and difficult for someone as ignorant as Miss Jan to follow. She states that Sir Leslie wasn't up to his normal form.

What an agnostic such as Sir Leslie would say publicly about Pascal's scepticism, about his 'wager' that if God does not exist, the sceptic loses nothing by believing in him, but that if he does, the sceptic gains, we can only guess at. But we *do* know what Sir Leslie Stephen wrote about Pascal. Although Stephen appreciated Pascal's position, he seriously criticised it:

> I see that Pascal's morality becomes distorted; that in the division between grace and nature some innocent and some admirable qualities have got to the wrong side; that Pascal becomes a morbid ascetic, torturing himself to death, hating innocent diversion because it has the great merit of distracting the mind from melancholy brooding, looking upon natural passions as simply bad . . . . the devotion of a man to an ideal which, however imperfect, is neither base, sensual, nor anti-social, which implies a passionate devotion to some of the higher impulses of our nature, has so great a claim upon our reverence that we can forgive, and even love, Pascal. We cannot follow him without treason to our highest interests.[46]

What is ironic about this analysis is that the behaviour Stephen ascribes to Pascal, he himself manifested – torturing himself to death', 'melancholy brooding', a morbid asceticism. We can ascertain that in 1897, according to Virginia Woolf's own testimony, her beliefs were closer to Pascal's than her father's; according to her father, her beliefs were 'treason' to her own interests. It is easy to see why she referred to herself in the entry in which she describes her father's lecture on Pascal as the ignorant Miss Jan. For, according to her father, 'No intelligent being had any right to continue to believe.'[47]

But her description of herself as Miss Jan takes on even greater significance, when one realises that Pascal was a *Jan*senist. Jansenists confronted the issue of the extent to which human beings were, in fact, free agents, free to control their own destinies, in a very different way from supporters of the theological position that they opposed – Counter-Reformation – and differently from that of the agnostics such as Sir Leslie Stephen. The Jansenist argued that human beings were simply not as free as the Counter-Reformers claimed they were; the Jansenist acknowledged that human destiny was arbitrary, and not the product of a certain human being making responsible choices about her or his own destiny. The Jansenist also argued that human beings were fundamentally depraved and that human nature was corrupt, especially by lust.

Given the life that Virginia Stephen was leading in 1897, given the fact that her own life had been rendered difficult by events over which she had no control, given the fact that she had been victimised by the uncontrolled sexual desires of her half-brothers, it is easy to see why such a doctrine as Jansenism had its appeal for the young Virginia. In the 1897 diary, Woolf very often articulates pessimistic attitudes about the nature of the world (which she refers to as Miss Janism) that are close to, if not identical with, Jansenism, such as this one, in her 16 October entry: 'Life is a hard business – one needs a rhinoceros skin – & that one has not got!'[48]

In reality, Woolf's world had been a dismal one, difficult to live in; and no amount of rationalist argument from her father about how that state of the world could be improved would convince her in 1897 that his views were correct. If any system of belief expressed reality as she herself had experienced it (and as he had experienced it as well), it was not his rationalist's expectation that the work of human beings could improve the world; Woolf herself had been victimised by fate too often by the time she was fifteen to be able to believe this. If any system of belief could help her through her very difficult time, it was not her father's agnosticism, which made him difficult to live with; rather, she would conceptualise for herself the God that she had need of. In fact, in 1897 she probably understood, like many adolescents aware of the contradictions displayed by their parents and their elders, the difference between her father's stated system of belief, and his actions; she probably knew in her own heart, although she was probably smart enough to keep it to herself, that in living with Sir Leslie Stephen, she was living with a hypocrite, and that none of his publicly professed views would be of much help to her.

It is clear that Woolf retained this mystical strain, which separated her from her father, and from all of the extreme rationalists in her life, thoughout her life, although it is likely that she did not share this strain with any but kindred spirits. In August 1929, when she was writing *The Waves*, for example, she shared with Vita Sackville-West, who would undergo her own religious conversion, this mystical side:

> These headaches leave one like sand which a wave has uncovered – I believe they have a mystic purpose. Indeed, I'm not sure that there isnt some religious cause at the back of them – I see my own worthlessness and failure so clearly; and lie gazing into the depths of the misery of human life; and then one gets up and everything begins again and its all covered over.[49]

'I see my own worthlessness and failure so clearly': it is worth noting that Woolf's mysticism, both in 1897 and in 1929, was hydra-headed. Part of her mysticism was a way she set herself apart from her father and his system of belief, part of it allowed her to accomplish the act of identifying her own ideas about the way the world functioned. But there was another side to 'The Eternal Miss Jan', a more pessimistic side to her discoursing on man's (and her own) need for a God. And that side was connected to her own 'worthlessness and failure' which allowed her, at the same time, to understand 'the depths of misery of human life' in general.

These unpublished diaries which Woolf kept during her adolescence and young adulthood record the difficult yet exhilarating process through which Woolf created herself as an adolescent, as a young woman, and as a writer. For me, these diaries are often difficult to read, difficult to deal with, because they remind me of something that I should prefer to forget: that a woman in the process of training herself to become a serious writer often considers herself a deviant – so much so that she has to hide behind the persona of a 'Miss Jan', so much so that she has to glue her diary into the pages of a book so that no one will read them.

What is striking, none the less, as one reads these early diaries, is the energy with which the young Virginia Stephen tried, against immense odds, and with amazing success, considering those odds, to become a writer, an independent thinker, a person apart. One is a first-hand witness to a truly remarkable portrait of a very courageous young woman; one is a first-hand witness to how Virginia Stephen used the persona of Miss Jan to turn herself into the mature and distinguished critic, novelist, biographer and social historian, whom we now celebrate as Virginia Woolf.

## NOTES

1. This essay has been substantially revised, following a letter from the Literary Estate refusing this writer permission to quote directly from Virginia Woolf's early diaries at the Berg Collection. The reader will be referred to the passages in the diaries at the Berg which are paraphrased. The exact quotations in this essay have appeared in print before, and the notes will provide information concerning where the extract has been published before. The diary is now in the Henry W. and Albert A. Berg Collection of English and American Literature of the New York Public Library, Astor, Lennox and Tilden Foundations. I should like to thank Lola L. Szladits, Curator, for her generous and gracious assistance and support. I should like to thank Jane Marcus, Melissa Hield, the Department of English, Women's Studies, College of Liberal Arts, and the Humanities Research Center of the University of Texas at Austin for inviting me to participate in their celebration of Virginia Woolf's centenary, 'Bloomsbury in Texas'. A portion of this essay was read at that celebration. I should like to thank, as well, an anonymous reader who invited me to rethink the issue of the significance of 'Miss Jan'.

I should also like to thank Ernest J. DeSalvo, Arthur Golden, Jane Lilienfeld, Jane Marcus, Frank McLaughlin, Susan Squier and Sara Ruddick for discussions which clarified the issues that are raised in this essay.

2. 1897 diary, entry for Saturday, 1 January 1898. For a discussion of this year in Virginia Woolf's life, see my '1897: Virginia Woolf at Fifteen: "the first really *lived* year of my life" ' in *Virginia Woolf: A Feminist Slant*, ed. Jane Marcus (Lincoln, Nebr.: University of Nebraska Press, 1983). For other views of Virginia Woolf's adolescence, see Quentin Bell, *Virginia Woolf: A Biography*, 2 vols (New York: Harcourt Brace Jovanovich, 1972); Jean O. Love, *Virginia Woolf: Sources of Madness and Art* (Berkeley Calif., and Los Angeles: University of California Press, 1977). For Woolf's later memories of certain of the incidents described here, see *MB*.

3. Diary entry for Monday, 18 January 1897 refers to how her present diary was now longer than the diary she had kept for 1896. The 1896 diary has not been located, to the best of my knowledge.

4. The journals are as follows:
(1) 1897 Diary. The diary is catalogued as '[Diary] Notebook

1897' in the Berg Collection. It consists of 277 holograph entries.

(2) Warboys Summer Holidays 1899. The journal is catalogued as '[Diary] Holograph notebook. Unsigned. Aug. 4–Sept. 23, 1899. No. 1.' It consists of forty-eight holograph entries in the form of a journal and writing notes. Berg Collection.

(3) Hyde Park Gate Diary. 1903? The diary is in the Berg Collection and is catalogued as '[Diary] Holograph notebook. Unsigned. June 30–Oct. 1, 1903? No. 2.' It consists of 157 holograph entries in the form of essays and writing exercises.

(4) Christmas, 1904–31 May 1905. Berg Collection. The diary is catalogued as '[Diary] Holograph notebook. Unsigned. Christmas, 1904–May 31, 1905. No. 3.' It consists of 135 holograph entries.

(5) Diary. Cornwall. 1905. Berg Collection. The diary is catalogued as '[Diary] Holograph notebook. Unsigned. Aug. 11, 1904–Sept. 14, [1905]. No. 4.' It consists of fifty-two holograph pages.

(6) Apr 1906–1–14 Aug 1908. Berg Collection. The journal is listed as '[Diary] Holograph notebook. Unsigned. April, 1906–Aug. 1–14, 1908. No. 5.' It consists of seventy-nine holograph entries.

(7) Greece/Italy. 14 Sept [1906]–25 Apr 1909. Original in the British Library. Typescript carbon copy in the Berg Collection where it is listed as '[Diary] Typescript (carbon) copy of unlocated original. Sept. 14, [1906]–April 25, 1909.' It is highly inaccurate copy of the British Library original, with many incorrect readings. I should like to thank the Keeper of the Manuscripts of the British Library for access to the original, and Catherine Smith for providing me with her microfilm so that I could further check my transcription against the original.

5. See my *Virginia Woolf's First Voyage: A Novel in the Making* (Totowa, NJ: Rowman and Littlefield, 1980; London: Macmillan, 1980) and my edn of *Melymbrosia (M)*.

6. See B. J. Kirkpatrick, *A Bibliography of Virginia Woolf*, 3rd edn (Oxford: Clarendon Press, 1980).

7. The official edition of Virginia Woolf's diaries, which has been published by the Hogarth Press in England, and by Harcourt Brace Jovanovich in the United States, ed. by Anne Olivier Bell, begins with the diary that Woolf kept in 1915. The Editor's Preface to the first volume mentions these seven volumes in passing, but gives no justification for their omission (*D*, I). In his *Biography*, Quentin Bell writes that 'these essays are not of biographic interest except in so far as they attest to the high seriousness and immense thoroughness with which Virginia prepared herself for the profession of letters' (I, 93.)

8. See, for example, Susan Squier's work on the significance of the city for Woolf, which is based, in part, upon her reading of these diaries in *The Politics of City-Space: Virginia Woolf and London* (Chapel Hill, NC:

University of North Carolina Press, 1985); William Herman, 'Virginia Woolf and the Classics: Every Englishman's Prerogative Transmuted into Fictional Art', paper presented at the Centenary Conference on Virginia Woolf, Morgantown, WV, 1982.

9. See, for a theory regarding women writing: Sandra M. Gilbert and Susan Gubar, *The Madwoman in the Attic: The Woman Writer and the Nineteenth-Century Literary Imagination* (New Haven, Conn., and London: Yale University Press, 1979). It is important to note, in this connection, that the centenary of Virginia Woolf's birth passed, almost without notice, in Britain. The same cannot be said for the centenary of James Joyce.

10. Carol Gilligan, *In a Different Voice: Psychological Theory and Women's Development* (Cambridge, Mass.: Harvard University Press, 1982).

11. DeSalvo, '1897: Virginia Woolf at Fifteen', in *Virginia Woolf: A Feminist Slant*.

12. Louise DeSalvo, 'Virginia Woolf's Politics and her Mystical Vision', review of Madeline Moore, *The Short Season between Two Silences* (Boston, Mass.: George Allen and Unwin, 1984), in *Tulsa Studies in Women's Literature*, IV:1 (Dec 1985). I should like to thank Shari Benstock, Editor, for her comments regarding this essay.

13. See, for example, Loren S. Barritt and Barry M. Kroll, 'Some Implications of Cognitive-Developmental Psychology for Research in Composing', in *Research on Composing: Points of Departure*, ed. Charles R. Cooper and Lee Odell (Urbana, Ill.: National Council of Teachers of English, 1978).

14. Gayatri C. Spivak, 'Unmaking and Making in *To the Lighthouse*', in *Women and Language in Literature and Society*, ed. Sally McConnell-Ginet, Ruth Barker and Nelly Furman (New York: Praeger, 1980) pp. 311–27. I refer to Spivak's essay because it demonstrates the persistence of the popular misogynist misconception of Woolf as a writer possessed by madness, despite the very careful, more balanced analyses of Woolf in the process of writing published in recent years. See Grace Radin, *Virginia Woolf's 'The Years': The Evolution of a Novel* (Knoxville: University of Tennessee Press, 1981), and Jane Lilienfeld, ' "The Deceptiveness of Beauty": Mother Love and Mother Hate in *To the Lighthouse*', *Twentieth Century Literature*, 23 Oct 1977, pp. 345–76, which really does what Spivak's essay purports to do: it is rooted in the author's knowledge of Victorian culture and Woolf's biography. An extremely important book on the issue of Woolf's madness is Stephen Trombley's *All That Summer She Was Mad* which argues convincingly that Woolf's so-called madness was a response to the drugs that were given her in her adolescence.

This section of my essay was first presented as a response to Blanche Wiesen Cook's paper, 'Biographer and Subject: a Critical Connection', at the Columbia Women's Studies Seminar. I should like to thank Blanche Wiesen Cook for helping me to think through the issues presented here, and Gaye Tuchman, for inviting me to respond to Cook's paper. Cook's paper has been published in *Between Women: Biographers, Novelists, Critics, Teachers and Artists Write about their Work on Women*, ed. Carol Ascher, Louise DeSalvo and Sara Ruddick (Boston, Mass.:

Beacon Press, 1984).

15. Spivak, 'Unmaking and Making', in *Women and Language*, p. 316; Bell, *Biography*, I, 65.

16. Quoted in Quentin Bell, *Virginia Woolf: A Biography*, I, p. 65. An extremely interesting entry because it discusses the mimetic function of art is that of 12 August 1899.

17. Moore, *Short Season*, p. 12.

18. *Virginia Woolf: 'The Waves'. The Two Holograph Drafts*, transcribed and ed. J.W. Graham (Toronto: University of Toronto Press in association with the University of Western Ontario, 1976) Draft 1, p.3. My quotation is not an exact transcription of Graham's edn. I have, rather, reproduced the sense of the passage.

19. Ibid., Draft 1, p. 16.

20. *WD*, p. 351.

21. Entry for 13 August [1899].

22. Entry for 7 August [1899].

23. Another version of this exists in Monk's House Papers, University of Sussex, England. According to the catalogue, it was 'written in 1899 & copied by VS in 1904 for Emma Vaughan'. It is MH/a.10, 'A Terrible Tragedy in a Duckpond: A Note of Correction & Addition to the above. by one of the Drowned'.

24. See Lilienfeld, ' "The Deceptiveness of Beauty" ', *Twentieth Century Literature*, 23 Oct 1977.

25. See my ' "A View of One's Own": Virginia Woolf and the Making of *Melymbrosia*', in *M*, for a fuller treatment of this issue.

26. *TL*, pp. 54–5.

27. Frederic William Maitland, *The Life and Letters of Leslie Stephen* (London: Duckworth, 1906).

28. *ND*, p. 16. See Jane Marcus, 'Enchanted Organs, Magic Bells: *Night and Day* as Comic Opera', in *Virginia Woolf: Revaluation and Continuity*, ed. Ralph Freedman (Berkeley, Calif., and Los Angeles: University of California Press, 1980).

29. For critical exploration of these characters, see my *Virginia Woolf's First Voyage*; Marcus, 'Enchanted Organs', in *Virginia Woolf: Revaluation and Continuity*. For analyses of Mr Ramsay in *To the Lighthouse*, see Maria Di Battista's essay in *Virginia Woolf: Revaluation and Continuity*; Lilienfeld, ' "The Deceptiveness of Beauty" ', *Twentieth-Century Literature*, 23 Oct 1977; Sonya Rudikoff, 'How Many Lovers Had Virginia Woolf?', *The Hudson Review*, Winter 1979, and my remarks in '1897, Virginia Woolf at Fifteen', in *Virginia Woolf: A Feminist Slant*. For a discussion of Colonel Abel Pargiter, see the essays in the Virginia Woolf Issue, ed. Jane Marcus, of *BNYPL*, LXXX, no. 2 (Winter 1977); Jane Marcus, 'Pargeting *The Pargiters*: Notes of an Apprentice Plasterer', *BNYPL*, and Radin, *Virginia Woolf's 'The Years'*.

30. For a discussion of fathers in Woolf's fiction, see Beverly Ann

Schlack, 'Fathers in General: the Patriarchy in Woolf's Fiction', in *Virginia Woolf: A Feminist Slant.*

31. See n. 8.

32. This entry has been quoted in 'Virginia Woolf at Fifteen', in *Virginia Woolf: A Feminist Slant*, p. 83.

33. Gilligan, *In a Different Voice*, pp. 51 and 30. For an important evaluation and critique of Gilligan's position, helping me arrive at some of the conclusions presented here, see Susan M. Squier and Sara Ruddick, 'In a Different Voice: Psychological Theory and Women's Development', *Harvard Educational Review*, LIII, no. 3 (Aug 1983) 338–41.

34. Gilligan, *In a Different Voice*, p. 30. Gilligan demonstrates this development by discussing the response of an eleven-year-old girl.

35. Gilligan (quoting Nancy Chodorow) in *In a Different Voice*, p. 8.

36. See my '1897: Virginia Woolf at Fifteen' in *Virginia Woolf: A Feminist Slant.*

37. Gilligan, *In a Different Voice*, p. 17.

38. The Miss Jan entries appear on the following dates in the 1897 diary: Sunday, 3 Jan; Monday, 4 Jan; Tuesday, 5 Jan; Friday, 15 Feb; Thursday, 11 Feb; Friday, 19 Feb; Tuesday, 20 Apr; Wednesday, 28 Apr; Sunday, 2 May. To my knowledge, Miss Jan does not appear after Sunday, 2 May. This means that Miss Jan as a figure does not appear in this diary after the death of Stella Duckworth. I have argued elsewhere that after Stella's death, Woolf was freer to pursue her own interests, and the absence of Miss Jan as a cover figure after Stella's death might support this observation.

39. Entry for Sunday, 8 Dec 1929, in *D*, III, 271; emphasis added.

40. Sir Leslie Stephen, *'An Agnostic's Apology' and Other Essays* (London: Smith, Elder, 1893) p. 41. Quoted in Noel Gilroy Annan, *Leslie Stephen: His Thought and Character in Relation to his Time* (London: Macgibbon and Kee, 1951) p. 173.

41. Ibid., p. 172. The words are Annan's and they summarise Stephen's agnostic views.

42. Ibid., p. 175.

43. For an illuminating analysis of how Woolf's process of grieving was arrested, see Mark Spilka, *Virginia Woolf's Quarrel with Grieving* (Lincoln, Nebr.: University of Nebraska Press, 1980); for Sir Leslie's private account, see *Sir Leslie Stephen's Mausoleum Book*, ed. Alan Bell (Oxford: Clarendon Press, 1977).

44. *MB*, pp. 40–1.

45. I should like to thank Jane Marcus for helping me clarify these issues. For an analysis of the impact of the life and works of Virginia Woolf's aunt Caroline Emelia Stephen, a great Quaker theologian, upon her work, see Jane Marcus, 'The Niece of a Nun: Virginia Woolf, Caroline Stephen, and the Cloistered Imagination', in *Virginia Woolf: A Feminist Slant.*

46. Stephen, quoted in Annan, *Leslie Stephen*, p. 195. See also Stephen, *'An Agnostic's Apology' and Other Essays*, pp. 338–80, and *Essays in Freethinking and Plainspeaking* (1873) pp. 360–2.

47. Annan, *Leslie Stephen*, p. 191. The words are Annan's summarising Stephen's position. Woolf owned several volumes of Pascal's works. See *Catalogue of Books from the Library of Leonard and Virginia Woolf Taken from Monks House, Rodmell, Sussex, and 24 Victoria Square, London and now in the possession of Washington State University, Pullman, U.S.A.* (Brighton: Holleyman and Treacher, 1975).

48. Quoted in my 'Virginia Woolf at Fifteen'.

49. 15 Aug [1929] in *L*, IV, 78.

# 7 'The Sacred Edifices': Virginia Woolf and Some of the Sons of Culture

ANGELA INGRAM

When we look at ancient works of art we habitually treat them not merely as objects of aesthetic enjoyment but also as successive deposits of the human imagination. It is indeed this view of works of art as crystallised history that acounts for much of the interest felt in ancient art by those who have but little aesthetic feeling and who find nothing to interest them in the work of their contemporaries, where the historical motive is lacking, and they are left face to face with bare aesthetic values.

(Roger Fry, 'Art and Life', 1917)

Let it be built on lines of its own. It must be built not of carved stone and stained glass, but of some cheap, easily combustible material which does not hoard dust and perpetrate traditions. Do not have chapels. Do not have museums and libraries with chained books and first editions under glass cases. Let the pictures and the books be new and always changing. Let it be decorated afresh by each generation with their own hands cheaply.

(Virginia Woolf, *Three Guineas*, p. 33)

Towards the end of that most political novel, *The Years* (1937), Eleanor Pargiter and her niece, Peggy, are passing 'public buildings; offices of some sort'. Waving her hand at them, Eleanor says, 'but what I want to see before I die . . . is something different, . . . another kind of civilization' (*Y*, p. 335). The association between 'public buildings' (what could, following Roger Fry, be termed 'crystallised history') and what passes for 'civilization' is a

125

constant factor in Virginia Woolf's writing. Such buildings are always features in her landscape, and a few of them, chiefly those of Cambridge and London, loomed monumentally over her life. It is clear that she felt their material, 'public' mass with varying emotions, however much she simultaneously felt the necessity for a private place for women – an actual 'place' of bricks and mortar, or simply a place/space women could share, a 'magical garden of women'.[1] There seems never to have been a time when she didn't see public edifices as 'symbolic' – of the cramping of the mind, or of the freeing of the spirits of people to whom such buildings were 'appropriate'. With regard to Cambridge especially, this 'symbolic' aspect must have been apparent early in her life. In her biography of Roger Fry, she notes how 'depressed' he was by the 'hygienic hideousness of the new limestone buildings' of Clifton (his public school), and how 'liberated' he felt by the beauty of Cambridge: 'His mind had opened there; his eyes had opened there' *(RF*, pp. 38,60). Fry's ideas about 'art and life' formed rapidly at Cambridge. He helped start a newspaper there, and designed the cover illustration. It consisted of 'a tremendous sun of culture rising behind King's College Chapel' (p. 56).[2]

To Virginia Woolf, Cambridge meant something other than the 'liberation' of young men and the 'sun' – not to mention the sons – of culture. Preparing a sequel to *A Room of One's Own* in the 1930s she had to become, says Brenda Silver, 'a systematic reader of her culture';[3] and it is clear that, systematic or not, Virginia Woolf was *always* a 'reader of her culture', and that she 'read' accurately the massive presence of the buildings 'her' culture valued. The buildings of Cambridge, most especially King's College Chapel, did not merely represent men's 'psychic space', but were actual spaces enclosed by actual walls with stones smoothed and validated, often, by the 'six hundred years' which spelled the existence of the fictitious St Katharine's College, Oxford, one of the settings for *The Years*.[4]

More obviously political than Roger Fry, the reviewer of a recent book on American architecture tells us that

> the best of our past architecture asks us to confront our public ideologies . . . [And] to the extent that such ideologies are the province of institutions, architecture can embody them in the buildings that it erects to house those institutions. That has been one of the central roles of architecture through history: to

hold up before us a focused image of the role an institution plays in our lives, the nature of that institution and the character of its works.[5]

Virginia Woolf knew, of course, that the 'public ideologies' are those of the Men's House and that the buildings are fabricated in such a way as to make them sacred structures, whose plan, whose *logos*, is in heaven. For her the 'sacredness' of those structures has a very mundane counterpart, which inevitably partakes of the sacred, so symbiotic is the relationship. That counterpart is explained, and its importance insisted on in *Three Guineas*, which explicitly links male domination – whose most extreme expression is European Fascism – with men's education and all it encourages: competition for 'honours', elitist, militaristic, classist and sexist attitudes, and a religiously sanctioned definition of country and of patriotism with which Virginia Woolf, a middle-class woman, an outsider insisting on her freedom from unreal loyalties, refuses to identify. The identification of these attitudes, one with the other, is made very simply by St John Hirst in *Melymbrosia*. It is perhaps significant that the response are a laugh and a 'vehement rejoinder':

'I calculate . . . that if every man in the British Isles has six male children by the year 1920 and sends them all into the navy we shall be able to keep our fleet in the Mediterranean; if less than six, the fleet disappears; if the fleet disappears, the Empire disappears; if the Empire disappears, I shall no longer be able to pursue my studies in the university of Cambridge.' (*M*, p. 218)

The associations are always present; the mundane counterpart of the sacred structures of men's ideology is 'Arthur's Education Fund', the centuries-old accumulation of money which sends the sons of prominent men to public school and to university.[6] Contributed to so much and for so long by the unschooled daughters of educated men, the Fund casts its shadow over the entire landscape. The result is, she tells the treasurer of the society 'to prevent war and preserve cultural freedom' (a man educated, she imagines, at one of the great public schools and at the university),

that though we look at the same things, we see them differently.
What is that congregation of buildings there, with the semi-
monastic look, with chapels and halls and green playing fields?
To you it is your old school: Eton or Harrow; your old
University, Oxford or Cambridge; the source of memories and
of traditions innumerable. But to us, who see it through the
shadow of Arthur's Education Fund, it is a schoolroom table;
an omnibus going to a class; a little woman with a red nose who
is not well educated herself but has an invalid mother to
support; and an allowance of £50 a year with which to buy
clothes, give presents and take journeys on coming to maturity.   (*TG*, p.5)[7]

But the treasurer is probably concerned only with 'obvious fact',
and so, although 'the fact that Arthur's Education Fund changes
the landscape – the halls, the playing fields, the sacred edifices – is
an important one . . . that aspect must be left for future discussion'
(p.5).

The future, as we say, is now, just as it was then. And, because
Virginia Woolf saw those 'sacred edifices' through the shadow of
Arthur's Education Fund, she would say to the treasurer of the
woman's college rebuilding fund, 'Let it be built on lines of its own
. . . not of carved stone and stained glass, but of some cheap, easily
combustible material which does not hoard dust and perpetrate
traditions.' The question here is whether to send money to help
rebuild the women's college or whether money should be
earmarked for 'Rags. Petrol. Matches' with which to burn the
college to the ground. Built on the lines of the old, male colleges it
would teach people 'the old poisoned vanities and parades which
breed competition and jealousy', the competition which leads to
war, not to its prevention (p. 35).[8] Ultimately she sends the
guinea, unconditionally, because the rebuilt women's college,
'imperfect as it may be', is 'the only alternative to the education of
the private house' (p. 39).[9] One guinea sent by a woman to help
rebuild a women's college is one small contribution to set against
the endowments of centuries. And with endowments we are led,
perforce, back to Cambridge, where it all starts (and where, in
Virginia Woolf's writing, it continues, even if, in *The Years*, we
have to call if Oxford).[10]

The apparent sense of conflict in *Three Guineas*, and the
outsider's viewpoint defined there, characterise Virginia Woolf's

perceptions of the 'great universities', of Oxbridge. *Jacob's Room* (1922) was her first novel set, in part, in the university; in it she first 'found her voice' as a novelist. Jacob Flanders, the 'hero' of what Judy Little has recently called a comic, even a parodic *Bildungsroman*, moves from childhood, through Cambridge, a position in the City, holidays in Greece, to an early death in the First World War. As Judy Little cleverly suggests,

> In *Jacob's Room* the traditional male growth-pattern, full of great expectation, falls like a tattered mantle around the shoulders of the indecisive hero, heir of the ages. The musing and amused narrator mocks the structure of her story; she mocks the conventions of the hero's progress; and, by implication, she mocks the values behind those conventions.[11]

It is, I think, in the voice of this 'musing and amused' narrator that Virginia Woolf often directs her own voice against the hallowed buildings of the sons of culture:

> They say the sky is the same everywhere. Travellers, the ship-wrecked, exiles, and the dying draw comfort from the thought. . . . But above Cambridge – anyhow above the roof of King's College Chapel – there is a difference. Out at sea a great city will cast a brightness into the night. Is it fanciful to suppose the sky, washed into the crevices of King's College Chapel, lighter, thinner, more sparkling than the sky elsewhere? Does Cambridge burn not only into the night, but into the day?
>
> (*JR*, pp. 31–2)

Jacob himself, Judy Little suggests, is 'somewhat on the outside', never quite absorbed into the atmosphere of Cambridge.[12] And, if Jacob is 'somewhat on the outside', he is seen from the point of view of an outsider roughly three times removed. ('I'm a complete outsider', wrote Virginia Woolf to Goldie Lowes Dickinson of King's, when he said how 'good tempered' he thought *A Room of One's Own – L*, IV, 106.) And so, at an ever-so-orderly Chapel service, Jacob, his mind wandering because of the 'several hat shops and cupboards upon cupboards of coloured dresses . . . displayed upon rush-bottomed chairs', muses thus:

> But this service in King's College Chapel – why allow women to

take part in it? . . . No one would think of bringing a dog into church. For though a dog is all very well on a gravel path, and shows no disrespect to flowers, the way he wanders down an aisle, looking, lifting a paw, and approaching a pillar with a purpose that makes the blood run cold with horror (should you be one of the congregation – alone, shyness is out of the question), a dog destroys the service completely. So do these women – though separately devout, distinguished, and vouched for by the theology, mathematics, Latin and Greek of their husbands. (*JR*, pp. 32–3)

So incongruous do the dons' wives seem to Jacob – 'vouched for' though they are, their presence is an affront to his 'inherited' sense of 'old buildings and time' (p.45) – that his own version of Dr Johnson's dog walking on its hind legs slips in quite naturally.

Women do not, as far as I know, urinate on the 'pillars' of King's College Chapel, but they might stray off the gravel paths (no longer gravel, since the 'improvements' of the 1950s) onto the grass of the Court. And they are flushed off. 'He was a Beadle; I was a woman. This was the turf; there was the path' (*AROO*, p.6).[13] And from the path, the narrator of *A Room of One's Own* focuses on the roof of an unnamed but clearly defined chapel:

As you know, its high domes and pinnacles can be seen, like a sailing-ship always voyaging never arriving, lit up at night and visible for miles, far away across the hills. Once, presumably, this quadrangle with its smooth lawns, its massive buildings, and the chapel itself was marsh too, where the grasses waved and the swine rooted. Teams of horses and oxen . . . must have hauled the stone in wagons from far counties, and then with infinite labour the grey blocks . . . were poised in order one on top of another, and then the painters brought their glass for the windows and the masons were busy for centuries up on that roof. . . . Every Saturday somebody must have poured gold and silver into their ancient fists. . . . An unending stream of gold and silver . . . must have flowed into this court perpetually to keep the stones coming and the masons working. . . . And when the age of faith was over . . . still the same flow of gold and silver went on . . . more chairs, more lectureships in the university where [merchants and manufacturers] had learnt their craft. Hence the libraries and laboratories; the observatories, the

splendid equipment of costly and delicate instruments which
now stands on glass shelves, where centuries ago the grasses
waved and the swine rootled.   (pp. 9–10)[14]

The 'stream of gold and silver' here is as important as are the
eccentric dons, the 'rare types' able to survive only in the
university, who make up the congregation – the recipients,
however indirectly, of the 'treasure'. But, when the congregation
is inside, 'the outside of the chapel remain[s]', and 'the outside of
these magnificent buildings is often as beautiful as the inside' (pp.
9,8). To this narrator, as to the narrator of *Jacob's Room*, what
remains is the 'ship' of King's College Chapel. That chapel,
which, Her Majesty's Commissions declared in 1959, 'is amongst
our most important possessions . . . being one of the four most
sumptuous buildings of Royal foundation of the period',[15]
remains a dominating physical presence, both 'crystallised history' and the thing itself.

The outside of the chapel, the stones of the chapel, and the
money with which the chapel was built are, indeed, inseparable.
Thus it is the *building* which the narrator 'explains' as she sits in
another room in another building where

> the real interest of whatever was said was . . . a scene of masons
> on a high roof some five centuries ago. Kings and nobles
> brought treasure in huge sacks and poured it under the earth
> . . . and then . . . the great financial magnates of our own time
> came and laid cheques and bonds, I suppose, where the others
> had laid ingots and rough lumps of gold. All that lies beneath
> the colleges down there, I said; but this college, where we are
> now sitting, what lies beneath its gallant red brick and the wild,
> unkempt grasses of the garden?   (*AROO*, pp. 19–20)

The 'gallant red brick' belongs, of course, to both Newnham and
to Girton, whose founders did well to 'raise bare walls out of the
bare earth' (*AROO*, p.23). Of the original Girton (not Hitchin)
buildings, a newspaper correspondent wrote in 1874, 'The new
College for Women, which has excited so much interest of late, is
of plain red brick, and has as yet no claims to beauty, though it is
hoped that when the trees, which are already planted around it,
grow up, the spot will not look quite so bare'.[16] Of a photograph
taken in the same year, E. E. Constance Jones (who became
Mistress in 1903) remarks, 'No wonder the *Graphic* correspondent

thought it so bare!'[17] Here the 'amenities had to wait', and there were to be, at first at least, 'no chapels'.[18]

In 1928, however, at Newnham (as well as at Girton), the gardens were 'wild and open, and in the long grass, sprinkled and carelessly flung, were daffodils and bluebells, not orderly perhaps at the best of times'; here one might have seen 'J–H– herself', whose bent figure had been real enough.[19] Around the 'fictitious' college, 'all was dim, yet intense too, as if the scarf which the dusk had flung over the garden were torn asunder by star or sword – the flash of some terrible reality leaping, as its way is, out of the heart of spring. For youth–'. Here, the narrator's soup arrives (that thin, plain soup served in the women's college), and it is October, not spring. And yet the bent figure in the wild garden, the gallant red brick, the invocation of 'youth', help establish Virginia Woolf's counterweight to the ages and ages of the 'great universities'. Jane Harrison died in April 1928; at her funeral 'a bird sang most opportunely; with a gay indifference, & if one liked, hope, that Jane would have enjoyed' (*D*, III, 181). Spring, anywhere, may conventionally be a beginning, but October is the 'birth of the year', not only in accordance with those ancient Greek ceremonies described by Jane Harrison,[20] but also according to the university calendar. So it is fitting that Virginia Woolf, speaking at the women's colleges in October, should deliberately confuse, conflate these two, these three, 'births': it is the women's college which must be built of 'some cheap, easily combustible material', must have its books and pictures 'new and always changing', must be 'decorated afresh by each generation with their own hands'. It is the women's college which must be not a 'sumptuous' edifice to the monarch and his God, not a showpiece of English Perpendicular, but must be built on lines of its own, making use of any cyclical beginning it can. These things bespeak re-volution, even (perhaps especially) over thin soup and prunes and custard.

The 'rare types' like those of the King's congregation are, later in Woolf's writing, ossified into their places, part of the stone and the ages which they inherit. And, since youth is 'wild', there is little to do, sometimes, but laugh at them. In *Jacob's Room* we were invited to look at them as they went into service: 'What sculptured faces, what certainty, authority, controlled by piety, although great boots march under the gowns. In what orderly procession they advance' (*JR*, p.32). The combination of sculpture, order, and, implicitly, feet of clay – or perhaps the jackboot on the neck – gives way, in *The Years*, to gargoyles.[21] These, Beverly Ann Schlack has suggested, constitute 'an apt metaphor for [Woolf's] scornful strategies in this novel, where laughter is often rather grim, gargoyle-faced, and many-clawed'.[22] (In this connection, Joanna Lipking has pointed out that the Pargiter sons appear 'in later life with the lineaments of statues or portraits'. And, in a lovely reading of the '1914' City chop-house scene, she points to how, in Martin's *mis*reading of Sara's appraisal of the chop-house clientele, we have, with his 'Were you looking at the monuments?', the 'petrification of the stockbrokers'.)[23]

To these suggestions I would add that we should remember that gargoyles have a specific architectural function. Since rainwater threatens to rot roofs, gutters are built to collect it, and it then runs down spouts to be spewed out, away from the roof. Gargoyles, grotesquely carved animal or human heads, 'ornament' the ends of the spouts, and from their mouths pours, or gurgles, the unwanted, roof-rotting water. Being gutter ornaments, gargoyles are naturally rather out of touch with the solid ground, and in Virginia Woolf's buildings are thus perfect representatives of the 'rare types' who make up the congregations of all sorts of privilege-ridden male institutions.

Early on in *The Years* it is raining in Oxford (and in Cambridge):

> Over the vast domes, the soaring spires of slumbering University cities, over the leaded libraries, and the museums . . . the gentle rain slid down, till, reaching the mouths of those fantastic laughers, the many-clawed gargoyles, it splayed out in a thousand odd indentations. (*Y*, p.47)

When Kitty Malone, daughter of the Master of St Katharine's, has been to the ugly, little houses of Miss Craddock, who makes a living teaching history, and of Professor Robson's family, whose working-class background sets them apart from conventional 'Oxford', her distaste for the great university is confirmed. Returning from 'outside' territory, Kitty reaches a familiar part of Oxford: 'But for a moment all seemed to her obsolete, frivolous, inane. The usual undergraduate in cap and gown with books under his arm looked silly. And the portentous old men, with their exaggerated features, looked like gargoyles, carved, medieval, unreal' (p. 74).

The fixity and the unreality are not new, of course, in Virginia Woolf's Oxbridge. Two weeks after her 'Modern Fiction' lecture to the Heretics, she wrote to Jacques Raverat,

> Do you feel kindly towards Cambridge? It was, as Lytton would say, rather 'hectic'; young men going in for their triposes; flowering trees on the backs; canoes, fellows' gardens; wading in a slightly unreal beauty; dinners, teas, suppers; a sense, on my part, of extreme age, and tenderness and regret; and so on and so on. We had a good hard headed argument, and I respect the atmosphere and I'm glad to be out of it. Maynard is very heavy and rather portentous. . . . (*L*, III, 114)

Virginia had obviously visited Trinity often enough as a young woman, but surely, too, Leonard's Cambridge became part of her 'copy'. In 1960 Leonard recalled his initial loneliness when he went up in 1899; the only other Paul's scholar of his year was, after all, someone he scarcely knew. But 'suddenly everything changed and almost for the first time one felt that to be young was very heaven. . . . It began casually in what was called the screens, the passage through the Hall from Trinity Great Court to Neville's Court.' There, he met Saxon Sydney-Turner.[24] 'Brilliant young men, whose lights had been kindled at Cambridge, . . . burnt all of them precisely in the same way', reported Virginia Woolf to Violet Dickinson in 1907, and so it is no surprise to find Richard Dalloway, whom Jane Austen puts to sleep, declare in *Melymbrosia* (c.1910), 'I suppose the most momentous conversations of my life took place while perambulating the great court at Trinity.'[25]

Endless repetition, momentous Wordsworthian revelations, the same 'liberating' environment – these things ossify, petrify. It is no wonder then, that the undergraduate philosophising of Jacob and his friends was 'hard, yet ephemeral, as of glass compared with the dark stone of the Chapel' (*JR*, p.45). The narrator tells us this because Jacob, after Sunday lunches, after dinners, teas, feels 'such steady certainty', such 'reassurance from all sides, the trees blowing, the grey spires soft in the blue', because Jacob, after a night of talk, was the 'only man who walked at that moment back to his rooms, his footsteps rang out, his figure loomed large' (pp.36, 46). The 'old stone' echoes his footsteps with 'magisterial authority'. Any young man, any man, looms large not because he is especially buttressed by his own intrinsic worth, but because he has behind him, as it were, a piece of the rock.

We could 'check' on the accuracy of Virginia Woolf's perceptions, particularly with regard to King's, in a variety of ways. We might obtain statistics relevant to the annual numbers of visitors to King's Chapel; or count the money put into the ancient chest – near the postcard stand – which is marked 'for the restoration of the Chapel'; or chronicle the nervous stories of outsiders who come to Cambridge – defining as an outsider anyone whose 'destiny' has not always been Cambridge, whose gender, colour, class is 'wrong', whose university is 'red brick' rather than old stone. But books are *much* more convincing. In 1922, the year of *Jacob's Room*, the Lowell Institute in Boston, Massachusetts, funded a course of lectures by one Albert Mansbridge (a Royal Commissioner on the universities, 1919–20). The lectures were published as *The Older Universities of England: Oxford and Cambridge* in 1923. Of the book's eight illustrations, six are of Cambridge. One, of a 'Washington Memorial' in Little St Mary's, is obviously included for an American audience. The others show the Pepysian Library at Magdalene (small, and sweet, and 'quaint'), the Queen's College Bridge (an engineering 'marvel' in wood), and the 'bridge of Trinity College', 'Under the Library, Trinity College' and 'A Part of Cambridge'. This last, sketched in the manner of a seventeenth-century drawing, shows part of Great St Mary's (the University Church, within ten miles of which all students must reside in order to fulfil residence requirements), St John's College, Trinity College (and Trinity Bridge), Caius College, and the Senate House (where students take their degrees and where men voted in huge numbers to keep women from receiving degrees). All this takes up, at most, five-eighths of the picture. The rest is of King's Chapel, so centrally placed that 'A Part of Cambridge' might as well be a sketch of that sacred edifice.

The Chapel is not Cambridge, but to the outsider it represents Cambridge. I suppose Virginia Woolf would appreciate the irony of tourists' Cambridge being her Cambridge, because she was not, of course, a tourist in the way that tourists are . . . tourists.[26] Being shut out of the Wren Library at Trinity (where the Milton Minor Poems manuscript is 'locked up'), and being made aware, from her position on the gravel path, of the massive weight of masonry (1875 tons of chapel-vaulting alone[27]), rising above the turf on which no one may walk 'unless accompanied by a Senior Member of the College', she obviously saw things differently from the way male members of the Stephen line – and their intimates – saw them.[28]

When, in *Three Guineas*, she tells the treasurer that women see a 'congregation of buildings' differently, it is partly because they have a 'semi-monastic look'. It is precisely the monastic exclusiveness of men's universities ('men . . . living . . . in little communities of their own' – *P*, p.107), and what they bestowed on their sons, that Virginia Woolf perhaps envied but then comprehensively rejected. The colleges are 'monasteries', used to confirm the power of the Church and of the monarch and then, too, the power of the 'proper' (reformed) religion. Just as St Katharine's, 'symbolized' by the Lodge, 'owed a good deal to money that had been given to the College by the Church before the Reformation, or taken from the Church after the Reformation' (*P*, p.106), so King's and Trinity were completed and augmented by Henry VIII with the help of money taken from the 'dissolved' monasteries.[29] Virginia Woolf knew and we know that 'The Church's one foundation / Is Jesus Christ her Lord', but we also know that it was not water and the word that produced the king's 'chirche' in Cambridge but 'money [which] was poured liberally to set these stones on a deep foundation' (*AROO*, p.9). (It is wonderfully apt that of the buildings pulled down to clear a space for Henry VI's King's College, one was a 'small college called God's House'.[30]) The 'monastic look', though, serves to remind people that behind the political and economic power these buildings represent is, ostensibly, another greater, spiritual power. And the 'look' itself is sometimes attractive, even to outsiders. So, returning from Oxford, where she had stayed with her 'priestly' (also 'hollow') cousin, Herbert Fisher, Virginia Woolf admits that 'there was a certain monastic dignity about the cloisters in the moonlight (not that I like colleges)' (*L*, V, 254).

The very stones, of course, reflect the ways in which the 'sacred' and the politically powerful join in the architecture of the universities, and especially in King's College Chapel. A modern architectural historian tells us of the 'lasting monastic influence' over British architecture. He shows how, while this influence continued unabated, other, more secular architectural syntax asserted itself: 'Heraldic decoration appears for the first time on a large scale in the spandrels of the wall arcading the later parts of Henry III's work in Westminster Abbey.' And this element, evidence partly of the 'layman's taste', becomes more apparent in both religious buildings and in 'domestic architecture which had hitherto been purely practical, either in the nature of the grandiose centre for the administration of an estate or practical in a purely military sense'.[31] Thus the Crown, whose military and administrative power we can, obviously, characterise in the language of *Three Guineas*, exerts its influence from the late thirteenth century down to the sixteenth century, so that by the time Henry VII and Henry VIII have done their work on King's we have a production about which a recent commentator says, 'it is not unreasonable to propose that the vaulting, along with the sculpture, should be understood as a political document which attests to the legitimacy of the Tudor dynasty'.[32] And the ante-chapel 'has a wealth of heraldic decoration exalting the Tudor family and its Beaufort connexions'.[33] Anyone wanting to be a tourist and to bring a little of this back can, at the stand set up in the light of the Chapel's lovely west window, buy a postcard of one of the decorations in the series under the windows. There, between the crowned Tudor rose and the Beaufort portcullis, are wonderful carvings of the Welsh dragon and the English greyhound, each with its little penis much in evidence, supporting the arms of Henry VII.

The monarchical presence in Cambridge, confirmed by the completion of King's College Chapel, had been established earlier by the endowment of 'The King's Hall'. This, in 1546, was joined with Michaelhouse to become Trinity College – the 'grandest of all English colleges' according even to A. L. Rowse, a man almost obsessively attached to Oxford.[34] It is Trinity which has 'the most spacious College court in existence', a fountain which is 'perhaps the finest thing of its kind in England', and a Great Gate surpassing any other in 'either' university.[35] Exhibiting the arms of Edward III and his six sons, and a statue of Henry VIII, the Great Gate inspires one commentator to remark that 'no street – no town – in England presents anything like this "boast of heraldry" which Gray had always under his eye in Cambridge. It is a permanent record of the two royal groups in England who preferred this university; the gateway of Trinity being the *trait d'union* between them'.[36]

It was 1944 when G. M. Trevelyan published *Trinity College, An Historical Sketch*. It is a great pity it came too late for Virginia Woolf to comment on it. One wonders how she might have responded to the reviewer who confessed that anyone familiar with the Trinity buildings was aware of

> the difficulty of explaining this intimate relationship in which
> . . . at least the function of the buildings consists. It is not
> merely a question of the sentimental affection with which a man
> regards the material setting of his first adult experience; it is the
> sense that *succeeding generations have recognized that a community
> devoted to learning is as deserving of splendour as the politically or the
> economically powerful*, and of this the Great Court and Nevil's
> Court at Trinity are the most magnificent witnesses. King's
> Chapel is perhaps a greater piece of architecture than any of the
> buildings that form these courts, Wren's Library not excepted,
> but it is a monument to Royal Piety rather than to the dignity of
> learning, and it is the latter quality which is so admirably
> brought out by the author of this book.[37]

Ah yes! Men 'whose lights had been kindled at Cambridge . . .
burnt all of them precisely in the same way'.

Given her conflicting responses to the sacred edifices of male
academe, it is interesting that, on the face of it, Virginia Woolf
pays more attention to King's College Chapel, with its brass to the
memory of J. K. Stephen, than to Trinity, with all its Stephen and
'Bloomsbury' connections, and its library.[38] It is perhaps for
reasons she presents in *A Room of One's Own*, whose narrator is
barred from seeing the 'Lycidas' manuscript by a donnish
'guardian angel', a 'deprecating, silvery, kindly gentleman'
(*AROO*, p. 7). The building which the narrator then curses is not
the original library, but the 'modern' one, begun only in 1676 by
Christopher Wren. It is *that* building which forms the riverward
boundary of Neville's Court – the court on which Adrian Stephen
had his rooms, and where his visiting sister had heard 'the sound
of Grace coming through the windows . . . in the summer when we
were young!' (*L*, III, 555) There was, perhaps, even more to these
associations than the impulse to remind us that, where the chapel
now stands, once the swine rootled.

Back to his rooms came Jacob, and the old stone echoed with
magisterial authority; back from Girton came Virginia Woolf on
27 October 1928, to record in her diary,

The corridors of Girton are like vaults in some horrid high church cathedral – on & on they go, cold & shiny – with a light burning. High gothic rooms; acres of bright brown wood; here and there a photograph.

And we saw Trinity & King's this morning. Now to concentrate on English Literature. . . .   (*D*, III, 201)

Women's Cambridge does *not* burn into the day, the burning of unnecessary lights being expensive, and funds low. We are back in 'reality', which, for a writer who has to earn her living, must sometimes be 'English Literature', and which should always consist in standing very firmly on the turf and remembering the importance of particular edifices, perhaps the importance of burning them to the ground, even if, at times, they pretend to be inoffensive pieces of furniture. Like chairs.

In May 1940, Virginia Woolf tried to explain to members of the Workers' Educational Association how it was that 'English Literature' was changing, or how it should be changing. Concerning the 'representative names' of the time, and those writers who form the family to which they belonged, she said, in part,

> a chair is a very important part of a writer's outfit. It is that chair that gives him his attitude towards his model; that decides what he sees of human life; that profoundly affects his power of telling us what he sees. By his chair we mean his upbringing, his education. It is a fact, not theory, that all writers from Chaucer to the present day, with so few exceptions that one hand can count them, have sat upon the same kind of chair – a raised chair.[39]

Having tallied up the masculine pronouns here, all we need to do is remind ourselves that, although it had to be explained to Mrs Chailey, in *Melymbrosia*, 'to her considerable though mute amazement . . . that no gentleman could read Greek in a high chair' (*M*, p.16), a voice issuing from a 'raised chair' is a voice issuing *ex cathedra*. And, with regard to 'the cathedral', whether it be chapel, a library,[40] or merely the hallowed turf, Virginia Woolf urges her listeners to 'Trespass at once!' The alternative to trespassing is building, and here there are two paths we can take. If the women's college is to be built on the lines of the old male colleges, the 'sacred edifices' of the sons of culture, we might send a contribution, but

> this note should be attached to it. 'Take this guinea and with it burn the college to the ground. Set fire to the old hypocrisies. Let the light of the burning building scare the nightingales and incarnadine the willows. And let the daughters of educated men dance round the fire. . . . And let their mothers lean from the upper windows and cry, 'Let it blaze! Let it blaze! For we have done with this "education"!' (*TG*, p. 36)

Or, we might still help build a college, but only one that is 'built on lines of its own . . . built not of carved stone and stained glass, but of some cheap, easily combustible material which does not hoard dust and perpetrate traditions'. Not 'crystallised history', but bluebells in October.

## NOTES

1. The phrase is taken from Ellen Hawkes, 'Woolf's "Magical Garden of Women" ', in *New Feminist Essays on Virginia Woolf*, ed. Jane Marcus (London: Macmillan; Lincoln, Nebr.: University of Nebraska Press, 1981) pp.31–60. Hawkes borrows the phrase from Woolf's 'Friendship's Gallery' (1907). This was published in *Twentieth Century Literature*, XXV, nos 3–4 (Autumn–Winter, 1979) 270–302.

2. Ibid., p.56. The paper, the *Cambridge Fortnightly*, ran to only five issues, from 24 Jan to 13 Mar 1888. The cover illustration, shown on only four issues, is a rather distorted view of Cambridge with, centre, King's Chapel and a huge sun, rising into a cloudy sky, surrounding it like a halo. (I am grateful to J. E. Lambert of the Photography Department, Cambridge University Library, for sending me photocopies of all five covers and a photograph of the four-times-repeated illustration.)

3. Brenda Silver, *Virginia Woolf's Reading Notebooks* (Princeton, NJ: Princeton University Press, 1983) p. 22. (I'm extremely grateful to Jane Marcus for, among other things, lending me her copy of the pre-publication proofs.)

4. With regard to 'psychic and physical space', see also Jane Marcus, 'Thinking Back through Our Mothers', in *New Feminist Essays on Virginia Woolf*, pp.5–6.

5. William Hubbard, 'The Meaning of Buildings', review of Marcus Whiffen and Frederick Koeper, *American Architecture 1607–1976*, in *New Republic*, 18 Nov 1981, p.30.

6. For an incisive run-down on the 'professional men' spawned by the

Fund, as Woolf saw them, see Beverly Ann Schlack, ' "Fathers in General": The Patriarchy in Virginia Woolf's Fiction', in *Virginia Woolf: A Feminist Slant*, ed. Jane Marcus (Lincoln, Nebr.: University of Nebraska Press, 1983).

7. Even when she is on holiday, Miss Allen (in *Melymbrosia*) has to 'keep in touch with the classics because she made her living and supported an invalid sister by teaching girls in the north modern language and English Literature' (*M*, p.80)

8. With both *The Years* and *Three Guineas* much on her mind, Virginia Woolf wrote to Julian Bell in March 1936, 'As for your Apostles, much though I respect them singly, I begin to think that these Societies do more harm than good, merely by rousing jealousies and vanities. What d'you think? It seems to me the wrong way to live, drawing chalk marks round ones feet, and saying to the Clives etc you can't come in' (*L*, VI, 20.). Cf. the 'chalkmarks' in *Y*, p.56.

9. A letter dated 19 Feb 1936 from 'J. P. Strachey' asks Virginia Woolf to 'join the Committee of Patrons who will launch Newnham's first public appeal for money' (Silver, *Reading Notebooks*, LIX, B, 10). In a letter to Pernel Strachey dated four days later, Virginia Woolf says, 'perhaps now I'm a patron, I shall be asked to lay a brick' (*L*, VI, 15).

10. Virginia Woolf's own experience of Cambridge and of Oxford is, in *The Years* and *The Pargiters*, 'fleshed out' by her reading of Mrs Humphry Ward's *A Writer's Recollections* (New York and London: Harper, 1918). See, for example, *P*, p.106; and Jane Marcus, 'Pargeting *The Pargiters*: Notes of an Apprentice Plasterer', *BNYPL*, LXXX, no. 3 (Spring 1977) 432. The *Recollections* seem to have been, to Virginia Woolf, both detestable and a 'masterpiece without rival' (*L*, II, 307), the 'blare and pomp' having an irksome effect on her (*D*, I, 300). It is not at all surprising that, in the 1930s, 'reading her culture', she should have gone back to Mrs Ward's memories of the 'stately dignity and benignant charm' of the Bodleian, echoing to 'the voices of the bells outside, as they struck each successive quarter from Oxford's many towers', or of a 'dinner at Balliol' where she found herself 'sitting next the great man Taine' (*Recollections*, I, 149, 155). Not surprising that Mrs Ward's experience should be 'read' in entirely the opposite way by Kitty Malone, who feels 'rather guilty' about doing the Bodleian 'so quick' in the company of the sympathetic Mrs Fripp, who 'hated the sound of the bells; . . . a dismal sound' (*Y*, pp. 59, 61). 'King's bell saying very pompously all through the night the hour', Virginia Woolf recorded in her diary after a week-end in Cambridge (*D*, II, 230). And of the 'great man' Kitty wants to say, 'Did you really like the way he spits when he talks?', and can remember 'the damp feel of a heavy hand on her knee' (*Y*, pp.57, 66).

11. Judy Little, '*Jacob's Room* as Comedy: Woolf's Parodic *Bildungsroman*', in *New Feminist Essays*, p. 105.

12. Ibid., p. 111.

13. A matter of women and children last, obviously. Gwen Raverat recalls, 'The climax of all earthly pleasures came when we received a letter from Ralph [Wedgewood, her cousin], written in invisible ink, inviting us to tea in his rooms at Trinity. After that tea-party poor Charles went through a terrible ordeal, for Felix threw his cap on to the grass in the Great Court, and dared him to go on to it to fetch it. Walking on the sacred college grass is about the worst crime a Cambridge child can commit; however, Charles did it and survived' – *Period Piece* (New York: Norton, 1951) p. 235.

14. This is, of course, an accurate historical account of the building of the Chapel. Its foundation stone laid in 1446 by Henry VI, the Chapel was chiefly the work of Henry VII and Henry VIII; indeed, King's scholars had to remind Henry VII, in 1499, that his uncle's great work 'was abandoned, an unsightly fragment'. Stone was certainly hauled from 'far counties': Henry VI's builders used stone from two quarries near Leeds, Yorkshire, and Henry VII's, from Weldon, Northamptonshire. The painters 'brought their glass' only in 1515; when they finished, in 1531, the Chapel had the 'greatest proportion of glass to stone' of any English church.

As to the 'unending flow of gold and silver', there are some figures extant. Henry VII spent £1700 between May 1508 and April 1509, and, in March 1509, sent another £5000. In February 1511–12 his executors granted the College a further £5000, having been directed in 1509 to deliver as much additional money as was necessary to finish the work. In 1508–9 there were some 150 workers employed, about ninety of them masons. The master carver's annual salary was £13 16s 8d., as was the 'Comptroller's'. Between 1509 and 1513, the master carver (the King's Joiner) had an annual salary of £18 5s. Masons working on the bays in the main vault got £100 for each bay, and in 1515 the King's Glazier was given an advance of £100. Henry VIII's expenses began when the College petitioned him for money to complete the decorations and fittings (excluding glazing). The estimate (which included fifty-six statues of kings – never executed) was for £2893 14s. Paving alone was estimated at £868.

Additions and changes continued through the following four centuries. The choir, for instance, was repaved in 1702, and, also in the eighteenth century, the woodwork and stonework at the Chapel's east end were 'rearranged' for a mere £1652. Only in 1879 was the west window filled with coloured glass – a representation of the Last Judgement. At the time when Virginia Woolf spoke at Girton and at Newnham the most recent addition had been – what else? – the King's College Chapel War Memorial to the fallen of the First World War.

See relevant sections of *Royal Commission on Historical Monuments, England: An Inventory of the Historical Monuments in the City of Cambridge*, 2 vols (London: Her Majesty's Stationery Office, 1959) I; T. D. Atkinson and J. W. Clark, *Cambridge Described and Illustrated* (London: Macmillan 1896); M. A. R. Tuker, *Cambridge* (London: Adam and Charles Black, 1907); Brian W. Downs, *Cambridge Past and Present* (London: Methuen, 1926); Edmund Vale, *Cambridge and its Colleges* (London: Methuen, 1959).

15. *Royal Commission . . . Cambridge*, I, 105.

16. Quoted in E. E. Constance Jones, *Girton College* (London: Adam and Charles Black, 1913) p. 6.

17. Ibid., p.7.

18. The 'amenities' are mentioned in *AROO*, p. 21, citing Ray Strachey, *The Cause* (1928). 'Do not have chapels', quoted at the head of this essay, is from *TG*, p.33, and the note there refers to Lady Stanley's forbidding the use of funds at Girton for a chapel rather than for educational purposes.

19. For the importance of Jane Harrison to Virginia Woolf's thinking, see Jane Marcus, '*The Years* as Greek Drama, Domestic Novel, and Götterdämmerung', *BNYPL*, LXXX, no.2 (Winter 1977) 276–301, and 'Pargeting *The Pargiters*', *passim*. Jane Marcus further explores Virginia Woolf's recognition of the radical elements in Jane Harrison's classical studies in 'Liberty, Sorority, Misogyny', in *The Representation of Women in Fiction*, ed. Carolyn G. Heilbrun and Margaret R. Higonnet, Selected Papers from the English Institute, 1981, n.s., no.7 (Baltimore: Johns Hopkins University Press, 1983) pp. 60–97.

20. See Marcus, 'Pargeting *The Pargiters*', *BNYPL*, LXXX, no.3, 420. In another essay, Jane Marcus says, 'As we move from October to June, we realize that it is not only the year which is academic. (But this male "academic" year is paralleled by a "female" matriarchal year, deriving from Jane Harrison's studies of pre-classical Greece and structuring the time sequence of all the novels' – 'Enchanted Organs, Magic Bells: *Night and Day* as Comic Opera', in *Virginia Woolf: Revaluation and Continuity*, ed. Ralph Freedman (Berkeley, Calif., and Los Angeles: University of California Press, 1978) p.109.

I must confess to having attentively read this essay 'too late' to avoid my inevitably identifying the year's beginning in October with the beginning of Michaelmas Term. Most people associated with the men's university would, I imagine. Of course, a glance at Jane Harrison tells us that the October festival was the Thesmophoria, the autumn festival of sowing (*Prolegomena to the Study of Greek Religion*, ch.1), and that Demeter, whose title was Thesmophoros, 'laid down a law or Thesmos in accordance with which it was incumbent upon men to obtain and provide by labour their nurture'. We find, too, that pigs were let down into clefts in the earth and left to rot, in order that the civilising rites might be accomplished (ibid., ch. 4). This is rather nice in view of those swine which 'rootled' in King's courts, as well as of more recent feminist epithets for the opposition.

21. Of interest here, perhaps, is a change Virginia Woolf made in the manuscript of 'The Journal of Mistress Joan Martyn' (1906). Susan Squier and Louise DeSalvo point out in their introduction that in changing 'with one foot raised as though he were ready to kick her if she turned', to '& his boot seemed ready to . . . crush her', the 'revision not only truncates and supplants the earlier, longer, cancelled passage, it introduces the figure which also signifies male domination' – *Twentieth Century Literature*, XXV, nos 3–4 (Autumn–Winter 1979) 238.

22. Beverly Ann Schlack, 'Virginia Woolf's Strategy of Scorn in *The Years* and *Three Guineas*', *BNYPL*, LXXX, no.2, 147.

23. Joanna Lipking, 'Looking at the Monuments: Woolf's Satiric Eye', ibid., pp. 141, 143–4.

24. Leonard Woolf, *Sowing: An Autobiography of the Years 1880 to 1904* (New York: Harcourt Brace Jovanovich, 1960) p. 103.

25. L, I, 300, and *M*, p. 47 (see also *VO*, p.64).

26. Several months after I had written this I came across Brian W. Downs, *Cambridge Past and Present* (1926). It would be nice to think Virginia Woolf had glanced at it while she was preparing notes for 'Women and Fiction'. Downs begins his account of the Chapel thus: 'To most visitors to Cambridge the word "King's", sometimes the word "Cambridge" too, stands for nothing more than this College Chapel, certainly the most imposing monument in the town and University, and perhaps the finest specimen in England of the architecture of its time' (p.152). Downs's commentary places some emphasis on the diverse counties whence the stone was brought, and on Henry VI's 'dream of splendour', his intention 'to endow [the College] with wealth and privileges before which every other College would seem but a mean thing'.

27. *King's College Chapel* (London: Jarrold, for King's) p.9.

28. In 'A Sketch of the Past' Virginia Woolf records, 'All our male relations were adepts at the game. They knew the rules and attached immense importance to them. Father laid enormous stress upon schoolmaster's reports, upon scholarships, triposes and fellowships. The Fishers, the male Fishers, took every prize, honour, degree' (*MB*, p.132).

29. See, for instance, A. G. Dickens, *The English Reformation* (London: Collins, 1967) p.211.

30. Tuker, *Cambridge*, p.101, and Vale, *Cambridge and its Colleges*, p.94.

31. Geoffrey Webb, *Architecture in Britain: The Middle Ages* (Baltimore: Penguin Books, 1956) pp.27,157.

32. W. C. Leedy, Jr, 'Building Accounts of King's College Chapel, Cambridge, 1508–1515', *Society of Architectural Historians Journal*, XXXV (Dec 1976) 257.

33. Webb, *Architecture in Britain*, p.198.

34. A. L. Rowse, *Oxford University in the History of England* (New York:

G. P. Putnam's, 1975) p.49.

35. *Royal Commission . . . Cambridge*, II 215; Theodore Fyfe, *Architecture in Cambridge* (Cambridge: Cambridge University Press, 1942) p.69.

36. Tuker, *Cambridge*, pp. 103–4.

37. Geoffrey Webb, review of *Trinity College. An Historical Sketch* (1944), in *Architectural Review*, Apr 1944, p. 112; emphasis added.

38. With reference to the brass to J. K. Stephen, see Leslie Stephen, *The Life of Sir James Fitzjames Stephen* (New York: G. P. Putnam's Sons, 1895) p. 477; and Jane Marcus, 'Taking the Bull by the Udders', below, Ch.8.

39. Virginia Woolf, 'The Leaning Tower', in *'The Moment' and Other Essays* (New York: Harcourt Brace Jovanovich, 1948) p. 136.

40. In her 'little piece of rant' about Morgan Forster's reminding her of Mrs Green's being on the Committee of the London Library and her being 'so troublesome' that Leslie Stephen said 'never again', Virginia Woolf wrote, 'The veil of the temple – which, whether university or cathedral, was academic or ecclesiastical I forget – was to be raised, & as an exception she was to be allowed to enter in. But what about my civilisation? For 2,000 years we have done things without being paid for them. You cant bribe me now' (*D*, IV, 297–8).

# 8 'Taking the Bull by the Udders': Sexual Difference in Virginia Woolf – a Conspiracy Theory[1]

JANE MARCUS

> It has been with a considerable shaking in my shoes, and a feeling of treading upon a carpet of eggs, that I have *taken the cow by the horns* in this chapter, and broached the subject of the part that the feminine mind has played – and minds as well, deeply feminized, not technically on the distaff side – in the erection of our present criteria. For fifteen years I have subsisted in this to me suffocating atmosphere.
>
> (Wyndham Lewis, *Men without Art*, 1934)

Reviewing *A Room of One's Own*, Rebecca West saw Virginia Woolf 'braced against an invisible literary wind' blowing from the direction of Bloomsbury. She saw this 'uncompromising piece of feminist propaganda' as the 'ablest' written in a long line of feminist pamphlets from Millicent Garrett Fawcett in the middle of the Victorian Age until the actual winning of the vote, in 1928. And so indeed it must be seen, as a product of thinking back through those Victorian mothers in the context of the history of those pamphlets. It is an exact demonstration of her own socialist thesis in *A Room* that 'masterpieces are not single and solitary births' but are 'the outcome of many years of thinking in common, of thinking by the body of the people, so that the experience of the mass is behind the single voice' (*AROO*, pp. 68–9). Woolf's voice is not single in this essay, but collective, and she speaks for seventy years of struggle. Rebecca West praised Woolf's courage, which 'defied a prevalent fashion among the intelligentsia, which is particularly marked in the case of her

146

admirers', and 'all the more courageous because anti-feminism is so strikingly the fashion of the day among intellectuals'.[2] Dame Rebecca pointed out that 'Before the war conditions were different. The man in the street was anti-feminist, but the writers of quality were pro-suffrage.' Her explanation defines the change as 'due to the rising tide of effeminacy which has been so noticeable since the war. The men who despised us for our specifically female organs chastised us with whips; but those to whom they are a matter for envy chastise us with scorpions.'

Wyndham Lewis and Rebecca West agreed on little. Here are voices from the Right and the Left calling the Bloomsbury Liberals effeminate and blaming them for the 'feminisation' of British culture. Apologists for Bloomsbury's pacifist ethos of friendship have ignored its rampant anti-feminism, the chill wind that froze the author of *A Room of One's Own* into isolation. But it is my contention that what is called 'feminisation' is really another form of patriarchal power – a homosexual hegemony over British culture derived from the values of the Cambridge Apostles and King's College and anti-feminist with a difference – scorpions, not whips. This hegemony, in the Gramscian sense,[3] was as oppressive to women such as Virginia Woolf as the whips of her uncle Fitzjames had been to Millicent Garrett Fawcett. It is a mistake to call this cultural softening 'feminisation', when the homosexuals who exercised this power were loyal to the patriarchy. Wyndham Lewis might have more correctly said 'sodomisation' as an example of the 'erection of criteria' for art which were less robust than he wished, though that is as offensive a term as his own.

Virginia Woolf felt that cold wind of Bloomsbury anti-feminism and in *A Room of One's Own* she gathered a collective counter BLAST (with apologies to Mr Lewis) in the breathing-together of women in a conspiracy to huff and puff and blow down the walls of Cambridge and deflate its chief villain, Oscar Browning.[4] Oscar Browning was conveniently *not* Lytton Strachey or Morgan Forster, but he was their philosophical father. In puncturing that pompous overstuffed boy-loving patriarch, Virginia Woolf symbolically attacked her 'friends', and rid herself of the illusion, surely dispelled by Desmond MacCarthy's attack on her and all women artists in the *New Statesman*,[5] that the elite homosexuals of her world were allies with women in oppression. They may have been pouting, self-pitying patriarchs, but they were patriarchs none the less.

'Taking the bull by the udders' (a phrase dropped in a letter) is one of those astonishingly 'lupine' locutions in Virginia Woolf's writing, so funny, outrageous and 'true' for the woman reader, that they haunt the imagination. Like a Freudian slip, her deliberate verbal 'mistakes' seem to tap a primal spring in the unconscious. In the role of asides or jokes in letters, these slips reveal that she is aware that she writes from within the prison house of patriarchal language. Woolf's jokes, slips and asides are signals to the woman reader, who laughs in recognition or nods in assent over the page, that we are together, woman reader and woman writer, conspiring against the power of patriarchal language. As the comedian needs our laughter to continue mocking authority, Woolf needs her audience's assent and she courts us unashamedly to participate in the plot against phallocentric language.

This conspiracy of woman reader and woman writer is literally a 'breathing-together' as we rock or are rocked to the rhythm of her words. In *A Room of One's Own*, the conspirators are also the inspiration for her talks to women students. In this paper, which, like Woolf's, is a written version of a talk, I want to explore the ways in which she makes sexual difference an asset for women, makes the male the other, defines his language as different from the natural, normal speech of women together, and asserts the superiority of women's speech as a demotic and democratic instrument of communication, as opposed to the egotistical male 'I' which lies like a 'shadow' across the page, 'a straight dark bar' (*AROO*, p. 123) on the prison house of language. For our texts we shall take 'taking the bull by the udders', a seemingly casual spoken phrase recorded in a letter; 'A Woman's College From The Outside', an essay written at the same time as the lectures that compose *A Room of One's Own* and also concerned specifically with women's education; and a section of *The Pargiters*, originally intended to be part of *The Years*. My concern is with Woolf's role as a feminist literary critic, her experiments with a female grammar and with a rhetorical strategy which I have called 'sapphistry',[6] which masters the principles of classical rhetoric and subverts them at the same time.

Sexual difference for Woolf is not a simple matter of male and female, power and desire. Lesbianism and homosexuality are equal others, and androgyny is a privileged fifth sexual and literary stance. In her life as in her work, celibacy is also singularly important in her own sense of sexual difference.[7]

One may argue, moreover, that class difference extends her five-finger exercise to the other hand. For the salient sub-text in every Woolf novel is the voice of the working-class women, the heroic charwomen mythologised into a collective Nausicaa washing the dirty linen of the patriarchal family, her perpetual subject. The caretaker's children who sing for their supper at the end of *The Years* speak in tongues with the hard 'ks' of Greek chorus, a prophecy of the British mother tongue's responsibility for the exploitation of her colonial children. If women speak to each other in 'a little language unknown to men' because of the male control of language, Britain's future workers, the Indians, Africans and West Indians of her former Empire, speak to each other in pidgins and creoles, languages less 'little', but equally 'unknown' to the powerful. Their music, their art, may be a mystery to the elite, but it is a culture of its own. *A Room of One's Own* may appear to be merely a primer for valorisation of female difference, but its eloquent peroration to the absent women washing up the dishes, assuring us that Shakespeare's sister will be born of the uneducated classes, declares that it will also serve as a manual for the subversion of class difference and racial difference.

## I HER SISTER'S VOICE

In this section I want to suggest that Virginia Woolf deliberately fashioned for herself a role in which reading, writing and speaking were feminist and radical acts, a role in which she, as novelist and as feminist critic, became *her sister's voice*, as Procne read the text of Philomel's woven story in the tapestry, and spoke for her against the patriarchy. Biographical accounts of Virginia Woolf's speaking voice stress her weakness and describe a high-pitched whinnying sound. Hearing her voice on a BBC tape which Nigel Nicolson played at the Woolf Centenary Symposium in Texas, I, like the rest of the audience, was shocked by the difference between this voice and the hesitant hysterical voice I had expected. Virginia Woolf's voice was a deep, rich, fruity contralto, bordering on the baritone. Two features stand out on this tape – the authoritative self-confident commanding tone of the born leader and public speaker, and the rhythmical musical range from low to high of the writer who loves the sounds of words. They roll off her tongue in accents betraying her class, of course, but also in liquid syllables suggesting a bubbling spring of laughter counter-pointing her cool control. The voice is so sure of itself, so eminently sane and healthy that it banishes for ever the biographer's hysterical invalid. (When this paper was read at the Berkshire Women's History Conference, 1984, at Smith College, Cora Kaplan responded with the point of view of English working-class women. To them, Woolf's voice on the tape represents class privilege, Kaplan argued, and the class identification outweighs any sense of gender solidarity for those women.)

Woolf's own odd phrase, 'taking the bull by the udders', which I have taken as my text here, may possibly have been a simple reaction to Wyndham Lewis's attack on her as a lesbian when he said he was taking '*the cow by the horns*'. One is amused that, inadvertently, Lewis had conjured up an image of the horned goddess, Hathor, the cow goddess of the ancient Egyptians, crowned with the moon. As Evelyn Haller has convincingly argued, the Egyptian myths surrounding the worship of Isis inform Woolf's thought as fully as *The Odyssey* informs *Ulysses* or the image of Byzantium occurs in Yeats.[8] The bull with udders may be drawn as well from Jane Harrison's extensive work on bulls and their association with ancient mother-goddess worship. Anthropologists have even suggested recently that on the grand nurturing figure of the 'Many Breasted Artemis' in Ephesus the 'many breasts were not breasts at all but bulls' scrota sacrificed every year to the Asian *magna mater* Kybela, goddess of fertility, and hung on her statue'. Woolf's nurturing male is thus opposed by a figure of a 'phallic mother'.[9]

In Woolf's letter, she attributes to her sister her own rewriting of Wyndham's Lewis's phrase. 'Taking the bull by the udders' is such a rebellious verbal gesture, thumbing its nose at the phallus, that Woolf denies responsibility for saying it. 'Not for attribution', she seems to say. Or 'off the record', as politicians say when they tell the truth. 'It's not my tongue that uttered it, not my hand that wrote it', Woolf the ventriloquist seems to claim in her attribu-tion/misattribution of these words to her sister, Vanessa Bell. Why, we ask, can Vanessa's voice say the unsayable, talk back to His Master's Voice (as we may call the patriarchal power over language)? The answer is part of Woolf's life-long myth of difference from her sister, a difference, for her, as powerful as actual and symbolic sexual difference. Woolf's companionate marriage protected her celibacy, but her deepest emotional relationships were with women; 'Women are my line', she was continually telling her sister:

> You will never succumb to the charms of any of your sex – What an arid garden the world must be for you! What avenues of stone pavements and iron railings! Greatly though I respect the male mind . . . I cannot see that they have a glowworm's worth of charm about them – the scenery of the world takes no lustre from their presence. They add of course immensely to its dignity and safety: but when it comes to a little excitement –!   (*L*, III, 281)

Vanessa, constructed by Virginia as the 'normal woman' to whom she was 'other', was married, a mother, and had sexual relations with several men (including homosexuals). She was what all men want women to be (as Woolf said of the Angel in the House). Although she often dares her own anti-phallic discourse, in putting anti-phallic discourse in her sister's mouth on this occasion Woolf doesn't risk male disapproval ('She's a feminist; she's a sapphist; she's a man-hater'). By putting these words in the mouth of a 'womanly woman', she gets to say them loud and clear and be protected from male displeasure at the same time. A woman such as Vanessa Bell couldn't possibly suggest castration, the male reader thinks. The lover of men, the mother of sons – she is not suspect. By this rhetorical ventriloquism, Woolf as a feminist is able to express in the voice of one of the patriarchy's pet women the wish to castrate the symbol of male power. Thus the 'normal' woman becomes her political sister, is 'on her side' and joins in her feminist protest. The difference is erased. She is then not really 'other', or different from her sister. They are bonded by a mutual attack on men.

Part of Woolf's self-made myth of difference from her sister, is not only Vanessa's 'real' womanhood as opposed to her own largely unacted lesbian identity, but her division of the artist's body into the verbal and the visual. As Woolf conceives and enforces these roles in a lifetime of letters to and about her sister, she and Vanessa are one body in her continually reiterated desire to merge with her sister as Lily Briscoe wants to be one with Mrs Ramsay ('like waters poured into one jar'). Vanessa, the painter, is the eye and the hand, and she, the writer, is the ear and the mouth. If we did not have Quentin Bell's biography, only Virginia's letters, we should see Vanessa as Virginia verbally constructed her, completely inarticulate, deaf and dumb, except with a brush in her hand, a child in her lap or a lover in her arms. Obviously, the real Vanessa Bell was not inarticulate, but Virginia Woolf continued to create her as a modern Mrs Malaprop.[10]

Woolf commonly attributes to her sister the mixing of two old saws or folk sayings, some of which are very funny, and obviously the invention of someone who wants to be her sister's voice, someone who is inventing a role and writing the dialogue. Writing the script of her sister's life in this small way, Woolf enacted her desire to control what she had no control over, and simultaneously *spoke for* Vanessa as the representative of all the common women she felt she was writing for and to, as a feminist. The mistakes attributed to Vanessa, the mixed truisms, one feels, are meant to suggest that Vanessa, by mistake, stumbles on a deeper wisdom than the verbally adept can ever command. Her slips tap into a deep reservoir of old wives' tales and women's folk wisdom not available to the sophisticated (and, by extension, more shallow) writer. Vanessa Bell certainly played her role well in her sister's script. The following quotations are from one letter to Virginia in response to *To the Lighthouse*: 'I don't flatter myself that my literary opinion is really of any interest to you . . .'; In fact, I think I am more incapable than anyone else in the world of making an aesthetic judgment on it'; 'I am very bad at describing my feelings'; 'I don't feel capable of much analysis'; 'I daresay you'll think all I've said nonsense. You can put it down to the imbecile ravings of a painter on paper' (*L*, III, 572–3). Simultaneously Woolf glorifies her sister as the dumb goddess mumbling the oracular wisdom of the ages, a Cassandra in Sussex, and reaffirms herself as artist–god, because she has put the unverbalised into words, written the script for the prophetess. Vanessa is Every-woman, stuttering out of her historical silence, and Virginia then is legitimately women's spokeswoman. 'Anonymous' is always a woman and *she* speaks for Anonymous. Through this rhetorical strategy, she satisfies the feminist's desire to be her sister's voice and it is only another bold leap from blood sisterhood to political sisterhood.

The actual phrase 'taking the bull by the udders' revises the old imperative to meet difficulty head on, bravely to confront a powerful adversary, to take the bull by the horns, an aggressive action not commonly associated with women. The bull is the ancient symbol of the phallus, representing male power and sexuality. The horns symbolise the genitals and also can be dangerous and deadly to the attacker. Traditionally, a person who takes the bull by the horns is coming to grips effectively with an enemy or an obstacle. Woolf's language implies the removal of the horns (castration), which deprives the bull of his power to kill. The horn is also a speaker, an instrument to project the voice, the sign of phallic control over language. She silences it, cuts it off, udders it, utters it. She does not say 'we shall share speech'. She says 'You shall be silent. I will speak.' (One wonders why Americans use a reference to a bull's excrement to mean exaggerated speech or lies.) Is the lie (all fiction?) a prerogative of male speech? The silent replacement of the bull's genitals with udders leaves him not only castrated but 'cowed'. He can be milked; he is maternal. The bold act of taking the bull by the udders means not only depriving him of evidence of phallic power, horns and genitals, but also replacing them with organs of nurturance. The phrase asks the question, 'How can I deprive the fathers of their phallic power, their threatening masculinity?' and answers itself, 'By turning them into mothers.' In other words, bull–horn–genitals is paralleled by cow–udder– what? What is *absent*, where the *difference* lies, is female genitality – yet another instance of Woolf's reverence for female chastity. She gives us a mythical androgynous beast, a bull with udders. In real life this is what Woolf did to her husband. She married the only virile and intensely masculine man in her circle, Leonard Woolf, and cast him in the role of the bull with udders, the maternal male. He is a nurturing figure throughout their married life, appearing in her letters and diaries as a version of the Lady with the Lamp, maternalised, 'uddered', the Husband with the Glass of Milk.

The verbal act of castrating/silencing the bull seems to me analogous to the myth of Procne and Philomel (which Woolf revises in *Between the Acts*).[11] The rapist cuts out the tongue of his female victim so that she cannot speak of his sexual crime. This phrase deprives the phallic voice of its power to speak/kill but replaces it with the power to nurture. The female version replaces one power with another, while the male version not only does violence to the female, but cuts off her power to relieve the hurt by telling her story. She saves herself by her skill in weaving, which is a kind of telling. Her sister is the reader. And the reader–sister speaks and acts for the silenced and oppressed sister. So Virginia speaks for Vanessa as Procne speaks for Philomel. The narrative voice in Woolf's novels is the voice of the sister–reader–speaker; she is the swallow who sings for all the silenced nightingales: 'I am my sister's keeper.' She is the tongue of the tongueless ones.

Geoffrey Hartman, following Plato, has described Philomel's cry against oppression as the universal 'voice of the shuttle'. I have argued that the weaving of the tapestry is a specifically *female* art which is 'read' by a specifically female person, just as the violence Procne's husband does to her is a rape of her female body. The voice of the shuttle is a gendered voice. But what concerns me here is the role of Procne as *reader* of her sister's text, translator of the invisible (to men) stitches in the *peplos*, secret sharer of a 'little language unknown to men', the language of weaving: 'a native loom she found, / And hung the warp; and weaving on the white / With crimson threads, set forth her piteous plight' (Ovid, *Metamorphoses*, 133–4). Procne reads and is struck dumb; in horror, she disguises herself (significantly) as a follower of women's biennial 'Bacchic rites', with vine leaves in her hair and dressed in a fawn skin (like the savage virgin sisterhood of Artemis). She disguises Philomel in the same costume with an ivy mask and rescues her from her prison in the forest. As a huntress, she contemplates cutting out her husband's eyes, tongue or penis, but decides to punish the patriarchy, kills her son and serves him to his father to eat so that the father's body becomes 'his son's unhallowed tomb' (ibid., 136).

Procne, reader and actor, is her sister's severed tongue, which 'strangled utterance made': 'The remnant twitched; the tongue with muffled sound / Muttered its secret to the blackened ground, / And writhing still, like a cut snake, it tried / To reach her where she stood, before it died' (ibid., 133). Like many feminist critics after her, Virginia Woolf was the reader of the 'scraps, orts and fragments' of women's texts and lives, of the oppressed, raped and silenced. Writing/writhing is a kind of feminist poetics. In *A Room of One's Own* she is Procne to the Philomel of Judith Shakespeare. Procne's voice is sometimes undeniably venomous, 'like a cut snake'; sometimes 'strangled'. She does desire to castrate the rapist, to kill. She cannot restore her sister's virginity or sew the severed tongue back to its root. She can flaunt the severed head of her son in the face of her horrid husband; she can deny him his fatherhood.

In *A Room of One's Own* we hear the swallow ('Mary Hamilton') singing of the nightingale (Judith Shakespeare). Woolf produces and reproduces a woman's reading-practice here. Our collaboration in this process is surely why the book has become the one standard text in Women's Studies classes.

## II   THE TRIOLOGIC IMAGINATION

In *A Room of One's Own* Virginia Woolf deconstructs the lecture as a form. The lecture was another version of the discourse of male domination. 'Lecturing', she wrote, 'incites the most debased of human passions – vanity, ostentation, self-assertion, and the desire to convert.' 'Why not create a new form of society founded on poverty and equality?' she asked.

> Why not bring people together so that they talk, without mounting platforms or reading papers or wearing expensive clothes or eating expensive food? Would not such a society be worth, even as a form of education, all the papers on art and literature that have ever been read since the world began? Why not *abolish* prigs and prophets? Why not invent human intercourse?   (*DM,* pp. 227–34)

The lecture as conversation (between women) rather than the dictation of the expert to the ignorant, is enacted in *A Room of One's Own*, as she puts that protesting 'But' in the mouths of the supposedly silent student audience before uttering a word in her own voice. She abolishes the prigs and prophets, the absent father, the absent grandfather, the absent male professor. As *abolitionist* of the slavery of the listener to the speaker, she echoes her grandfather, abolitionist of British slave trade, and her father, would-be abolitionist of the servitude of the Cambridge don to the Church of England. As she shows us by her use of pronouns that the lecturer's 'one' is not impersonal, gender-free and universal, but male, she also shows us that the 'lecture' as 'a form of education' is a one-way street. Communication is not reciprocal: when *he* stands, *they* sit; while *he* speaks, *they* listen. *A Room of One's Own* invents human intercourse on a model of female discourse, as a conversation among equals. By what narrative magic can she do away with the whole authoritarian patriarchal structure of domination in the system of academic lectures? Has she really rid herself of those four deadly sins, those debased passions roused by the power of the podium? She does limit her own authority in that she speaks only as herself and not as the collective 'Mary' when she speaks as a writer and as a reader.[12]

In *Three Guineas* Woolf suggests refusing to lecture as a pacifist's political act, because of the university's collusion with the war machine. She calls the system of lecturing 'vain and vicious', and then qualifies this in a footnote which I shall quote at length because it addresses two issues of concern to us today, the illiteracy of students and the viciousness of literary criticism:

> No one would maintain that all lecturers and all lectures are 'vain and vicious'; many subjects can only be taught with diagrams and personal demonstrations. The words in the text refer only to the sons and daughters of educated men who lecture their brothers and sisters upon English literature; and for the reasons that it is an obsolete practice dating from the Middle Ages when books were scarce; that it owes its survival to pecuniary motives; or to curiosity; that the publication in book form is sufficient proof of the evil effect upon the lecturer intellectually; and that psychologically eminence upon a platform encourages vanity and the desire to impose authority. . . . Again, the violence with which one school of literature is now opposed to another, the rapidity with which one school of taste succeeds another, may not unreasonably be traced to the power which a mature mind lecturing immature minds has to infect them with strong, if passing, opinions, and to tinge those opinions with personal bias. Nor can it be maintained that the standard of critical or of creative writing has been raised. . . . None of this applies, of course, to those whose homes are deficient in books. If the working class finds it easier to assimilate English literature by word of mouth they have a perfect right to ask the educated class to help them thus. But for the sons and daughters of that class after the age of eighteen to continue to sip English literature through a straw, is a habit that seems to deserve the terms vain and vicious; which terms can justly be applied with greater force to those who pander to them. (*TG*, pp. 155–6)

Woolf was not 'vain and vicious', we assume, ten years earlier lecturing at the women's colleges, because they were so young and poor, and therefore comparable to the working class in the 1930s. But, if I, who lecture upon English literature, take her seriously, then I am a cross between a soda jerk and a pimp, providing my 'mentally docile' listeners with Miltonic milkshakes and Shakespearean sodas. Even as I lecture about her, she is lecturing me (in the sense of admonishing and chastising me) and she wants to abolish my trade altogether. Her notion of a 'conspiracy' between her 'common reader' and the writer against professors of literature and critics was not just a pretty rhetorical device, but a serious attack on professionalism, which she saw would be as dangerous to women as it had been to men. So I shall try to avoid vanity and viciousness, to keep my feet firmly planted in the margins of this text, to come out from behind the podium and acknowledge your 'But, what does "taking the bull by the udders" have to do with sexual difference and Virginia Woolf?'

Woolf deconstructs her own lecture with the opening words of *A Room of One's Own* as she includes the audience in conversation by articulation of their question: 'But, you may say, we asked you to speak about women and fiction – what has that got to do with a room of one's own?' The audience, the 'you' with its question, comes first. She says she will 'try' to explain. She relaxes her authority, gives up the stance of the expert. Her opening sentence is the continuation of an interrupted conversation in which she is only an equal partner. In her written text, she keeps the conversation going. The reader is included in the 'you', so the text becomes a three-sided conversation between the woman writer, the woman students in the audience, and the woman reader. Without us, we are made to feel, she cannot speak. Using Bakhtin's concept of 'the dialogic imagination', I shall argue that our role as readers is to collaborate in this conversation, to conspire with the woman writer and the women students to overthrow the formal rigidity of the lecture as 'an educational device'. It is not a monologue. It is not even a mock Platonic dialogue, but a *trio-logue*. The woman's text asks the reader to share in the making of the text as the lecturer includes the listeners in her speaking. She abdicates her power of suspense by giving her conclusion first, and in the simplest possible language. 'A woman must have money and a room of her own if she is to write fiction.' We could rewrite this as an 'expert' might say it: 'Let us examine the role of gender and capital to the production of culture.' If she had opened this way, and there is no doubt, given the hectoring, lecturing tone of the footnote from *Three Guineas*, that she *could* have, we should have a lecture, not what she called 'talks to girls'.

After tripling the power of her own voice by including her readers and her student audience, she triples it again: 'call me Mary Beton, Mary Seton, Mary Carmichael or by any name you please'.[13] She is not Virginia Woolf standing on the platform but the voice of the anonymous female victim of male violence throughout the ages. In the text she tells us that 'Anonymous' was most often a woman. On the platform she becomes 'Anonymous' in person. She transforms herself in the narrative to the object of her narration.

Once the three-sided conversation is established, its informality and collectivity implicitly mocking the formal egotism of the absent male professor's lecture, her illegitimacy as a lecturer proclaimed, she can say 'I'. 'I have shirked the duty of coming to a conclusion', she confesses. This disingenuous pose disarms us into thinking her far more truthful than an authoritative lecturer. Humbly, she abjures expertise: 'women and fiction remain – so far as I am concerned – unsolved problems'. Now she has all her women readers and listeners in the palm of her hand. To 'make some amends' for posing as a lecturer, 'I am going to do what I can to show you how I arrived at this opinion'; 'I am going to develop as fully and freely as I can the train of thought which led me to think this.'

Confidences thus exchanged – among women – Woolf moves to the impersonal 'one', the two generalisations then proposed (*AROO*, p. 4) are an extrapolation from the single and collective female. 'One' is robbed of its impersonality as a gender-free pronoun: '*One* can only show how *one* came to hold whatever opinion *one* does hold. *One* can only give *one's* audience the chance of drawing their own conclusions as they observe the limitations, the prejudices, the idiosyncracies of the speaker' (emphasis added). The linking of the questioning *you* and the responding *I* to make a female *one* reminds the audience of the absent other whose educational process we imitate and remake in female terms. The authoritative, supposedly gender-free impersonal 'one' of the male professor, the British authority, is *not* gender-free but male, and made by a conflation of the *I* and *you* of the male lecturer and his male students. We know this because she has 'fully and freely' engendered and gendered her 'one' out of herself and some women students. We know also that the 'One' in her title, *A Room of One's Own*, is as female as the 'one' in 'Between puberty and menopause *one* menstruates once a month' (emphasis added). She is making the female the universal norm in this title, but she can only do this with our consent, and we are very well aware that in a mixed audience the assent would not be granted her, and the response would be of the kind produced by 'Between puberty and menopause one menstruates once a month.' But Woolf's most exciting act in *A Room of One's Own* is its collective narration.

In the March 1929 issue of the *Forum*, Woolf published an essay called 'Women and Fiction' which must have been a draft of part of *A Room of One's Own*. It is curiously flat and lifeless compared to the book, solely because of its single omniscient narrator. Reading it, one becomes aware that her book's brilliance is based on its *triologue*, the three-fold narration of speaker, reader and audience, as well as the multiple Marys of her own persona. The essay in the *Forum* is more openly political, complains of the 'distortion' of 'someone resenting the treatment of her sex and pleading for its rights' in *Middlemarch* and *Jane Eyre*. 'This brings into women's writing an element which is entirely absent from a man's unless, indeed, he happens to be a working man, a Negro, or one who for some other reason is conscious of disability.' But she predicts that women's novels, now that they have the vote, will 'naturally become more critical of society, and less analytical of individual lives':

> We may expect that the office of gadfly to the state, which has been so far a male prerogative, will now be discharged by women also. Their novels will deal with social evils and remedies. Their men and women will not be observed wholly in relation to each other emotionally, but as they cohere and clash in groups and classes and races.

The *Forum* exhibits a strong concern with women's education. The previous issue had an article by the President of Smith College in favour, but, in March, W. Beran Wolfe, a psychiatrist, claimed that unnamed sexual vices were rampant: 'They spell out a terrific indictment of women's colleges.' He describes the frustrated scholar 'with the feeble glory of a Phi Beta Kappa key' who 'projects her social discouragement to the next generation'. If she isn't a scholar

> college teaches her the futility of being a woman, and when she
> graduates, she swells the growing number of neurotic women
> who fill the divorce courts and mental sanitaria. These women
> miss the opportunity to learn social and sexual adjustment
> during the most significant years of their development, because
> women's colleges offer them the sickly pablum of archeology
> and art appreciation instead of the robust material of human
> cooperation.

Though *A Room of One's Own* may have seemed a redundant
reissue of the pamphlet literature of the suffrage movement, it is
clear from the *Forum* that misogyny was alive and well in 1929.
The January issue contained a piece by D. H. Lawrence,
'Cocksure Women and Hensure Men', blaming male impotence
on intellectual women, begging women to obey their biological
imperative in a barnyard lecture on the evil of brains in women.[14]
In 'Professions for Women', her speech before the London
National Society for Women's Service in January 1931, Virginia
Woolf, who despised lectures, again gave a lecture to an all-female
audience. It was another fishing-trip into the female element, into
the arms of mother water, a submerged merger of several female
selves, 'waters poured into one jar'. Whether one reads this talk as
a description of creativity, as amniotic bliss or as an example of a
woman writer's 'fluid boundaries', it does dramatise the under-
water world of a woman writer's imagination, and answers a
question which has puzzled feminist critics: 'What sex is the muse
of the woman writer?' Virginia Woolf's muse is female and the
relation between her two selves (here reason and imagination) is
distinctly sexual. The muse of the woman writer, her guide into
the unconscious realms of female sexual experience, is a mermaid.
Their relationship, the writer as 'fisherwoman', and the muse as
diver, is distinctly lesbian. She gives two scenarios (*P*, pp.
xxxviii–xxxx) – a fishing-trip and a reverse striptease. In one she
was 'letting her imagination feed unfettered on every crumb of her
experience; she was letting her imagination sweep unchecked
round every rock and cranny of the world that lies submerged in
our unconscious being'. The 'imagination' comes to the surface,
floating 'limply and dully and lifelessly'. When reason says, 'What
on earth is the matter with you?' the naked muse 'began pulling on

its stockings and replied, rather tartly and disagreeably, it's all your fault'. The novelist apologises for her lack of experience.

In the second scenario, the mermaid darts away into the depths. 'The reason has to cry "Stop!" the novelist has to pull on the line and haul the imagination to the surface. The imagination comes to the top in a state of fury.' The novelist replies, ' "My dear, you were going altogether too far. Men would be shocked." Calm yourself, I say, as she sits panting on the bank – panting with rage and disappointment.' She says it will be fifty years before a writer can use 'this queer knowledge' about 'women's bodies' and their 'passions' in her writing, not, in fact, until 'men can be educated to *stand* free speech in women'. The use of the word 'stand' brands male intolerance as the source of women's reticence. The mermaid is impatient but resigned. 'Very well says the imagination, dressing herself up again in her petticoat and skirts, we will wait. We will wait another fifty years. But it seems to me a pity.' She is not sure that men can be civilised or 're-educated' to allow women to be artists. That problem 'lies on the lap of the Gods, no not upon the laps of the Gods, but upon your laps, upon the laps of professional women'.

Here, as in *A Room of One's Own*, Woolf flirts with her female audience, seductively suggesting that with the support of women readers the woman writer can tell 'the truth about the body'. This dramatisation of the relation between a woman artist and her muse, the rational feminist and the sexually liberated unconscious, parallels Woolf's relationship with Vita Sackville-West – the daring dive, the pull of convention, the hasty retreat and exchange of bad temper.[15]

Woolf then dramatises a conspiracy of women against the male breadwinner, a conspiracy to win them the right to work. Having aroused her audience, she then cautions patience. She claims that there actually *are* 'men with whom a woman can live in perfect freedom', yet she concludes with a romantic description of the working woman's room as an escape from the patriarchal house: 'I suspect that the sofa turns into a bed; and the wash stand is covered with a check cloth by day to look as much like a table as possible.' The next step is

a step upon the stair. You will hear *somebody* coming. You will open the door. And then – this is at least my guess – there will take place between you and *someone else* the most interesting, exciting and important conversation that has ever been heard. But do not be alarmed; I am not going to talk about that now. [Emphasis added; note that this is the original speech, not that included by Leonard Woolf in *CE*.]

What sex is 'somebody'? What sex is 'someone else'? Why is this 'alarming'? This lecture as lupine plot, feminist conspiracy, is another seductive sapphistry. It stops just short of sedition. It writes a script with missing lines like the ellipses in 'Chloe liked Olivia. They shared a . . .' The audience (or the reader) supplies the missing dialogue in 'the *most* interesting, exciting and important conversation that has ever been heard'. Has Chloe come to visit Olivia after the laboratory has closed? Will that 'conversation' become a conspiracy?

The lectures we have looked at were public addresses and they show Woolf's rhetorical strategies at their best. Now let us look at 'A Woman's College from the Ouside', a sketch of Newnham published in *Atalanta's Garden* (though its first sentence appears in *Jacob's Room*) in 1926. Here the chip on her shoulder at never having had a formal education ('from the *Outside*') weighs down Woolf's shoulder and sprains her writing-arm. The scene is a 'drama in muslin', if we may borrow George Moore's title, in which the woman in the moon gazes on a pure white virginal world of Newnham and its garden bathed in a 'vapour' which is the *breath* of women laughing together, issuing from the windows, attaching itself 'by soft elastic threads to plants and bushes'. It is another 'conspiracy', the breathing of women, sleeping together, laughing together. Their misty breath veils the garden so that the moon may unveil her face: 'as none but women's faces could meet her face, she might unveil it, blank, featureless and gaze into rooms where at that hour, blank, featureless, eyelids white over eyes, ringless hands extended upon sheets, slept innumerable women'. The Tennysonian 'innumerable' aches with the kind of nostalgia which comes, not from memory of experience, but from a wish for the memory of experience. It is the way one would describe a castle in Spain if one had never seen a castle in Spain and always longed for a glimpse of it. It is doubtful if any actual graduate of Newnham would conjure up that virginal mist, the communal nun's bridal veil which blankets the world of the women's college. The 'blank, featureless' face of the woman in the moon is mirrored by the 'blank, featureless' faces of the sleeping women. Like the white square name cards on the women's doors, the virginal sleeping faces are blank pages – their history has not been written.[16]

The moon sees Angela (Miranda in the typescript) kiss her bright reflection in the glass, her identity, 'visible proof of the rightness of things', 'a lily floating flawless upon Time's pool', 'the bright picture hung in the heart of the night, the Shrine hallowed in the nocturnal blackness'. Angela's identity, her being 'glad to be Angela', comes from the community of women in which her selfhood can be developed. The shrine of female identity is in the sleeping-quarters of the women's college. The dormitory of the women's college is a 'white hotel' in which the sleepers are watched by the blank-faced moon – Watch-woman, what of the night?: 'night is free pasturage, a limitless field, since night is unclouded richness, one must tunnel into its darkness. One must hang it with jewels.' The narrative nightwatch of the outsider and her eyeless lunar companion scans names as well as faces in one of the most unabashedly romantic passages ever to come from the ironic pen of Virginia Woolf:

> A. Williams – one may read it in the moonlight; and next to it some Mary or Eleanor, Mildred, Sarah, Phoebe upon square cards on their doors. All names, nothing but names. The cool white light withered them and starched them until it seemed as if the only purpose of all these names was to rise martially in order shoud there be a call on them to extinguish a fire, suppress an insurrection, or pass an examination. Such is the power of names written upon cards pinned upon doors. Such too the resemblance, what with tiles, corridors, and bedroom doors, to dairy or nunnery, a place of seclusion or discipline, where the bowl of milk stands cool and pure and there's a great washing of linen. (pp. 6–9)

There she is again, that recurrent figure in Woolf's work, the virgin mother, the moon chaste yet protective, the nunnery and dairy, asexuality and maternal nurturance – the insistent note in all her writing, of *sexual difference as sexual abstinence*. (I don't really mean abstinence, but a kind of sexual autonomy associated with the goddess Artemis in the wilderness.) Why is this passage on purity so seductive? 'Elderly women slept, who would on waking immediately clasp the ivory rod of office . . . reposing deeply they

lay surrounded, lay supported, by the bodies of youth . . . .' It is
that mother superior or headmistress and her 'ivory rod' who
rouses the unawakened female desire for a haven under female
authority, the rule of the nunnery, the discipline of the headmistress in a community of work, the underlying sexuality of social
and political sisterhood.

Seductive as this sketch is, ending with nineteen-year-old
Angela sucking her thumb in 'this good world, this new world, this
world at the end of the tunnel', it does not finally work. The reader
is neither invited nor coerced into co-narration. Attractive as
Angela is, she is only a vision glimpsed in the mirror by the moon
and we are not invited to worship at her shrine, our breath does
not cloud her mirror. The rhetorical *trio-logue* of the lectures here
lacks a third party, and it takes three to make a conspiracy. Yet we
respond to the clean, white milky ambience of this world without
men. We do respond to Woolf's 'erotics of chastity',[17] if we read
'chastity' as ownership of one's own sexuality, despite her
idealisation of women's education. For the moon is shining on a
woman's space, a place where the name of the mother, the name of
the sister, are inscribed – instead of the name of the father, the
name of the brother. Angela's image does float like a lily 'flawless
upon Time's pool', fearless. 'The prim-voiced clock' issues ' *his*
commands' (emphasis added) and is disregarded – in the night,
women's time – when the real (and permanent?) bonds of
sisterhood will be forged.

Of course this utopian vision of women's education comes from
the uneducated 'daughter of an educated man'.[18] When Angela is
kissed by Alice Avery she is astonished that the Great Mother
herself has recognised her – by 'the incredible stooping of the
miraculous tree', and we are reminded of Lily Briscoe's adoration
of Mrs Ramsay. That ivory rod could, one suspects, chastise its
daughters as well as rule them. (What would Virginia Woolf make
of Margaret Thatcher?) The fact was that women's colleges were
very poor; Somerville was infested with rats; and Woolf herself
tells us elsewhere the effects of poverty and discouragement on
women would-be geniuses. Angela can love Alice because she has
learned to love herself. The moonlight on the mirror is an
archetypal reflection of how women come to know themselves and
their bodies through the cycles of the moon. Woolf's notion of
sexual difference is caught here emotionally. As she analysed
difference and asserted female superiority rationally and political-

ly in other texts, in this one she exposes her passionate longing for purity, for female community, and expresses a deep desire for the discipline of female authority. The relationship of childlessness to female genius is one which Woolf explores in *A Room*. It is interesting that the essay which fails valorises chastity, while the one which succeeds celebrates sexuality (though, as I argue in 'Sapphistry', it is lesbian sexuality). (Feminist critics have analysed the absent mother in many texts – perhaps we should explore as well the figure of the absent child. Judith Shakespeare is not only a suicide but a pregnant suicide.)

It is also interesting to note the view of a woman's college from the *inside* in Dorothy Sayers's *Gaudy Night* (1936; New York: Avon, 1968). A Somerville graduate herself, Sayers mocks all the romantic feminist visions of female scholarly community which Woolf's two essays celebrate. I do not know if it was meant as a deliberate reply to Woolf's book, but it is an effective attack on women's education. In 'Shrewsbury College', the shrews are buried by poison-pen letters and the excretal brown paint of obscene graffiti on the walls as well as the destruction (by pen) of a feminist scholar's proofs. The individual rooms are violated as well as the common rooms, and a critique of Woolf's view of women's writing-practice is presented in the text's obsession with other forms of women's writing than fiction – anonymous letters, mystery stories, literary and historical scholarship, psychology, love letters, term papers and the disturbing brown obscenities on the library walls. Harriet's poem is finished by Wimsey as she does the research and he solves the crime. The best example of Sayers's attack on female creativity is the scene where Harriet pays Wimsey's nephew's bills by writing out the cheques, which he *signs*.

While *A Room* is concerned with thinking back through our literary mothers, *Gaudy Night* asks, 'how many great women have had great fathers and husbands behind them?' 'Dear me! Being a great father is either a very difficult or a very sadly unrewarded profession' (p. 48). Harriet Vane is less romantic about the sleeping women: 'On the doors were cards, bearing their names: Miss H. Brown, Miss Jones, Miss Colburn, Miss Szleposky, Miss Isaacson – so many unknown quantities. So many destined wives and mothers of the race; or, alternatively, so many potential historians, scientists, schoolteachers, doctors, lawyers . . . .' (p. 92). Instead of bowls of milk, Sayers sees shoes and 'little heaps of soiled crockery' outside the women's rooms. The dons present a different version of female authority from that the outsider imagines. Woolf's dream of a lesbian utopia in a woman's college is in Sayers's hands a nightmare of repressed sexuality, jealousy and hatred (one is reminded here of Woolf's own phrase, 'words the defilers') and the class enmity of women.

The failure of 'A Woman's College from the Outside' is a failure to share narration with her subject and her audience (to give the audience a voice in the text), as well as an imaginative failure, and it underlines the brilliance of Woolf's 'sapphistry', her *'triologue'* in *A Room of One's Own*. In *A Room of One's Own* Woolf's narrative strategy builds such a strong collective presence of women co-narrators of her text, a chorus of oppressed and victimised women – Mary Beton, Mary Seton, Mary Carmichael, the women students in the audience, the women professors and the implied women readers – that her feminist voice is continually valorised by their presence and she seems invincible to the patriarchy. Indeed the platform is so crowded with conspirators that when Woolf says 'I' we read it and hear it as 'we', and her written 'I' has no five-o'clock shadow, no resemblance to the 'straight dark bar' on the patriarchal cage.

I have suggested that the male reader is forced to deny the superiority of his gender if he is to read *A Room of One's Own* sympathetically. But I should like to point out some exceptions to this rule, Geoffrey Hartman in 'Virginia's Web' and J. Hillis Miller's reaffirmation of its argument in *Fiction and Repetition*.[19] Aside from the absence of references to feminist critics, note that the essays centre on the passage in *A Room* which describes a man and a woman getting into a taxi. Woolf herself describes her fascination with the 'rhythmical order' with which she invests the scene. Both men see this passage as descriptive of the source of Woolf's creativity, a recognition of a 'force' in nature. Frankly, every woman reader I know sees this passage as Woolf's mnemonic device to force herself out of her feminist and lesbian fantasy world, back to a vision of 'heterosexuality makes the world go round'. That couple is Woolf's rude reminder to herself that most women are not part of a woman's community but are isolated from each other in relation to individual men. It is a reminder to herself that the male reader is out there, and she placates him with this mysterious heterosexual romance. It signals to the female reader that this is the stuff of reality, that this is the stuff of fiction: a man and a woman getting into a taxi. The scene accentuates her own difference and the difference of her text from the stream of life represented by the rhythmical meeting of the couple in the crowd, and its reference to the stream at Oxbridge on whose banks she first began to puzzle out the problems presented by her lecture. This passage is the 'little fish' she promised her listeners as their prize. Women's assertion of difference, perhaps in lesbianism, in militant feminism or in celibacy, will alienate them, as she is alienated, from the mainstream, from the order and rhythm of everyday heterosexual life. It is significant that male critics pounce on this passage of romantic heterosexuality, the modern version of the lines from Tennyson and Rossetti which she mocks, as evidence of Woolf's creativity, when it is clear from her letters and diaries that she herself feels (whether rightly or wrongly it is impossible to say) that her own creativity lies in the experience of madness and of difference (her sympathy with lesbianism and her sexual abstinence).

By collaborating in the three-way dialogue of the narration of *A Room*, we women readers have validated our own gender-derived reading-experience. We have not only gone fishing but also learned to reproduce our fishing-trip in our imaginations. So empowered, we can also join Virginia Woolf in uddering/uttering the bull.

## NOTES

1. A version of this paper was given at the 1982 Brown University Virginia Woolf Centenary Conference, organised by Elizabeth Weed and Roger Henkle. It is a companion piece to 'Sapphistry: Narration as Lesbian Seduction in *A Room of One's Own*', forthcoming in my *Virginia Woolf and the Languages of Patriarchy* (Bloomington, Ind.: Indiana University Press). I should like to thank Louise DeSalvo, Angela Ingram, Nancy Harrison and Elizabeth Abel for their helpful comments; a longer version appears in my book.

2. Rebecca West, 'Autumn and Virginia Woolf', in *Ending in Earnest* (New York: Doubleday, 1931) pp. 208–13.

3. For a discussion of this point, see my 'Liberty, Sorority, Misogyny' in *The Representation of Women in Fiction*, ed. Carolyn G. Heilbrun and Margaret R. Higonnet, selected papers from the English Institute, 1981, n.s, no.7 (Baltimore: Johns Hopkins University Press, 1982).

4. I discuss the Oscar Browning passage in 'Sapphistry'.

5. *New Statesman*, 2 Oct 1920, p. 704. Woolf's reply is repr. in *D*, II, Appendix III. See also *New Statesman*, 16 Oct 1920. For a fine analysis of how Woolf's anger is used in *A Room of One's Own*, see Alice Fox, 'Literary Allusion as Feminist Criticism in *A Room of One's Own*', *Philogical Quarterly* (Spring 1984) pp. 145–61.

6. I coined this word in 'Liberty, Sorority, Misogyny' (1981), published in *The Representation of Women in Fiction*, and Susan Gubar has taken it up and used it in a slightly different way in her current work.

7. For Woolf's concern with celibacy, see my 'The Niece of a Nun: Virginia Woolf, Caroline Stephen and the Cloistered Imagination', in *Virginia Woolf: A Feminist Slant*, ed. Marcus (Lincoln, Nebr.: University of Nebraska Press, 1983).

8. See Evelyn Haller, 'Isis Unveiled', ibid.

9. See Sandra Shattuck's essay on Jane Harrison in this volume. The quotation is from Diether Cartellieri, *TLS*, 16 Dec 1983, p. 1403.

10. For one example of Virginia's ventriloquism with Vanessa, see *L*, III, 375. For another view of Vanessa, see Angelica Garnett's *Deceived by Kindness* and Louise DeSalvo's fine review in *The Women's Review of Books*, vol. II, no. 11 (August 1985).

11. For a fuller discussion of the Procne and Philomel myth in *Between the Acts*, see my 'Liberty, Sorority, Misogyny'; for a theory which uses the myth, see my 'Still Practice, A/Wrested Alphabet: Toward a Feminist Aesthetic', in *Tulsa Studies in Women's Literature*, Spring/Fall 1984; also forthcoming in book form from Indiana University Press, edited by Shari Benstock.

12. Richard Bauman has pointed out to me that Erving Goffman does a deconstruction of the lecture similar to my analysis here, though it is done in strictly patriarchal terms in *Forms of Talk* (Philadelphia: University of Pennsylvania Press, 1982).

13. I discuss the ballad and other aspects of the lecture form in 'Sapphistry'.

14. D. H. Lawrence's typescript is in the Humanities Research Center, University of Texas at Austin.

15. In May 1927 Vita had gone with Virginia to lecture at Oxford. She wrote to Vanessa (*L*, III, 380) of her admiration for her aristocratic friend's ability to take her stockings down at dinner and rub her legs with ointment, because of the midges, with no embarrassment. Her dramatisation here is of the naked muse forced to put her stockings on for fear of telling the truth about women's bodies. For the relations of Virginia Woolf and Vita Sackville-West, see Louise DeSalvo, 'Lighting the Cave', *Signs: Journal of Women in Culture and Society*, VIII, no.2 (Winter 1982).

16. One could make a similar point about the blank shelves in the British Museum indicating the absence of women's books. As we go to press 'A Woman's College from the Outside' has appeared in *The*

*Complete Shorter Fiction of Virginia Woolf* (London: Hogarth Press, 1985) pp. 139–42.

17. The 'erotics of chastity' in Woolf is a concept I discuss in 'The Niece of a Nun' in *Virginia Woolf: A Feminist Slant*.

18. For a brilliant study of women's education in England, see Martha Vicinus's *Independent Women: Work and Community for Single Women 1850 to 1920* (University of Chicago Press, 1985). A completely opposite reading of *Gaudy Night* as a love story, 'a reworking of the primary intimate bond between a mother and her child', appears in Lee Edwards, *Psyche as Hero* (Middletown, Conn.: Wesleyan University Press, 1985).

19. Geoffrey Hartman, 'Virginia's Web', in *Beyond Formalism* (New Haven, Conn.: Yale University Press, 1970), and J. Hillis Miller in *Fiction and Repetition* (New Haven, Conn.: Yale University Press, 1982). The taxi passage (*AROO*, pp. 100–2) is her way of relieving the 'strain' of feminist thinking. It leads directly to the 'big fish' of 'a woman writing thinks back through her mothers' and the trial of 'the androgynous mind of the artist' as a solution. She warns her students of the split and alienated feelings of the feminist 'when from being the natural inheritor of that civilization, she becomes, on the contrary, outside of it, alien and critical'. The couple in the taxi is a relief, a fiction of co-operation between the sexes which she forces herself to imagine because the pain of exclusion and male contempt for women which her reading and experience have taught her are too much to bear. The preceding chapters have been a feminist reading-lesson. The fiction of the taxi is not the source of Woolf's creativity but a fictional device of imagined male–female natural union, to keep her, and her readers/listeners from despair. Nelly Furman reads the passage 'as a spatial metaphor for the library shelves', a vision of balance in the representation of the two sexes in culture in ' "*A Room of One's Own*": Reading Absence', *Women's Language and Style*, ed. Butturf and Epstein (University of Akron Studies in Contemporary Language, 1978). See also Woolf's short story 'The Introduction' in *Mrs Dalloway's Party*, where Lily Everit, the would-be critic, is despised and rejected as a woman but refuses to back off, realising that 'this civilization depends on me'. This passage is discussed in more detail in *Virginia Woolf and the Languages of Patriarchy* (Indiana University Press, 1986).

# 9 'Cam the Wicked': Woolf's Portrait of the Artist as her Father's Daughter

ELIZABETH ABEL

> I'm now all on the strain with desire to stop journalism & get on to *To the Lighthouse*. . . . the centre is father's character, sitting in a boat, reciting We perished, each alone, while he crushes a dying mackerel – However, I must refrain.    (Entry for 14 May 1925, *D*, III).

> Then one day walking round Tavistock Square I made up, as I sometimes make up my books, *To the Lighthouse*; in a great, apparently involuntary rush. . . . I wrote the book very quickly; and when it was written, I ceased to be obsessed by my mother. I no longer hear her voice; I do not see her . . . .
>      Certainly, there she was, in the very centre of that great Cathedral space which was childhood; there she was from the very first.    ('A Sketch of the Past', 1939)

If *Mrs Dalloway* is constructed such that 'every scene would build up the idea' of its central character, *To the Lighthouse* is in doubt about its centre.[1] Resisting a unitary focus, the text enacts the problematics of recounting a family history whose plural subject fosters diverse narratives. *To the Lighthouse* dramatises the contradictions between Woolf's prospective and retrospective definitions of its centre. The lacuna 'Time Passes' offers as a textual centre is only the most striking manifestation of a discontinuity sustained more discretely through the multiple histories Woolf hoped would counteract the sentimentality threatened by her theme: 'The word 'sentimental' sticks in my gizzard. . . . But this theme may be sentimental; father and mother and child in the

170

garden; the sail to the Lighthouse. I think, though, that when I begin it I shall enrich it in all sorts of ways; thicken it; give it branches – roots – which I do not perceive now' (entry for 20 June 1925, in *D*, III, 36). Woolf's metaphors of textual enrichment have changed since *Mrs Dalloway*: the 'beautiful caves' that were to deepen private history have been exchanged for metaphors of thickening drawn from the interdependent parts of a tree: a family tree that will ironise the family romance by matching its plural subject to a plural narrative.[2] Chronology has also grown more complex, for the straightforward movement of history, which reverses Woolf's evolving vision of the text by progressing from mother to father, is countered by the multiple acts of retrospection that advance the narrative by moving back.

It is this heterogeneity, this insistence on representing its own narrative ambivalence, that has been neglected in the criticism, which has concentrated primarily on specific aspects of Woolf's 'theme', usually focusing either on the variations on androgyny played by the Ramsays (not only male/female, but also its permutations: fact/imagination, reason/intuition, truth/beauty, [mock] heroism/domesticity, farsightedness/myopia, and so on) or on the dilemma of the woman artist dramatised by Lily Briscoe.[3] Although analyses of genre have taken as their starting-point Woolf's own uncertainty about the appropriate label for her text, they have tended to translate her indecision into an assertion. Thus, the question mark disappears from her claim that 'I am making up *To the Lighthouse* – the sea is to be heard all through it. I have an idea that I will invent a new name for my books to supplant "novel". A new – by Virginia Woolf. But what? Elegy?' (entry for 27 June 1925, in *D*, III, 34).[4] Circumscribing genre unifies a text whose origins and broadest patterns may be elegiac, but whose fractured explorations of elegiac subjects resists consolidation as a single genre or theme.

Like other critical perspectives on this text, a reading that focuses on self-reflexive narrative anticipates *A Room of One's Own*, where Woolf conflates the dynamics of the family romance with those of narrative by mapping family metaphors onto literary processes: 'we think back through our mothers if we are women' (*AROO*, p.79). In *To the Lighthouse* the familial context, accentuated by the island setting, is also the arena of self-conscious narrative, though here the claims of patrilinearity compete with those of matrilinearity. It is this extended overlap, not the episodic and explicit Freudian allusions critics have decried, that makes this Woolf's most profoundly psychoanalytic text.[5] *To the Lighthouse* is shot through with scenes of reading, writing and painting, inconspicuous yet germinal scenes from which memory spins its tale, textual moments (in Lily Briscoe's words) 'ringed round, lit up, visible to the last detail, with all before it blank and all after it blank, for miles and miles' (*TL*, p.254). This is a text concerned not only with the genesis of narrative, but with different models of textuality and their relation to their narrator's and subject's sexuality. These links among family history, narrative and gender constitute the psychoanalytic substance of this text, which refracts its author's narrative concerns among its disparate characters. Thus, Woolf's two most explicit textual representatives – Lily and Cam – inherit her competing narrative loyalties. Lily is her vehicle for thinking back through her mother. Heir to her author's original plan of centring her text on 'father's character, sitting in a boat, reciting We perished, each alone', Cam enables Woolf to dramatise the narrative plight of the daughter who thinks back through her father.

Because critics have systematically neglected Cam in favour of Lily and James, who are accented and counterpointed in the text, this essay plucks her from the web of narrative to illuminate, and account for, her obscurity.[6] By her name and her position as the youngest Ramsay daughter, Cam is Woolf's most literal narrative counterpart, her self-portrait as her father's daughter, yet she is powerfully, though erratically, submerged.[7] Minimally outlined in Part I, Cam nevertheless joins the finale in Part III – and yet, as such a shadowy, attenuated presence that it is not clear why she is included. The arrival at the Lighthouse caps James's drama exclusively: Cam has never desired this journey and drifts suspended between the text's dual resolutions: the arrival at the Lighthouse and the completion of Lily's painting. Yet, rather than a sign of aesthetic incoherence, her plight brilliantly discloses one intersection of psychoanalysis and narrative: the imaginative field delimited by the daughter's shift from pre-Oedipal mother to Oedipal father. In this later, more self-conscious work, Woolf has rewritten Clarissa Dalloway's story to accent an eroticised relation with the body of the father's texts.[8] Paternal violence has softened to a seduction that is more textual than sexual, but that cuts the daughter as decisively from her maternal past. Purposefully obscure, Cam anticipates the problematic Woolf who announces two years later in *A Room of One's Own*: 'It is useless to go to the great male writers for help, however much one may go to them for pleasure. . . . The ape is too distant to be sedulous' (*AROO*, p.79).

Cam is an enigma throughout the text. Less central than James, she is also less psychoanalytically programmatic: no ritualistic images (such as the axes, knives and pokers with which James fantasises murdering his father) allegorise her consciousness. As a child, she is fiercely independent: 'She would not "give a flower to the gentleman" as the nursemaid told her. No! no! no! she would not' (*TL*, p. 36). Hence her appellation by Mr Bankes: 'Cam the Wicked' (p. 83). Indecipherable even to her mother (and perhaps the only character who is), Cam seems wholly present to herself as she dashes through Part I like a projectile guided by some urgent private desire: 'She was off like a bird, bullet, or arrow, impelled by what desire, shot by whom, at what directed, who could say? What, what? Mrs Ramsay pondered, watching her' (p. 84). This defiant energy has dissipated by Part III; Cam sits passively in the boat while her brother navigates, her father reads and chats with Macalister, and Macalister's boy catches fish. Like the boat that bobs up and down in place, Cam's thoughts circle back on themselves as she aimlessly dabbles her hand in the water and watches the fish that objectify her feeling of entrapment.[9] Whereas the narrative holds James psychically responsible for the inter-rupted progress of the boat by linking his drama of memory and repression to the rise and fall of the wind (section viii), thereby according him the task of reshaping the past to enable the future, Cam's internal drama (section x), which follows and depends on her brother's, is severed from this narrative teleology. James faces the Lighthouse and navigates toward it; Cam sits in the bow and gazes back toward the island. Though brother and sister share the task of reconstructing memory, Cam's efforts do not impinge on the action. Her project is purely historical.

At the beginning of 'The Lighthouse', the cowed and angry siblings share a single will, though Cam's syntactic subordination – 'He would be impatient in a moment, James thought, and Cam thought' (p. 242), 'So James could tell, so Cam could tell' (p. 245) – indicates the hierarchy. Woolf chooses the occasion of an interpolated story to introduce Cam as an independent conscious-ness. Macalister's tale of maritime rescue and disaster, prompted by Mr Ramsay's questions about the great storm at Christmas, weaves an alliance between the two old men, overcoming class and ethnic difference to constitute a homogeneous narrative voice as Mr Ramsay adjusts his gaze and speech to Macalister's and mimics his Scottish accent. Shared pleasure in the sexual division of labour and its representation in narrative outweighs other differences: Mr Ramsay 'liked that men should labour and sweat on the windy beach at night . . . he liked men to work like that, and women to keep house and sit beside sleeping children indoors, while men were drowned, out there in a storm' (p. 245). Woolf dramatises the impact of this story not on James, who can aspire to a future role in it, but on its more problematic female auditor, whose access to this explicitly masculine discourse requires mediation. The imaginative arena the story opens frees the carefully guarded love Cam feels for her father, but this release is qualified by the mental act it presupposes. Cam can enter this discourse only by displacing herself as its potential subject, transferring her childhood love of adventure to an idealised image of her (elderly) father, with some consequent mystification of her own emotions. 'Cam thought, feeling proud of him *without knowing quite why*, had he been there he would have launched the lifeboat, he would have reached the wreck. . . . He was so brave, he was so adventurous' (p. 246: emphasis added). Woolf marks Cam's emergence in the third part of her text as a reaction to a masculine 'text' that grants her the gendered relationship to narrative explored in *A Room of One's Own*.

Cam's idealisation of Mr Ramsay, moreover, provokes a return of what it has repressed: the knowledge of his tyranny. This knowledge is Cam's as well as James's, and the 'compact' that declares it and that suddenly checks her surge of affection for her father has presumably been forged by both siblings, who had 'vowed, in silence, as they walked, to stand by each other and carry out the great compact – to resist tyranny to the death' (*TL*, p. 243). Yet Cam perceives the agreement as a text she can neither revise, revoke, nor fully endorse, a coercive force that evolves into 'the tablets of eternal wisdom' lying on the knee of James the lawgiver, silencing her (p. 251). Cam is complicit in this silencing. Though the compact *does* represent James's perspective more fully than her own, and *does* reflect his greater authority, Cam's desire to evade her own anger obscures her part in the creation of an unwritten text that records a strand of her relation to her father. As she projects her former adventurousness onto her father, she projects onto her brother her former defiance, the voice that had said 'No! no! no!' to the gentleman, dividing her salient childhood traits between two men and two texts in which participation leads to alienation. Denying herself the roles of both protagonist and author, she colludes with the assumptions of patriarchal textuality.[10] The scene on the boat suggests some prior learning.

Paralysed by the stand-off between her father and her brother, Cam recovers her own memories only after this drama is resolved in section viii and the boat is speeding toward the Lighthouse once again. In section x the motion sparks Cam's imagination, which converts the growing distance into time and reverts to a single privileged scene, her counterpart to James's epiphanic vision of his mother 'saying simply whatever came into her head. She alone spoke the truth; to her alone could he speak it' (p. 278). Cam, however, remembers her father, not her mother; scenes of reading and writing rather than of speech; and a study rather than a garden. Eden to her is the garden's aftermath, though the narrative suggests this revision is delusion. Her memory focuses on her father's study. 'Sometimes she strayed in from the garden purposely to catch them at it. There they were (it might by Mr Carmichael or Mr Bankes who was sitting with her father) sitting opposite each other in their low armchairs . . . . Just to please herself she would take a book from the shelf and stand there, watching her father write' (p. 281). In Cam's imagination, fathers know best, and they speak the knowledge of the printed text. 'They were crackling in front of them the pages of *The Times*, when she came in from the garden, all in a muddle about something some one had said about Christ, or hearing that a mammoth had been dug up in a London street, or wondering what Napoleon was like' (p. 281). 'Straying' from garden to study, from nature to culture, from the private muddle to the public text, Cam re-enacts Clarissa Dalloway's symbolic moment of transition from pastoral Bourton to urban London, and from Sally Seton to Richard Dalloway, the moment sealed during Clarissa's retreat from her party to the private room in which she assimilates Septimus Smith's death by renouncing the hold of her past. Explicitly, the two scenes are linked through the reference to *The Times*, which reassures the female spectator that the flux of experience can be securely captured in the authoritative idiom of the daily patriarchal text. Clarissa's speculation that 'Even now, quite often if Richard had not been there reading the *Times*, so that she could

crouch like a bird and gradually revive ... she must have
perished' prepares for the startling reversal: 'And once she had
walked on the terrace at Bourton. It was due to Richard; she had
never been so happy' (*MD*, pp. 281–2).[11] More profoundly, the
scenes are linked by the desire to mark the closure of a
developmental era.

In Cam's memory, closure is gentle, a gradual transition from
one sphere to another, a gradual translation of experience to
thought that unfolds organically like a leaf that has gained, not
lost, its natural environment. As a child in the study Cam had felt
that 'one could let whatever one thought expand here like a leaf in
water; and if it did well here, among the old gentlemen smoking
and *The Times* crackling then it was right' (*TL*, p. 282). Yet the
tension between her metaphor and her literal description under-
cuts her evolutionary model, reasserting a distinction she would
blur. Throughout the text Cam associates the leaf with Mrs
Ramsay. In 'The Window' Cam carries a leaf when she responds
to her mother's call; in 'The Lighthouse' the leaf is her recurrent
image for the island that incarnates the receding past. 'It lay like
that on the sea, did it, with a dent in the middle and two sharp
crags, and the sea swept in there, and spread away for miles and
miles on either side of the island. It was very small; shaped
something like a leaf stood on end' (p. 280). Cam's simile revises
but does not conceal a prior, less overt metaphorisation of the
island as a female body, a womb, from which she is drawn slowly
away. With a sea-swept dent in the middle of two crags, the island
hovering behind the leaf is a figure of the mother. As a child, Cam
hoped to extend, articulate and assess the past identified with the
garden and the mother by translating the leaf into the language of
the father – and in so doing to imitate her father's own translations
of hedges into periods, of geranium leaves into 'scraps of paper on
which one scribbles notes in the rush of reading' (p. 66), of nature's
leaves into the pages of a book. When she repeats this gesture in
the present, a fissure surfaces. It is the image of the leaf-shaped
island that triggers her adolescent memory: 'Small as it was, and
shaped something like a leaf stood on its end with the gold-
sprinkled waters flowing in and about it, it had, she supposed, a
place in the universe – even that little island? The old gentlemen in
the study she thought could have told her. Sometimes she strayed
in from the garden ...' (p. 281). The rift between the gold-
sprinkled island and the old men in the study reveals what has

been lost in the translation and what now is lost more emphatically in Cam's attempt to situate one domain of experience within the discourse of another.

Only these repercussions of the past in the present lend credibility to the hints of a Fall. If the young Cam 'strays' from the garden in search of information, this knowledge is not forbidden, nor is she expelled. The garden, moreover, is no unfallen natural paradise, for voices within it have produced the muddle that sends her in search of clarification. If there is a Fall, it pertains not to the search for knowledge, or even to its source (the study is a logical, perhaps inevitable, resource to enlist), but to its consequences. The historical questions that arise in the garden – about Christ, Napoleon and a prehistoric mammoth – are appropriately carried to the study, but they differ from the issue the older Cam mentally refers to the same place: a question of personal history, of the private past, of the mother's place 'in the universe'. However passionately motivated her search for knowledge, and however legitimate her indebtedness to her father, Cam's apprenticeship in the study ensnares as well as liberates her, sanctioning certain modes of thought, discouraging others, creating an intellectual framework that becomes her single frame of reference. The old gentlemen in the study reinforce Cam's interest in history, priming her for the position she assumes in the boat.[12] Studying the past, she also learns to privilege it. By 'The Lighthouse' Cam is expert at gazing backward, at translating images of a shifting present into the framework of the past, at repeating in adolescence patterns learned as a child.

The scene in the study both mirrors and prepares the scene in the boat. Cam's psychological position in the present, as well as her literal one, moreover, finds a precedent in her father's study. In both situations Cam's curiosity and responsiveness draw her imaginatively into a conversation between men, with a consequent erosion of her own subjectivity. As the two scenes blur in her mind, similarities emerge between her relation to the story spun by Mr Ramsay and Macalister, and her relation to the dialogue between Mr Ramsay and an old gentleman 'who might be Mr Carmichael or Mr Bankes', whose identity matters less than his structural position opposite her father, Macalister's position. (We are told this location obliquely through stage directions: when James fears his father's admonition about a slackening sail, he imagines that Mr Ramsay 'would say sharply, "Look out! Look out!" and old Macalister would turn slowly on his seat – presumably to look at the drooping sail; when Mr Ramsay listens to Macalister's story, he leans forward – presumably to catch every word [p. 244].) In the study, ambiguity obscures who talks with whom. Cam wants to believe that her questions received answers, but the text suggests that the gentlemen conversed primarily with one another. Whom did they address when they turned their papers, crossed their knees, 'and said something now and then very brief' (p. 281)? An almost identical phrase in the next sentence records a conversation between the two old men: Mr Ramsay said something 'briefly to the other old gentleman opposite' (p.282). Only in Cam's final recapitulation of the scene does someone explicitly answer her question: 'The old gentleman, lowering the paper suddenly, said something very brief over the top of it about the character of Napoleon' (p. 283). Is this a wishful secondary revision, part of her project of rescuing her father from James's hostile fantasy? The substance of the interaction reinforces its structural ambiguity. Cam's only question to be answered, and the only specified content of any verbal exchange, concerns the character of Napoleon, ominous in light of Woolf's subsequent depiction of this historical figure. In *A Room of One's Own* Woolf explains that 'mirrors are essential to all violent and heroic action. That is why Napoleon and Mussolini both insist so emphatically upon the inferiority of women, for if they were not inferior, they would cease to enlarge' (*AROO*, p.36). By *The Years*, 'the character of Napoleon' has evolved into 'the psychology of great men', exemplified explicitly by Napoleon, that obstructs the knowledge of 'ourselves, ordinary people' (women, homosexuals, foreigners, in this context), which would enable us to make 'laws and religions that fit' – in contrast, presumably, to such homogenising codes as the 'tablets of eternal wisdom' transmitted from father to son (*Y*, pp. 281–2). For Woolf, Napoleon incarnates the attitude that writes women out of a history defined as exchanges between (great) men. That his character should be the climax of a scene in which Cam struggles to learn history reveals the pathos of her eagerness for access to a discourse whose terms diminish her, and for a place in an exchange that calls into question her status as interlocutor.

The apprenticeship in the study is not the only source of Cam's attenuation in language. It may be her fate as youngest daughter to serve as a vehicle of messages rather than their sender or recipient, and her willing metamorphosis into a blank page encourages her use as a transparent medium. The significant variable is the gender of the speakers. In 'The Window' Woolf briefly sketches an alternative semiotic context for Cam. When sent by Mrs Ramsay to ask the cook if Andrew, Paul, and Minta have returned from the beach, Cam mimics for her mother the cook's exact response. But between the question and the answer she inserts her own story, and 'it was only by waiting patiently, and hearing that there was an old woman in the kitchen with very red cheeks, drinking soup out of a basin, that Mrs Ramsay at last prompted that parrot-like instinct which had picked up Mildred's words quite accurately and could now produce them, if one waited, in a colourless singsong' (*TL*, p. 85). A diminutive female Hermes shuttling between two female speakers, Cam nevertheless succeeds in imposing her own embryonic narrative. Its subject, 'an old woman in the kitchen', resonates against Woolf's first description of the centre of her text, the vision to which Cam is heir: the father in a boat. The text associates the red-cheeked old woman with the bibulous elderly cleaning-woman Mrs McNab, who in 'Time Passes' remembers being 'always welcome in the kitchen' where the cook, at Mrs Ramsay's request, kept a plate of milk soup for her.[13] Though stripped of Mrs Ramsay's arabesquing consciousness, Mrs McNab serves in 'Time Passes' as a bare corporeal remainder and reminder of her mistress, an incarnation of memory who tears the 'veil of silence' that has fallen on the Ramsay home (p. 196). As the lowest common denominator of female artistry, the work of preservation whose psychological correlate Mrs Ramsay calls 'the effort of merging and flowing and creating' (p. 126), Mrs McNab is the figure who by sheer determination rescues the Ramsay's home from 'the sands of oblivion' and connects the first part of the novel to the third (p. 209).[14] As Cam's kitchen muse, she fleetingly inspires a story that refuses to be squelched. In the same way that her position in the novel inscribes the traces of female labour in a bleakly inhuman textual centre, her position in Cam's circuit as messenger raises the prospect of a third rendition of the novel's three-part form. Cam's vision of the island as a sea-swept dent between two crags hints at this rendition. The configuration of mass and space shows a family resemblance with Lily Briscoe's 'question ... how to connect this mass on the right hand with that on the left' (p. 83) and James's 'night's darkness' between two days (p. 9), but Cam represents the centre as a place of origin. Her glimpse of the island shares with her miniature narrative a buried notion of female engendering. These echoing accounts could evolve into Cam's counterpart to the narrative formulas offered by Lily and James; they could become Cam's story, her meta-narrative, her version of history. But this nascent narrative design never emerges, and cannot emerge. Cam's muted presence in the text is no accident, for it is precisely when she first perceives the island as a body – 'She had never seen it from out at sea before' (p. 280) – that she turns to the memory of the study.

Cam's poignancy derives from a narrative perspective that blends sympathy with irony. It is less that we see options to which Cam is blind (to whom should she refer her questions about history?) than that we can gauge the cost of choices she has made, interpret metaphors opaque to her, and register her pleasure as an index of her innocence. Though Cam's course may look easier than James's, since the death of their mother appears less devastating to her and her father is less peremptory with her, we can also observe that, if her suffering is less acute and articulate, it is also less empowering. If James renounces a privileged bond with his mother and the unsullied truth her language signifies to him, and accepts in their place the poverty and power of linguistic signs (the tablets he inherits from his father), Cam never fully accedes to this symbolic register. Her own metaphors betray that her father's study, in which she takes such pleasure, offers her the material of language more readily than its significance. Within this sanctuary, Cam relishes tangible signs with no expectation that their content is available. She represents the old gentlemen's clarification of her muddle as a tactile, rather than a verbal, intervention: 'Then they took all this [muddle] with their clean hands (they wore grey-coloured clothes; they smelt of heather) and they brushed the scraps together . . .' (p. 281). Instead of reading the book she takes from the shelf 'just to please herself', she watches her father write and admires the evenness of his lines without attempting to decipher their meaning. The scene on the boat mirrors this relation to paternal texts. Cam is both thoroughly familiar with, and ignorant of, the book in which her father is engrossed, 'the little book whose yellowish pages she knew, without knowing what was written on them. It was small; it was closely printed. . . . But what might be written in the book which had rounded its edges off in his pocket, she did not know. What he thought they none of them knew' (p. 283). The father as text, like the father's texts, remains hermetic to her, and her attempt to generalise this condition cracks against James's conviction that he and his father 'alone knew each other' (p. 275). Cam's image of the tiller's transformation into tablets marks her only conscious recognition of their father's differing legacies. These differences crystallise in the children's final interactions with Mr Ramsay. Cam's relationship with her father culminates in a silent gesture of paternal courtship, as Mr Ramsay hands her 'a gingerbread nut, as if he were a great Spanish gentleman, she thought, handing a flower to a lady at a window (so courteous his manner was)' (p. 305). The father–son relationship concludes with the breaking of silence in the long-withheld 'Well done!' that answers James's unspoken desire for paternal recognition and praise (p. 306). Despite (or because of) Cam's delight in her father's courtly gesture, this resolution of their relationship implies that her apprenticeship did not fulfil its promise. Revising a Keatsian model of treacherous seduction as the failure of a (feminine) imagination to sustain its offer of transcendence, Woolf's father–daughter narrative outlines a seduction by a (masculine) tradition that reneges on its equation of knowledge and authority.

The 'most touching' of the 'life-giving affinities' between Leslie Stephen and his youngest daughter, according to Leon Edel, was Sir Leslie's gift on Virginia's twenty-first birthday of a ring and a declaration: she was, he averred, 'a very good daughter'. Oblivious to the dissonance of his metaphors, Edel explains, 'It was as if there were a marriage and also a laying on of hands, a literary succession. The father . . . performed a marriage between Virginia and the world of letters.'[15] Woolf herself, however, was well aware that being wed to a tradition was not being its heir, and she dramatised this difference in the Ramsay children's destinies. The personal inclinations of daughter, and of father, have little relevance to the course of events; Cam's education in the study prepares her to inherit her mother's position rather than her father's. Whether overtly enacted as dialogue, or mediating more subtly between a masculine authorship and readership, the textual tradition transmitted by the study returns its female initiate to the original female position between two gentlemen: between Ramsay and Macalister, between Ramsay and the generic old gentlemen, between Ramsay and his son – the nuclear masculine pair. The daughter's position thus slides imperceptibly

into the mother's.[16] Though the father–mother–son triad that
prevailed in 'The Window' gives way in 'The Lighthouse' to a
father–daughter–son triad, the median feminine position is
unchanged. As the scene on the boat gradually re-creates its
predecessor at the window (*TL*, I, vii), the characters psychically
alter their positions. Having explicitly established that Mr
Ramsay sits 'in the middle of the boat between them (James
steered; Cam sat alone in the bow)' (p. 242), Woolf inconsistently
rearranges the protagonists to conform with the emotional
topography. Cam's 'brother was most god-like, her father most
suppliant. And to which did she yield, she thought, sitting
between them, gazing at the shore . . .' (p. 251). As Cam inherits
her mother's middle position, for which her training in the study
paradoxically has groomed her, Woolf dissects the configuration
that silences the daughter.

Ostensibly, Mr Ramsay tries during the boat trip to engage his
daughter in conversation, but Woolf portrays the scene as an
unvoiced dialogue between Mr Ramsay and his son. After Mr
Ramsay's opening question, we shift directly to James's response:
'Who was looking after the puppy today? he [Mr Ramsay] asked.
Yes, thought James pitilessly, seeing his sister's head against the
sail, now she'll give way. I shall be left to fight the tyrant alone' (p.
250). Mr Ramsay's second question similarly returns us to
James's consciousness. Sliding pronouns ('she', 'her', 'they',
'somebody') replace Cam with Mrs Ramsay as the pressure of the
struggle recalls its prototype, Mr Ramsay's interruption of
James's idyll with his mother.

> She'll give way, James thought, as he watched a look come
> upon her face, a look he remembered. They look down, he
> thought, at their knitting or something. Then suddenly they
> look up. There was a flash of blue, he remembered, and then
> somebody sitting with him laughed, surrendered, and he was
> very angry. It must have been his mother, he thought, sitting on
> a low chair, with his father standing over her . . . a man had
> marched up and down and stopped dead, upright, over
> them.    (pp. 251–2).

Having blurred his sister with his mother, James succeeds in
adolescence where he failed as a child and prevents his father's
victory. Torn between the irreconcilable demands of her father

and his son, Cam succumbs to silence, unable to find a language for her own split desire.

In the present scene, Mr Ramsay is humble, not apparently engaged in any struggle, eager only to converse with his daughter. His motivation, however, mirrors his son's: like James, he uses Cam to replay and repair the past, though he tries to compensate to his wife through his daughter rather than exacting compensation from her. When Cam's uncertainty about the points of the compass recalls Mrs Ramsay's imprecision about the weather, Mr Ramsay merges daughter and mother: 'He thought, women are always like that; the vagueness of their minds is hopeless . . . . It had been so with her – his wife' (p. 249). Grieving for his wife, and feeling remorse over his anger at her, Mr Ramsay craves the solace of his daughter's approval. The scene on the boat thus becomes a scene of seduction that locates Cam between two men struggling to redo their relation to her mother: 'I will make her smile at me, Mr Ramsay thought' (p. 250). His manner is courteous, but his project is coercive. Though he struggles to suppress his longing for confirmation, Cam reads it clearly. 'And what was she going to call him [the puppy]? her father persisted. He had had a dog when he was a little boy, called Frisk . . . she wished, passionately, to move some obstacle that lay upon her tongue and say, Oh, yes, Frisk. I'll call him Frisk' (p. 252). In this competition for her tongue, Cam can be silenced by Mosaic tablets or echo a paternal language that suggests an Adamic ritual of naming: 'So she said nothing, but looked doggedly and sadly at the shore. . . . They have no suffering there, she thought' (p. 253).[17]

Ironically, Cam's education in the tradition that situates her in a silent centre enables her to gloss the ramifications of this situation. Assuming her mother's place between Mr Ramsay's 'entreaty – forgive me, care for me' and James's exhortation, 'Resist him. Fight him', Cam feels herself divided not only between father and son, but also between the claims of pity and those of justice, the binary opposition that conventionally disting-uishes the Christian from the Judaic tradition. The terms are transposed (the son advocates justice, the father pity), but their reversibility does not alter the female position as a pivot between two dispensations, a place where centrality amounts to mediation.[18] Cam's allusive language also echoes classical tragedy, especially the Sophoclean trilogy that has been a reservoir of cultural paradigms. The 'god-like' brother and the 'suppliant' father between whom Cam imagines herself seated suggest incarnations of the same individual: Oedipus the King, regal law-maker, god-like in his splendour, who becomes the blind old man, the homeless suppliant of *Oedipus at Colonus*, an aged hero guided by his daughter. Woman again is pivot of this transformation. Mother and daughter to both father and son, Cam also assumes these overlapping roles within the implied Oedipal drama. As stand-in for her mother, she holds the place of Jocasta to both Mr Ramsay and to James, who betters his father in the conflict over her. As daughter, she must also be Antigone (both daughter and half-sister to Jocasta), and forgive, nurture, and protect her father in his frail old age. As sister, however, she must be Antigone to James and select her role from the last play of the trilogy, where sororal loyalty to brother over 'father' (both her father's brother and her prospective father-in-law) is the principled, heroic choice of living death over ethical compromise.[19] Cam wants to play both Antigone's roles, to be the loyal sister and the loving daughter, but James forbids her to play Antigone to her father, and Mr Ramsay tries to dissuade her from the bond with her brother. Paralysed between father and son, between two manifestations of a patriarchal God and two incarnations of Oedipus, Cam is the ambiguous mother and maid whose body is a fulcrum in the sequences of history and a page on which the tests and texts of masculinity are inscribed.[20] The only escape is out of the body, the desire motivating the suicidal fantasy (another echo of Jocasta and Antigone) latent in Cam's envious gaze at the island, where people, it seems, 'had fallen asleep . . . were free like smoke, were free to come and go like ghosts' (p. 253).

Cam is released from these fantasies only after James resolves the conflict with his father that places her between the two men. Section x opens with a sense of liberation: to describe it, Cam tentatively adopts, and then rejects, a narrative model drawn from Macalister, a story about escaping from a sinking ship. Her search for images more appropriate to her own sense of adventure begins by echoing the language of her mother in Mrs Ramsay's only solitary scene, the moment of visionary eroticism elicited by the Lighthouse beam ('The Window', xi):

What then came next? Where were they going? From her hand, ice cold, held deep in the sea, there spurted up a fountain of joy at the change, at the escape, at the adventure (that she should be alive, that she should be there). And the drops falling from this sudden and unthinking fountain of joy fell here and there on the dark, the slumbrous shapes in her mind; shapes of a world not realised but turning in their darkness, catching here and there, a spark of light; Greece, Rome, Constantinople. (pp. 280–1)[21]

Gazing at the past illumined by this anticipation of the future, at the leaf-shaped island transformed by 'gold-sprinkled waters', Cam identifies her distinctive narrative task: to hinge the maternal shape of the past with the fleetingly illumined shapes of the future by articulating the central place she occupies, turning her historical aptitude to an unwritten history. It is here that she remembers her father. The section ends with the disappearance of the island: 'the leaf was losing its sharpness. . . . The sea was more important now than the shore' (pp. 283–4). The final words return to Macalister's story and to Mr Ramsay's refrain, as Cam 'murmured, dreamily, half-asleep, how we perished, each alone' (p. 284).

Unable to assume an adversarial stance toward a masculine narrative tradition, Cam only gestures toward a story she cannot tell. Through a different 'daughter' and heir to Mrs Ramsay, Woolf glosses Cam's dilemma by indicating the strategies that must be employed to record the 'slumbrous shapes . . . of a world not realised' but fleetingly disclosed in a moment of release. Minta Doyle, an enigmatic figure revealed primarily through other female characters, shares Cam's role as a submerged vehicle for Woolf's meditation on female narrative. The most overtly erotic figure in the novel, a vibrantly attractive 'golden-reddish' girl who sparks Mr Ramsay's gallantry and Mrs Ramsay's jealousy, Minta is also the most opaque. Like the hole in her stocking that signifies her unruly sexuality to the proper Mr Bankes, Minta's subjectivity is a hole in the text, a sign of a story that resists direct narration.[22] Hinted at through images similar to Cam's, Minta's experience is filtered primarily through the consciousness of Cam's older sister Nancy, who grasps just enough to articulate the limits of conventional narrative.

Woolf chooses the most traditional strand of her text, the story of Minta Doyle's and Paul Rayley's courtship, as an occasion for revealing how fictional conventions can serve the unconventional

female narrator. It is not simply that the Rayley marriage
eventually fails; courtship, more significantly, offers a reservoir of
tropes and sequences for Woolf to problematise. The climax of
this plot, and the only traditional scene of passion in the novel, is
ingeniously located behind a rock. We see the event that
celebrates Paul's and Minta's engagement exclusively through
Nancy Ramsay's shocked, indignant eyes, and even this eye-
witness report is uncertain. Nancy is 'carried by her own
impetuosity and her desire for rapid movement right behind a
rock and there – oh, heavens! in each other's arms, were Paul and
Minta kissing *probably*' (p. 115: emphasis added). Minta's own
reaction to the engagement remains yet more ambiguous. Woolf
represents it exclusively through the most conventional trope for
female sexual initiation, Minta's loss at the beach of 'the sole
ornament she possessed' (p.116). Yet Minta's loss is undecodable,
for her grandmother's brooch, a weeping willow set in pearls,
suggests not only the conventional virginity, but also a female
heritage, disrupted equally by marriage.[23] If the allegorical value
of the metaphor directs us to one loss, its quotidian particulars –
'the brooch which her grandmother had fastened her cap with till
the last day of her life' (p. 116) – directs us to another. When the
loss is scrutinized obliquely through Nancy's consciousness,
uncertainty is all that can be ascertained: 'Nancy felt, it might be
true that she [Minta] minded losing her brooch, but she [Minta]
wasn't crying only for that. She was crying for something else. We
might all sit down and cry, she felt. But she did not know what for'
(p. 117). Finally, Minta's experience can only be represented as
an unspecifiable 'something else'.[24]

   This is true of Minta's future, as of her past. Woolf's framing of
the unseen scene behind the rock, enclosed by matching processions to and from the beach, distinguishes between male and
female relationships to narrative. The procession home at night-
fall is presented through the consciousness of Paul, who effortless-
ly translates an immediate temporal sequence into the signifiers of
a future one: 'And as they came out on the hill and saw the lights of
the town beneath them, the lights coming out suddenly one by one
seemed like things that were going to happen to him – his
marriage, his children, his house' (p. 118). No gap divides the
unrepresented scene from the significance Paul attaches to the
neutral chain of lights. His desire finds expression in a list that
designates the (con)sequences of patriarchal courtship: though

things will happen *to* him, they will nevertheless be *his*. Paul imagines conducting a silent Minta, psychically as well as physically effaced by him, through the links of this chain: 'they would retreat into solitude together, and walk on and on, he always leading her, and she pressing close to his side (as she did now)' (p. 118). The movement toward the scene behind the rock, by contrast, points to Minta's future only obliquely through a Morse code transmitted by her intermittent pressure on her companion Nancy's hand. Nancy poses the central question for her: 'What is it that she wants?' (p. 112). (What does a woman want? And, we might add, from whom?) The difficulty of formulating an answer is represented as a gap dividing women from language. Standing on the site from which Paul sees 'his marriage, his children, his house', Nancy tries to decipher Minta's future. Her images prefigure Cam's.

> When Minta took her hand and held it, Nancy, reluctantly, saw the whole world spread out beneath her, as if it were Constantinople seen through a mist, and then, however heavy-eyed one might be, one must needs ask, 'Is that Santa Sofia?' 'Is that the Golden Horn?' So Nancy asked, when Minta took her hand, 'What is it that she wants? Is it that? And what was that?' Here and there emerged from the mist (as Nancy looked down upon life spread beneath her) a pinnacle, a dome; prominent things without names.   (pp. 112–13)

Unlike Paul, who unproblematically attaches word to image, Nancy can visualise, but not designate, the novel shapes of Minta's desire. To record in language these 'things without names' requires an antithetical strategy of playing figures against themselves. Cam, more than Nancy, lacks this strategy. When she swerves away from a story that would link the 'shapes of a world not realised' with the shapes of a feminine past beyond the study, Cam reveals her enclosure in the textual tradition she would need to contest to write a different history.

'If we continue to speak the same language to each other, we will reproduce the same story . . .', Luce Irigaray insists. 'If we continue to speak this sameness, if we speak to each other as men have spoken for centuries, as they taught us to speak, we will fail each other. Again . . . . Words will pass through our bodies, above our heads, disappear, make us disappear.'[25] A certain circularity marks Cam's narrative activity, for the story she tells is the story of how she came to tell that story. It is a paradigmatic story of the daughter who thinks back through her father, a story of narrative imprisonment.[26] Woolf's feat in this text is to read the Oedipal narrative as an account of the daughter's shift to her father's dialogue with his son(s), a discourse that situates her (like her mother) in a median position between two men. The Oedipal narrative now accounts for an attenuated female language as well as sexuality, for a language that itself attenuates women's sexuality.

As Woolf's conception of the centre of her text shifted from father to mother, her narrative attention gravitated to the figure of Lily Briscoe, a peripheral character in the holograph manuscript.[27] Mr Ramsay in a boat reciting, 'We perished, each alone', became a focus of the third part of a text whose longest, richest, opening portion is dominated by his wife, psychically and aesthetically resurrected in Part III by her surrogate daughter Lily, rather than by Cam. Though Cam is overshadowed by this more successfully articulate 'sister', she nevertheless performs a vital function in disclosing the narrative costs of paternal filiation. Through Cam as well as Lily, then, Woolf adumbrates the claim from which much of her current pre-eminence in feminist literary history derives: 'we think back through our mothers if we are women'.

## NOTES

1. Virginia Woolf, 18 June 1923, entry in holograph notebook dated variously from 9 Nov 1922 to 2 Aug 1923; cited in Charles G. Hoffmann, 'From Short Story to Novel: The Manuscript Revisions of Virginia Woolf's *Mrs Dalloway*', *Modern Fiction Studies*, XIV, no. 2 (Summer 1968) 183.

2. On the 'beautiful caves', see *D*, II, 30. That the tree was understood to be the governing metaphor for *To the Lighthouse* is suggested by the original dust jacket designed by Vanessa Bell. On the family tree as the subject of Lily's painting, see Susan Gubar, 'The Birth of the Artist as Heroine: (Re)production, the *Künstlerroman* Tradition, and the Fiction of Katherine Mansfield', in *The Representation of Women in Fiction*, ed. Carolyn G. Heilbrun and Margaret R. Higonnet, Selected Papers from the English Institute, 1981, n.s., no. 7 (Baltimore: Johns Hopkins University Press, 1983) p. 48.

3. The many readings of androgyny in *To the Lighthouse* include Nancy Topping Bazin, *Virginia Woolf and the Androgynous Vision* (New Brunswick, NJ: Rutgers University Press, 1973); Avrom Fleishman, *Virginia Woolf: A Critical Reading* (Baltimore: Johns Hopkins University Press, 1975); Ralph Freedman, *The Lyrical Novel: Studies in Hermann Hesse, Andre Gide, and Virginia Woolf* (Princeton, NJ: Princeton University Press, 1973); and Maria DiBattista, *Virginia Woolf's Major Novels: The Fables of Anon* (New Haven, Conn.: Yale University Press, 1980). The focus on Lily is more recent. Here, the outstanding text is Jane Lilienfeld, ' "The Deceptiveness of Beauty": Mother Love and Mother Hate in *To the Lighthouse*', *Twentieth Century Literature*, XXIII, no. 2 (Oct 1977) 345–76. See also Sara Ruddick, 'Learning to Live with the Angel in the House', *Women's Studies*, IV, nos 2–3 (1977) 181–200; Phyllis Rose, *Woman of Letters: A Life of Virginia Woolf* (New York: Oxford University Press, 1978); and Gayatri C. Spivak, 'Unmaking and Making in *To the Lighthouse*', in *Women and Language in Literature and Society*, ed. Sally McConnel-Ginet, Ruth Borker and Nelly Furman (New York: Praeger, 1980) pp. 311–27. These two focuses simply identify dominant critical trends; they by no means exhaust the criticism of this text.

4. In *Virginia Woolf's Major Novels*, Maria DiBattista offers a comprehensive and persuasive reading of *To the Lighthouse* as an elegy for both of Woolf's parents, yet, by slighting the tensions between the narratives engendered by each parent, she posits a more unified text than I perceive.

5. Critics are often embarrassed by the explicitly Oedipal framework surrounding James's narrative. Thus, for example, Avrom Fleishman tries to explain it away: 'We do not take seriously the images of slaying the father by knife or ax (12, etc.) which come to James's mind (although they are elaborated in the broad stream of imagery of mutilation and destruction which runs through the text)' (*Virginia Woolf: A Critical Reading*, p. 121n). Thomas G. Matro similarly dismisses the Oedipal structure as 'an already too obvious Oedipal pattern and a facile resolution' and argues that it is part of a larger pattern of confronting the tyranny of symbols – 'Only Relations: Vision and Achievement in *To the Lighthouse*', *PMLA*, XCIX, no.2 (Mar 1984) 221. Other critics have embraced a psychoanalytic framework as an adequate explanatory context for the text. See, for example, Helen Storm Corsa, '*To the Lighthouse*: Death, Mourning, and Transfiguration', *Literature and Psychology*, XXI (Nov 1971) 115–32; and Ernest S. Wolf and Ina Wolf, 'We Perished, Each Alone. A Psychoanalytic Commentary on Virginia Woolf's *To the Lighthouse*', *International Review of Psycho-Analysis*, VI (1979) 37–47. For psychoanalytic readings that apply a Jungian rather than a Freudian lens, see Lilienfeld, ' "The Deceptiveness of Beauty" ', *Twentieth Century Literature*, XXIII, no. 2; and DiBattista, *Virginia Woolf's Major Novels*.

6. For a reading of the multiple strands of this web, see my *Virginia Woolf and the Fictions of Psychoanalysis* (forthcoming from the University of Chicago Press), which devotes individual sections to James, Lily, Mrs Ramsay and Cam.

7. Cam's full name is undoubtedly Camilla, the name of Virginia's counterpart in Leonard Woolf's novel *The Wise Virgins, A Story of Words, Opinions, and a Few Emotions* (London: Edward Arnold, 1914). Camilla is also the name of a legendary maiden in the *Aeneid* (VII. 803, 11.539–828). A huntress brought up by her father who, to protect her from their tribal enemies, tied her to a javelin, dedicated her to Diana, and threw her across the Amasenus river, she has a clear affiliation with patrilineage. This affiliation, and its discontents, are also suggested by the nickname of Woolf's character, the name of the river identified with the university attended by generations of Stephen males. I am grateful to Jane Marcus for pointing these associations out to me.

8. Freud describes the daughter's shift from mother to father in his three essays on female sexuality: 'Some Psychical Consequences of the Anatomical Distinction Between the Sexes' (1925), 'Female Sexuality' (1931) and 'Femininity' (1933), conveniently collected in *Women and Analysis: Dialogues on Psychoanalytic Views of Feminity*, ed. Jean Strouse (New York: Grossman, 1974). For a reading of this shift in *Mrs Dalloway*, see Elizabeth Abel, 'Narrative Structure(s) and Female Development: The Case of *Mrs Dalloway*', in *The Voyage In: Fictions of Female Development*, ed. Elizabeth Abel, Marianne Hirsch and Elizabeth Langland (Hanover, NH: University Press of New England, 1983) pp. 161–85.

9. We see these fish only through Cam's eyes; even the bracketed section vi, which reports from an omniscient perspective the mutilation of a fish, interrupts her train of thought: 'They have no suffering there, she thought', ends section iv; 'They don't feel a thing there, Cam thought', opens section viii. The fact that in Woolf's original plan Mr Ramsay catches the fish underlines the helpless daughter's identification with them. For a different reading of the mutilated fish, see John Burt, 'Irreconcilable Habits of Thought *In A Room of One's Own* and *To the Lighthouse*', *ELH*, XLIX, no. 3 (Fall 1982) 889–905.

10. On the distinctive problems of this (inevitable) collusion, generated by women's '(ambiguously) non-hegemonic' relation to the dominant discourse, see Margaret Homans, ' "Her Very Own Howl": The Ambiguities of Representation in Recent Women's Fiction', *Signs: Journal of Women in Culture and Society*, IX, no.2 (Winter 1983) 186–205; and Rachel Blau DuPlessis and Members of Workshop 9, 'For the Etruscans: Sexual Difference and Artistic Production – the Debate over a Female Aesthetic', in *The Future of Difference*, ed. Hester Eisenstein and Alice Jardine (Boston, Mass.: G. K. Hall, 1980) pp. 128–56. On the question of Woolf's own evasion of anger in her literary theory and practice, see Elaine Showalter, 'Virginia Woolf and the Flight into

Androgyny', in *A Literature of their Own: British Women Novelists from Brontë to Lessing* (Princeton, NJ: Princeton University Press, 1977) pp. 263–97. Woolf's account in 'A Sketch of the Past' of her acquiescence to Thoby's tyranny provides an explicitly autobiographical parallel to Cam's relationship to James. See *MB*, p. 71.

11. For a detailed reading of this scene, see Abel, 'Narrative Structure(s) and Female Development' in *The Voyage In*.

12. Woolf's account of Cam's relationship to Mr Ramsay has deeply autobiographical roots. In *Virginia Woolf: A Biography* (New York: Harcourt Brace Jovanovich, 1972), Quentin Bell recounts the famous anecdote about the young Virginia's alleged preference for her father (p. 26). In 'Virginia Woolf and Leslie Stephen: History and Literary Revolution', *PMLA*, XCVI, no. 3 (May 1981) 351–62, Katherine C. Hill discusses Sir Leslie's appointment of Virginia as his literary heir and his insistence that she study *history* and *biography*. One letter that Hill cites from Leslie Stephen's correspondence with his wife is especially revealing: 'Yesterday I discussed George II with Ginia. She takes in a great deal and will really be an author in time; though I cannot make up my mind in what line. History will be a good thing for her to take up as I can give her some hints.' Hill points out that Woolf's earliest literary ambition was to write 'solid historical work', and documents the impact of Sir Leslie's historical orientation on Woolf's critical assumptions. Some direct lines of descent are apparent in Woolf's essay 'Hours in a Library', titled after her father's book, and in 'Leslie Stephen', which recounts Sir Leslie's unusual decision to allow 'a girl of fifteen the free run of a large and quite unexpurgated library' – precisely Cam's experience (*CDB*, p.74). Hill's commitment to redeeming Sir Leslie undervalues the other side of his literary influence on his daughter, however. This side is represented by Woolf's famous journal entry, 'His life would have entirely ended mine. What would have happened? No writing, no books – inconceivable' (entry for 28 Nov 1929, in *D*, III, 208). Cam's relationship to Mr Ramsay also powerfully reveals this aspect of paternal tyranny. For an illuminating account of the autobiographical sources of the father–daughter relationship in *To the Lighthouse*, see Louise A. DeSalvo, '1897: Virginia Woolf at Fifteen', in *Virginia Woolf: A Feminist Slant*, ed. Jane Marcus (Lincoln, Nebr.: University of Nebraska Press, 1983) pp. 78–108.

13. In the holograph version of the novel, a Mrs McLeod is visiting the cook when Cam brings Mrs Ramsay's message to her. Cam describes Mrs McLeod, who has come to get blankets for her dying mother, as 'a very old woman . . . in the kitchen who wore bugles'. That between the holograph and printed versions of the text Woolf eliminated Mrs McLeod's name and changed her characteristic traits from bugles and blankets to red cheeks and soup suggests an intention to point to her identity as Mrs McNab. See Virginia Woolf, *'To the Lighthouse': The*

*Original Holograph Draft*, transcribed and ed. Susan Dick (London: Hogarth Press, 1983; Toronto: University of Toronto, 1982) p. 94.

14. In both the holograph version of 'Time Passes' and the French translation published in *Commerce* in the winter of 1926, Mrs McNab plays a more central and heroic role than in the printed English text. A primitive, enduring, female life force analogous to the rusty pump in *Mrs Dalloway*, Mrs McNab articulates the text's commitment to heterogeneity: 'Walking the beach the mystic, the visionary, were possessed of intervals of comprehension perhaps. . . . The truth had been made known to them. But Mrs McNab was none of these. She was no skeleton lover, who voluntarily surrenders and makes abstract and reduces the multiplicity of the world to unity and its volume and anguish to one voice piping clear and sweet an unmistakable message' ('Time Passes', a translation of the French text, forthcoming in *Twentieth Century Literature*). For a study of Woolf's 'metaphor of the artist as charwoman to the world', see Jane Marcus, 'The Years as Greek Drama, Domestic Novel, and Götterdämmerung', *BNYPL*, LXXX, no.2 (Winter 1977) 276–301. Jane Marcus has also observed that by opening female communication across class lines, Cam anticipates Woolf's own role in her 'Introductory Letter' to *Life as We Have Known It, By Co-Operative Working Women*, ed. Margaret Llewelyn Davies (London: Hogarth Press, 1931).

15. Leon Edel, *Bloomsbury: A House of Lions* (New York: Avon Books, 1979) p.90.

16. This slippage occurs in Freudian theory as well. The compensation Freud claims women seek for their 'castration' blurs the distinction between daughter and mother: the daughter 'slips – along the lines of a symbolic equation, one might say – from the penis to the baby', from being the daughter of a father to being (if she is fortunate) the mother of a son, to being the inactive centre of the Oedipal triangle. See 'The Dissolution of the Oedipus Complex', *The Standard Edition of the Complete Works of Sigmund Freud*, XIX, trs. James Strachey (London: Hogarth Press, 1961) p. 179. For an exposition of Mrs Ramsay's median position between husband and son, see Abel, *Virginia Woolf and the Fictions of Psychoanalysis*.

17. As an account of women's silencing, the scene on the boat recurs in diverse guises throughout Woolf's corpus. For readings of the Philomel and Procne myth as Woolf's primary vehicle for disclosing the rape of the female tongue, see Jane Marcus, 'Liberty, Sorority, Misogyny', in *The Representation of Women in Fiction*, pp. 60–97, and ' "Taking the Bull by the Udders" ', Ch. 8 above; and Patricia Kleindienst Joplin, 'The Voice of the Shuttle is Ours', *Stanford Literature Review*, I, no.1 (Jan 1984) 175–86.

18. On Christianity's reduction of the Great Mother to the mother of God – that is, to a mere hinge between the Old Testament and the New – see Mary Daly, *Beyond God the Father: Toward a Philosophy of Women's*

*Liberation* (Boston, Mass.: Beacon Press, 1973) pp. 91–6. On Woolf's affinity with a mystical tradition that focuses on 'A Woman Clothed with the Sun', in contrast to a patriarchal God, see Madeline Moore, *The Short Season between Two Silences: The Mystical and the Political in the Works of Virginia Woolf* (Boston, Mass.: George Allen and Unwin, 1984) esp. pp. 27–31. See also Catherine F. Smith, '*Three Guineas*: Woolf's Prophecy', Ch. 12 below.

19. As the political struggles of the 1930s intensified, Antigone became Woolf's recurrent figure for the silenced female hero who resists masculine dictatorship. See, for example, *TG*, pp. 81, 141, 169–70; and *Y*, pp. 135–7. For discussions of Antigone's place in Woolf's politics and aesthetics, see the essays in *BNYPL*, LXXX, no.2 (Winter 1977).

20. Iconography in *To the Lighthouse* frequently superimposes Christian and psychoanalytic traditions. The subject of Lily's painting, the mother and child that to Mr Bankes are 'objects of universal veneration' (*TL*, p. 81), explicitly functions in both frames of reference. Cam's allusive incorporation of these traditions is not anomalous. On the trope of woman as the page awaiting the male pen, see Susan Gubar, ' "The Blank Page" and the Issues of Female Creativity', in *Writing and Sexual Difference*, ed. Elizabeth Abel (Chicago: University of Chicago Press, 1982) pp. 73–94. Cam's position as a fulcrum between two men is reinforced by another resonance of her name: 'a curved wedge, movable about an axis and used for forcing or clamping two pieces together' (*Webster's Third New International Dictionary*). I am grateful to Judith Kegan Gardiner for bringing this definition to my attention.

21. Jane Marcus has pointed out that at this moment Cam's writing arm is submerged and stimulated, which augurs well for Cam by associating her with Woolf's figure of the woman as a fisherwoman in *A Room of One's Own* and 'Professions for Women' (*DM*, pp.235–42).

22. The hole in Minta's stocking bears a clear resemblance to the metaphors Margaret Homans cites of women's 'nonrepresentational alternatives' to a linguistic tradition understood as male: for instance, the cry that concludes Toni Morrison's *Sula*, 'a fine cry – loud and long – . . . just circles and circles of sorrow', and the photograph of the concentric circles of the Sojourner's stump that concludes Alice Walker's *Meridian*. See Homans, ' "Her Very Own Howl" ', *Signs*, IX, no.2, 191–5. I am grateful to Catherine Gallagher for calling my attention to the importance of Minta's stocking.

23. The metaphor of jewels repeatedly celebrates female, especially generational, bonding in Woolf's texts. The brooch belonging to Minta's grandmother recalls the 'diamond, something infinitely precious' that emblematises Sally Seton's erotic gift to Clarissa Dalloway (*MD*, pp. 52–3). In *To the Lighthouse* the 'little ceremony of choosing jewels, which was gone through every night' ritualises Rose's relation to her mother, giving form to 'some deep, some buried, some quite speechless feeling

that one had for one's mother at Rose's age' *(TL*, pp.122–3). For a different account of jewels as metaphors of female identity, see Bonnie Zimmerman, ' "Radiant as a Diamond": George Eliot, Jewelry, and the Female Role', *Criticism*, XIX (1980) 212–22.

24. Minta effectively demonstrates the problem of women's language examined by French feminist theory, which argues that women's sexuality is repressed by a phallocentric discourse, and that a female writing would open up the process of signification to the plurality that constitutes female sexuality. For one account of this theory that focuses on metaphor as a mode of enunciation that operates by saying 'something else', see Mary Jacobus, 'The Question of Language: Men on Maxims and *The Mill on the Floss*', in *Writing and Sexual Difference*, pp. 37–52.

25. Luce Irigaray, 'When Our Lips Speak Together', trs. Carolyn Burke from *Ce sexe qui n'en est pas un*, in *Signs*, VI, no.1 (Autumn 1980) 69.

26. This is the paradigmatic nineteenth-century story that Sandra M. Gilbert and Susan Gubar massively document from a more textual point of view in *The Madwoman in the Attic: The Woman Writer and the Nineteenth-Century Literary Imagination* (New Haven, Conn.: Yale University Press, 1979).

27. In this version the character of Lily first appears as 'Miss Sophie Briscoe, a kindly and rosy lady who spent much of her life sketching'. She is a fifty-five year-old spinster with middle-class tastes, a dilettante. See *To the Lighthouse: The Original Holograph Draft*, p. 29. Only as Woolf determined to make Mrs Ramsay central did she transform and elaborate Lily into an adequate vehicle of a mother–daughter narrative. In his Gayley Lecture at the University of California at Berkeley, 1983, Alex Zwerdling pointed out Lily's tenuous status in the holograph draft of the text. I am indebted to him for this insight and for generously lending me his copy of the recently published draft.

# 10    This is the Room that Class Built: the Structures of Sex and Class in *Jacob's Room*[1]

### KATHLEEN DOBIE

The year of 1921 was a year of domestic turmoil for Virginia Woolf. In October, her two family servants, Lottie and Nelly, were sick with influenza. Then, in December, they were both in bed again with German measles. In addition to nursing the servants, Woolf was busy with such household chores as cleaning and painting the dining-room, baking bread, and scrubbing down the earth closet. Woolf writes in her diary on 11 December 1921,

> Yes, I ought to be doing the beds; but Leonard insists upon doing them himself. Perhaps that's Lottie on the stairs? Ought I go out & scold her for not staying in bed? Is the hot water on? Well, soon it will be time to go out and eat a plate of meat in the restaurant in the passage. In other words, both the servants have German measles, & for 3 days we have been servants instead of masters. (*D*, II, 148)

This domestic situation was one that would cause Woolf to ask her friend Roger Fry, 'Do other people go on like this, I sometimes wonder, or have we somehow . . . slipped the coil of civilization? I mean, we've jumped the lines' (*L*, II, 484, no.1196).

If Woolf 'jumped the lines' within her household, she used that experience to depict those social lines and their impassability within English society. For 1921 was also the year that Virginia Woolf completed her third novel, *Jacob's Room*, which provides an elaborate description of the breeding and education of a male child in England and ends abruptly with his death as a soldier in the First World War. Within this text, Woolf both describes a society which breeds its sons for patriotic death on the battlefield, and reveals the foundation of this society to be the relationship of

servants to masters. The dynamics of this servant–master relationship are explored by Woolf in terms of the relationship of the
lower classes to the upper, and the relationship of women to men.

*Jacob's Room* is a thorough examination of class and sex in
English society, in which the upper class feeds on the lower and, as
it feeds, the upper-class male grows stronger; while the upper-
class male sucks his power from the lower class, particularly the
lower-class woman, his female counterpart grows even more
fragile and sickly. This view of women in a hierarchical English
society is best delineated through particular characters and
relationships in *Jacob's Room* – through the complex pattern of
interrelationships of the Barfoots, Dickenses and Betty Flanders,
of the Pascoes and the Durrants.

The class of the female characters in *Jacob's Room* is, significantly, not always easy to ascertain. Betty Flanders is a widow with
three sons. Like lower-class women and men she is profoundly
dependent upon upper-class men. Through her association with
wealthy and well-connected men, her son Jacob is able to attend
Cambridge and her son Archer enters the Royal Navy. The fact
that her sons gain a firm foothold in the privileged class marks
Betty Flanders's experience as different from that of the working
classes.

Yet, Mrs Flanders is not herself upper-class; she merely
transfers that status from educated and influential men to her
sons. It becomes obvious, then, that the ability to claim a powerful
status and the power to confer status on another belongs to men.

Women are allowed to claim a lower-class status. They are
allowed working-class earnings and never any more than that.
There is no question in *Jacob's Room* which women belong to the
lower classes. And, unlike Mrs Flanders and Mrs Durrant, these
women are never defined in terms of their association with a man.
The occupations of the husbands of Betty Flanders and Mrs
Durrant are needed to define these two women, while Nanny,
Rebecca and Mrs Papworth are identified by their work alone.

Women are not allowed membership of the middle and upper
classes in their own right. They are wives of members of the
middle and upper classes. Without incomes of their own, these
wives of clergymen and merchants form an outside class. Their
position is equivalent to that of privileged servants living within
the master's home. They live in comfortable, even lavish,
surroundings with only one man, the master–husband, between

them and that society in which they will never be allowed more than a working-class wage; if, in fact, they will be allowed a wage at all.

It is actually through the depiction of Betty Flanders's ambiguous position that Woolf exposes the no-man's class these wives of clergymen and merchants live in. Because she is a widow and not a farmer's wife, or a banker's, one cannot pinpoint her class quickly. One is left examining her relationship to various men and finding the sum is greater than the parts. Her relationship with Captain Barfoot, a local politician, boosts her son into the elite preserve of Cambridge and, yet, she remains a woman alone with three sons and no income of her own. In Betty Flanders's life the effect of empowered men is clearly visible. So, too, is her essential inability to generate wealth. The social and economic position of widows and mistresses is merely the position of the wife, exposed and magnified.

Betty Flanders's situation does not serve as an illustration of men's kindness to helpless widows and their children. Her situation is, instead, one consequence of a societal dictate that women are not to have power of their own. Ellen Barfoot is the daughter of James Coppard, former mayor and town-benefactor. Though her father had money and political influence, it is not Ellen who benefits but her husband. Captain Barfoot steps into her father's shoes and becomes a town councillor. Again, power and its privileges are merely transferred by a woman from man to man. She is not allowed to exercise these privileges herself.

Like Betty Flanders, Mrs Durrant is a widow. But, unlike Betty, she is a wealthy widow: her husband was a banker. Mrs Durrant is the most authoritarian and mobile woman in *Jacob's Room* because she has money of her own and, unlike Ellen Barfoot, no man. So her money and her influence are not taken over by a husband. However, women alone with money make men nervous, so, in order to keep her money and influence, Mrs Durrant must give the appearance of planning to remarry. Throughout the novel, she is visibly courted by a number of old men.

In contrast, Captain Barfoot is clearly a powerful male, in charge of things, marching up through the political ranks in Scarborough. He has an invalid wife, is himself crippled by war, and visits Betty Flanders on Wednesdays. For twenty years, his wife knows, and the town approves the fact, that 'Wednesday was Captain Barfoot's day' (*JR*, p.24).

Why does the Captain visit the widow? What does Betty Flanders have that Ellen Barfoot doesn't? Milk, sex and sons. It is for these that Captain Barfoot goes to Betty Flanders and it is for these that the upper-class male preys on the lower-class woman and women such as Betty Flanders who are women alone without incomes of their own and are, thus, equally dependent on the 'largesse' and whims of men.

According to Woolf, milk is a resource compelling intrusion. In describing the small cottage of Mrs Pascoe, the white-haired farmer's wife, she writes, 'Although it would be possible to knock at the cottage door and ask for a glass of milk, it is only thirst that would compel the intrusion' (p. 52). Captain Barfoot is compelled to Betty Flanders's door by this same thirst. Betty's milk is both nourishment (of the ego, of the spirit) and an index of her capacity to mother. It is only with Betty that the Captain discusses his day at the office. He airs his political aspirations and can be seen, pipe comfortably in hand, sinking deeply into her soft and accepting armchair. Here, he is still called 'the Captain' – and after twenty years!

Mrs Flanders also offers sons and sexuality. Betty Flanders's figure ripens and enlarges. Ellen Barfoot, however, *issues* dull words 'like crumbs of dry biscuit' (p. 25). She herself 'bears' a tumour while Betty has borne three sons. This sterility of women protected by marriage or class and the fertility of the lower classes is echoed again and again in *Jacob's Room*.

Mrs Durrant's daughter, upper-class Clara, is a virgin, 'semi-transparent, pale' (p. 62). However, Florinda, who is without family and lives in cheap rooming houses, becomes pregnant. Mrs Papworth, a housemaid, is the mother of nine; Mrs Pascoe is viewed at the well and grows cabbages and flowers in stony ground; Mrs Dickens, the rheumatic wife of the Barfoots' manservant, also has children but she has had the bad luck of bearing daughters.

Though Mrs Dickens and Betty Flanders are of a lower class than Mrs Barfoot and both possess the fertility assigned by Woolf to lower-class women, Mrs Dicken's lot more closely resembles that of Mrs Barfoot. Both are crippled and both are left at home while their husbands journey out to other and more hospitable places. Mr Dickens, a man of the lower classes, finds that 'he had much in common with Mrs Barfoot' (p. 25), and, while he calls the Captain his master, he sees himself as 'in charge' of the Captain's wife. A woman's lot is not decided by class alone. Marriage is an important variable. Even though Ellen Barfoot is of a privileged and politically influential class, she is married, and so has no independence. As economic reality limits the world of the lower-class person, so this reality, in addition to custom and law, limits that of the married woman. She has no rights but is a commodity and, like the lower-class individual, is dependent upon the patronage and protection of those with more power. Both women and the lower classes may labour but may never possess. The lower class create monetary profit for the benefit of their employers; the married woman tends a house that belongs to her husband, labours with children who will bear her husband's name.

Both Mrs Barfoot and Mrs Dickens are imprisoned in this institution of marriage that Mrs Jarvis, the unhappy wife of a clergyman, calls a 'fortress'. As Betty Flanders roams around the Roman encampment, occasionally choosing to sit in the tumble-down fortress, so she uses the financial protection of Barfoot but otherwise wanders freely, coming late when the Captain visits, talking openly, at ease in his presence.

Compare this freedom to that of the other two women – Mrs Dickens is caged within a small room and, further, within a twisted, rheumatic body; Mrs Barfoot is 'civilization's prisoner' (p. 25), imprisoned within a bath chair and at the mercy of a man. Marriage cripples women as surely as the war has crippled the men. Dickens is 'in charge' of a woman, aiding the Captain 'at the front'. Even the title 'Captain' shows a domestic war, and Woolf's use of war terminology points to another war – a war, yes, between the sexes, that is just as cruel and frightening as any openly declared war fought 'over there'.

Compare Mrs Barfoot with Mrs Durrant, another upper-class woman, and the variable of marriage in class structure is brought into even further relief. Mrs Durrant, whose husband is dead, is seen travelling freely in coaches and even driving one herself. She attends the opera, throws parties, discusses politics with an endless stream of sociable old men. Ellen Barfoot, on the other hand, tastes not a single fruit of her family's wealth. She *knows* she will never see the town attractions and must rely on the words of an infinitely more mobile, lower-class man to bring her news of the world. Though her father's name is always associated with water – witness his gift of the town's drinking-fountain, his name 'painted upon municipal watering-carts' (p. 25) – she is dry, both in word and in womb.

Mrs Barfoot's imprisonment can be seen as a respected English tradition. After all, male heirs are everything, and, if one's wife can't or doesn't co-operate, then the man is expected to go elsewhere. Note the understanding and sympathy of the townsfolk who blame Ellen and say, 'A man likes to have a son – that we know' (p. 15). She is, of course, reminiscent of those unproductive queens of England, locked in the Tower, living out their days in high-class, 'comfortable' imprisonment.

There is a subtle twist to this arrangement in that Mrs Barfoot is fully aware of her husband's whereabouts on Wednesdays. Perhaps she prefers it this way? The townsfolk say 'She doesn't put herself out for no one' (p.15). Perhaps she doesn't enjoy the attentions of a lame and three-fingered man and her illness is a withdrawal from him – an eternal and momentous headache. Upper-class women may be only too glad to send their crippled husbands off to be 'serviced'. It is a privilege only they can afford.

In going to the lower classes for sex, men are following the pecking-order within larger English society. Men enshrine/ imprison their wives and fuck the women beneath them. It is quite clear that sex is equated with power when Dickens is described as not being without the 'feelings of a man' as he walks Mrs Barfoot around the esplanade. These are not sexual impulses that he feels but those of power: 'He, a man, was in charge of Mrs Barfoot, a woman' (p. 26).

Men relegate their sexuality to a lower sphere. How do they satisfy these 'base needs', then, without themselves becoming base? They remain above these needs by fulfilling them while maintaining their superiority within the class structure. If sex is a beastly need, the lower-class woman is a beast and man travels down through the social circle to 'fuck her'. He can then rise above the animal instincts by moving back up to his higher class. Thus, Jacob exits the bedroom *before* Florinda, looking both 'clear' and 'authoritative' (p. 92). Not only is he the first to leave the sexual encounter behind, but, 'cleared' of his animalistic desires, he is quick to recover his position of authority.

Jacob has a series of such affairs with lower-class women and prostitutes but he places upper-class Clara high on a ladder, haloed in beautiful light. He describes his dilemma thus: 'The body is harnessed to the brain. Beauty goes hand in hand with stupidity' (pp. 81–2). What he is saying is that what is beautiful or sexually attractive to him is that 'stupidity' or, rather, the uneducated female – the lower-class one. Jacob's problem is that sexuality is, in fact, an expression of power. He can 'express himself' to women of the lower class but Clara is above him on the social ladder. She must be seen as angel – honoured but not desired.

Jacob imagines that Florinda is chaste until he realises her 'stupidity'. In other words, Florinda is allowed her virginity until she is discovered to be of the lower classes. She literally can't afford chastity, unlike the wealthy Mrs Barfoot, who sends her husband down the street for sex. At the novel's close, Florinda is pregnant and she is compared to an animal, reinforcing the image of lower-class women as breeders.

*Both* upper- and lower-class women are defined in their breeding-capacities. While the lower-class women breed sons, the upper-class women 'nurse cancer' (p.104) and 'bear tumours'. Denied the realm of action, women have only their nurturing-capacities. Lacking children, they feed their diseases.

Two questions arise here. Why don't upper-class women have children in this novel? That is, what is the metaphorical significance of this for Woolf? And why, lacking children, must they turn their lives in on themselves? Clara Durrant's life sheds some light on both questions.

Clara has been brought up as upper-class women are in England – set on an endless round of parties, tied to a teapot, busily arranging her own 'doom', as Edwin Mallet, one of her suitors, names it: that of courtship and marriage. She is, as Jacob clearly sees her, 'a virgin chained to a rock' (p. 123). Totally uneducated sexually, Clara becomes hysterical and faints in the presence of the very sexual image of the pounding, riderless horse. When Jacob approaches her, when they are alone in the grape arbour, Clara flees, crying that he is 'too good – too good' (p. 63).

Clara does not know how to dismount the pedestal she has been placed on. Male society has split love into romantic and earthy halves and Clara has been given her place in the 'higher' sphere. Jacob's honourable intentions toward Clara are indeed 'too good' for her. *Her* sexuality has not been satisfied elsewhere and it cannot be satisfied elsewhere. *She* still has sexual desire but is not allowed to be a sensual being.

However, custom has decreed that Clara is not to be loved but to be married. She is given an endless round of social duties and so is never left alone with Jacob to let her feelings blossom naturally. The only time 'alone' with a potential mate granted in upper-class society is time arranged and chaperoned. Jimmy and Helen, a couple at Clara's party, for instance, are 'invariably separated' (p. 96) by the tea table and English custom. They are brought together at parties and counselled separately over breakfast and 'nothing happens'! It is no mistake that the two are compared to 'fine collie dogs' (p. 96), for, as in the breeding of pedigree dogs, the male and female are brought together for a short amount of time in a controlled environment in order to mate.

If all this wasn't cause enough for frigidity, there is the custom of arranging marriages with homosexual or older men. Clara suffers the attentions of her mother's friends Mr Bowlby and Mr Wortley, and is thought by the local matchmakers to be the right kind of woman for the homosexual Dick Bonamy. 'But sometimes it is precisely a woman like Clara that men of that temperament need . . .', one suggests (p. 154). 'A woman like Clara' is a woman who has had her sexuality refined right out of her and is too frightened and sexually in the dark to make any demands on Dick.

So why are so many upper-class marriages sexless and sterile? Woolf seems to point to the elevation of upper-class women into the non-corporeal realm, the lack of sexual education and the arrangement of marriage – both the impersonal manoeuvring and the disregard for the sexual feelings of young women. Even if Clara retained any sexual appetite, what chance for consummation with an old man such as Bowlby or a homosexual male?

How do these upper-class women deal with this situation? Some nurse illness. Miss Rosseter not only nurses her cancer: she paints. Miss Perry has hired five servants and a butler to help wind out the time that is 'issued to spinster ladies of wealth in long white ribbons' (p. 103). These long hours are the real burden of upper-class women. They are bred to a delicacy that renders them unfit for any activity more strenuous than lifting a teapot and are taught only the skills needed for an ornamental existence. While lower-class women deal with the upper-class males' sexuality and, often, even bear the children, upper-class women have been refined right out of existence. They have no societal purpose except carrying on the family name and family wealth when there is no male heir.

But they must be kept busy and in the dark about their useless state. Thus, the parties and arrangements of marriage over which there have been 'more coachmen's lives consumed, more hours of sound afternoon time vainly lavished than served to win us the battle of Waterloo' (p. 84). Again, this is the war at home in which Clara is surely one of its victims. Her typical day is described thus: 'Clara Durrant procured the stockings, played the sonata, filled the vases, fetched the pudding, left the cards, and when the great invention of paper flowers to swim in finger bowls was discovered, was one of those who most marvelled at their brief lives' (p. 84). She does not have the time really to excel or to learn anything well. After all, knowledge above the level of 'feminine accomplishment' might even raise her status and would certainly open her eyes to her condition. But she is kept busy enough. 'Italian remained a hidden art, and the piano always played the same sonata' (p. 84).

Clara, like Julia Eliot, who 'shared the love of her sex for the distressed; liked to visit death-beds' (p. 168), is kept occupied by caring for the ill and the poor. Denied the flesh-and-blood existence of her lower-class sisters, the upper-class woman becomes increasingly ghost-like and intimate with death and disease. Not only does this occupation (or preoccupation) fit her image as angel, now one of mercy, but it helps maintain the status quo. The nurturing, feminine quality is set to work bandaging the wounds of society without making any structural changes in society. Thus, Jimmy's body 'feeds crows in Flanders and Helen visits hospitals' (p. 97). The wrongs are never decried or righted; they are merely covered, temporarily succoured.

So, to society, Clara's life, as an upper-class female, is merely a problem of years to be disposed of. First, the upper-class female is engaged in marriage arrangements. Then, there is marriage. Clara's crying jag at Edwin Mallet's proposal reveals that she has no illusions about that particular fortress. And Woolf's use of the name Mallet for the male suitor clearly shows *his* courtship to be *her* destruction.

If marriage is a fortress peculiarly designed to keep the women in and let the men out, then class is equally peculiar in its structure. In *Jacob's Room*, the lower class is open to entry from the upper classes, who come down to plunder sex and sons. But the door clangs shut when the lower class tries to move out. Mrs Pascoe has a gate, but it only serves to keep *her* in. Mrs Durrant enters that gate to take Mrs Pascoe's nephew for coachboy just as the minister also entered to take Mrs Pascoe's son. Yet, as *they* leave, Mrs Pascoe is left inside the gate. She looks right and left as if to spot the next raiding-party.

Woolf tells us that the only thirst that would compel one to knock at Mrs Pascoe's door is the thirst for milk – that is, the need for nurturance, the need for sons. From the Betty Flanderses and the Mrs Pascoes, English society gets its future servants and soldiers. From the Florindas, it gets sex. And Mrs Papworth (Dick Bonamy's housekeeper) and Nanny mother the children of the upper class. They are the milk that has dried in the upper-class breast. And milk is what the upper classes are clamouring for: not only nurturance but also the biological ability to mother. The lower classes nurture the children of their oppressors and bear them sons.

By nurturing them, lower-class women keep the families of the wealthy intact. It is no accident that all the wealthy in *Jacob's Room* can trace their family lines and link distant relatives with ease. The lower-class family, on the other hand, is *not* intact. There is constant reference to illegitimate children. Florinda and Fanny must settle for 'godmothers', and Rebecca, the housemaid, is totally without family.

The contrast is sharply apparent in the example of Mrs Papworth and Mrs Pascoe. While Mrs Papworth muses on her own stillborn children, she is mothering Dick and Jacob. As Mrs Pascoe sits alone in her home, nephew and son long taken away, Mrs Durrant prepares for the homecoming of her son, Timothy.

The lower-class woman is appraised according to her service to the upper-class. Note the placement of the old blind woman with her illegitimate daughter against an English bank. *They* are the unvalued by-products of English society. In a social order where sons are needed to man the machine and females are needed to reproduce and satisfy sexual needs, old women are of no use, and the use of their daughters is limited.

Possession is definitely a question of economics. Men with enough money can afford to imprison their wives and keep their children. Mrs Pascoe is poor and is completely open to assault and plunder. Mrs Durrant enters the gate easily and it is her right to take what ever pleases. Mrs Pascoe is left with the doubtful defence of degrading her property in the hope that it will appear undesirable. Thus, she looks 'deprecatingly' (p. 55) at the bush that Mrs Durrant admires.

Not only are chastity and possession stated in economic terms:

Woolf discerns that communication has a price tag as well. Mrs Durrant talks incessantly, imperiously. Mrs Pascoe is silent throughout. Even when she is with her nephew Curnow, they are only allowed their dumb glances. Not only has the boy been taken by the Durrants, but communication across class lines is not allowed. This insures the status quo by nullifying any advantage the working class might glean from the migration of one of their own into an upper-class home.

In her silence, Mrs Pascoe is described as a miser who has 'hoarded her feelings within her own breast' (p. 54). Unlike the 'nimble witted' townsfolk, she has no method by which to express her feelings. It is her uneducated speech which shames and silences her. For Mrs Pascoe, education is a luxury. Thus, she is miserly with her emotions because she truly cannot *afford* to express them.

In her enforced silence, the lower-class woman can be named by others. Without communication, she cannot assert her self and her very being is co-opted by others for use in image-making.

The tourists see Mrs Pascoe as picturesquely lonely and the 'sophisticated people' set her up as the 'flesh and blood of life'. She becomes what is necessary for them. If the wealthy can see her as 'hard, wise and wholesome' (p. 54), they can deny the harsh loneliness of her life. The tourists also romanticise the loneliness by imagining her and the lament of the waves in winter. But Woolf reminds us that 'Even on a summer's day you can hear them murmuring' (p. 53).

This inability to assert the self affects all women. Mrs Durrant is certainly more potent than Mrs Pascoe. In the hierarchy of vision, *she* haughtily watches the tourists who watch and mythologise Mrs Pascoe. Yet, when Mrs Durrant reaches the hilltop after leaving Pascoe's cottage, she loses her vitality. Her drop into apathy at the very moment of its climax must be seen against Jacob's meditations on top of the Acropolis. Sitting there, *he* asks, 'Why not rule countries?' (p. 150). The view that inspires him, freezes her.

There is also within the text repeated reference to the lack of schooling and the inarticulateness of the women in Jacob's life. Clara writes like a child, Fanny is baffled by *Tom Jones* and 'the impediment between Florinda and her pen was something impassable' (p. 94). That expression and assertion of self wear a price tag is further demonstrated by Fanny's description of *Tom*

*Jones* as a mystic book that costs three and sixpence.

When women *do* write, they write letters that Woolf describes as both the unpublished art of women and 'the sheet that perishes' (p. 93). The message is clear: women work in what is perishable. Even when they can afford self-assertion, the results are fragile.

Assertion, then, is a male privilege and *Jacob's Room* shows that, pushed to its extreme, assertion becomes war. As Mrs Papworth correctly diagnoses, 'Book learning does it' (p. 102) and the boys' educated joust for words spills over into a very physical wrestling-match. This parallels the connection made by Woolf between a Cambridge education and war. Both war and the university are institutes of English society fuelled by the lives of unwitting English boys.

A Cambridge education is also a schooling for war. Before going to battle, Bonamy and Jacob shoot words at each other, such as 'objective', 'absolute', 'justice', and 'punishment'. This type of thinking runs in direct opposition to that of the women. With the exception of Mrs Durrant, whose mind is compared to a hawk's, the women's minds tend, like Mrs Pascoe's, to adhere to their 'solitary patch' (p. 56). Mrs Papworth muses over a sink of dirtied soap suds; Mrs Flanders ignores the view of moors and sea, looking up from her sewing only to suck on the thread. Her thoughts tangle round the boys, money, the present hour. They are pulled down to the task at hand, ever mindful of the body and its wants and needs. How opposed to masculine thought, which is freed from these bonds of necessity!

And who will clean the bloody mess exploded from educated, masculine thought? Woman, of all classes, will. Mrs Papworth will first sweep up the broken coffee pot and then she will raise another generation in the continuing 'conspiracy of hush and clean bottle' (p. 13).

Only the conspiracy that Woolf writes about between Betty and Rebecca is more than the act of nurturing life in a violent and technological society. It is the actual meeting of women across class lines. When women are divided into classes and then defined as opposites, the chances of their communicating are slim. But it is only through this meeting that they will become, as women, whole. Woolf suggests that, whenever two women come together, a conspiracy is taking place, for this is a revolutionary act that must be done in secret and against the whole of English society.

This division between women is clearly tied up with the division within man's psyche. There, the divorce of mind and body, sensuality and intellect, leads to war. Thus, the conspiracy of women is life-affirming in the most far-reaching way. To conspire means – literally – to breathe together. The hope held out in *Jacob's Room* is the endurance of human society. From the occasional and whispering 'breathing together' of Rebecca and Betty might rise the only possibility for the continued existence, the 'breathing together' of the human race.

## NOTE

1. This paper was originally written for a course on Virginia Woolf taught at Hunter college by Louise DeSalvo. I am indebted to Louise DeSalvo for first inspiring me to look at the issues of sex and class in literature. For her brilliance, her generous support and her editor's eye, I wish to thank her.

# 11 Woman's Sentence, Man's Sentencing: Linguistic Fantasies in Woolf and Joyce[1]

## SANDRA M. GILBERT

The words we seek hang close to the tree. We come at dawn and find them sweet beneath the leaf. (Virginia Woolf, *JR*, p. 93)

What can he do with these terrible dames? Poor Saint James Joyce. (James Joyce[2])

One of the most famous yet most opaque passages in *A Room of One's Own* appears in Chapter 4, when Virginia Woolf introduces her notoriously puzzling concept of 'a woman's sentence'. Observing that 'we think back through our mothers if we are women', she remarks that the early nineteenth century woman novelist found that 'there was no common sentence ready for her use', since the 'man's sentence' inherited by 'Thackeray and Dickens and Balzac' from 'Johnson, Gibbon and the rest' was as alien to her mind as 'the [hardened and set] older forms of literature' were to her imagination (*AROO*, p.79). The remark – like the literary history in which it is embedded – seems appealingly empirical. Those of us who wish to understand the relationship between genre and gender, Woolf seems to imply – even those who wish to examine the more ontological connection between sexuality and creativity – need merely analyse and classify linguistic structures. And yet in practical fact, though I may be here revealing my ignorance, I know of no serious research

208

into empirical linguistics that has actually disclosed what might be the special traits of 'a woman's sentence' or that has even revealed those secondary sexual characteristics which define Woolf's normative 'man's sentence'.

Indeed, we seem to come much closer to the heart of the matter when we abandon such projects altogether and study those theories about the 'hierarchized oppositions' of patriarchal language that have been so compellingly articulated by Hélène Cixous and other contemporary French feminists.[3] At the same time, however, where the moderate claims of empirical linguistics are both too moderate and too empirical to reveal the theoretical fullness Woolf's passage seems to promise, the words of Cixous and, say, Luce Irigaray often seem almost immoderately theoretical, even mystical, in their straining to imagine a female language *'which is constantly in the process of weaving itself, at the same time ceaselessly embracing words and yet casting them off to avoid becoming fixed, immobilized'*.[4] Woolf is (isn't she?) too practical for such imaginings to illuminate hers. She talks about architecture, food, greenery. And sentences, the primordial structures of speech, practical as paths through the college garden. But what, then, does she mean when she dreams of, yet doesn't define, 'a woman's sentence'?

Briefly, provisionally, I want to suggest here that Woolf used what was essentially a *fantasy* about a utopian linguistic structure – 'a woman's sentence' – to define (and perhaps disguise) her desire to revise *not woman's language but woman's relation to language.* In fact, I want to argue that when, toward the end of chapter 5 of *A Room of One's Own*, she elaborates upon her dream of the wonder-ful woman writer Mary Carmichael, who has 'broken the sequence' *'as a woman who has forgotten that she is a woman'* (emphasis added), Woolf at least half-consciously means that her fictive Mary Carmichael has triumphed not by creating a new sentence-as-grammatical-unit but by overturning the sentence-as-'definitive-judgement', the sentence-as-decree-or-interdiction, by which woman has been kept from feeling that she can be in full command of language. The utopian concept of woman's grammatical sentence is thus a sort of mask for the more practical idea of woman's legal sentence. Moreover, the ambiguity of the phrase 'woman's sentence' – for who is being sentenced?, and who is sentencing whom? – is a veil behind which Woolf may be imagining feats of epic prestidigitation: woman, who has been sentenced by man, will now sentence man; and woman, who has been sentenced to confinement and dispossession, to staying in the parlour of domesticity and keeping off the grass of culture, will now sentence herself to freedom and £500 a year. Finally, I want to suggest that in articulating this visionary revision of the 'common' English sentence – that is, the common patriarchal sentence – Woolf was working in a mode and with material that has been increasingly important since the turn-of-the-century feminist movement overturned a number of communal Victorian decrees about female sexuality. Especially in the twentieth century, I shall argue, women try to come to terms with the urgent need for female literary authority through fantasies about the possession and command of language, fantasies that articulate the slowly emerging idea of a mother tongue.

To illustrate my points about woman's relation to language and the woman writer's sense of her own need to claim authority by reclaiming her own command of language, I shall consider what seems to me to be a crucial, if subtextual, dialectic implicit in the linguistic fantasies of the two great twentieth-century artists whose centenaries we have lately celebrated: James Joyce and Virginia Woolf. Because, as Carolyn Heilbrun has rightly noted, 'in their separate ways [these two figures] divide the modern genius between them',[5] they offer striking paradigms of, on the one hand, the attempt of the masculinist modernist to perpetuate man's engrained habit of sentencing woman, and, on the other hand, the struggle of the feminist modernist to contrive a viable and vital sentence of her own.

Before turning to the key twentieth-century battle of the books in which Woolf and Joyce were consciously or unconsciously embroiled, however, I should like for a moment to consider the central imagery of an 1895 oil painting by George de Feure called *The Voice of Evil*, for in significant ways the enigmatic iconography of this work summarises and emblematises the literary–historical dilemma that both Woolf and Joyce, along with many of their contemporaries, had to confront.[6] Painted by a leading designer of 'L'Art Nouveau' who was also a sometime disciple of Baudelaire, *The Voice of Evil* seems at first to be little more than a misogynistic piece of exotic *erotica* which depends for its *frisson* on the assimilation of a male fantasy about lesbian desire into a *fin de siècle* pattern of flowers, jewels and vaguely-hinted-at orientalia. Pale and severe, a woman sits before a writing-table, facing a blank sheet of paper and a quill pen. She seems to have discarded her jewels (or is she about to put them on?) and a tall, Art Nouveau flower rises surrealistically to one side of her, framing her and (in its emblematising of forbidden desire) framing her up. In the background toward which her dreaming gaze is turned, a dark-skinned red-haired horned woman makes love to a pale woman who certainly seems to resemble this dreaming foreground woman. And both the woman in the fantasy scene and the woman in the no-less-fantastic reality are attending, it appears, to 'the voice of evil'.

The *voice* of evil: especially in the context I wish to create, that title is crucial. For Baudelairean as this erotic painting seems, it also makes an important statement about the dreaming woman – the potential artist – and her relation to language. By the turn of the century, European men were anxiously aware that a great change had taken place in Western culture; as Woolf notes, again in *A Room*, it was a change 'of greater importance than the Crusades or the Wars of the Roses'. Within the last hundred years, 'the middle class woman [had begun] to write'(*AROO*,p. 68), and thus to create a literature and a history of her own. But, not unnaturally, European men were unnerved by the formation of a female literary community along with the breaking of the sequence of silence that such a community implied. To male artists from James to Joyce, Eliot, Lawrence, and Hemingway, it must have seemed that the voice of woman's linguistic desire, like the speech of her mysteriously alien sexual desire, might be the voice of evil. De Feure, for instance, fears that, as the horned muse-woman in the dream whispers and touches her troubled rapt, desirous friend, the musing woman in the foreground may lean forward, sweep away the mind-forged manacles of her rings and bracelets, and begin to write her alien and autonomous woman's words. So he has elegantly indicted and sentenced her before she can indite the sentence of her own freedom.

De Feure's is, I think, a representative *fin de siècle* male fantasy about female speech, usefully condensed into a single graphic image, a narrative tableau, and it adumbrates many modernist male fantasies. As Susan Gubar and I have suggested elsewhere, it has affinities with James's hint in *The Bostonians* – dramatised through his depiction of the relationship between the ardent feminist Olive Chancellor and the inspirational speaker Verena Tarrant – that there is a perverse connection between female speech and lesbianism; it predicts, also, James's more Draconian assertion in the same novel, made through the lips of the struggling writer Basil Ransom, that 'The whole generation is womanized; the masculine tone is passing out of the world; it's a feminine, a nervous, hysterical, chattering, canting age . . . .'[7] Similarly, it looks forward to Lawrence's portrayals in *The Rainbow* of the reptilian schoolmistress of words Winifred Inger, and in *Women in Love* of the sinister miniaturist Gudrun Brangwen. In paradoxical ways, moreover, it explains the fantasies about female language which marked James Joyce's career, from his early creation of the linguistically näive Maria, whose pathetically platitudinous consciousness is rendered with such fine irony in 'Clay', to his mid-career characterisations of such linguistically lame or liquefied women as Gerty MacDowell and Molly Bloom, to his final construction of the 'hithering thithering' babble of Anna Livia Plurabelle.

'I hate intellectual women', Joyce once 'pointedly told Mary Colum', who was herself one of that species, and, despite (or perhaps because of) his famous dependence on such patronesses as Lady Gregory and Harriet Shaw Weaver, he generally evaded the threat of female 'high culture' posed by a thought-tormented figure such as de Feure's intellectual *femme fatale*. As Heilbrun observes, the 'one' voice he 'never heard and never could catch' was 'the voice of a woman passionately intellectual'.[8] To be sure, besides writing a rebelliously 'severe' review of her *Poets and Dreamers*, Joyce poked scathing fun at the woman he was sardonically to call 'Gregory of the Golden Mouth' and 'that old hake Gregory' in a deliberately ungrateful limerick:

> There was a kind lady called Gregory,
> Said 'Come to me, poets in beggary',
> 　　But found her imprudence
> 　　When thousands of students
> Cried 'All, we are in that category.'[9]

Moreover, in the Nighttown section of *Ulysses*, whose 'womancity' of a brothel is haunted by 'nudities very lesbic',[10] he explored Bloom's politically parodic nightmare of becoming a 'new womanly man' (p. 493) and thickened the atmosphere of comic horror with brief speeches by 'A Feminist' and 'A Virago'. Finally, in 'Penelope', he literally embedded and implicitly attacked Molly's memory of sleeping in the arms of a slightly older woman significantly called Hester Stanhope. Named after a notorious early-nineteenth-century eccentric – a traveller, an intellectual, a cross-dresser – this sapphic and sinister figure evidently introduced the young Marion Tweedy to a range of popular novels, including Mrs Henry Wood's best-selling *East Lynne*. Worse still, she apparently attempted, along with her husband, to seduce the girl, defining herself as a 'dog' and addressing Molly playfully as 'Doggerina' (pp. 755–6), as if to emphasise the connection between female depravity and the metamorphosis of god into dog that Stephen enacts during the Black Mass in 'Nighttown's' brothel.[11]

Despite such excursions into anti-(female) intellectual parody, however, Joyce for the most part defended himself against the female voice of evil – a voice which, as in *The Bostonians*, implies self-consciousness, intentionality, and a malevolent attempt to usurp male linguistic as well as sexual authority – by reconstituting the female and her voice as intellectually inferior, 'natural' (and hence amoral). 'Woman', he once told his brother Stanislaus, quoting a current Dublin witticism, 'is an animal that masturbates once a day, defecates once a week, menstruates once a month, and parturates once a year.'[12] The remark looks forward to his well-known plan for the linguistic structure of 'Penelope', whose 'four cardinal points' were to be 'the female breasts, arse, womb and cunt expressed by the words *because, bottom* (in all senses, bottom button, bottom of the class, bottom of the sea, bottom of his heart), *woman, yes*', as an expression of what he elsewhere called the 'pre-human' and 'post-human' qualities of the female earth and the earthy female.[13] In addition, though, the remark explains why, as Fritz Senn has observed, most of the women in *Ulysses*, from Miss Douce and Miss Kennedy to Gerty MacDowell and (even) Molly Bloom articulate their experience with what is in some sense the same naïveté, the same banality.[14]

Of course the barmaid–sirens Miss Douce and Miss Kennedy speak in vulgarly giggly shrieks, while Gerty thinks and dreams with a prissy gentility that Joyce himself described as a 'namby-pamby jammy marmalady drawersy ... style',[15] and Molly's imaginings (like those of her descendant Anna Livia Plurabelle) leak out in long sensuous unpunctuated streams of consciousness. Thus Gerty's language, like that of Maria in 'Clay', both appropriates and parodies what Joyce and many of his contem-

poraries saw as the debased style of a best-seller such as Maria
Cummins's *The Lamplighter,* one of the novels (produced by what
Hawthorne called a 'damned mob of scribbling women') which
most definitively established a threatening female centrality in the
literary market place, while Molly's embodies the male-
constructed female desire central to the pornographic imaginings
of her favourite author, Paul de Kock, whose 'nice name' she notes
and admires. In all cases, however, what marks these women's
words is a kind of essential emptiness, a vacancy which expresses
the world and the flesh to which Joyce sentences them.[16]

Molly's bewilderment at the high classical concept of 'metempsychosis' and her implicit metamorphosis of it into the babble of
'met him pike hoses' is one example of the parrot-like blankess
with which these characters respond to patriarchal ideas.
Another, and perhaps more poignant example is their inability to
name, and thus claim, even the functions of their own bodies, an
incapacity manifested in Gertie's speculation that 'that thing
must be coming on' (*Ulysses,* p. 361) and Molly's similar worry
about 'getting that thing like that every week' as well as her
bemusement by the word 'vagina' and her significant transformation of 'emissions' into 'omissions' (p. 770). But the 'omission' of
intellect such problems represent is probably best summarised by
Bloom's musicological meditations, in 'Sirens', first on the notion
that female singers 'can't manage men's intervals' and have a '*Gap*
in their voices too' (emphasis added); then on the 'chamber
music' of his wife's 'tinkling', which leads him to conclude that
'Empty vessels make most noise', then on the virgin female's
'Blank face' which needs to be written on like a 'page' for 'If not
what becomes of them?', and finally on the female body as a 'flute
alive' on which man must 'Blow gentle' or 'Loud' because 'Three
holes all women' (p. 285). Clearly, in endowing Bloom with such
speculations, Joyce is taking upon himself the Holy Office of
pronouncing that woman, both linguistically and biologically, is
wholly orifice. And it was against such a definition of the female
voice of 'omission' as well as against James's or de Feure's equally
problematic definitions of the female voice of 'evil' that a woman
writer such as Virginia Woolf had to contend, in a dialectic of the
sexes that centred on the crucial issue of woman's command of
language as against language's command of woman.

But, if the speculations of feminists started with the same
problem that haunted and harassed masculinists – what is the

nature and meaning of a woman's sentence? – they came, as one would expect, to very different conclusions. As Joyce himself observed in *Finnegans Wake*, while the father spins his 'yarns' to the son 'on the swishbarque waves', the mother might be 'spelling her yearns' to the daughter 'over cottage cake'.[17] And indeed, from the middle of the nineteenth century to our own era, such disparate women as Elizabeth Barrett Browning and Edith Wharton, Emily Dickinson and Gertrude Stein, HD and Hélène Cixous have formulated utopian fantasies whose visionary and revisionary 'yearns' imagine a way in which woman might sentence herself to a sentence of her own. As far back as the 1850s, after all, Elizabeth Barrett Browning created in *Aurora Leigh* a woman poet whose different script 'from female finger-tips burns blue' and yet 'strike[s] out' as strong as 'masculine white heat' to 'quicken' both male and female readers, while only a decade or so later Emily Dickinson, refusing either to publish or to punctuate in conventional ways, insisted on the 'different dawn' of unorthodox meters whose 'jingling', as she told Thomas Wentworth Higginson, 'cools my tramp'.[18]

Similarly, in our own century Edith Wharton wrote a sardonic short story called 'Xingu' about the disruption of a genteelly male-identified ladies' literary lunch by a woman who dreams up a fantasy of 'Xingu' which may be a religion, a river – or a landscape.[19] And of course, not long after Wharton recorded this disruption, Gertrude Stein notoriously ruptured the syntax of tradition, announcing that the 'sentence' of 'patriarchal poetry' which was 'sent once' might be left 'in pieces'; might, indeed, even be 'finished tomorrow' if women would agree 'Never to be what he said' but instead to 'Reject rejoice rejuvenate', for, when women lovers transcribe their own loving language, 'In the midst of writing there is merriment.'[20] Still more recently, too, as Susan Gubar has pointed out, HD spelled out visions of a female-centred world in which, through the 'echoing spell' of her alchemical art, old words mysteriously dissolve into new ones.[21] Most recently, moreover, Hélène Cixous, the author of the massive study *The Exile of James Joyce*, has re-Joyced in proposing a revisionary redefinition of Joyce's idea of femininity by deliberately and rebelliously Mollifying herself with the fantasy of a language written in the 'white ink' of woman's milky imagination.[22]

Not surprisingly, however, it is Virginia Woolf herself whose works most consistently meditate on both the problems and the possibilities of woman's language. For, even while she cried out for a new 'woman's sentence', decried the semi-literate sentences of such women as Florinda and Clara in *Jacob's Room* (*JR*, p. 91), and – as Elizabeth Abel has ably demonstrated – condensed a uniquely female vision of woman's psychic development into the 'gaps' and 'silences' of *Mrs Dalloway*, Woolf continually interpolated female linguistic 'yearns' into her revisionary narratives of women's histories. Seeking, in Jane Marcus's words, to untie 'the Mother Tongue, [to free] language from bondage to the fathers and [return] it to women', she produced, on the one hand, fantasies of linguistic alienation, and, on the other hand, fantasies of linguistic exhilaration, but as we shall see, these fantasies were significantly interdependent.[23]

To begin with, a profound sense of linguistic alienation pervades almost all Woolf's novels. In *The Voyage Out*, Rachel Vinrace – falling ill with an unnamed tropical disease whose symptoms notably recapitulate Woolf's own spells of madness – hears her lover reading the magisterial words of *Comus* and thinks that 'it was painful to listen to them; they sounded strange; they meant different things from what they usually meant (*VO*, p. 326). In *Mrs Dalloway*, a sky-writing aeroplane famously produces an ambiguous trail of smoke which might mean 'Glaxo', 'Kreemo', 'toffee' or 'KEY' (*MD*, p. 38). In *To the Lighthouse*, Lily Briscoe translates Mr Ramsay's metaphysically grammatical concern with 'subject and object and the nature of reality' into an enigmatic vision of a kitchen table suspended among the trees (*TL*, p. 38). In *The Years*, the sibylline Sara Pargiter insistently asks, 'What's "I"?' (*Y*, p. 140). In *The Waves*, Rhoda sees figures on a blackboard as 'white loops' through which she steps 'into emptiness alone' (*W*, p. 189). In *Between the Acts*, the tormented Miss La Trobe imagines 'words of one syllable' rising from mud, 'words without meaning – wonderful words' (*BA*, p. 212). All these Woolfian heroines, then, and sometimes even Woolf's heroes, experience themselves as excluded or dispossessed from the 'ordinary' sense of language, which becomes (as in Rhoda's and Woolf's own moments of existential crisis) a patriarchal puddle over which they cannot step.

At the same time, though, if we compare their feelings of exclusion with the mystified mouthings which manifest the linguistic exclusion of Joycean women from Maria to Gerty to Molly, we can see at once that there is a key difference between the alienation of Woolf's characters and that of Joyce's. For, while Joyce's heroines blankly accept or reject the male-defined linguistic systems into which they cannot really enter, Woolf's women consistently interrogate and evaluate such systems. From Lily's point of view, after all, the alphabet of Mr Ramsay's intellectual activity is as silly as Gertrude Stein thought the patriarchal sentence was; with Stein, indeed, Lily would no doubt wish to substitute the possibility that 'any letter is an alphabet' for the linguistic linearity of Mr Ramsay's paradigmatically patriarchal schemes.[24] Thus, where Joyce engenders his alienated women as empty vessels whose only alternative to echoing Babel is the resounding silence of Molly's slow sleepy lapse into the '*yes*' of unconsciousness or Anna Livia Plurabelle's long and increasingly incoherent drift into the 'moananoaning' of a primordial father's voice, Woolf consistently offers her heroines, and a few heroes, the amazing grace of fantastic new languages, tongues which sometimes redemptively, sometimes sardonically, incarnate extraordinary sense in ineffable shape, sound, syntax.

In *Night and Day*, for instance, Mrs Hilbery, the presumably eccentric daughter of a 'great poet', decides that 'Anne Hathaway had a way, among other things, of writing Shakespeare's sonnets' (*ND*, p. 305), while her daughter, Katherine, articulates her joy in life and love through enigmatic visions of 'algebraic symbols, pages all speckled with dots and dashes and twisted bars' (p. 300), and Katharine's suitor, Ralph Denham, conveys strong feelings via drawings of 'blots fringed with flames meant to represent – perhaps the entire universe' (p. 487). Similarly, in *Mrs Dalloway*, the shell-shocked Septimus expresses his strong feelings in pictographic 'writings' that consist of 'Diagrams, designs, little men and women brandishing sticks for arms, with wings – were they? – on their backs; circles traced round shillings and sixpences – the suns and stars . . .' (*MD*, pp.223–4), while an ancient woman 'opposite Regents Park Tube station' transforms what J. Hillis Miller thinks might be Richard Strauss's 'Aller Seelen' into a famously enigmatic song that goes 'ee um fah um so / foo swee too eem oo' (p. 122). Again, in *The Years* the two 'children of the caretaker' – descendants of the tube-station crone – provide a fitting climax to the Pargiter's family reunion with a shrill ditty that begins 'Etho passo tanno hai / Fai donk to tu do . . .' (*Y*, p. 429).

Throughout her *oeuvre*, moreover, Woolf insists that both the

alienation from language her books describe and the revision of
lexicography her books detail are frequently functions of the fact
that women's historical dispossession has allowed them to create a
linguistic culture not in opposition to nature but, instead, in
collaboration with nature. Among her most striking female
artists, for instance, are ancient singers such as the tube-station
crone in *Mrs Dalloway*, whose 'voice bubbling up without
direction' sounds like the voice of 'an ancient spring spouting from
the earth' (*MD*, p. 122), and the 'old blind woman' who, in *Jacob's
Room*, sits singing long past sunset outside 'the Union of London
and Smith's Bank . . . from the depths of her gay wild heart' (*JR*,
p. 67). Both figures, like Molly and Anna Livia Plurabelle, might
be said to incarnate the natural force of female desire. But where
the words of Molly and Anna Livia Plurabelle wash away into the
needs of a 'childman weary' or the tides of a 'cold mad feary
father', these earth mothers sing for the sake of their own songs,
chant to assert the authority of their own experience. Unlike
Bloom's Sirens, they have no 'gap' in their voices, and they
negotiate their own 'intervals' with triumphant precision to
articulate melodies whose meaning Woolf, at least, understands.

Less directly, but just as dramatically, the new hieroglyphs and
new histories of characters in other Woolf novels are also
facilitated by the co-authorship of nature. Lily's pictographic
inscription of her vision at the end of *To the Lighthouse*, for example
– itself an aesthetic revelation which involves a goddess-like
revision of nature (for in order to recapture Mrs Ramsay she
decides that she will 'move the tree' in her long-deferred painting)
– is made possible by the intervention of those two tuneful, if
elderly, muses Mrs McNab and Mrs Bast, who resurrect the
Ramsay's summer house in a 'rusty laborious birth' (*TL*, p. 210)
as they stoop, rise, groan, sing, slap and slam. In *Between the Acts*,
moreover, Miss La Trobe's play is repeatedly redeemed when, as
the Reverend G. S. Streatfield puts it, 'Nature takes her part' (*BA*,
p. 192), with the bellows of 'moon-eyed' cows providing a crucial
refrain at one point, and a 'sudden profuse' shower offering a
telling *dénouement* at another. And, perhaps most mystically and
most mysteriously, Bernard and Susan are vouchsafed a significantly linguistic vision in *The Waves*, when they escape from their
schoolroom and flee through the forest to discover the magically
fluent queendom of Elvedon, where a 'lady sits between . . . two
long windows, writing'. Against the 'Nightlessons' of *Finnegans
Wake*, where Shem and Shaun learn the old verities of patriarchal

history while their sister Issy studies the ancient subordinations of 'Granma's grammar', Woolf sets this epiphany of the new, delivered by and within a 'ringed wood': gazing at the regal scribbling woman of Elvedon, Bernard breathlessly affirms 'We are the first to come here. We are the discoverers of an unknown land' (*W*, p. 186).

Finally, then, it is no wonder that Woolf's most explicit *fantasy* – *Orlando* – is a book of revelation about a new manly woman whose life primarily articulates a fantasy about the passion and possessions of language. *Orlando* is of course a text complementary to *A Room of One's Own*, a narrative that tells the whole amazing history of Mary Carmichael, who here turns out to be not a poor young woman writing her first novel in a dingy bedsitting-room but an ageless man/woman who actually is Woolf's own lover–muse, writing and rewriting *the* poem of England about (and in a sense in collaboration with) a druidical oak tree on her own hereditary estate. Neither Shakespeare's sister nor anyone's niece, this woman *is* English letters, the commander and inheritor of her own language, and, interestingly enough, she has certain affinities with the sinister sapphist who introduced Joyce's Molly to literature and (implicitly) to 'lesbic' love. For, like the real Lady Hester Stanhope, whom Woolf memorialised as 'the last of the great English aristocrats' in a 1910 review of her biography, Orlando is a 'great English aristocrat' who sets 'sail for the East' in order to change her life and her sex as well as 'shake her fist at England' ('Lady Hester Stanhope', in *BP*, pp. 195–200).

But where both Joyce's depraved Hester and Woolf's more positively portrayed Lady Hester are in some sense defeated by their travels (Joyce's Hester becomes a 'dog', the real Lady Hester – at least as Woolf saw her – a half-mad 'Turkish gentleman'), Woolf's revisionary heroine gains in power, achieving redemption as she distances herself from both father land and mother tongue in order to repossess both on and in her own womanly terms. Finally, become definitively and powerfully female, this insouciantly authoritative author wires her husband a comically encoded comment on the meaning of literary achievement: '"Rattigan Glumphoboo", which summed it up precisely' (*O*, p. 282). By the end of the book that tells her story, moreover, when she speaks a word she has learned to speak its power, to evoke and invoke its essence: 'when she called him . . . "Bonthrop" it should signify to the reader that she was in a solitary mood' (p. 259). 'Then she called "Shelmerdine" and the word went shooting this

way and that way through the woods and struck him where he sat'
(p. 260). '"Marmaduke Bonthrop Shelmerdine!" she cried,
standing by the oak tree. The beautiful, glittering name fell out of
the sky like a steel blue feather' (p. 327).

Yet Orlando, like Woolf herself, speaks in ordinary sentences.
She is not duplicitous. Her words don't caress each other or weave
and unweave themselves like the spells of some erotic sorceress.
On the contrary, she speaks what Adrienne Rich has called 'the
oppressor's language'[25] and speaks it with Shakespearean ease
and exuberance. The fantasy Woolf enacts through her is thus a
definitive statement of the 'yearn' that I think underlies so many
nineteenth– and twentieth–century women's words, a fantasy of a
woman's sentence that clothes a fantasy of a woman who
sentences, a fantasy of woman's language that splits open to reveal
a fantasy of the possession and command of this language, this
language in which I am writing, our own language, our mother
tongue.

That this language might be a *mother* tongue, however, suggests
a further impetus for the kind of male fantasising I mentioned
earlier, discussing the worries of de Feure, James and Joyce about
women's entrance into the literary market place, for such a point
reminds us that, especially in the last century, male artists have
had to contend with their own linguistic anxieties through the
invention of fantasy languages not just for women but for
themselves – languages, that is, which did not (like the language of
Joyce's women) primarily diminish femaleness but principally
aggrandised maleness. Of course, as Walter Ong's recent account
of the relationship between the common *materna lingua* (or mother
tongue) and the 'civilised' *patrius sermo* (or father speech) implies,
European male writers have, since the high Middle Ages, been
integrally involved in a struggle into and with the vernacular
which has continually forced them to examine, usurp and
transform the daily speech of women and children so as to make it
into a suitable instrument for (cultivated) male art.[26] Clearly,
though, this defensive process has intensified in recent centuries.
As Ong also points out, the *patrii sermi* of Latin and Greek, along
with the agonistic processes of education in such 'classical'
tongues, functioned as linguistic signs of gender demarcation at
least until the middle or late nineteenth century. But by the time
such novelists as James and Joyce began to write, male *literati* had
to confront their own awareness that they shared not only the
market place but also the language of women, and (not surprisingly) they met this awareness with intensified fantasies about, and

mystifications of, what they as men could uniquely do with such a 'common language'.

From James to Pound, and Eliot to Joyce, therefore, male modernists attempted to achieve what Lawrence called 'the mastery that man must hold' by an occulting of language through the deliberate and elaborate deployment of allusions, puns, deconstructions and reconstructions, an occulting that would transform the mother tongue itself into a kind of 'father speech'. But Joyce in particular achieved such mastery, and he achieved it because, as Gertrude Stein put it, 'He is incomprehensible and anyone can understand him', because, that is, he had produced a book that retells the old patriarchal 'yarns' in a language that can be understood only through a diligent process of analysis analogous to that required by Greek and Latin classics such as the *Odyssey* and the *Aeneid*.[27] In other words, if I may risk a phrase in 'father speech', Joyce effected a 'metempsychosis' of the *patrius sermo*, for, even before *Finnegans Wake* condensed most European (and some oriental) tongues into a neologistic language whose Viconian loops form a perfect Möbius strip of what we might call patrilinguistic history, *Ulysses* reincarnated the patriarchal power of Homer's classical Greek in a new and equally difficult language which functioned (just as surely as Homer's had until the mid-nineteenth century) to occult and authenticate the high cultural 'yarns' of the father as against the commoner 'yearns' of the mother.

It would be impossible and most likely unnecessary to review all the verbal strategies by which Joyce performed this feat of legerdemain in which the mother tongue dissolved and resolved itself into a newly empowered 'father speech'. In any case, for our purposes here, the most striking example of his linguistic prestidigitation consists of the series of dazzling parodies he incorporates into the scene at the Dublin Lying-in Hospital, the section of *Ulysses* called 'The Oxen of the Sun', which records the conception, incubation and birth – 'Hoopsa Boyaboy Hoopsa' – of a magical-sounding boy through stylistic metamorphoses which seem to prove that (male) linguistic ontogeny recapitulates (male) linguistic phylogeny. The borning 'Boyaboy' *is* his language, a patriarchal word made flesh in the extended *patrius sermo* of history, and, though he is undoubtedly torn out of the prostrate *materna lingua* represented by silent Mrs Purefoy, he is victoriously flung (in a Carlylean birth passage) into 'God's air, the Allfather's air' because of the 'man's work' performed by his human father, Theodore Purefoy, who is defined as 'the remarkablest progenitor, barring none in this chaffering all including most farraginous chronicle' (*Ulysses*, p. 423).

Given the ferocity of such male defensiveness, where does this dialectic of linguistic fantasies leave the woman writer, with her desire for not just a room but a sentence of her own? For one thing, despite the apparently innovative rhetoric of the male avant-garde, it obviously leaves the woman as the only true exponent of the new. At one point in the 'Nighttown' of *Ulysses*, Bella/Bello, the horrifyingly manly Madame, scornfully describes Leopold Bloom as a 'Manx cat' (p. 541), threatening him with the literal and linguistic castration he and his creator so profoundly fear. But in a perhaps semi-consciously revisionary gesture, Woolf centrally places the same Manx cat in one of the early sections of *A Room of One's Own* (p. 11), as an emblem not of the deformed posterior of the old but of the reformative posture (and possibility) of the new. To be different – that is, to be female – is not to be castrated or deformed, says her fantasy of a woman's sentence; it is simply to be in command of oneself and one's words, as Miss La Trobe is, or as the lady of Elvedon is, that figure so iconographically like de Feure's woman and yet so ideologically unlike her.

As Carolyn Heilbrun has observed – speaking, indeed, of Woolf and Joyce – 'no critical display is more offensive than that which praises one author only by damning another',[28] and I hardly wish to defend Woolf's visionary fluency by damning Joyce's equally fluent visions. Yet if I could choose a linguistic system to inhabit (and I like to think that by thinking about authors such as Woolf and Joyce I can so choose) I should yearn not for Molly's bed but for Woolf's Elvedon. I should choose not the reiterated *yes* of the nursery where 'Granma's Grammar' is taught but the 'unknown land' where a new woman sits 'between . . . two long windows' writing the sentence of her own freedom.

## NOTES

1. This essay began as an attempt on my part to think through Woolf's famous concept of a 'woman's sentence', but it quickly evolved into part of a collaborative project with Susan Gubar. Portions of the present work appear in two collaborative papers – 'Sexual Linguistics: Gender, Language, Sexuality' and 'Ceremonies of the Alphabet: Female Grandmatologies and the Female Authorgraph'. 'Sexual Linguistics' has appeared in *New Literary History* (Spring 1985) and 'Ceremonies' has been published in the *New York Literary Forum* (Fall 1983). Besides being

grateful to *New Literary History* and to the *New York Literary Forum* for permission to reprint selected passages here, I am also deeply grateful for the inspiration and advice of Susan Gubar, though all failures in research, argumentation and formulation in the essay that follows are entirely my own.

2. James Joyce, 'As I was going to Joyce Saint James's', quoted in Richard Ellmann, *James Joyce*, rev. edn (New York: Oxford University Press, 1982) pp. 634–5.

3. See excerpt from Cixous, 'Sorties', in *New French Feminisms*, ed. Elaine Marks and Isabelle de Courtivron (Amherst: University of Massachusetts Press, 1980) pp. 90–1.

4. See excerpt from Irigaray, *Ce sexe qui n'en est pas un*, ibid., p. 103.

5. Carolyn Heilbrun, 'James Joyce and Virginia Woolf: Ariadne and the Labyrinth', in an unpublished paper. I am grateful to Carolyn Heilbrun for allowing me to quote from this essay.

6. *The Voice of Evil*, together with a brief discussion of its history and iconography, appears in *Femme Fatale: Images of Evil and Fascinating Women*, ed. Patrick Bade (New York: Mayflower, 1979) fig. 12 and p. 122.

7. Henry James, *The Bostonians*, ed. Alfred Habegger (Indianapolis: Bobbs-Merrill, 1976) p. 318.

8. Joyce's comment to Mary Colum is quoted in Ellmann, *James Joyce*, p. 529; Heilbrun, 'James Joyce and Virginia Woolf'. According to Ellmann, 'Joyce objected to Budgen that the female was attempting to usurp all the functions of the male except that which is biologically preempted, and even on that, he said, she was casting jealous, threatening eyes. "Women write books and paint pictures and compose and perform music. And there are some who have attained eminence in the field of scientific research"', he noted, adding defensively, 'But you have never heard of a woman who was the author of a complete philosophic system, and I don't think you ever will' (*James Joyce*, p. 634n).

9. Ibid., p. 112.

10. James Joyce, *Ulysses* (New York: Vintage, 1961) p. 570; subsequent citations will appear in the text. For a more detailed analysis of 'Nighttown' and especially of the sex changes it dramatises, see Sandra M. Gilbert, 'Costumes of the Mind: Transvestism as Metaphor in Modern Literature', *Critical Inquiry*, VII, no.2 (Winter 1980).

11. For further discussion of Joyce's Hester Stanhope, see Fr Robert Boyle, SJ, 'Penelope', in *James Joyce's Ulysses: Critical Essays*, ed. Clive Hart and David Hayman (Berkeley, Calif., and Los Angeles: University of California Press, 1974); Boyle observes that 'Joyce may have wished to bolster Molly's remark on women's inherent bitchiness, and thus he names this Hester after a really bitchy woman and has her call herself a dog and Molly doggerina in order to imply not only bitchiness but a further example of the god-dog contrast' (p. 411n).

12. Ellmann, *James Joyce*, p. 162.

13. *Selected Letters of James Joyce*, ed. Richard Ellmann (New York: Viking, 1975) pp. 285, 289.

14. Fritz Senn, 'Nausicaa', *Joyce's Ulysses: Critical Essays*. For further comment on this issue, see also Colin MacCabe, *James Joyce and the Revolution of the Word* (London: Macmillan, 1978) esp. pp. 125–6; and Anthony Burgess, *Joysprick: An Introduction to the Language of James Joyce* (New York: Harvest, 1973) esp. pp. 102–3.

15. Ellmann, *James Joyce*, p. 487.

16. Hawthorne's remark is quoted in Caroline Ticknor, *Hawthorne and his Publishers* (Boston, Mass.: Houghton Mifflin, 1913) p. 142; as Burgess observes (*Joysprick*, p. 103), Gerty has read Maria Cummins's sentimental bestseller *The Lamplighter* (1854), whose style is closely akin to that of her own stream of consciousness and whose heroine, significantly, is named *Gerty*. For a fuller analysis of woman's symbolic 'blankness', see Susan Gubar, '"The Blank Page" and the Issues of Female Creativity', *Critical Inquiry*, VIII, no.2 (Winter 1981).

17. James Joyce, *Finnegans Wake* (New York: Viking, 1939) p. 620.

18. Elizabeth Barrett Browning, *Aurora Leigh*, VII. 567–8; Emily Dickinson, 'There is a morn by men unseen' (Johnson no. 24), and letter to Thomas Wentworth Higginson.

19. Edith Wharton, 'Xingu', in *'Xingu' and Other Stories* (New York: Charles Scribners' Sons, 1916).

20. *The Yale Gertrude Stein*, ed. Richard Kostelanetz (New Haven, Conn.: Yale, 1980) pp. 123, 146, 121, 111, 54.

21. Susan Gubar, 'The Echoing Spell of HD's *Trilogy*', *Contemporary Literature*, XIX, no.2 (1979).

22. Hélène Cixous, 'The Laugh of the Medusa', in *New French Feminisms*, p. 251.

23. Elizabeth Abel, unpublished paper on *Mrs. Dalloway*. I am grateful to Elizabeth Abel for allowing me to quote from this essay. Jane Marcus, 'Thinking Back through our Mothers', *New Feminist Essays on Virginia Woolf*, ed. Marcus (London: Macmillan; Lincoln, Nebr.: University of Nebraska Press, 1981) p. 1, and see also pp. 2–4, 16–19.

24. See Lily's meditation on the 'alphabet' of Mr Ramsay's mind in *TL*, pp. 53–5; Stein remarks that 'Any letter is an alphabet' in 'Lifting Belly', *The Yale Gertrude Stein*, p. 48.

25. Adrienne Rich, 'The Burning of Paper instead of Children', in *Poems: Selected and New, 1950–1974* (New York: Norton, 1975) p. 151.

26. Walter Ong, *Fighting for Life* (Ithaca, NY: Cornell University Press, 1981), esp. pp. 36–7.

27. For Stein on Joyce, see Ellmann, *James Joyce*, p. 529; see also Woolf's remark about Joyce that 'A first-rate writer . . . respects writing too much to be tricky'.

28. Heilbrun, 'James Joyce and Virginia Woolf'.

# 12 *Three Guineas*: Virginia Woolf's Prophecy[1]

## CATHERINE F. SMITH

My university, like many others, is planning a core curriculum. It will begin with Great Books. Nationally, the Endowment for the Humanities, experiencing budget cuts, has established new guidelines for funding educational projects in the United States, with a focus on supporting main structures and mainstreams. 'We have been through a period of innovation in the seventies', said a director of the Endowment recently, 'and now in the eighties we must support traditional humanistic values. We need', he quoted Oliver Wendell Holmes, 'more education about the obvious and less embellishment of the obscure.'[2] Both my university and the Endowment, it seems, ask my help in preserving intellectual tradition, if not intellectual freedom. I am asked to make up reading-lists of Great Books, to teach them, to increase our library acquisitions of them.

I can't do it without *Three Guineas* on my reading lists. When the Endowment advocates 'teaching the obvious', a phrase from that book wells up in me, muttering, 'paid-for culture' (*TG*, p. 90). The gap appears. What I have to teach is the gap, and *Three Guineas*. I know from students' experience in a centenary seminar on Woolf in the spring of 1982, however, that *Three Guineas*, like all great books, is difficult to read. Therefore, I want a strategy for teaching it that makes it accessible and shows its powerful reinvention.

I find what I want by identifying the genre of *Three Guineas* as prophecy, a literary mode peculiar to cultural crisis. Like its biblical models, prophecy has continued to emerge in modern times of destruction and dislocation. It points away from immediate threats to expose corrupt underlying assumptions, symbols and institutions. It envisions new culture, new history, new self. And, after the New Testament, the prophet's own irradiated consciousness serves as the model for general human transformation.[3] Uses of prophecy in English literary history,

225

especially by the women writers whom I shall discuss later, provide a context for identifying this aspect of Woolf's art.

*A Room of One's Own* and *Three Guineas* are Woolf's prophecies. In them, she is a visionary teacher, appropriately didactic. Like a lecture in the new college for women, *Three Guineas* models a way of seeing, a structure of imagining to underlie new moral choice and political action. Woolf's collective solution to cultural crisis is fearless women. Her prophetic task in *Three Guineas*, therefore, is to create them as readers, to raise women's collective consciousness of strength. This purpose and this audience determine her rhetorical form. *Three Guineas* is phenomenological narrative presenting a model of the subject being talked about, the fearless asymmetry of the mind of an outsider.

War is prevented, Woolf argues, by changing the social mechanics, by making society equitable and just. Equity begins with empowering, not only enfranchising, women. Woolf's method of empowering is visionary. In *Three Guineas*, ideas are imaged and dramatised. Mental forms act. For example, 'Arthur's Education Fund' is 'a fact so solid that it cast a shadow over the entire landscape', a landscape fretted by women's suffrage, which keeps women moving about, trudging in processions, working in offices, speaking on street corners, countermarching the processions of educated men's sons, mounting the steps, passing in and out the doors, ascending the pulpits of the Bank, Parliament, St Paul's (*TG*, pp. 5, 14, 18).

The mental world of these phenomena is the mind of the narrator, a woman at a table, writing. She is answering a letter from an educated man requesting her help in preventing war and preserving culture and liberty. Between the narrator's 'I' and the man's 'you' moves the archetype who dramatises the narrator's perspectives, an educated man's daughter. Her vision darkened by a triple shadow – the shadow of Arthur's Education Fund, of the 'veil that St Paul still lays upon our eyes', and of the private house – she explores an imagined terrain of powerlessness, or feminine spiritual territory conditioned by lack of education, lack of property, and patriarchal religion at the root of both (pp. 5, 18, 62). From the threshold of the private house, or from distant vantages on bridges over the Thames or the Cam, she peers with a victim's distortion at a surreal male world. Like Alice in a looking-glass world of male power, she artlessly exposes violence and absurdity. Her perspective connects with Lily Briscoe's, watching Mr Ramsay charge and chant; with Rose Pargiter's after the encounter with the man at the pillarbox. Falling, Alice lets out the line of her imagination and finds it stopped by the wall of conditions.[4]

This spiritual traveller is the first form of the narrator's consciousness in *Three Guineas*. Her cracked innocence expresses dark, witty conceits: the weird processions, costumes, and rituals of the powerful male; the odour of domestic tyranny like a male cat's stink; the mulberry tree of property with its circling caterpillars, and – truly fallen women – rich ladies who endow the pleasures, causes and colleges of men.

But falling Alice, the educated man's daughter, is also potentially powerful, again like Rose Pargiter, 'a sturdy little girl . . . [who] grew enormously . . . & ate enormously . . . and was a . . . tomboy (*P*, p. 47). The talisman is in her purse,

> one bright new sixpence in whose light every thought, every sight, every action looked different. . . . In imagination perhaps we can see the educated man's daughter, as she issues from the shadow of the private house, and stands on the bridge which lies between the old world and the new, and asks, as she twirls the sacred coin in her hand, 'What shall I do with it? What shall I see with it?' Through that light everything she saw looked different. . . . The moon even . . . seemed to her a white sixpence, a chaste sixpence, . . . the sacred sixpence that she had earned with her own hands herself.   (*TG*, p. 16)

If guineas are old moons, part of a waning world, they birth a chaste, poor new one, rich with comic vision: dances and songs; a house with no shadows; psychometers to measure the atmosphere of possibility; a glowing womanshape in the evening sky, signifying 'Rats' in radiant hail to mark living conditions in women's colleges, and – truly redeemed women – rich ladies who endow the pleasures, causes, and colleges of women. In this new world, born-again daughters of uneducated mothers and grandmothers 'dance round the new house, the poor house . . . [they] sing "We have done with war! We have done with tyranny!" And their mothers will laugh from their graves, "It was for this that we suffered obloquy and contempt! Light up the windows of the new house, daughters! Let them blaze!"' (p. 83).[5]

*Three Guineas*, like *To the Lighthouse*, is in three parts. Part I

uncovers contradictions of being female in a male world. Part II
envisions the community of women and ends in the apocalypse of
the daughters' dance. Part III reveals the means to a new world
hidden, though scattered, in the current one. The Outsiders'
Society, like Lily Briscoe's perspective in the third part of *To the
Lighthouse*, unifies phenomena. More precisely, with its disciplines
of poverty, chastity, derision, and freedom from unreal loyalties,
the Society universalises and affirms particular experiences of
letting-go, of detaching from male worlds in order to see
differently, to think differently. Radiant, separate, the Outsiders'
Society is the full revelation of the narrator's consciousness. It is
another kind of mind, granite and rainbow. It is irradiated
feminine consciousness, or the visionary substructure of rational
feminist politics.

The vision utilises epistolary form. Addressed to an identified
audience, the concerned, educated man, *Three Guineas* reaches
through his partial awareness to the women in his shadow. The
narrator answers two letters from women before completing her
reply to him. Like moons pulling the tide of her argument, like
collaborators, the women she answers and the women they
represent are the narrator's real audience, receivers of her verbal
propositions endowing imagination, her visionary forms
dramatic.

An implied feminine audience in *Three Guineas* perhaps includes
Woolf's mentor in feminine mystical political tradition, Caroline
Emelia Stephen.[6] No figure in Woolf's early life did more to shape
her vocation or more haunted her imagination than her aunt, the
Quaker theologian. By 1904, when Virginia visited Caroline for
an extended period following Leslie Stephen's death, her father's
sister was recognised as the revitaliser of English Quakerism, a
popular speaker (especially to the young at Cambridge), the
author of *Quaker Strongholds* and, later, *The Light Arising: Thoughts
on the Central Radiance*, and *The Vision of Faith*, a collection of essays.
Woolf's ideas of mental chastity, celibacy, and the language of the
inner light, as well as her life-long model of the woman writer – a
woman at a table, alone in a room, writing – might all be traced to
her aunt. In a 1906 letter to Madge Vaughan, Virginia acknowledges Caroline's primitive power.

I have just come back from a Sunday with my Quaker aunt . . .
we talked for some nine hours; and she poured forth all her

spiritual experiences, and then descended and became a very wise and witty old lady. I never knew anyone with such a collection of stories – which all have some twist in them – natural and supernatural. All her life she has been listening to inner voices, and talking with spirits, and she is like a person who sees ghosts, or rather disembodied souls, instead of bodies. She now sits in her garden, surrounded with roses, in voluminous shawls and draperies, and accumulates and pours forth wisdom on all subjects. All the young Quakers go and see her, and she is a kind of modern prophetess. I think you would like her very much; and her grey dressing gowns.    (*L*, I, 229).

Stephen's narrative skill, particularly concerning spiritual experiences, and her 'rational mysticism' discussed in her books on religious experience may have as much to do with the poetics of *Three Guineas* as they have with those of *The Waves*. (Woolf was concluding *The Waves* in 1931 when the idea occurred that eventually became *The Pargiters: A Novel–Essay, Three Guineas* and *The Years*.) The archetypal narrator of *Three Guineas*, the giant female 'I', the woman at a table writing whose consciousness is a new kind of mind, is perhaps Woolf's elegy for her aunt, reinventing her as a fearless woman. A prophecy, *Three Guineas*, is the spiritual autobiography of a feminist, correcting an inherited vision.[7]

Reinvention and correction of her aunt's vision were demanded by Woolf's disagreement with Caroline Stephen's social proposals for women. In 1871, drawing conclusions from her social work prior to her Quaker ministry, Stephen published *The Service of the Poor*, arguing for professionalising nursing and the social work done by economically independent, unmarried women. However, she also argued that women's best political influence was indirect, working through family and class ties to male legislators and jurists with actual power to aid the poor. In both *A Room of One's Own* and *Three Guineas*, Woolf vigorously objects that women *are* the poor, regardless of their fathers' or brothers' property. She vigorously refuses to advocate women's indirect influence, regardless, again, of their male relatives' positions of power. Lengthy attacks in *Three Guineas* on indirect influence as legitimate political action – at times, it seems to be a book primarily about the nature of women's influence – suggest not only Woolf's conscious disagreement with her aunt's Victorian compromise, but also perhaps also an unconscious struggle with Stephen's imaginative influence on her. These substantive disagreements are evidence of *Three Guineas*' conceptual kinship with Stephens's *The Service of the Poor*, just as Woolf's visionary form reflects Stephens's *The Light Arising*.

I noted earlier that other English women writers' uses of prophecy help to identify Woolf's. I want to turn now from critical analysis of her prophecy to its historical precedents. Specifically, I shall discuss English women prophets of the seventeenth century, particularly Jane Lead. These women illuminate Virginia Woolf's imagination, and she theirs.

As far as I know, Woolf did not know about Jane Lead, though she could have easily imagined her.[8] Passages on women prophets near the end of *Three Guineas* suggest that Woolf was at least aware of such women. Born to Hamond and Mary Calthorpe Ward in 1623, descended through both parents from generations of landed families in Suffolk and Norfolk, Jane Ward was one of twelve children growing up in the prelude to civil war. She lived in a manor house much like Blo' Norton Hall, the setting for an early short story by Woolf, in the same landscape, the flat, misty fens and bogs of East Anglia.[9] In the medieval period, the region was extraordinary for its number of religious houses and its visionaries, such as Julian of Norwich. Wars, religious and political, English or continental, passed frequently through sixteenth and seventeenth century East Anglia as a coastal region close to Europe, much like Woolf's Sussex in the 1940s.

The most significant event of Jane Ward's young life, by her own account, occurred when she was sixteen and dancing in the Christmas festivities at her parents' hall. Suddenly, she recorded, she was overcome by 'a warm, sensitive sadness . . . and softly I perceived the words: Withdraw from all this: I know of another dance I shall lead you to, for this is vanity.'[10] The depression that followed lasted three years, during which she scoured public and private religious meetings in Norfolk and Civil-War London for resolution to her spiritual crisis. Relief came, eventually, in another ecstatic moment. She determined to be a bride of Christ, saying she found earthly marriages repulsive.[11] However, perhaps for economic reasons, in 1644 she married a cousin, William Lead, and lived an apparently happy life as a London merchant's wife with four daughters, though in a city and country torn by revolution. Her extraordinary inner life continued on its course. When in 1663 she joined a private, non-conformist group gathered around Dr John Pordage in London, she was already recognised as a spiritual explorer whose 'Gift of Revelation y Dr gave great regard to and attended upon'.[12]

In 1670, William Lead died at forty-nine, leaving his widow at forty-seven, two surviving daughters, and no will. Thus, inheritance was blocked. Jane Lead was made administrator of the estate, but her legal powers were meaningless. As she recalled in an autobiography written nearly thirty years later,

> since he had entrusted most of his worldly possessions to a factor overseas, and they were received by the same, the widow and orphans were stripped of their rights. He did not relinquish anything. Due to these circumstances, I was left to dire and extreme want, which forced me even more to place my assets in Heaven. I determined to remain a Widow in God . . . .[13]

Her decision was shaped by the second most significant event in Jane Lead's life. While walking in a country place in April 1670, two months after her husband died, she envisioned 'an overshadowing bright Cloud and in the midst of it the Figure of a Woman'. Three days later a luminous reappearance gently commanded, 'Behold me as thy Mother.' Six days later, in London, came the promise, 'I shall now cease to appear in a Visible Figure unto thee, but I will not fail to transfigure my self in thy mind; and there open the Spring of Wisdom and Understanding.'[14] The relationship continued over thirty-four years: 'I have learned to observe her Times and Seasons, I witness her opening as in the Twinkling of an Eye, a pure, bright, subtil, swift, Spirit, a working motion, a Circling Fire, a penetrating Oil.'[15] Between 1674 and 1681, with John Pordage, Lead directed a congregation, experienced sympathetic visions, studied, and wrote extended commentary on the theology of the sixteenth-century Protestant mystic Jacob Boehme. She also wrote a journal of visions nearly 2000 pages long.

After Pordage's death when she was fifty-eight, Lead continued writing and publishing alone until, around 1695, when she was seventy-two and partially blind, a new, younger group of enthusiasts formed the Philadelphian Society under her spiritual guidance and began publishing her remaining work, including her journal. She died in 1704, continuing in vision, at eighty-one.

Jane Lead was described by her contemporaries as a prophet. She herself was ambivalent about the title, believing that her own 'inward Deep' as she called it, was but a Type, and her exploration only an example. Her aim was to stimulate such exploration universally. 'Everyone a prophet' was her message, supported by the mystic theology she studied and explicated. Apart from her self-perception, however, Lead can be grouped with the large number of visionaries and prophets, including some Quakers, who were prominently part of the history of England's social, economic and cultural crisis in the seventeenth century. She shared those prophets' sense of crisis, their sense of election as 'weaker vessels' chosen to reveal the meaning of the times, and, with other women preachers, she shared public persecution.[16] She and these others are a neglected, diverse, early group of women verbal artists in England, the link that Virginia Woolf wanted to find in women's literary history between the Renaissance poets and the eighteenth-century novelists. Their writing, indebted to scripture, oral tradition and their own dreams, expands the origins of modern prose narrative.[17]

Lead's prophecy was not primarily concerned with immediate events. She did not foretell. Rather, she interpreted the times. She was both ecstatic and learned, self-educated both in the spirit and in scripture. She particularly studied the Book of Revelation and its interpretative scholarship, to which she contributed.[18] A contemporary of Milton's, she responded to many of the same events and intellectual sources as he. However, her revision of those sources differs markedly from Milton's. For example, redeeming or 'raising' Eve, as she says, was her aim in retelling the creation story.[19]

Her exegesis of biblical metaphor, in fact, takes her out of Milton's line of vision and places her in Virginia Woolf's. Biblical metaphor, conditioned by her own experience as a woman in seventeenth-century England, gave Jane Lead a tradition of symbolism, but more significantly, a voice remarkably like the narrator's in *Three Guineas*. Beth Nelson, in describing another seventeenth-century prophet, Lady Eleanor Davies, remarks on her 'simultaneous exegesis of the merged and single text of Scripture and her own history'.[20] The comment captures Lead and Woolf as well. Woolf's extended footnotes in *Three Guineas* arguing against Paul on women, her running references to patriarchal religion, and her lineal tracing of women writers back to ancient prophetesses – all give the pamphlet *Three Guineas* a strong tonal resemblance to seventeenth-century tracts by Lead and her contemporaries.

The most striking common element in this pamphlet literature of feminist prophecy from Lead to Woolf is an emphasis on economic fact and its related vision. Jane Lead began life as the daughter of an educated, propertied man. In principle, she was part of his property under coverture. Next she became a middle-class wife, part of her husband's property. Then she was an impoverished widow caught in a common situation for seventeenth-century English women, most of whom married, were widowed (often more than once) and frequently did not receive the widow's annuity. Lead expressed her changes in circumstances by adapting traditional biblical metaphors of the feminine – the soul as Christ's Bride and the redeemed spirit as the Woman Clothed with the Sun. Recall her personal economic history as you listen to these quotations from her journal, *A Fountain of Gardens*, and two commentaries, *A Tree of Faith* and *The Enochian Walks with God, Found out by a Spiritual Traveler*:

Being Dead wherein we were held fast, we should serve in the Newness of Spirit; as being discharged from the Law of the first Husband, to which we were married, after the Law of a Carnal Command: Whence we are now free to be Married unto him that is raised from the Dead, and so shall become the Lamb's Wife, jointured unto all the Lands and Possessions that he hath. The Eternal Revenues are belonging to her, whether Invisible or Visible: all Power in Heaven and Earth is committed her . . . whether it be Gifts of Prophecy, or of Revelation, or of Manifestation, or of Discerning of Spirits: or that high Tongue of the Learned, which only speaks from Wisdom's Breath.

At which Opening, my Spirit even failed within me, as desponding ever to get rid of my First Husband . . . that first Husband who so long hindered my Marriage with the Lamb.[21]

Believe that Christ will settle upon this Espoused Bride all that is his: that she shall have a mutual Interest with him, in what the Father hath put into his Hand, which is all Power, and

Wisdom to manage that Power; which reacheth to a dominion, and over all created Beings, and things, whatever: herein for a certainty she will be put into a Joint-possession, with the Lord her bridegroom as her Propriety.[22]

Having given an Account of what the Spirit of Christ hath given in, as to what is expected and required for the accomplishing such as are to make up for an Espousal Bride to him . . . it is absolutely needful that we should be furnished out with such Powers and Gifts, as may qualify for such a High Marriage-Union, with the First Begotten-Son and Heir of the High God, who doth most willingly give . . . that so a Stock of Spiritual Goods being taken in, may be to support, and carry on the Heavenly Calling withal; which if found diligent in, may mount to a mighty Encrease, for the making of a Dowry so great and large, as may somewhat agree with him, with whom we are to be matched unto.[23]

In these selections, male primogeniture, coverture and dower rights – the three legal principles governing women's economic status in the seventeenth century – are revised. Lead improves the Bride's status at every point. The Bride is freed of carnal obligations. The Groom is the most advantageous mate, God's 'First Begotten-Son and Heir', who can offer an undivided estate. The Bride is assured of a large dowry that she administers. Though Christ is the proprietary husband, it is the bride's 'Business and Employment' to manage her own estate. With equal contribution to the union, and with autonomous management of their separate investments, the partners have 'mutual Interest' in their merged assets. Completing the analogy, Christ's death entitles the Bride's soul to 'a certainty' of inheriting 'all the lands and possessions that he hath', not merely the promise of a widow's portion.

Lead's imaginative improvements in marital economy can be viewed in the context of women's worsening position in the actual economy, particularly in relation to marriage. Dowries and jointures, which are prominent in her metaphor, illustrate continuing erosion of women's status beginning in the late Renaissance.[24] After the twelfth century, dowries were usually cash, rather than land. They were also usually the daughter's only inheritance from the parental estate. As pressure to find sources of investment money increased in the market economy of the seventeenth century, dowries as a form of capital inflated extraordinarily.[25] Marriageable daughters became financial liabilities, exacerbated by a higher percentage of females than males in the population.[26] In addition, traditional dower rights changed. Replacing the widow's life interest in a third or more of the conjugal estate was the jointure, a contract made at the time of marriage to establish the widow's annuity in ratio to the size of the dowry. Investment of the dowry was expected to yield the annuity. As dowries inflated, the ratio increased, deflating the jointure. Moreover, as control over capital passed increasingly to males through successions of statutes defining the economic implications of coverture and primogeniture, widows were less likely to receive the jointure at all.[27] Even though entitled to the annuity, widows had to be assigned it within forty days of the husband's death by the heir or guardian of the estate, leaving them vulnerable to conflicting interests and claims. The jointure might be reduced or forfeited if the widow remarried or 'committed incontinency'. Men inheriting their wives' property were not limited in either of these ways.[28] Two kinds of public records show that jointures often were not received: calendars of litigation in equity courts and the case literature of astrologers reporting visits by both wives and widows to learn when or if a jointure would be awarded.[29]

As already noted, Jane Lead knew these general circumstances at first hand. The Bride of Christ expressed her experience. But the Woman Clothed with the Sun transformed it. Taken from Revelation, this metaphor had a long history in mystical tradition as an image for the Wisdom of God. Lead sometimes called her 'the Wonder Woman'.

> This is the great Wonder to come forth, a Woman Clothed with the Sun . . . with the Globe of this world under her feet . . . with a Crown beset with stars, plainly declaring that to her is given the Command and Power . . . to create and generate spirits in her own express likeness.[30]

Lead says in her journal that the bright Woman first appeared in a vision two months after William Lead's death in 1670. Its outlines in the economics of disinheritance and displacement were clear from the beginning.

She said on this wise, That I was greatly beloved, and she would be my Mother and so should I own her and call her, who would now be to me as Rebecca was to Jacob, to contrive and put me in a way how I should obtain the Birth-right-Blessing . . . .

Know then (saith the same Voice) thou shalt supplant thy brother Esau, who according to the Figure, is a cunning Hunter in the out-birth and field of Nature. While he with his subtility is seeking it abroad, in the wild Properties of the External Region, I will now help thee to it near at Hand, even in thy own enclosed Ground.[31]

In Lead's conjunction of the two metaphors, it is the mother wit of Wisdom, and not God the Father, who properly endows the soul to be Christ's bride.

I resolve to make my Application, as not to be put off with anything less than the Kingdom and Reigning-Power of the Holy Ghost . . . and . . . to grasp in with Love-violence, this my fair, wise, rich and noble Bride, well knowing her Dowry was so great it would . . . set me free.[32]

Jane Lead significantly adapts her Wisdom figure to include concern for the property aspects of marriage.[33] These were mortal necessities for seventeenth-century women. As elaborated by male contemporaries such as Lead's close associate John Pordage and her two followers Francis Lee and Richard Roach, Wisdom is more an eroticised, alchemical feminine image for passive human reason stimulated by active, masculine divine will. Their usage closely follows that of Jacob Boehme, the Protestant mystic who influenced Lead and her circle. Jane Lead's Wisdom, on the other hand, draws on older forms of the ideal in Judaeo-Christian mysticism – proverbs, or practical rules for living in a paradoxical world – combined with the Wisdom tradition's final theological expression in Revelation as irradiated consciousness.[34] Granite and rainbow.

With this powerful, doubled conception of Wisdom, Jane Lead built a coherent philosophical and emotional understanding of paradoxical reality in which a feminine ideal might be Bride of Christ while female people were essentially powerless. Lead analysed her needs and demonstrated one form of female emancipation: wed the feminine self. In her resolute celibacy, she did.

Jane Lead, Caroline Emelia Stephen and Virginia Woolf are prophets by analogy, three women in three centuries of English culture who arrived at similar visions. But my point is not to frame Woolf in a historical comparison. She differs from her two predecessors in one important actuality: they were both preachers, a role she avoided. My point is to show a line of women's vision – I'm tempted to call it a golden thread – that continues to evoke vision in readers. Students in our centenary seminar reported desire, excitement, and courage as results of reading *Three Guineas*, even though they found it difficult. Obscurity in the pronouncement and illumination in the hearer are characteristic of prophetic utterance. Or, perhaps more accurately, because it removes this discussion from Judaeo-Christian tradition – not a comfortable framework for discussing Woolf – these qualities characterise shamanic utterance. The shaman, according to Mircea Eliade, is elected, often involuntarily, by out-of-body experience to become a technician of ecstasy and bearer of collective vision.[35] Virginia Woolf, a technician of language, apprentice to a technician of ecstasy in Caroline Stephen, might be considered a shaman. In 'Anon', her unfinished history of English literature, she observed that writers speaking to their readers, like the anonymous singers and their audiences who came before, stir the deepest human instincts. 'The passion with which we seek out these creations and attempt endlessly, perpetually to make them, is of a piece with the instinct that sets us preserving our bodies with clothes, food, roofs, from destruction.' A note in the margin adds 'twin to the bodies instinct'.[36] By 1935, simultaneously working on *The Pargiters: A Novel–Essay*, *The Years* and *Three Guineas*, she made clear that she understood literary form to reconstruct consciousness:

It struck me tho' that I have now reached a further stage in my writers advance. I see that there are 4? dimensions; all to be produced; in human life; and that leads to a far richer grouping and proportion; I mean: I and not I: the outer and the inner – no I'm too tired to say: but I see it . . . new combinations in psychology and body . . . .  (*D*, IV, 353).

Reading *Three Guineas*, we see it, too. That's why I define the work as prophecy and suggest that Woolf's literary form has evolutionary significance. In the 1930s, not usually described as a high point of her creativity, she herself thought she was closer than ever to a fully human art 'corresponding to the dimensions of human being'. She had found a form to work the whole brain, she said (*D*, IV, 346–7). She also felt curiously serene, detached: 'have a feeling that I've reached the no man's land that I'm after and can pass from outer to inner and inhabit Eternity. A queer, very happy feeling . . . . So what does it mean?' (*D*, IV, 355).

Cultural anthropologists study symbolic form in experiential terms, asking, 'Where does it come from?' and 'What do people do with it?' For Jane Lead and Virginia Woolf, metaphors such as the Woman Clothed with the Sun, or the Woman at a Table Writing, clearly have psychosocial origins and serve as an adaptive strategy, enabling them to create and renew their lives.[37] If readers' reactions – my own, students', others' – are any indication, those metaphors are still generative, still prophetic. It is possible to finish reading *Three Guineas* with a queer, very happy feeling, looking out, asking, 'What shall I do with it? What shall I see with it?'

## NOTES

1. I am grateful to Katherine Howell, Jean Huster, John Kelly, Brenda Miller, Robin Satterly, Diana Stout, Sylvia Sukop and Nancy Weyant, students in a 1982 centenary seminar on Virginia Woolf, Bucknell University, for the discussion that led to this essay. Versions of the essay were presented at the 1982 Modern Language Association Convention, Los Angeles, and the 1983 National Women's Studies Association Convention, Columbus, Ohio.

2. Richard Ekmann, at the National Endowment for the Humanities Grantees' Conference, 12–14 Dec 1982, Washington, DC.

3. For prophecy in biblical tradition, see Gerhard von Rad, *Old Testament Theology*, I, trs. D. M. G. Stalker (Edinburgh: Oliver and Boyd, 1962), and *The Message of the Prophets* (New York: Harper and Row, 1965). For literary prophecy, see Joseph Anthony Wittreich, Jr, *Visionary Poetics: Milton's Tradition and his Legacy* (Huntington Library, Calif., 1979); and David V. Erdman, *Blake: Prophet against Empire*, rev. edn (New York: Doubleday, 1969).

4. Alice as a falling and rising goddess figure has been proposed by Nina Auerbach, lecturing on 'Falling Alice and Fallen Women', Bucknell University, 1981. The figure is further discussed in Auerbach, *Woman and the Demon: The Life of a Victorian Myth* (Cambridge, Mass.: Harvard University Press, 1982).

5. Jane Marcus suggestively applies the phrase 'born again' in this context, referring to Woolf herself in 1904, in 'The Niece of a Nun: Virginia Woolf, Caroline Stephen, and the Cloistered Imagination', in *Virginia Woolf: A Feminist Slant*, ed. Marcus (Lincoln, Nebr.: Nebraska University Press, 1983).

6. Ibid.

7. Wittreich in *Visionary Poetics* argues that prophecy as a literary form engages a chain of intra-poetic relationships, or imaginative kinship, in which prophets correct earlier prophets' visions.

8. However, Madeline Moore, in *A Short Season between Two Silences: The Mystical and Political in Virginia Woolf* (Boston, Mass.: George Allen and Unwin, 1983), notes that in the 1930s Woolf took out of the Dr Williams's Library of English Religious Nonconformity, Gordon Square, two works referring to Lead, J. H. Overton's *Life of Law* and Alexander Whyte's *Characteristics of William Law*. In addition, *The Dictionary of National Biography*, ed. Leslie Stephen, contains a biography of Lead.

For Jane Lead's life and writing, see my 'Jane Lead: Mysticism and the Woman Clothed with the Sun', in *Shakespeare's Sisters: Feminist Essays on Women Poets*, ed. Sandra M. Gilbert and Susan Gubar (Indianapolis: Indiana University Press, 1979) pp. 3–18.

9. 'The Journal of Mistress Joan Martyn', ed. and intro. Susan M. Squier and Louise A. DeSalvo, in *Twentieth Century Literature*, XXV, nos 3–4 (Fall–Winter 1979) 237–69.

10. 'Lebenslauff der Autorin', attached to the German edition of six tracts by Lead, Herzögliche Bibliothek zu Gotha, A297 and 229 (*Facsimilia collecta opera Ernesti Salamonis Cypriani* [Coburg, 1711]), unpaginated. I am grateful to Annelies E. Gray for translating this sole extant version of Lead's 'Life of the Author'.

11. Nils Thune, *The Behmenists and the Philadelphians: A Contribution to the Study of English Mysticism in the Seventeenth and Eighteenth Centuries* (Uppsala, 1948).

12. Désirée Hirst, *Hidden Riches: Traditional Symbolism from the Renaissance to Blake* (New York: Barnes and Noble, 1964) pp. 107–8.

13. 'Life of the Author' (see above, n.10)

14. Jane Lead, *A Fountain of Gardens Watered by the River of Divine Pleasure, and Springing up in All Variety of Spiritual Plants . . .* (London, 1697–1701) I, 18–21.

15. Ibid., p. 27.

16. Keith Thomas, 'Women and the Civil War Sects', in *Crisis in Europe 1560–1660*, ed. Trevor Aston (New York, 1965) pp. 317–40, and *Religion and the Decline of Magic* (New York, 1971) *passim*; Beth Nelson, Department of English, University of Colorado, 'Without Honor: Seventeenth Century Women Prophets and the Emergence of the Woman Writer', unpublished paper presented at the 1978 meeting of the Modern Language Association, New York.

17. Catherine F. Smith, 'Jane Lead: The Feminist Mind and Art of a Seventeenth Century Protestant Mystic', *Women of Spirit: Female Leadership in Jewish and Christian Traditions*, ed. Rosemary Ruether and Eleanor McLaughlin (New York: Simon and Schuster, 1979), 184–203.

18. Jane Lead, *The Revelation of Revelations Particularly as an Essay Towards the Unsealing, Opening, and Discovery of the Seven Seals, the Seven Thunders, and the New Jerusalem State* . . . (London: A Sowle, 1683).

19. Lead, *Fountain*, II, 105–7.

20. Nelson, 'Without Honor'.

21. Lead, *Fountain*, I, 69–71, 118, 77–8.

22. Lead, *A Tree of Faith* (London, 1699) pp. 24–5.

23. Lead, *The Enochian Walks with God, Found Out by a Spiritual Traveler* (London, 1694) p. 30.

24. Eleanor Riemer, 'Women and Capital Investment: The Economic Decline of Siennese Women at the Dawn of the Renaissance', unpublished paper presented at the Fifth Berkshire Conference of Women Historians, Vassar College, 1981.

25. Lawrence Stone, *The Crisis of the Aristocracy 1558–1691* (Oxford, 1965) pp. 632–49; *Family and Inheritance: Rural Society in Western Europe 1200–1800*, ed. Jack Goody, Joan Thirsk and E. P. Thompson (London, 1976), esp. the essays by J. P. Cooper, Joan Thirsk and E. P. Thompson.

26. Roger Thompson, *Women in Stuart England and America: A Comparative Study* (London, 1974) 31–5.

27. E. P. Thompson, in *Family and Inheritance*, pp. 352–3; G. E. Mingay, *English Landed Society in the Eighteenth Century* (London, 1963) p. 35.

28. Ibid.

29. Suits for the jointure are noted in Doris Mary Stenton, *The English Woman in History* (London, 1957) pp. 34–5. Astrologers' records are discussed in Thomas, *Religion and the Decline of Magic*, p. 315.

30. Lead, *Fountain*, I, 27; IV, 106–7; II, 126; I, 470.

31. Ibid., I, 24–5.

32. Ibid., I, 69–78, 118, 77–8.

33. Catherine F. Smith, 'Women, Property, and Prophecy in Seventeenth Century England', paper presented at the Fifth Berkshire Conference of Women Historians, Vassar College, 1981.

34. Catherine F. Smith, 'Jane Lead's Wisdom', in *Poetic Prophecy in Western Literature*, ed. Raymond-Jean Frontain and Jan Wojcik (Fair-

leigh-Dickinson University Press, 1983).

35. Mircea Eliade, *Shamanism*, trs. William R. Trask (New York, 1964), 23.

36. 'Anon' TS. fragment with the author's corrections, unsigned and undated, 8pp., Berg Collection, folder 5, p. 3.

37. Jane Lilienfeld, reviewing Stephen Trombley's *All that Summer she was Mad: Virginia Woolf, Female Victim of Male Medicine*, discusses the close relationship of body and language in Woolf's aesthetic in *Virginia Woolf Miscellany*, Fall 1982. In 'Women, Property, and Prophecy' (see above, n.33) I discuss the background of Jane Lead's metaphor and her uses of metaphor in learning new ways to live.

# 13 The War between the Woolfs[1]

## LAURA MOSS GOTTLIEB

Virginia Woolf was 'the least political animal that has lived since Aristotle invented the description'.[2] That is the well-known assessment of her husband, Leonard Woolf, whose credentials as a political observer and commentator were impeccable. Disillusioned with his experience as a colonial administrator in the Ceylon Civil Service between 1904 and 1911, he joined the Fabian Society in 1916 and wrote for it the book which became the blueprint for the League of Nations.[3] He also served for many years as secretary for the Labour Party's prestigious Advisory Committee on International Affairs. His career as a writer was predominantly political as well, consisting of a steady stream of books and articles on world events, in addition to the editorship of such journals as *War and Peace*, the *Nation*, and *Political Quarterly*.

Leonard's view of Virginia has been challenged only in the last decade by scholars who have unearthed in Virginia's novels an amazingly consistent and quite radical political analysis buried beneath her 'evasive' and 'impressionistic' literary style.[4] In bringing Virginia's feminist views to light, scholars such as Naomi Black have noted Leonard's inability to recognise his wife's political concerns, observing that this inability may have been related to 'a more general dismissal of women because they are not much involved in the few activities which men are prepared to recognise as politics': matters relating to government or party organisation.[5] But Leonard's disregard for his wife's political views may also have been related to his resentment of her intrusion into the field he had designated as his own. Having given up his strictly literary efforts early in their marriage, Leonard may have felt that, if his wife was going to be the literary genius in the family, he was entitled to be the sole political commentator.

We know that Virginia Woolf was alienated by the traditional masculinist politics her husband participated in. She wrote in her

242

diary in 1935, 'Yesterday we went to the L[abour] P[arty] meeting at Brighton, & . . . I have refused to go again this morning . . . . Why? The immersion in all that energy & all that striving for something that is quite oblivious of me; making me feel that I am oblivious of it' (entry for 2 Oct 1935 in *D*, IV, 345). Virginia's sense that such groups did not so much exclude her from their political concerns as ignore her own, led her to advocate major power shifts between sexes, classes, races and castes. In advocating such upheavals in society, Virginia Woolf subscribed to a more revolutionary politics than her husband.

Only two scholars seem to have compared Virginia's and Leonard's political writings, and these have ignored the conflict between their views. Both Josephine O'Brien Schaffer and Selma Meyerowitz have briefly sketched parallels between Leonard's study of communal psychology, *Quack, Quack!*, and Virginia's anti-war pamphlet, *Three Guineas*,[6] and Meyerowitz has gone on to speculate that their shared political views 'created a substantial bond in their marriage'.[7] Unfortunately, in straining to find similarities between Virginia's and Leonard's political views, Meyerowitz has had to generalise to such an extent that important differences between the Woolfs are obscured: she has had to overlook Virginia's most significant contribution to political discourse – her radical feminism – and to deny Leonard's assessment of Virginia's political thinking. I believe that it is important to analyse the political differences between the Woolfs, first, because it is only in such an analysis that their distinct political identities emerge, and, second, because it may shed light on the way Leonard and Virginia communicated with each other.

Fortunately for us, then, within the space of five years Leonard and Virginia each published a work on exactly the same subject: how to prevent war. The better-known book is *Three Guineas* (1938), a polemical pamphlet which locates the origins of war in male psychology as institutionalised in patriarchal, capitalist culture. Completely overlooked, however, has been Leonard's contribution to *The Intelligent Man's Way to Prevent War* (1933).[8]

Essentially a plea for an international government modelled on the League of Nations as the rational arbiter of inevitable international disputes, *The Intelligent Man's Way to Prevent War* is introduced by Leonard Woolf and includes essays by seven well-known British political writers, professors and statesmen. Although some of the articles are now dated, this fifty-year-old volume, taken as a whole, remains surprisingly apt, its theories and arguments even more convincing today in view of the arsenal of chemical, biological and nuclear weapons which have been developed since the book's publication. The topicality of this book, in fact, only underlines the complete lack of progress made toward disarmament and the peaceful resolution of international conflicts in the past half-century.

The book has been ignored since it was first published. Receiving only three brief reviews when it first appeared in 1933, it received no mention in Virginia's letters or diary and is alluded to only parenthetically in Leonard's autobiography.[9] Duncan Wilson's political biography of Leonard Woolf (published in 1978) refers to *The Intelligent Man's Way* only in an appendix of Leonard's books and pamphlets, where it appears in last place, out of alphabetical order, apparently as an afterthought.[10] Even more surprising is its total absence from Selma Meyerowitz's 1982 book on Leonard.

Leonard's *own* neglect of *The Intelligent Man's Way* can probably be explained by his limited involvement with the book: the idea was not his own, the book was brought out quite rapidly, and Leonard's editorial responsibilities were few. Knowing that Leonard was sympathetic to his own political views, Victor Gollancz, the dynamic left-wing British publisher, first proposed the book to Leonard on 21 November 1932, saying that, since G. D. H. Cole's *The Intelligent Man's Guide through World Chaos* (1932) had been so successful, he would like to publish a book 'uniform with [it, but] . . . dealing with the prevention of war'.[11] Gollancz's proposal was specific:

> I want it to be about 200,000 words long: to be published at 5/–: and to be so simply written that it is perfectly intelligible to the 'man in the street', and yet neither vague nor lacking in detail. My idea is that the book should be divided into seven or eight big sections, and that there should be as many, or nearly as many, contributors. I have jotted down on the accompanying sheet some very rough suggestions . . . .

He stressed that he would like to have the manuscript in his hands by the end of March, and that, although the chapters would be written on a variety of topics, he did not want the book to be 'a mere symposium' – he wanted it to be a unified argument leading up to the view that 'ultimately the most important thing of all is the working for international socialism'. After a brief exchange of letters clarifying Leonard's exact responsibilities and revising the list of chapter headings and contributors, Leonard Woolf and Victor Gollancz signed the contract for the book on 26 November 1932, five days after the book was first proposed. As Gollancz's daughter wrote to me, 'They did things quickly in those days!'[12]

*The Intelligent Man's Way to Prevent War* for the most part met the criteria set for it by its publisher. In his Introduction, Leonard Woolf described each of the chapters and briefly stressed the urgency of the problem of preventing war in view of contemporary events. Sir Norman Angell contributed a chapter entitled 'The International Anarchy', Professor Gilbert Murray advocated 'Revision of the [Versailles] Peace Treaties', C. M. Lloyd discussed 'The Problem of Russia', Charles Roden Buxton wrote about 'Intercontinental Peace', Viscount Robert Cecil promoted 'The League [of Nations] as a Road to Peace', Will Arnold-Forster discussed the problems of 'Arbitration, Security, [and] Disarmament', while Sir Norman Angell pointed out the 'Educational and Psychological Factors' that would have to be taken into account when trying to prevent war. Professor Harold J. Laski, a Marxist, contributed the final chapter, 'The Economic Foundations of Peace', arguing that 'there is nothing inherent in the organisation of Socialist states, as there is in capitalist states which makes . . . [war] inevitable' (Leonard's summary of Laski's argument, *Intelligent Man's War*, p. 17). The common theme of the book, though, is not so much a plea for international socialism, as Gollancz had intended, as an appeal for the creation of an international government whose decisions regarding relations between sovereign states would be universally recognised and obeyed. This appeal is underscored by the appendix, the Covenant of the League of Nations.

Like *The Intelligent Man's Way to Prevent War*, *Three Guineas* can also trace its origins to the early 1930s. Although it was not published until 1938, Virginia first conceived a book in 1931 to be about 'the sexual life of women'. Calling it at various times, 'Professions for Women', 'On Being Despised', her war pamphlet, and 'What Are We to Do?'[13] she began collecting materials for it in scrapbooks in the early 1930s but was not able to begin piecing together her material on these apparently disparate subjects until 1935 (and not intensively until 1936 and 1937). Every insult to women, every whiff of war, every hint of fascism's approach rekindled her desire to write the book (see, for one example, the entry for 11 Feb 1932, in *WD*, p. 174). But she was finishing *The Waves*, writing 'A Letter to a Young Poet', editing the second *Common Reader*, and writing *Flush* and *The Years*. Interestingly enough, the Labour Party meeting at Brighton from which Virginia felt excluded was another critical spur to the writing of *Three Guineas*. Now calling it 'The Next War', she wrote in her diary: 'Did I say the result of the L.P. at Brighton was the breaking of that dam between me and the new book, so that I couldn't resist dashing off a chapter; stopped myself; but have all ready to develop – the form good I think – as soon as I get time?' (entry for 15 Oct 1935, in *WD*, p. 248). But it wasn't until the spring of 1937 that she was able to devote herself exclusively to *Three Guineas*.

Like *The Intelligent Man's Way*, *Three Guineas* is based on the belief that war is a social phenomenon. As Leonard puts it,

> War is not a 'natural' catastrophe like a tidal wave or an earthquake. It is not inevitable; it is preventable in Europe like cannibalism, cholera, or witchburning, all of which, though once common in this continent, have been abolished by civilization. War depends upon the human will, . . . upon how [human beings] decide to order their society and to arrange their relations with their fellows.   *(Intelligent Man's Way*, p.9)

In a similar vein in *Three Guineas*, Virginia asks, '[What] kind of society, [what] kind of people . . . will help to prevent war[?]' (*TG*, p. 33).

Although Leonard recognises that 'ultimately . . . a world order to prevent war requires a different psychology', the general thrust of his book is toward envisioning new 'structures, organisations, [and] systems . . . for peace' (*Intelligent Man's Way*, p. 16). It is Virginia who uses her 'psychological insight . . . to decide what kind of qualities in human nature are likely to lead to war' (*TG*, p. 58). It is a difference in emphasis which leads to a radical difference in conclusion. For Virginia argues that war is an exclusively male activity and that the same social conditions which encourage war are those which permit men to dominate women economically, sexually, and intellectually. So, while Leonard argues for the League of Nations (one *more* patriarchal institution) as a means of arbitrating international disputes,

Virginia advocates the elimination of the patriarchal system altogether as a way of altering human psychology and of abolishing war.

Leonard and Virginia not only drew different conclusions about ways to prevent war, but they also wrote for different audiences. As the title indicates, *The Intelligent Man's Way* was written exclusively by men for men. Flattering its male readers (they must be intelligent), it ignores women as readers, as contributors, and as possible peace-makers. Although Leonard occasionally uses the terms 'human beings' and 'ordinary people' in his Introduction, it is clear that he hopes the serious reader will be 'the intelligent man'. The exclusion of women from every aspect of Leonard's book, as well as its narrow approach to ending war, may have been yet another spur to Virginia's desire to continue writing *Three Guineas*. Certainly it is suggestive that the fictional person she addresses in epistolary form in *Three Guineas* is a man, who, Virginia rather pointedly says, has written 'a Letter perhaps unique in the history of human correspondence, since *when before has an educated man asked a woman how in her opinion war can be prevented?*' (*TG*, p. 3: emphasis added).

Ostensibly addressing a male in *Three Guineas*, Virginia actually addresses women – specifically, the 'daughters of educated men': women, like herself, who were raised among middle-class brothers and fathers, but whose own education, financial and emotional independence, professional advancement, and quality of life had been sacrificed to ensure their brothers' class and sex privileges. Angered by the assumption in the man's letter ('How in your opinion are we to prevent war?' – *TG*, p. 3) that 'we' – he and Virginia – would approach the problem in the same way, Virginia immediately draws a distinction between 'you' (men) and 'us' (women – see p. 3). Pointing out the many differences in social conditioning, opportunity, and values between brothers and sisters, husbands and wives, men and women, she chooses to interpret this question as 'How can the daughters of educated men help men to prevent war?' (paraphrase of p. 44). This distance, repeatedly placed between herself and her male inquirer in *Three Guineas*, contrasts sharply with the strong and immediate identification she makes with women, consistently using the first person plural when writing of her own sex.

And what does she say when she speaks to women of the special contribution they, as a sex, can make to ending war? Examining

the patriarchal capitalist system, its '"civilization"', its ceremonies, and its professions, Virginia finds that men arouse the
emotions which lead to war by displaying their superiority over
other people. She then turns to the lives of nineteenth-century
women to demonstrate that although their formal education had
'great defects', it also had 'great virtues . . . for we cannot deny
that these, if not educated, still were civilized women' (*TG*, p. 79).
Ironically, poverty, chastity, derision, and freedom from what
Virginia calls 'unreal loyalties'[14] were the teachers of these
Victorian daughters of educated men, teachers still providing
valuable lessons in the prevention of war. Clinging to their
lessons, Virginia says, might enable women to enter universities
and professions closed to them, to retain their civilised nature, and
perhaps even to convince men of the usefulness of these characteristics in preventing war. Thus, while she supports the goals of her
correspondent's organisation, she declines to join, preferring the
duties of the 'Society of Outsiders', that elusive, unorganised
group of individuals – primarily women – who are not only
excluded from power but also subordinated to those who wield it.
Women's unique contributions to the cause of peace, she says,
may well be the values they learn by being outsiders.

Nigel Nicolson has expressed himself at a loss to understand
why Virginia felt so strongly about women's rights, for 'nothing in
her own life', he says, 'quite explains it'.[15] The explanation can be
found by comparing Virginia Woolf's career with those of the
male contributors to *The Intelligent Man's Way*. Of the eight men, all
were well educated, at least four having attended Cambridge or
Oxford.[16] Certainly all were either members of the 'Establishment' or on its fringes. *All* members of the chief prevailing
parliamentary parties,[17] they either edited important journals
(such as the *New Statesman, Foreign Affairs*, the *Nation*, and the
*Political Quarterly*[18]), taught at prestigious universities,[19] or served
the government in some capacity.[20] Additionally, Sir Norman
Angell and Lord Cecil won the Nobel Peace Prize in 1933 and
1937, respectively, while Professor Murray was awarded the
Order of Merit in 1941 and Cecil accepted the Companion of
Honour in 1956.

That these contributors are 'insiders' is no surprise, since
Leonard relied in part on his contributors' prominence and
respectability to persuade readers of the importance and sound-
ness of their cause. But what *is* striking is the discrepancy between

their credentials and Virginia Woolf's. In spite of the fact that her name will probably outlive theirs, she never went to university (although she was superbly self-educated), never joined a political party (though she participated in several women's organisations), never edited a prominent journal (though she helped to found the Hogarth Press), never taught at a prestigious university (though she taught night classes at a college for workers), and never served her government in any official capacity. Of the few honours which came her way, she rejected all but one.[21] This discrepancy underscores the points Virginia makes in *Three Guineas* about the relative positions of middle-class men and women in early-twentieth-century Britain and helps to explain her commitment to feminism.

Perhaps Leonard and Virginia would inevitably disagree on their approaches to ending war, for, as Virginia noted, 'since [men and women] are different, our help must be different' (*TG*, p. 143). Leonard, repeatedly insisting that 'the problem of preventing war is essentially simple' (*Intelligent Man's Way*, p. 10), offers a narrow solution to the peaceful resolution of international disputes. His suggestion only requires the obedience of sovereign states to some world governmental body which would, presumably, issue de-crees in some rational and disinterested manner, but would not necessarily initiate any major changes in the status quo. His solution would probably not address the sexual inequities with which Virginia was concerned.

Virginia, seeing a connection between the causes of war and patriarchy, urges adoption of the values of Outsiders: withdraw-ing from participation in many of society's functions, re-establishing universities and professions on new values, and promoting women's economic and social rights. Virginia's book is a more speculative, polemical and complex analysis of the causes of war than Leonard's, and her solution implies a fundamental shift in social values, customs and relations. In some ways, *Three Guineas* is almost more anti-fascist than anti-war, since its attack on fascism is rooted in its feminism. Virginia viewed patriarchal society as inherently fascist (and therefore war-mongering). To stamp out patriarchy is to stamp out fascism; to stamp out fascism, according to Virginia, is to stamp out war.

Alienated as Virginia was from the kind of politics which Leonard practised, she nevertheless respected his political goals and longed for his approval. Her report of their exchange

concerning *Three Guineas* lends support to Susan and Edwin
Kenney's assertion that Virginia played the role of dependent but
rebellious child to Leonard's role of stern parent throughout their
marriage.[22] Hoping to win Leonard's endorsement of her political
views, but perhaps suspecting that he would take them as a
personal challenge, in 1935 Virginia discussed with him her
thoughts for the anti-fascist pamphlet which became *Three
Guineas*. She reported in her diary, 'He was extremely reasonable
& adorable, & told me I should have to take account of the
economic question' (entry for 26 Feb 1935, *D*, IV, 282). The
uncharacteristically gushy adjectives she uses to describe his
reaction appear to be sarcastic and suggest the condescension
with which her ideas were apparently greeted. Why shouldn't he
be 'reasonable' about his wife's political views? Why is he
'adorable' when he listens to what she has to say? Why does he ask
her to 'take account of the economic question' when surely he was
aware that she knew about the economic inequality of men and
women from bitter personal experience? Again, describing in her
1937 diary the torrent of arguments, emotions, and words pouring
from her pen in *Three Guineas*, she frequently uses words associated
with horses, such as cantering or galloping (entries for 21 Feb, 7
Mar 1937, in *WD*). However, when Leonard 'gravely approves
*Three Guineas*', saying that, of course, 'it's not on a par with the
novels', she sadly concludes that it's only 'a good piece of
donkeywork' (entry for 4 Feb 1938, in *WD*). It takes her two
months to admit to her diary that 'I didn't get so much praise from
L[eonard] as I hoped' and to regain her confidence in the work
(entry for 11 Apr 1938, in *WD*).

   Bested by his wife in strictly literary endeavours, Leonard
Woolf may have felt threatened by his wife's invasion of the
territory he had staked out for himself: the realm of politics. In any
case, it appears that Virginia never won from him recognition of
her political astuteness – much less approval of her political views.
But perhaps the fault was not entirely Leonard's. For, although
*Three Guineas* and *The Intelligent Man's Way to Prevent War* reveal
political points of view markedly different in fundamental
assumptions, approaches and conclusions, neither Woolf seems to
have openly acknowledged their political differences. Leonard's
denial of Virginia's political vision and Virginia's disdain for
Leonard's political activities suggest that the war between the
Woolfs may have been more than just a battle of books.

NOTES

1. I should like to express my appreciation and affection to the members of the Morgantown (WV) Women's Studies Research Group (Gail Adams, Anne Effland, Clay Pytlik, Anna W. Shannon, and Linda Yoder) for their support, advice, good humour, fine food and forthright critical judgements. Special love and thanks to Elaine K. Ginsberg as well.

2. Leonard Woolf, *Downhill All the Way: An Autobiography of the Years 1919–1939* (New York: Harcourt, Brace and World, 1967) p. 27.

3. S. J. Stearns, Introduction to reprint of *The Intelligent Man's Way to Prevent War* (New York: Garland, 1973) p. 6. See also below, n.8.

4. 'Woolf, Virginia', in *Chambers's Biographical Dictionary*, ed. J. O. Thorne and T. C. Callocott, rev. edn (Edinburgh: W. & R. Chambers, 1974).

5. Naomi Black, 'A Note on the Feminist Politics of Virginia Woolf', *Virginia Woolf Miscellany*, Spring 1980, p. 5.

6. Josephine O'Brien Schaeffer, '*Three Guineas* and *Quack, Quack!* Read Together', *Virginia Woolf Miscellany*, Spring 1977, pp. 2–3; Selma Meyerowitz, *Leonard Woolf* (Boston, Mass.: Twayne, 1982) pp. 18–19.

7. Ibid., p. 19.

8. *The Intelligent Man's Way to Prevent War*, ed. and intro. Leonard Woolf (London: Victor Gollancz, 1933). References in the text refer to this edn.

9. The three reviews I have been able to locate appeared in the *TLS*, no. 719 (1933); *The Times*, 24 Oct 1933, p. 19; and the Mar 1934 issue of the *Millgate Monthly* (a magazine of the British Co-operative Movement). For Leonard's parenthetical reference to the book, see his *Downhill All the Way*, p. 196.

10. Duncan Wilson, *Leonard Woolf: A Political Biography* (New York: St Martin's, 1978).

11. Letter from Victor Gollancz to Leonard Woolf, 21 Nov 1932, in the archives of Victor Gollancz Ltd. Quoted with the kind permission of Livia Gollancz, his daughter, to whom I am grateful for the promptness and generosity with which she has written to me.

12. Letter from Livia Gollancz to the author, 4 Mar 1983. Quoted with the permission of Livia Gollancz.

13. For a complete list of Virginia's working titles for *Three Guineas*, see *D*, IV, 6, n.8.

14. Virginia defines 'freedom from unreal loyalties' as 'freedom from loyalty to old schools, old colleges, old churches, old ceremonies, old countries' (*TG*, p. 78).

15. Nigel Nicolson, Introduction, *L*, V, xv.

16. Norman Angell was educated abroad; Arnold-Forster, son of a Tory MP, was educated at the Slade. I haven't been able to find out the

educational background of Lloyd or Buxton, but I judge that their education was good by the positions they held: Buxton was Principal of Morley College, 1902–1910, a lawyer and an MP, while Lloyd, a journalist and teacher, was assistant editor of the *New Statesman* and taught in the Social Science Department of the London School of Economics. All the information on these men comes from three sources: *Chambers's Biographical Dictionary; Webster's Biographical Dictionary* (Springfield, Mass.: G. C. Merriam, 1976); and Stearns, Introduction to reprint of *The Intelligent Man's Way*, pp. 5–15.

17. All were members of the Labour Party except Cecil, a Tory, and Murray, a Liberal. Woolf and Arnold-Forster were also members of the Fabian Society.

18. C. M. Lloyd edited the *New Statesman*, Norman Angell edited *Foreign Affairs*, and Leonard Woolf edited *The Nation* and the *Political Quarterly*.

19. Murray taught at Oxford, Laski and Lloyd at the London School of Economics.

20. Cecil and Buxton were Members of Parliament; Arnold-Forster was Cecil's secretary and had served in the Royal Navy during the First World War; Lloyd had served in the Army during the First World War; and Leonard Woolf, as has been stated, served in Ceylon for seven years as a colonial administrator.

21. According to Nicolson (Introduction, *L*, V, xvi), Virginia turned down the Companion of Honour, a degree at Manchester University, and the Clark lectureship at Cambridge. She did accept the Femina–Vie Heureuse Prize for *To the Lighthouse*.

22. Susan M. Kenney and Edwin J. Kenney, Jr, 'Virginia Woolf and the Art of Madness', *Massachusetts Review*, Spring 1982, pp. 161–85. See esp. pp. 174–5.

# 14 The Remediable Flaw: Revisioning Cultural History in *Between the Acts*

JUDITH L. JOHNSTON

On 13 August 1940, while enemy bombers were flying overhead, Virginia Woolf put aside her draft of *Pointz Hall* to write to Benedict Nicolson, fiercely defending her own and Roger Fry's artistic careers against Nicolson's allegation (quoted by Woolf) that Fry 'shut himself out from all disagreeable actualities and allowed the spirit of Nazism to grow without taking any steps to check it' (*L*, VI). In replying by pointing to Nicolson's privileged education at Eton and Oxford and his elegant job as Keeper of the King's Pictures, Woolf attributes his pose of superior political morality to his culture. Her culture was different, though she studied the same books.

As a woman born in 1882, Virginia Stephen Woolf was not given an university education. Writing proudly, 'I never went to school or college. My father spent perhaps £100 on my education', she distinguishes herself not only from her correspondent, Ben Nicolson, but from all others whose cultural values, political ideas, and social prejudices were formed by a university education.[1] The daughter of Leslie Stephen was a privileged woman, both financially and intellectually. She was well, if cheaply educated. With access to her father's private library, and the benefit of private tutors, she read Greek and studied the classic texts of the humanist tradition – however, she studied them alone, not in the company of fellow university students.[2] Unlike Ben Nicolson, educated at Oxford, unlike her Bloomsbury friends educated at Cambridge, and unlike the brothers with university degrees, whose education, she once argued, was paid for by depriving their sisters, she maintained an outsider's perspective on the humanist tradition.

As an outsider, she believed that the values of humanism were

253

grounded in the dominance of a cultural elite from which she was excluded as a woman. Not only did Woolf doubt the validity of Matthew Arnold's assertion, in *Culture and Anarchy* that 'the men of culture are the true apostles of equality', she argued, in 1938, that the men of culture, supported by society, had systematically denied equality of education and opportunity to women. Her perspective on men's and women's roles in cultural history discerned a cycle of domination and victimisation rather than a process of civilisation progressing from Greece to Rome to Norman England to the British Empire. She saw politics and culture not as separate arenas – which is the assumption underlying Ben Nicolson's critique of Roger Fry – but rather as inextricably bound together.

Among her fictional characters, she creates a few defiant outsiders, such as the painter Lily Briscoe, but many characters who acquiesce to dominant cultural tradition, and also domineering characters who see themselves as conservators of their cultural patrimony. Like Mr Ramsay, these conservators are self-confident, overly rational, arrogant people who fail to address the urgent problems of contemporary life. In most of her published fiction, her anger is muted, especially when compared with earlier and more radical drafts. Her feminist essay published in 1929, *A Room of One's Own*, maintains a tone of polite, controlled indignation, but she does connect Mussolini, as one who despises women, with the misogynist Oxbridge professors who have authored the studies of women found in the British Museum (*AROO*, pp. 25–30). In 1938, responding to contemporary politics and to the explicitly political writings of the literary young men of the 1930s, she mounted in *Three Guineas* a public, angry critique of the patriarchal humanist tradition, linking the authoritarian family with nationalism, militarism and the rise of dictatorships. Personal and political relations, she argues, are shaped by the same cultural forces. Virginia Woolf's complex responses to the rise of fascism in the 1930s encompassed her rejection of a patriarchal culture fostered, she believed, by both Oxford and Cambridge.

Few of her friends in Bloomsbury applauded her ideas or her rhetoric in *Three Guineas*. Woolf's analysis contradicts the pacifist stance and ameliorative history that had come to be identified with the older Bloomsbury generation, an optimistic vision of culture articulated by Clive Bell in his 1928 *Civilisation*. She also rejects the imperative to employ revolutionary force against repressive violence, the activist stance and apocalyptic history envisioned by the younger Bloomsbury generation, as articulated by Julian Bell in his oddly unsympathetic Introduction to *We Did Not Fight* (1935), an edition of memoirs by conscientious objectors. Julian further distanced himself from the elder Bloomsbury generation to his 1936 essay 'War and Peace: A Letter to E. M. Forster', in which he advocated opposing war and fascism by force. Acting on his conviction, Julian Bell participated in the civil war defending against fascist attack the Spanish Republic; he was killed in July 1937. Virginia Woolf felt the connection between her powerful grief at her nephew's death and her indignation against all forms of repression. In *Three Guineas*, citing Creon's authoritarian speech against his niece Antigone, Woolf envisions contemporary violence not as an interval in the progress of civilisation, but as part of a continuous history of repressive personal and political relationships, rooted in a patriarchal culture. Instead of distinguishing British culture from German or Italian, and arousing nationalistic hatred of the other, the enemy, Woolf asks us to examine the photographic image of a virile uniformed man, his hand on a sword: 'He is called in German and Italian Führer or Duce; in our own language Tyrant or Dictator. And behind him lie ruined houses and dead bodies.' She calls upon our response as human beings, to see the connection between ourselves and that menacing figure (*TG*, p. 142).

The rhetorical form of her three essays in *Three Guineas* suggests inner debate and revision. She interrupts the essayist's monologue to consider the reader's response, and she explores several hypotheses sequentially. In *Three Guineas*, Woolf not only expounds her critique of the dominant cultural values, she also creates an essay form which embodies a polyvocal alternative to the single authoritarian voice of polemical essays and political speeches. As S. P. Rosenbaum has suggested, 'the literary history of Bloomsbury is, to an unusual extent, a history of prose', and the nonfictional prose deserves the same careful critical attention that has been given to the fiction.[3]

Understanding Woolf's experimental design and her political vision in *Three Guineas* makes possible a more appreciative reading of those essays and of her final novel. That she spent many hours writing letters rebutting attacks and explaining the radical analysis of *Three Guineas* indicates the strength of her commitment to her thesis. None of her other concerns, neither her grief over Julian Bell's death in the Spanish Civil War, nor her frustration at the disparate demands made on her as Roger Fry's biographer, nor doubts about her major revision of *The Pargiters* into *The Years*, nor the urging by Clive Bell and E. M. Forster and younger Bloomsbury friends that she participate in their political protests kept her from what she clearly regarded as an urgent task. As she explained in a letter to Margaret Llewelyn Davies, 'to sit silent and acquiesce in all this idiotic letter signing and vocal pacifism when there's such an obvious horror in our midst – such tyranny, such Pecksniffism – finally made my blood boil into the usual ink-spray' (4 July 1938, in *L*, VI). Her allusion to Dickens' hypocritical bully connects the literary world of the Victorian era with the political world of Mussolini's era; further, her choice of Pecksniff, who sought to dominate Mary by marriage in *Martin Chuzzlewit*, is consistent with her denunciation of tyrannical husbands and fathers.

Continuing the analysis she had begun in her non-fictional prose, Woolf worked on her final novel, *Between the Acts*, responding to contemporary historical events from 1938 to 1940. As her drafts progressed, she introduced changes that clarified a complex portrait of familial and political bonds within two frames: a literary history of British culture and the approach of a Second World War. In the composite form of *Between the Acts*, mixing authorial narration, characters' thoughts, dramatic verse parodies, and dialogue, she creates alternatives to one tyrannical authorial voice. As Woolf revised *Pointz Hall* into *Between the Acts*, she strengthened her political critique of British culture.[4]

Woolf's urgent tone in *Between the Acts* has three, interconnected origins: her recognition of the crisis in contemporary politics, her assumption that, as she was a writer, she must express her response in her writing (as E. M. Forster, John Lehmann, George Orwell, Stephen Spender and W. H. Auden were doing at the time), and her perception that, as a woman, her analysis of the flaws in her culture differed significantly from that of her male counterparts. A comparative study of Virginia Woolf and her contemporaries Elizabeth Bowen, Gertrude Stein, Anna Seghers, Marguerite Yourcenar, Willia Cather, Djuna Barnes, Louise Rinser, Nathalie Sarraute, Rebecca West, Jean Rhys, Zora Neale Hurston and Simone de Beauvoir, uncovers similar cultural revisions in their fiction written during the years 1936–42. These novelists examine bonds between authoritarian and submissive characters, make allusions to the rise of fascism or the approach of war, and embed cultural critiques in their fictional histories. Their novels demonstrate Woolf's proposition in *Three Guineas* that 'we can best help you to prevent war not by repeating your words and following your methods but by finding new words and creating new methods' (*TG*, p. 143).[5]

Virginia Woolf's response to domestic and international politics may be contrasted with that of other members of the Bloomsbury Group, even though she shared some of their concerns. In January 1935, she responded to a request that she support an anti-fascist exhibition initiated by the Cambridge Anti-War Council by asking why the 'woman question' was eliminated, and she was angered by the assumption that opposition to Hitler's fascism could be separated from feminist concerns (*D*, IV, 273). She did attend a planning meeting for that anti-fascist exhibition, but her political activity did not often include attending conferences, signing petitions or supporting candidates, for reasons she gave in *Three Guineas*. From her perspective, a more fundamental revision of cultural hierarchy was required.

Woolf argued in *Three Guineas* that the menace of fascism was found at home, nourished by the patriarchal family and by a male-centred culture. Her letters offer further evidence of her consistent political and cultural analysis. Writing to Ethel Smyth on 7 June 1938, Woolf found 'blatant Hitlerism' in the expulsion of women musicians from the Bournemouth orchestra (*L*, VI). In her letter dated 2 December 1939 to her niece Judith Stephen, Woolf advocated attacking 'Hitler in his home haunts. . . even with only the end of an old inky pen' (*L*, VI). By 'home haunts', Woolf meant Britain, and her main theme in the letter is the continuing discrimination against women students at Cambridge. Her references to fascism in her own culture are neither careless nor flippant. During Mussolini's invasion of Abyssinia, while British politicians were debating whether to impose sanctions against Italy, Woolf's diary entry makes the connection between British isolationist sentiment and a resurgence in the popularity of the British fascist Sir Oswald Mosley.[6] Because she did not regard fascism as a foreign or aberrant intrusion into the dominant cultural tradition, her response to German and Italian fascist aggression differed from the response of E. M. Forster.

She resisted Forster's pressure to attend the International Congress of Writers in Paris in June 1935. He headed the British delegation, but Woolf would not give her energy to an anti-fascist meeting that did not address the roots of fascism. Forster's 1939 essay 'What I Believe', allowing only two cheers for democracy, includes an assertion basic to his philosophy but antithetical to Woolf's analysis: 'I realise that all society rests on force', he wrote. 'But all the great creative actions, all the decent human relations occur during the intervals when force has not managed to come to the front.[7] Woolf did not concede so much. In *Between the Acts*, she portrays the cultural achievements of the Elizabethan Age, of the Age of Reason, of the Victorian Age not as 'intervals', but as epochs of a domineering civilisation. In his 1939 essay 'The Menace to Freedom', Forster deplores the tyrant and the coward, but argues that human nature is determined by its evolution from other forms of life; instead, he offers the utopian hope of a Beloved Republic of Individuals. Woolf also recognised a complicitous bond between tyrant and slave, but she connected it with that bond between the patriarch and the siren, and she suggested that dominance craved submission (*TG*, p. 129). Her perspective on evolutionary history was less deterministic than Forster's, for in her parodic *Outline of History*, in *Between the Acts*, she mocked the theory that contemporary man's bestiality derived from his origins among the apes. As an outsider to the educational system enshrining Platonic social theory, Woolf remained sceptical of his utopian republic in which the myth of metals establishes at birth a rigid social hierarchy ruled by philosopher kings. Consistent with Forster's view of civilisation is his nostalgic historical pageant *This Pleasant Land* (1940), which contrasts sharply with Miss La Trobe's satirical pageant portraying England's commercial exploitation of labour, colonial peoples, and women. As if mocking all traditional celebrations of the sweet island nation, Woolf begins her novel with her characters' complaints about the cesspool.

Woolf plunged into writing *Between the Acts* in 1938, immediately after the September Munich conference at which Hitler threatened war unless Chamberlain and Daladier allowed him to annex the Sudetenland, part of Czechoslovakia with many ethnic German residents. She had begun to draft her novel in early April, just after Nazi Germany's annexation of Austria, which she described as 'this riot of horror drumming in at the window' (letter

to Ethel Smyth, 18 Mar 1938, in *L*, VI). Her work intensified after
September 1938, and it is appropriate to consider her writing in
the context of the assertion made by Samuel Hynes in his study of
male authors: 'The Munich Crisis of September 1938 was a
symbolic event. . . . After Munich, writing in England had a
different tone: the last calls to political commitment had been
sounded, and had failed, and there would be no heroic actions.
The waiting for the end would begin in earnest.'[8] *Between the Acts*
conveys the repressed fear of an impending catastrophe and the
impatient desire for release from the tension of waiting. Woolf's
letters describing the Munich Crisis indicate that she expected
war, debated Chamberlain's motives at Munich, dreaded war's
consequences for her culture, and participated in self-
examination.

As she continued to work on her novel, the international crisis
intensified. Refugees from fascist states poured into England, and
in February 1939 Woolf sold her manuscript of *Three Guineas* to aid
them. In March, Hitler invaded Czechoslovakia, violating the
Munich accord. In her letter of 17 April to Ling Su-Hua, Woolf
deplored Italy's territorial aggression against Albania, writing
that unless President Roosevelt's appeal for peace is heeded,
'there is nothing can prevent war' (*L*,VI). In her letter of 16 July to
Ling Su-Hua, Woolf describes her response to the expected war:
'By this time one is so numb that it seems impossible to feel
anything, save that dull vague gloom' (*L*, VI). Woolf continued
writing after the Second World War began and completed her
final draft in the winter of 1940–1, interrupted by air-raid sirens
signalling bombing-attacks by German aeroplanes, which destroyed her houses at 37 Mecklenburg Square and 52 Tavistock
Square, as well as Vanessa Bell's studio at 8 Fitzroy Street. Her
letters during the period 1938–41 reveal her anxious and informed
response to the international political crisis, her dread of another
European war, and her ferocious defence of a life devoted to art,
such as Roger Fry's life and her own, as possibly the best way to
counteract an authoritarian, bellicose culture. She refused to
admit a false division between political and cultural values.

Her novel, set in June 1939, the summer before the war, became
her response to these contemporary historical events.[9] Both her
central plot involving the Oliver family and her play-within-the-
novel, Miss La Trobe's historical pageant recapitulating British
literary and imperial history, challenge the myth perpetuated by

Cambridge; that is, the humanist myth of a continuous cultural lineage from Greek to Roman to Norman to British empires. Correcting this partial cultural history, Woolf's fiction alludes to the alternative traditions that have been suppressed: the native Anglo-Saxon culture and the matriarchies of pre-Athenian Greece and Egypt. Woolf's achievement in *Between the Acts* rivals that of her friend Tom Eliot in *The Waste Land* (she deliberately reworks his fragmentary allusions to Philomela's rape, Shakespearean music and Baudelairean images), but her re-visionary historical fiction differs radically from his conservative, nostalgic elegy. The two other major novelists of her era, James Joyce and Marcel Proust, who produced fictions built upon autobiographical and realistic details, appear briefly in *Between the Acts*, in comic disguise, as the two nurses, gossiping (*BA*, 1969, p. 10). 'How cook had told 'im off about the asparagus' alludes to Proust's Françoise serving asparagus at Combray, and 'how it was a sweet costume with blouse to match' suggests Joyce's Gerty contemplating her own cunning outfit. Proust and Joyce, though concerned with the past, did not share Woolf's concern for connecting the culture's history with contemporary political events. Woolf's historical vision is pessimistic, but not deterministic; for she elucidates a cultural flaw which may yet be corrected, though not in 1941, and not by the characters she portrays.

Woolf attacks 'Hitler in his home haunts' in her portraits of Bart and Giles[10] Oliver, and she throws yet another ink pot at the 'Angel in the House' in her portraits of Lucy Oliver Swithin and Isa Oliver. Woolf envisions English cultural history in the Oliver family and in common villagers, in the library and in the great stone barn of Pointz hall, and in a rustic historical pageant created jointly by the villagers and a dictating playwright.

The Olivers, who can trace their name back only two or three hundred years, represent the rational humanists who forgot or devalued the rich native English cultural heritage. They belong to the ruling elite. Their family purchased Pointz Hall a few hundred years ago, and their French name suggests the change brought to Anglo-Saxon England by the Norman Conquest. England's native culture has been preserved in the Anglo-Saxon names of the working-class villagers, names which are found in the Domesday Book, that census ordered by William the Conqueror in 1086. The women of the Oliver family are closer than the men to England's native culture, for Isa, Giles's wife, is descended from the O'Neils, kings of Ireland, and Lucy, Bart's sister, married a Swithin. Saint Swithin was a ninth-century bishop of Winchester, and, as Lucy reminds herself, and the reader, 'The Swithins were there before the Conquest' (p. 31). Each year, Mrs Swithin retires to Hastings, the site of the battle where William defeated the Saxon king.

The conquest of Anglo-Saxon England by the Normans is mirrored in the domination of Lucy and Isa by Bart and Giles. Bart, the patriarch of the Olivers, bellows orders to his dog and masters his sister and daughter-in-law. Bart's mother introduced him to his literary culture, to Byron's poetry, but he now doubts the value of poets and books. Like Plato's mythical philospher who has seen the sun, Bart 'would carry the torch of reason till it went out in the darkness of the cave' (pp. 205–6). Putting his trust in the rational world of finance, he anxiously reads newspaper accounts of Daladier's manipulation of the franc. His son, Giles, anticipates the war but cannot imagine what action would serve to prevent the tragedy. Father and son embody the principle of mastery justified by reason. With self-confidence, they ridicule sentiment, passion, and poetic expression in the Oliver women. Bart, a retired colonial administrator, and Giles, a London stockbroker, with Streatfield, a minister, represent the three exclusively male professions Woolf names in *Three Guineas*. Their authoritarian personalities, which reflect the political situation, appear to be the product of their cultural education.

In the library at Pointz Hall, one finds evidence of the Olivers' modern university education, for, in addition to the shilling novels abandoned by guests, there are volumes by Donne, Keats, Byron, Shelley, Darwin, Eddington and Jeans, biographies of Wellington, Garibaldi and Lord Palmerston – male authors and subjects, all – and, of course, practical guides for the country gentleman, such as Hibbert on the Diseases of the Horse. The Oliver men, their university years behind them, no longer read books, but their library reflects their culture. Woolf worked on several drafts of the library description, but the evidence published in Mitchell Leaska's edition of *Pointz Hall* does not suggest radical revision. Woolf's final list of titles does represent the university education which she proposed to eliminate: 'not the arts of dominating other people; not the arts of ruling, of killing, of acquiring land and capital' (*TG*, p. 34). In *Three Guineas*, she voiced her fantasy of daughters and mothers uniting to burn down colleges fostering that nihilistic education. In *Between the Acts*, there are no heroic female agents of reform. The books rotting from the winter damp at Pointz Hall image a culture in natural decay.

Rejecting the narrow cultural history that regards Athenian Greece as the origin of English civilisation, Woolf reminds her reader of the alternative cultural roots that have been neglected. Her rendering of the great stone barn at Pointz Hall offers a clear example of her revisionary historical project. In a deadpan tone, Woolf's narrator reports, 'Those who had been to Greece always said it reminded them of a temple' (p. 26). Then that narrator describes the great barn in the alliterative, heavy-stressed line of Anglo-Saxon poetry: 'a hóllow háll sun-sháfted'. That barn is at least seven hundred years old, built long before the English renaissance revived interest in Greek architecture or quantitative poetic meters. Lucy, on p. 29 of the Earlier Typescript, asks, ' "Tell me, Bart, about the Renaissance. . . How did it show itself over here?. . . The crusaders", she hazarded. "Did they bring books back?. . . Greek and Latin texts?" ' At Pointz Hall, the barn and the carved arch of the former chapel (*BA*, 1969, p. 32) stand as monuments to native English culture.

Many early drafts of the barn description survive, as evidence that Woolf took great care with this scene. One wishes the drafts could be more precisely dated; however, from those dates Mitchell Leaska gives, Woolf seems to have revised her description into a more radical satire of cultural snobbism. The alliterative, heavy-stressed 'hollow hall sun-shafted' appears for the first time in the Later Typescript. In an early, undated version, the narrator calls the barn a 'temple', but Woolf later assigned the opinion to university-trained professionals: 'This noble building which reminded archaeologists of Greek temples' (Earlier Typescript, p. 126, first draft). In a holograph draft Leaska places in his appendix B (*PH*, p. 515), Woolf crossed out 'some archaeologists' and inserted 'everyone'. Finally, Woolf shifted the opinion to those 'who had been to Greece' (Later Typescript, p. 21). The final version thus gently ridicules those wealthy and erudite Englishmen whose pretentious and falsified cultural history traces their patrimony back to Greece, rather than claiming it in their native England. *Between the Acts* outlines a cultural history connecting 'this hollow hall' to contemporary England.

In June 1939, the violence of war threatens the landowners who have gathered for the villagers' rustic enactment of Miss La

Trobe's pageant. One member of the audience, alluding to the impending war, claims, 'No one wants it save those damned Germans' (*BA*, 1969, p. 151). Another asks, 'And what about the Jews, the refugees. . ?' (p. 121). Yet another voices the possibility of an invader crossing the Channel (p. 199). The unspoken question was: how could it happen again? How could the nations who had suffered so from the First World War be now facing the terrible threat of another? *Between the Acts* addresses that question, by offering an alternative history.

Miss La Trobe has written a pageant reviewing English literary history in four acts. Act I, presided over by Queen Elizabeth, contains a renaissance drama and portrays the colonialisation of that tobacco-producing colony, America. Act II, presided over by Queen Anne, imitates a restoration comedy, with its plot exposing the selfish greed and lust of young and old aristocrats. Act III, a Victorian melodrama of self-righteous missionaries carrying the white-man's burden of Christianity and Western civilisation to heathens abroad, is presided over by an odd figure of authority. This figure, wearing a long black garment, a row of medals, a domed hat, and a sceptre-like baton, appears as a caricature of Queen Victoria. He identifies himself, however, as a traffic constable guarding prosperity and respectability. He keeps the poor and disreputable in their places: 'Let 'em sweat at the mines; cough at the looms; rightly endure their lot. That's the price of empire' (p. 163). His speech connects the white man's civilising mission in the colonies with Victorian morality justifying class hierarchy. As the constable brandishes his truncheon, symbol of power in the Empire, his rule extends beyond colonial society, into families at home: enforcement of respectability and protection of prosperity is a 'white man's job' (p. 163).

The villager portraying the constable is named either Hammond (pp. 153, 206) or Budge (pp. 160, 161). Perhaps Woolf interchanged the names in error, as Mitchell Leaska suggests, but we can understand the connection in her imagination between a respectable, prosperous Budge and an infamous, prosperous Hammond, the proprietor of a homosexual brothel patronised by Prince Edward's intimate friend Lord Arthur Somerset, whom the Prince called 'Podge'. In addition to the similarity of 'Podge' and 'Budge', there is another association, one linked to Woolf's analysis of British culture. Budge suggests the dominant cultural chauvinism of the British Empire, for E. A. Wallis Budge

(1857–1934) was not only, as Mitchell Leaska notes, 'Keeper of Egyptian antiquities in the British Museum', but also responsible for removing 'The Book of the Dead' from Egypt to Britain, violating Egyptian laws protecting Egypt's national cultural heritage.[11] Budge embodies cultural imperialism, and his act may be interpreted as Britain's symbolic rape of Egypt.

Blatant though Act III's satire on Victorian society may seem to Woolf's reader, few in Miss La Trobe's audience recognise a direct challenge to their cultural values. Mrs Lynn Jones, thinking of her own father, defends the 'grand men', but Etty Springett concedes that child labour existed. Colonel Mayhew nearly comprehends the challenge as he asks, 'Why leave out the British Army? What's history without the Army, eh?' (p. 157), but his wife, perfectly reflecting her husband's patriotism, complacently expects the omission to be corrected in the finale, which she envisions as a rousing, nationalistic concluding scene: 'a Grand Ensemble. Army; Navy; Union Jack' (p. 179). She is disappointed.

Act IV, subtitled 'The Present Time. Ourselves', deviates from the pattern established by the first three acts. Miss La Trobe begins it daringly, with a stage empty of actors, illusions, and artifice. This scene, one of those Woolf added after completing the Earlier Typescript, suggests an alternative to most drama, in which the playwright fills the time with action and dialogue, thereby maintaining control.

This director whom the villagers have nicknamed 'Bossy' has been ordering them about for seven years (p. 22); as 1939 is their seventh pageant, the January in which she first claimed the terrace for her productions occurred in 1933. Having come to power in the same month and year as Hitler, Miss La Trobe strides about in June 1939 'with a whip in her hand' (p. 58). An energetic leader, she is pleased when she can impose her vision on others. By repressing her egotistical self at the beginning of the fourth act, she creates an extraordinary opportunity. Anything could happen.

In her experiment, breaking with theatrical convention, Miss La Trobe nearly becomes an artist who rejects patriarchal authority. 'Bossy' uncharacteristically abandons authorial control to nature – to the trees, to the cows, to the sky. She wants 'to douche them, with present-time reality' (p. 179). Woolf's diction cleverly and deliberately skirts the taboo. Miss La Trobe, however, desperately fears she might lose her audience. The ten minutes when she is not in control are painful to her. She suffers just as Cinderella's ugly step-sister suffers when, in order to make a good marriage with the Prince, she cuts off her own heel to fit into the glass slipper: 'Blood seemed to pour from her shoes' (p. 180). In the Later Typescript, the passage read not 'shoes' but 'veins', and, by changing one word in the Final Typescript, Woolf suggests the futile and self-hating sacrifice of a woman seeking safety in a husband. Her blood flowing down suggests self-mutilation, rather than a monthly cleansing or an annual ritual sacrifice preceding regeneration.

Miss La Trobe's panic ends when a brief rainstorm relieves the tension; however, Isa's response to that sudden, cathartic shower of rain is to envision giving up her life to end the suffering: 'On the altar of the rain-soaked earth she laid down her sacrifice' (*BA*, 1969, p. 181). In her unhappy marriage with Giles, she has sacrificed her life as an individual, and will continue to do so, since she regards history as an imprisoning cycle. Despite Isa's attraction for a martyred life, her sacrifice, an act of passive acquiescence to suffering, cannot forestall the war; indeed, Woolf's historical narrative suggests that submissiveness encourages the authoritarian use of force.

That shower also suggests the legend of St Swithin, Bishop of Winchester. Should it rain in July, on the anniversary of the day his buried bones were moved, it would rain for forty days. The brief shower in the summer of 1939 foreshadows the disaster of September, when Hitler's planes began bombing Poland. Similarly, the British war planes whose training-flight interrupts Mr Streatfield's speech portend the *Blitzkrieg*. Woolf recognised that the build-up of an armed airforce implied a nation readying for war, for in her letter of 27 July 1938 to Ling Su-Hua she wrote, 'People are tired of talking about war; but all the same we do nothing but buy arms. The air is full of aeroplanes at the moment' (*L*, VI). Before September 1939, the Japanese war on Manchurian China, the Italian invasion of Abyssinia and the Spanish Civil War had demonstrated to Woolf the terror of aerial bombardment.

Woolf's awareness of diplomacy's failure to prevent these wars is evident in Miss La Trobe's dumb show, inserted just after the shower. From former British colonies, representatives to the League of Nations appear to be talking, but do nothing. Neither

the agents schooled under the British Empire, nor the international forum for peace created in response to the First World War can
change the ominous plot of modern history.

After that important mime, the village children confront the
adults in the audience with reflecting mirrors. The next generation holds the present generation responsible for contemporary
history, in an action that realises the medieval definition of drama
as a mirror held up to the world, *speculum mundi*. Woolf thus places
the 1939 pageant within the ancient English tradition of miracle
and morality plays and *A Mirror for Magistrates*. Her didactic art is
not a modern innovation, not a propagandistic betrayal of her
culture.

Presiding over Act IV is no visible queen, but an unseen voice,
amplified by a megaphone. Although the speaker is not identified,
the author, Miss La Trobe, seems to be intruding her moral lesson
into the pageant. Through the megaphonic voice, Woolf parodies
the intrusive authorial voice in earlier fiction. Resuming total
control of her drama, Miss La Trobe addresses the audience
directly, exhorting them with a voice that masters the air and
prevents dialogue. What is spoken through a loudspeaker becomes the people's fate. This director seeks to dominate the people's
minds, just as Mussolini and Hitler did in their radio speeches.
Her pronouncement, 'A tyrant, remember, is half a slave' (*BA*,
1969, p. 187), admits that dictators depend on submissive masses.
In the historical context, British people obedient to the loudspeaker voice acquiesce just as German or Italian audiences cheered
their leaders' announcements.[12]

Throughout the pageant, Miss La Trobe's use of the gramophone to dominate her audience, to impose onto their
consciousness certain repeated phrases – such as 'Dispersed are
we' and 'no place like home' – recalls the propagandistic use of
recorded speeches and patriotic songs broadcast to radio audiences before and during the Second World War. The 'tick tick
tick' of the needle scratching on the record calls attention to the
mechanical reproduction of speech and suggests how repetition of
selected ideas and feelings blots out individual differences. Woolf
had used the same image in *Three Guineas* as she declined to join a
society: 'For by so doing we should merge our identity in yours;
follow and repeat and score still deeper the old worn ruts in which
society, like a gramophone whose needle has stuck, is grinding out
with intolerable unanimity "Three hundred million spent upon

arms"' (*TG*, p. 105).

In the Earlier Typescript (p. 210), Miss La Trobe confesses her highbrow pretensions: 'the rhyme, which has been inserted to entice you to believe that the author of this – by way of being honest – rhapsody has a university education'. In the final version, however, she flaunts her erudition as she asks her audience to question how 'this wall, . . . civilization' is to be built by 'orts, scraps and fragments like ourselves?' (*BA*, 1969, p. 188). She is alluding to Shakespeare's *Troilus and Cressida*, which builds dramatic tension around the possibility that the fall of Troy's wall might be prevented. This renaissance play, however, unlike Chaucer's version of the story, is built on the misogynist assumption of women's fickleness. Shakespeare's Cressida, like his Helen, leaves one lover for another. Troilus denounces his beloved, whom he believes has betrayed him and joined the Greek enemy: 'The fractions of her faith, orts of her love, / The fragments, scraps, the bits and greasy relics / Of her o'er-eaten faith, are bound to Diomed' (V.ii.158–60). In the same contemptuous tone of voice, Miss La Trobe's 'megaphonic, anonymous, loud-speaking affirmation' (*BA*, 1969, p. 186) denounces 'the gun slayers, the bomb droppers here or there. They do openly what we do slyly' (p. 187). In this harangue, she sounds like an authoritarian peace-monger, mounting an attack on the merchants of death. Even though she articulates a different message, she, like Mussolini or Hitler, encourages hostility, panders to her audience, and seeks to manipulate their sympathies. La Trobe's monologue ends, as the dictators' radio speeches often ended, with uplifting music.

Woolf heard Neville Chamberlain's speech broadcast from the airport, promising 'peace in our time' after yielding to Hitler's demand at the Munich conference on the Czechoslovak Sudetenland. She sarcastically records the 'frantic cheers, hysterical cries. . . bells pealing. . . perfectly infernal din' – but she notes that the villagers 'remained perfectly sure that it was a dirty business; and meant only another war when we should be unable to resist' (letter dated 3 October 1938 in *L*, VI). The villagers' pessimistic prediction proved correct in 1939.

In her novel, Woolf parodies Chamberlain's notorious radio broadcast of 1938 in the anti-climactic speech of Mr Streatfield. A magnificent mock-epic simile introduces the Reverend: 'As waves withdrawing uncover; as mist uplifting reveals; so, raising their eyes (Mrs Manresa's were wet; for an instant tears ravaged her powder) they saw, as waters withdrawing leave visible a tramp's old boot, a man in a clergyman's collar surreptitiously mounting a soap-box' (*BA*, 1969, p. 189). The only enlightenment this orator can offer is through the electric lights he hopes to put up in the church; otherwise, his speech merely repeats the message announced earlier in the amplified voice of authority, even as Neville Chamberlain repeated and granted Hitler's demand for the Sudentenland.

Dropping into the middle of that mock-epic simile, Mrs Manresa's tears, ravaging her powder, are no digression. In her shallow sentimentality, she, like the crowds cheering Chamberlain, expresses feelings that simplify a complex moral issue. Woolf's reader will remember that Mrs Manresa had recently used the mirror held up to her by a child to repair her make-up. Women who acquiesce to the role of seductress are, in a patriarchal culture, transformed into paragons of inconstancy. Manresa, like Cressida, has succumbed to that old plot. Although earlier in the narrative she seems to embody spontaneous sexuality, by the time she bids farewell to Giles, she is exposed as a creature of artifice whose pretentions to be a goddess of natural fertility fade: 'alas, sunset light was unsympathetic to her make-up; plated it looked, not deeply interfused' (p. 202). Her flirtatious behaviour is calculated to manipulate men, not to challenge the patriarchy. MANresa, from TasMANia, can define herself only in relation to a man. Her name and her luxuriant feminine image suggest she may have been modelled in part on Vanessa Bell and Katherine Mansfield (in earlier drafts, Manresa, like Mansfield, was born in New Zealand); however, the fictional Manresa lacks the creativity Virginia admired in Vanessa and Katherine. Mrs Manresa, like Milton's Eve, acts as the agent of a greater power.

Milton, blaming the loss of a natural paradise on Eve's weakness, not her challenge to divine authority, defines the postlapsarian world as one in which men shall dominate women, women shall bear children in pain, and men shall crush snakes underfoot. Woolf echoes Milton's description of Satan as 'squat like a toad' (*Paradise Lost*, IV, 799), as Giles crushes under his heel the snake and toad. A snake coiled in a circle, as this one is, in many cultures symbolises fertility and eternal life; however, Giles sees the snake choking on a toad as 'birth the wrong way round – a monstrous inversion' (*BA*, 1969, p. 99), and he kills it. Woolf's reader need accept neither Milton's history of the Fall, nor Giles's verdict and condemnation. In her portrayal of Giles's cowardly act of repulsion, Woolf mocks a traditionally heroic act. The image of St George slaying the dragon, used as a symbol of British national pride in the bellicose posters of the First World War, recalls the resurgence of aggressive nationalism in the 1930s. Giles's bloody shoe bears witness to petty tyranny, not glorious victory over evil.

Although she calls upon a commonly recognised association in St George crushing the dragon, Virginia Woolf built that symbol upon a vivid, private experience which she associated with contemporary politics. In her diary entry of 4 September 1935, after alluding to fascist propaganda, to Mosley's revived political activity, and to the League of Nations meeting to consider Mussolini's forceful invasion of Abyssinia, she recorded an extraordinary encounter: 'We saw a snake eating a toad: it had half the toad in, half out; gave a suck now & then. The toad slowly disappearing. L. poked its tail; the snake was sick of the crushed toad' (*D*, IV). A month later, she used that image in her letter to Julian Bell (14 Oct 1935), describing Ernest Bevin: 'like a snake whose swallowed a toad, denouncing him, crushing him' (*L*, V). At a Labour Party meeting, Woolf had heard Bevin denounce the pacifist George Lansbury over the question of imposing sanctions against Italy for the invasion of Abyssinia.[13] Woolf's memory links Mussolini's air raids with Bevin's verbal attacks, and her creative imagination transforms Leonard Woolf poking and Ernest Bevin crushing into Giles Oliver stamping. In reworking the image, she combined personal observation, domestic politics and fascist aggression. Giles Oliver's truimph over the snake embodies familial and international tyranny in a symbol traditionally identified with British culture.

Isa silently expresses her contempt for her husband's act: 'Silly little boy, with blood on his boots' (*BA*, 1969, p. 111), but Mrs Manresa endorses the bellicose myth by imagining herself a Queen and Giles her 'sulky hero' (p. 107). Woolf's revision sharpens her critique of Mrs Manresa as a woman in complicity with the tyrant, for in the Earlier Typescript only Isa notices the blood, but in the Later Typescript Mrs Manresa sees the blood and assumes he has performed an act of valour for her. Her response magnifies his male vanity and celebrates his act of forceful domination.

By his brief flirtation with her, Giles attempts to return to paradise, but Woolf deliberately sets his fling with this self-proclaimed 'wild child of nature' in a cultivated greenhouse garden.

The figures of natural fertility in this novel are the mothers, Lucy and Isa. They partially embody ancient, dual aspects of feminine power: the chaste warrior goddess of vengeance, who wields terrible weapons, and the goddess of nurturance, who comforts and eases pain. The Egyptian Isis, a terrifying and revitalising figure, and the Greek Diana, who punishes male voyeurism and who watches over women in childbirth, are present in their symbolic forms of the cow and the moon associated with Isa and Lucy.

Isa and Lucy only partially embody these goddesses, for they are nurturers, but not avengers. The power of British women to act has been diminished in a culture that idealises docile, passive, obedient girls. As the Victorian girls in the pageant sing, 'I'd be a butterfly', so Lucy acquiesces to her brother Bart's bullying, and Isa accepts Giles's domination. If that paradigm of submission to force is her only lot, then there is no alternative life for Isa, whose name echoes *aisa*, one of the Greek words for fate. With Isa, the reader feels that 'Surely it was time someone invented a new plot' (p. 215). Spain's Queen Isabella initiated a new plot by sponsoring exploration of the New World, but Giles's Isabel will repeat an old plot. The Egyptian Queen Cleopatra, who commanded a new plot, is a role enacted by Lillie Langtry, Eleonora Duse and Virginia Woolf, but not by Lucy Swithin.[14]

Midsummer should mark a turning-point. At midsummer, the goddess Proserpine leaves her mother Demeter to return to her husband who had raped her; she submits again to the god Pluto, in the Underworld, for six months of darkness. For Woolf, 'the profusion of darkness' imaged the approach of war – in the 'Time Passes' section of *To the Lighthouse*, Mr Carmichael, a cultural conservator, keeps reading Virgil while 'One by one all the lamps were extinguished.' Lucy, who is old enough to be Isa's mother, belongs to the generation who were adults during the First World War. Linking the public and private histories, Woolf specifies that the thirty-nine-year-old Isa is exactly 'the age of the century' (*BA*, 1969, p. 19). Her story represents the destiny of contemporary England. As the Second World War approaches, Isa re-enacts the tragic plot of separation from a maternal figure and submission to male authority on Midsummer's Eve 1939.[15]

Batty Lucy and dreamy Isa share a self-mutilating timidity. Their inability to rebel against forceful oppression is highlighted by Woolf's allusions to two women who did: Philomela and Procne. In the Greek version of the myth, Philomela, the virgin raped by her sister's husband Tereus, joins forces with Procne to enact terrible revenge: together, they kill Procne's child Itylus and serve up the boy's flesh for his father Tereus to eat. Fleeing the wrathful Tereus, Philomela is transformed into a swallow, Procne into a nightingale. Matthew Arnold's 'Philomela', following Roman versions of the myth, calls the nightingale Philomela and identifies her sister as the one who feels 'shame', Woolf blends characteristics of the two sisters as she connects them with Lucy and Isa.

Isa, haunted by the newspaper account of a young woman raped by solidiers, associates herself with the victim and, in her quotations of romantic poetry, repeats the sorrowful song of the nightingale. Like Arnold's Philomela, she moans about 'Eternal passion!' and 'Eternal pain!' Unlike the Greek mother, however, Isa never imagines sacrificing her son; indeed, she accepts Giles's continued domination because he is 'the father of her children' (*BA*, pp. 48, 215).

The swallow's migration and her constantly hopeful song are associated with Lucy. Bart, who calls his sister 'Cindy' (suggesting Cinderella among the ashes, still hoping for her prince), identifies her as 'Swallow, my sister, O sister swallow' (pp. 109, 115, 116), quoting from Swinburne's poem named for the sacrificed son, 'Itylus'. In that poem, the nightingale rebukes the swallow for forgetting Itylus, and Bart's allusion shifts his own feelings of guilt onto his sister, as if he is rebuking her for forgetting the sons lost in the First World War.

Woolf rejected the implication that mothers should feel guilt for sons lost in war; rather, the responsibility must be fixed on a culture that celebrated virility demonstrated in battle. When Bart, by wearing a newspaper helmet with a beak, attempts to arouse a display of fierce bravery in his grandson George, he is training the boy to become a man; that is, a fighter. Bart never questions the image of virility he acquired at school, reading the *Iliad*, or Arnold's version of combat, 'Sohrab and Rustum', in which the father, disguising his identity, engages in battle against the enemy's champion, whom he kills before he discovers his opponent is his own son, Sohrab. Rustum had not known of Sohrab's existence, because he believed that the child he had fathered had been 'one slight helpless girl'. The traditional exchange of boasts between these heroes identifies masculinity with courage but femininity with cowardice. Bart, sharing Arnold's culture, later 'looked at his son as if exhorting him to give over these womanish vapours and be a man, Sir' (*BA*, 1969, p. 133). Creon also identifies cowardice as womanly, when he rages against his son's appeal on behalf of Antigone. Both fathers, Creon and Rustum, unwittingly cause their sons' deaths, a parallel Woolf may have had in mind.

Bart, disappointed in his grandson's behaviour, vents his anger: ' "Heel!" he bawled, "heel, you brute!" And George turned; and the nurses turned holding the furry bear; they all turned to look at Sohrab the Afghan hound bounding and bouncing among the flowers' (p. 12). George and Sohrab are at first indistinguishable objects of Bart's commanding verb 'heel'. Woolf deliberately misleads her reader to assume the grandson is being addressed. The name 'Sohrab' appears in a late revision; earlier versions have traditional dog's names. Woolf strengthens her portrait of patriarchal culture by choosing the name Sohrab. As she knew, Matthew Arnold was the son of the educator Thomas Arnold, and the close friend of Arthur Clough. Matthew could boast to Arthur that he was imitating the rapidity of Homer's verse in 'Sohrab and Rustum', knowing that their common education allowed the comparison; however, Arthur's education, as Virginia Woolf had emphasised in *Three Guineas*, had come at the expense of denying an equal opportunity to Anne, his sister.

These mothers, Lucy and Isa, whose sons will carry on the patriarchal cultural tradition, bear a burden not of unearned guilt, but of complicity in what Winifred Holtby in 1935 described as the nationalistic cult of the cradle. In her *Women and a Changing Civilization*, published three years before Woolf's *Three Guineas*, Holtby analysed Mussolini's and Hitler's celebration of maternity, the cult of the cradle, in the context of Mosley's assertion, 'We want men who are men and women who are women', noting that all three fascists were advocating that women give up ambition for independent income and jobs outside the home. By connecting British with Italian and German reactionary politics, and by linking nationalism and militarism with hostility toward the equality of women, she anticipated the central arguments of *Three Guineas*. The female characters in *Between the Acts* enact only the restricted roles defined by a patriarchal culture; Isa's despairing wish that someone invent a new plot echoes Holtby's more blatant demand. 'What is there about women that should force them to become either queens or slaves?'[16]

If Lucy is correct in her belief that there is no historical change and people remain the same, then there can be no escape from the old plot that entraps her and Bart, and also Isa and Giles. In her conclusion, Woolf implicitly refutes the optimistic resolution of E. M. Forster's *Howards End*, where a new-born child symbolises hope for the future. Even if 'another life might be born', the reader cannot expect a third child fathered by Giles and grandfathered by Bart to transform the old story. In place of Forster's motto, 'Only connect', the audience hears the echo of 'We are dispersed' and 'Unity-Dispersity' becomes the fragmentary 'Un. . . dis. . .' (*BA*, 1969, p. 201).

As Isa and Giles prepare to repeat the cycle, the reader hears another allusion: 'first they must fight, as the dog fox fights with the vixen, in the heart of darkness, in the fields of night' (p. 210). Conrad's *Heart of Darkness*, like Woolf's novel, narrates a historical critique of imperialism. The terrifying movement backward in historical time at the end of Woolf's novel reflects Marlow's opening strategy in his narrative, drawing his audience back to an England that seemed uncivilised to a Roman commander. Marlow's intimate audience is a fellowship of men; he lied to Kurtz's fiancée. As long as women remain isolated from the horror, or pretend to ignore it, they continue to support the mastery of conquerors. To change the old plot, Isa must renounce the roles of vixen, nightingale and donkey; she must cease to be a patient vessel and passive victim.

Human history, rather than being determined by some immutable law of brutal nature, is the sum of human acts and speeches. Woolf's cultural vision is pessimistic, but not deterministic. Isa, like Lucy before her, acquiesces to force. Even though she, like St Augustine recalling his first sin, envisions the past in the rooted pear tree and in the hard green pears, Isa sees herself not as an independent soul challenging authority, but only as a donkey, like Mary, patiently bearing the burden. Although Isa sees no alternative history, she does hear one, which Woolf's readers share as an aural memory, 'murmured by waves; breathed by restless elm trees; crooned by singing women; what we must remember; what we would forget' (*BA*, 1969, p. 155). In the babble of voices and natural sounds between the pageant's acts, one can hear alternatives to the dictator's monologue.

In 1941, war seemed to repeat the tragedy of 1914, but Virginia Woolf, though she could see no future for herself, did elucidate the flaw in her cultural history that might be corrected. The cycle of dominance and victimisation enacted by Giles and Isa, and by Bart and Lucy, originates in the humanist tradition, as interpreted by the cultural elite Woolf associated with Cambridge. The assumption underlying *Between the Acts*, as *A Mirror for Magistrates*, is that change remains possible within the mutable world of history. Virginia Woolf's final novel demonstrates the power a woman can control 'even with only the end of an old inky pen'.

## NOTES

1. These sentences appear only in the typewritten draft (3633) of the letter (3634) to Benedict Nicolson dated 24 Aug 1940. In this assertion, Woolf deliberately echoes Mary Kingsley's complaint, 'being allowed to learn German was *all* the paid-for education I ever had. Two thousand pounds was spent on my brother's, I still hope not in vain.' Woolf had quoted Mary Kingsley in her first essay of *Three Guineas* (*TG*, p. 4). Woolf's n. 1 (*TG*, p. 145) also calls attention to Anne Clough, as another sister whose brother Arthur was educated at some expense, though little money was spent on her education. Woolf returns to the sister's unpaid-for education and the brother's paid-for education several times in *Three Guineas*.

2. For a persuasive analysis of the impact of her education on Woolf's development, see Jane Marcus's 'Liberty, Sorority, Misogyny', in *The Representation of Women in Fiction*, ed. Carolyn G. Heilbrun and Margaret R. Higonnet, Selected Papers from the English Institute, 1981, n.s. no. 7 (Baltimore: Johns Hopkins University Press, 1983) pp. 60–97.

3. S. P. Rosenbaum, 'Preface to a Literary History of the Bloomsbury Group', *New Literary History*, XII, no. 2 (Winter 1981) 334. Rosenbaum also asserts (p. 340) that, although 'she was more of a formalist than Forster, Virginia Woolf knew that there was no escaping history for women writers. When Bloomsbury's texts are looked at through succeeding ages, it is possible to describe not only how they developed in relation to one another but also how they are conjoined with contemporary events, including the publication of other texts.'

4. In making this assertion, I am relying on evidence drawn from

Mitchell A. Leaska's valuable scholarly edn of the Earlier Typescript and the Later Typescript of *Pointz Hall* (*PH*). In this essay, all quotations of the Earlier Typescript and Later Typescript are to Leaska's edn. His publication of these typescripts makes possible differing critical interpretations of Woolf's progressive revisions.

As I read the changes Woolf made, and compare the Earlier, Later and published versions of her novel, I find her critique of British culture becoming increasingly explicit and sharply worded. Mitchell Leaska has offered another interpretation: 'The Later Typescript, from which many deep folds of anger had been smoothed, became in effect a bridge of compromise between the Earlier and Final Typescripts. Virginia Woolf had indeed succeeded in suppressing the ferocity of her original plan. At what price, however, only she would finally know' (p. 29). His reading of the diaries, letters, and typescripts leads him to speculate that '*Pointz Hall* is the longest suicide note in the English language' (p. 451). I prefer to consider Woolf's novel in its historical and literary context.

5.  This essay on *Between the Acts* is drawn from my comparative study entitled 'Years that Ask Questions'.

6.  See Woolf's diary entry for 4 Sep 1935, in *D*, IV. In 1931, Mosley's party had enlisted the support of Harold Nicolson, who edited its newspaper *Action* and stood for Parliament as its representative. Harold was Benedict's father and Vita Sackville-West's husband.

The complexity possible within Woolf's vision of her flawed culture is evidenced in an unexpected statement, inserted into her tribute to man she regarded as a cultural guide. To some people, she wrote, this man seemed 'too ruthless, too dictatorial – a Hitler, a Mussolini, a Stalin. Absorbed in some idea, set upon some cause, he ignored feelings, he overrode objections.' The man so described was Roger Fry, in *RF*, p. 291.

7.  Reprinted in E. M. Forster, *Two Cheers for Democracy* (New York: Harcourt, Brace and World, 1951) p. 70.

8.  Samuel Hynes, *The Auden Generation: Literature and Politics in England in the 1930s* (New York: Viking, 1977) p. 334. Woolf's descriptions of the Munich Crisis are found in her letters to Vanessa, 28 Sep, 3 and 8 Oct 1938. Woolf was not the only woman novelist influenced by the Munich Crisis. Marguerite Yourcenar, French translator of *The Waves*, responded to Munich by writing her *Coup de Grâce* (1939), exploring the sexual politics through a historical fiction set in 1919. Elizabeth Bowen's *Death of the Heart*, a book Virginia Woolf received during the aftermath of the Munich Crisis (letter of 9 Oct 1938, in *L*, VI), reflects the growing fear of Italian and German fascism and the uneasy dread of war in the late 1930s. I treat the political parables of these novels in 'Years that Ask Questions'.

9.  Among critics convinced that Woolf deserves serious consideration as a political writer, those who have most influenced my reading are Jane

Marcus, in 'Art and Anger', and Berenice A. Carroll, in ' "To Crush him in our Own Country": The Political Thought of Virginia Woolf', both in *Feminist Studies*, IV (1978) 69–98 and 99–131, respectively. Alex Zwerding traced the allusions to the Second World War in his *'Between the Acts and the Coming of War'*, *Novel*, X (1977) 220–36.

10. That the name Giles is a form of Guillaume strengthens the evidence that Woolf had William the Conqueror in mind as she developed the symbolic historical significance of the Olivers. Despite Woolf's attention to the symbolism of names in this novel, however, I do not believe an analysis can be built upon the following coincidental connections: Lytton Strachey's first name was Giles, and his elder brother was named Oliver; Roger Fry's sister was named Isabel, and Julia Stephen's first cousin, Lady Isabel Somerset, supported women's right to work and to sexual freedom.

11. E. M. Forster had indignantly complained of Budge's theft in 'The Objects', *Athenaeum*, no. 4697 (1920) 599–600. I am indebted to Mitchell Leaska's scrupulous and copious note on Budge (*PH*, pp. 235–6); however, Leaska does not offer the same interpretation.

12. The origin of my reading here is Margaret Comstock's perceptive analysis, 'The Loudspeaker and the Human Voice: Politics and the Form of *The Years*', in *BNYPL*, LXXX, no.2 (Winter 1977) 252–75. During the Abyssinian crisis, Woolf recorded in her diary 'A very sensational voice on the loudspeaker last night. M[ussolini]. Closes the door' (entry for 5 Sep 1935, in *D*, IV). Her letters describing Londoners' response to the Munich Crisis include her memory of government messages delivered from loudspeaker vans: 'loud speakers slowly driving and solemnly exhorting the citizens of Westminster Go and fit your gas masks' (1 Oct 1938, in *L*, VI).

13. See Woolf's diary entries for 4 Sep and 2 Oct, in *L*, VI. The entry for 2 Oct includes her characterisation of masculine political actions as 'this weight of roast beef & beef' and of feminine political actions as 'a little reed piping' – perhaps an allusion to the myth of Syrinx, as reinterpreted by Ethel Symth in *Female Pipings in Eden*.

14. Woolf commented on Roger Fry's pleasure in the performances of Lillie Langtry and Eleonora Duse in the role of Cleopatra (*RF*, pp. 64, 67). Woolf writes of 'acting the part of Cleopatra' at a party (letter to Elizabeth Bowen, 29 Jan 1939 in, *L*, VI). Lilian La Trobe, like Lillie Langtry, came from the Channel Islands.

15. On Midsummer's Eve 1939, Woolf observed and participated in celebrations by French people in Bayeux, where she probably viewed the tapestry depicting Guillaume le Conquerant invading Saxon England. See her letters to Vanessa Bell and Ethel Smyth, 19 June 1939.

16. Winifred Holtby, *Women and a Changing Civilization*, repr. (Chicago: Academy Press, 1978) p. 172 (1st edn 1935); see also pp. 151–63 on the reactionary and anti-feminist politics of Hitler, Mussolini and

Mosley. It is possible that Lucy's project, installing electrical lights in the church, mockingly echoes Holtby's praise of 'the English woman electrical engineer, Miss Jeanie Dicks, who secured the contract for re-wiring Winchester Cathedral' (p. 178). Holtby dedicated her book to Ethel Smyth and Cicely Hamilton.

# 15 The Stage of Scholarship: Crossing the Bridge from Harrison to Woolf[1]

SANDRA D. SHATTUCK

> So far we might perhaps say that art was non-moral. But the statement would be misleading, since, as we have seen, art is in its very origin social, and social means human and collective. Moral and social are, in their final analysis, the same. That human, collective emotion, out of which we have seen the choral dance arise, is in its essence moral; that is, it unites.    (Jane Harrison, *Ancient Art and Ritual*[2])

> The gramophone was affirming in tones there was no denying, triumphant yet valedictory: *Dispersed are we*; who have come together. But, the gramophone asserted, *let us retain whatever made that harmony.*
>  O let us, the audience echoed (stooping, peering, fumbling), keep together. For there is joy, sweet joy, in company.    (Virginia Woolf, *BA*, 1969, p. 196)

It is an unsettling experience to read Jane Ellen Harrison's *Ancient Art and Ritual* side by side with Virginia Woolf's *Between the Acts*. The uncanny reverberations that traverse from the scholarly work into the pages of the fictional piece compound themselves until one would almost say that Woolf's work is a fictional rewrite of Harrison's scholarship. It is as if Woolf were staging Harrison's work, providing a theatre where creative scholarship and creative writing combine in their efforts at taking up questions about art, society, religion, the family, history, war.

Both works, in their own ways, articulate a grand search for origins: in Harrison, it is the illumination of art's origins in ritual;

278

for Woolf, it is the location of the origins of war in a patriarchal structuration of society that creates violence, domestic and global. Their shared urge to pose questions that get at an understanding of their world leads them to an agreement on the moral purpose of art – specifically, its ability to evoke communal experience with the possibility of collective action.

Woolf's last novel is a palimpsest of 'orts, scraps and fragments' (*BA*, 1969, p. 188) of Egyptian, Greek and Christian mythology, Greek and Elizabethan drama, English history and literature. It would therefore be foolhardy to claim that *Between the Acts* is a direct result of Woolf's reading of *Ancient Art and Ritual*. Nevertheless, the resonances of Harrison's work in Woolf's novel seem to me so striking that it is difficult to avoid concluding that the scholar had a strong influence on the writer. This I shall try to show by looking at the works themselves. To what extent Harrison affected Woolf is subject for research still to be done and lies outside the scope of this paper. If we look to the letters for clues to Harrison's and Woolf's personal relationship, we are left with a sparse sketch of dinners and visits. We know that Woolf's library contained an autographed copy of *Ancient Art and Ritual*, that Woolf read Harrison's *Epilegomena*, that Hogarth Press published Harrison's *Reminiscences of a Student's Life* in 1925. What place Harrison held in Woolf's imagination and thoughts on art, myth, ritual, we can only surmise. Immortalised by Woolf in *A Room of One's Own* as 'J. H.', Harrison must have held immense appeal as a role model and teacher. Woolf was acutely aware of the critical importance of education; she was equally eloquent on the discriminatory and repressive practices of educational institutions. She would have recognised the achievement that it was for Harrison to become a classical scholar and understood all too well the tyranny that kept Harrison out of the university classroom, confining her to teaching-positions in boys' schools. Woolf, the autodidact, and Harrison, the trained student, were both imaginative scholars who read in several different fields and who took up the questions posed by different disciplines.[3] *Between the Acts* reflects these many-layered influences; so also does *Ancient Art and Ritual*. Primarily known as a classical scholar,[4] Harrison's work is nevertheless filled with 'orts, scraps and fragments' from linguistics, anthropology, folklore, theology, philosophy and psychology. Harrison's passion for languages and her linguistic ability (she began learning Farsi in her seventies) must have been admired by Woolf, the artisan of words and student of languages herself. As a creator of goddess-like women in her works, and because she realised history was the story of heroes written by men, Woolf must have been entranced by the extensive scholarly work on goddesses that Harrison presents in her *Prolegomena* and *Themis*. Harrison's lifestyle must have also held some appeal for Woolf. For a theorist who found much to criticise in the nuclear family and romantic love, Woolf must have been struck by this passage from the *Reminiscences*:

> By what miracle I escaped marriage I do not know, for all my life long I fell in love. But, on the whole, I am glad. I do not doubt that I lost much, but I am quite sure I gained more. Marriage, for a woman at least, hampers the two things that made life to me glorious – friendship and learning. In man it was always the friend, not the husband, that I wanted. Family life has never attracted me. At its best it seems to me rather narrow and selfish; at its worst, a private hell. The rôle of wife and mother is no easy one; with my head full of other things I might have dismally failed. On the other hand, I have a natural gift for community life. It seems to me sane and civilised and economically right. I like to live spaciously, but rather plainly, in large halls with great spaces and quiet libraries. I like to wake in the morning with the sense of a great, silent garden round me. These things are, or should be, and soon will be, forbidden to the private family; they are right and good for the community. If I had been rich I should have founded a learned community for women, with vows of consecration and a beautiful rule and habit; as it is, I am content to have lived many years of my life in a college. I think, as civilisation advances, family life will become, if not extinct, at least much modified and curtailed.[5]

There are shades of Woolf's 'A Society' in Harrison's 'learned community' of women.[6] But whatever the proof of influence, personal and professional, between the two women, what I do find is that a reading of Harrison's *Ancient Art and Ritual* helps to shed light on Woolf's *Between the Acts*, a novel that presents more than its share of questions.

Just what is *Between the Acts*? How does it fit into our classificatory system of literary genres? Is it a novel, a play, the novelisation of a play? In this last novel, Woolf continues her drive to break the boundaries of the traditional novel form. *The Pargiters* shows us that *The Years* was to have been a novel-essay composed of fictional chapters describing the lives of women in a Victorian family followed by expository chapters in which Woolf presented the research and explained the rationale behind her fiction; the whole is a critique of the patriarchal family in Victorian England.[7] Because of Leonard Woolf's criticism and Virginia's own uneasiness with her attempt to combine what she termed the 'granite and rainbow' styles of writing, *The Years* never appeared in the form in which Woolf intended it.[8] Although not a combination of 'granite and rainbow', *Between the Acts* is nevertheless an interweaving of theatre and novel, perhaps more appropriately termed, according to Woolf's formula, a novel-play.

The novel begins and ends with the inhabitants of Pointz Hall. Within this framing we are given not only the entire text of the pageant presented on the lawn and terrace of Pointz Hall, but everything that goes around, through and between the pageant: the stage-setting; actors changing in the bushes; Miss La Trobe's stage directions and directorial curses and comments; the 'chuff chuff chuff' of the phonograph and the text it issues; the atmospheric and natural interruptions of cows, swallows, rain and planes; the village newspaper reporter's comments; the chorus's mutterings and movements; the comments and reactions of the spectators; the clergyman's speech; and, between the acts, the drama enacted by the figures of Pointz Hall.

Both the pageant and what goes on in the Pointz Hall scenes provide critiques of English history and society, with the family and personal relationships central to those critiques. Woolf does this by reworking drama and myth, by this attempt at a breakthrough in form. The pageant itself is made up of plays within plays, themselves comments on various dramatic traditions. In reading *Between the Acts* it would be wrong to separate out the prose and the drama, for it is precisely their intertwining that gives the novel-play its provocative form. We can visualise the pageant, see it performed in our minds; but the novel-play gives us what we could not get at a performance: the spectators' reactions, La Trobe's thoughts, the 'acts' between. By the same token, a novel without the pageant would not have the immediacy of dramatic impact which Woolf achieves. In proposing that *Between the Acts* is influenced by Harrison's work with Greek drama and ritual, it would be possible to view the time frame of the whole novel-play as that of a Greek drama, from sun-up to sun-down. It is also worth mentioning here that an analysis of *Between the Acts* is quite revealing if one keeps Brecht in mind; this is not entirely surprising, since Brecht's epic theatre is itself indebted to the Greeks.[9]

Before turning to the Greek elements in *Between the Acts*, I should like first to acknowledge the importance of Elizabethan drama in Woolf's novel-play. In a 1927 essay entitled 'The Narrow Bridge of Art'[10] Woolf challenges the critic to look at contemporary literature and to speculate on its future. Taking up the task herself, she says that modern literature is filled with some dissatisfaction and difficulty that stems from the failure of poetry to serve the contradictory experiences of the modern world. She asks if there was a form capable of expressing this attitude of 'contrast and collision' (p. 12) and replies that it existed in the Elizabethan poetic drama. Shakespeare is the model. As she states, Woolf sees in his drama the free and full expression of an unconfused mind. Woolf faults the modern poetic play and modern poetry for being unable to confront the present, for being confused and for presenting what she calls a distorted vision. She locates the writer's current unease in a world that is filled with 'incongruously coupled' emotions (p. 16) and conflicting, constantly jarring experiences. After offering the thought that perhaps poetry has become an inadequate art form for contemporary experience, Woolf then turns to prose. It is here that she succinctly describes *Between the Acts*, the novel she was to write over ten years after her essay:

> That cannibal, the novel, which has devoured so many forms of art will by then have devoured even more. We shall be forced to invent new names for the different books which masquerade under this one heading. And it is possible that there will be among the so-called novels one which we shall scarcely know how to christen. It will be written in prose, but in prose which has many of the characteristics of poetry. It will have something of the exaltation of poetry, but much of the ordinariness of prose. It will be dramatic, and yet not a play. It will be read, not acted. By what name we are to call it is not a matter of very great importance. What is important is that this book which we see on the horizon may serve to express some of those feelings which seem at the moment to be balked by poetry pure and simple and

to find the drama equally inhospitable to them.    ('The Narrow Bridge of Art', p. 18)

What Woolf attempts to outline in her essay is a literary form which 'will take the mould of that queer conglomeration of incongruous things – the modern mind' (pp. 19–20). It is through an inextricable blending of prose, poetry and drama that Woolf hopes to accomplish a vision that is simultaneously microscopic and macroscopic. According to Woolf, the three genres within this as-yet-unnamed novel have different tasks. It is up to prose to detail particularities, to 'give the sneer, the contrast, the question, the closeness and complexity of life' (p. 19). Poetry will find the least comfortable accommodations; its ability to present startling simple truths and beauty will perforce be sacrificed.[11] Drama will offer a logical cohesive ordering that will permit a broader view of life (Shakespeare is still the reference here) as well as create an 'explosive emotional effect' (p. 22). Woolf goes so far as to say that the desire of the writer is to draw blood from the readers. This is a somewhat violent turn of phrase for a pacifist, but perhaps it illustrates Woolf's belief in the crucial importance for her writing to get to the reader, to induce thought, discussion and the possibility of social change.

Woolf's expectations for this novel of the future do indeed describe a piece of literature we have seldom encountered. One could imagine Woolf's topic was film, not the novel, as she goes on to enumerate what she hopes this novel will dramatise:

the power of music, the stimulus of sight, the effect on us of the shape of trees or the play of colour, the emotions bred in us by crowds, the obscure terrors and hatreds which come so irrationally in certain places or from certain people, the delight of movement, the intoxication of wine. (p. 23)

I have discussed this essay at length, because I believe it helps to understand the creative theory behind *Between the Acts*. it also attests to the importance of the Elizabethan dramatic influence; La Trobe's work is after all called a 'pageant'. Harrison's *Ancient Art and Ritual* can also be of some help here. Although much of her work concerns Greek ritual and religion, in searching for the connections between art and ritual, Harrison looks to many other examples. In the third chapter of her book, 'Seasonal Rites: The

Spring Festival', Harrison discusses the spring festivals and May Day celebrations of Europe. These are festivals that welcome in the spring (food and fertility) and banish winter (hunger and barrenness). These pageants require a Queen of the May and a Jack-in-the-Green or King of the May. There are maypoles, either trees with greenery still on them, or poles decked with greenery and flowers, and a procession of townspeople who follow in the dance. It is in this light that I view the curious references to Mrs Manresa as queen of the pageant and Giles as her hero. Three times Manresa is called queen of the festival or pageant; twice she is described as being a goddess and once it is with 'flower-chained captives' following her. The first mention of Manresa and Giles together as queen and hero occurs at the moment of a May dance in the pageant; the chorus and actors are dancing around Queen Elizabeth on her soap box and singing the words 'a-maying, a-maying'. Manresa as queen and Giles as hero could have their political implications if we see them as parallels to the contemporary royal figures about whom the spectators comment. The flowers from the Coronation that decorate the barn, Manresa's 'flower-chained captives' and her appellation of 'queen', Giles as the warrior hero pleasing Manresa with his blood-stained tennis shoes, suggest a complicity between the Queen and King of a May festival and the actual monarchs of England. The layers of reference again are many, but the layer of ritual should not be ignored.

## I  THE IMPORTANCE OF RITUAL AND RELIGION

The concept of a bridge that links ritual and art is one that inhabits Harrison's imagination and theories behind her work. The image is strongly underlined in *Ancient Art and Ritual*, but perhaps more interestingly, it reappears in the *Reminiscences* as a strong motivating force. In speaking of her 'dabblings' in archaeology and anthropology, Harrison says,

> both were needful for my real subject – religion. When I say 'religion', I am instantly obliged to correct myself; it is not religion, it is ritual that absorbs me. I have elsewhere [*Art and Ritual*] tried to show that Art is not the handmaid of Religion, but that Art in some sense springs out of Religion, and that

between them is a connecting link, a bridge, and that bridge is Ritual. On that bridge, emotionally, I halt.   (*Reminiscences*, p. 84)

And further on:

I mention these ritual dances, this ritual drama, this bridge between art and life, because it is things like these that I was all my life blindly seeking. A thing has little charm for me unless it has on it the patina of age. Great things in literature, Greek plays for example, I most enjoy when behind their bright splendours I see moving darker and older shapes. That must be my *apologia pro vita mea*.   (pp. 86–7)

Those 'darker and older shapes' moving about in the background are evocative of Lucy Swithin's lumbering mastodons and mammoths travelling in the swamp that was England when there was no Channel to divide island and continent. Throughout *Between the Acts* there are allusions to a more 'primitive' and originary state: Giles kicking a 'barbaric' and 'pre-historic' stone before he kills the snake; Lucy's *Outline of History* and her searching-out of the beginning of history; Giles and Isa as the originary couple at the end of the novel standing like 'dwellers in caves'; La Trobe's as yet unformed play, a type of creation story with two figures and the first words. These moments in Woolf point to an impulse she and Harrison share – the impulse to explain the current state of affairs by reaching back into ancient history and pre-history. For Harrison this means an investigation into religion and ritual. Both these aspects are present in *Between the Acts*.

For Woolf and her vociferously anti-clerical stance, *Between the Acts* is strangely steeped in religion. But it is a religion as Harrison presents it in her work; that is, it is the creative and emotional, the mystical and social aspects that intrigue Woolf. In *Between the Acts*, it seems that Woolf is investigating the power of religion as a social force, its ability to unite people in some way. There is of course a condemnation of religion; the 'Picnic Party' scene, in which Edgar T. proposes to Eleanor Hardcastle so that as a young married couple they can travel to Africa and convert the 'heathens' together, is a devastating picture of organised religion as colonialism, as well as of the complicity of romantic love and marriage with imperialism. Nevertheless, religion, as exemplified by a syncresis of Egyptian, Greek and Christian elements, as well as the aspect of ritual and drama, does weave itself throughout *Between the Acts*. The pageant is put on for religious reasons; the proceeds will go towards the installation of electric light in the church. The pagaent is also a ritual that has been re-enacted over the last seven years. In Apuleius's *Golden Ass*, the incantation to Isis reveals seven as the fitting number; it is Isa who observes the ritual repetition of Bart and Lucy's exchange on the weather and the pageant. The barn is likened to a Greek temple: the play is enacted on what could be the scene of a Greek theatre. The chapel–larder with its carved arch in the cellar of Pointz Hall is described as having changed 'as religion changed' (*BA*, p. 32). Mr Streatfield, the clergyman, is sympathetically described, his individuality and human weakness marked by his tobacco-stained fingers. Streatfield is the one perceptive critic of La Trobe's work; he is astute and careful in articulating those aspects of the pageant which are crucial – the confusion, the question, the unity, the chorus, the contribution of nature, self-reflection, the barriers and bridges between spectator and actor. Then there is Lucy Swithin, the woman with the golden cross; she is the Isis–Madonna figure, the virgin mother who 'heals' Dodge. Lucy's religion is 'more of a force or a radiance' (p. 25), as Bart says, rather than the worship of a throne-seated figure called God. Isa even mistakes the nature of Lucy's religion, when she assumes Lucy's skyward gaze is a search for God, while Lucy is simply speculating on the possibility of rain. She is the one who attends to superstition, asking about the origins of the term 'knock on wood'. It is her ranging thoughts that allow her to engage in an 'imaginative reconstruction of the past' (p. 9); her religion unifies in 'a circular tour of the imagination – one-making' (p. 175). It is her thought and religion that exasperate the unimaginative and exacting ratiocination practised by Bart and Giles.

In *Epilegomena to the Study of Greek Religion*,[12] a forty-page sequel to *Prolegomena* and *Themis*, Harrison summarises her concepts of religion. She begins with the social origin of religion and insists that it be studied within that context. Ritual, because it is grounded in religion, is therefore a social art, precisely because it is performed as a community and for the collective good. The goal of religion is the preservation and continuation of life; ritual accomplishes this through two impulses which Harrison calls 'expulsion' and 'impulsion'. The rites performed, which can be folk plays, fertility dramas, children's games, peasants' festivals, work to expel evil, manifested in hunger and barrenness, and to bring in good, which is food and fertility. Expulsion and impulsion are the double edge of the same will to live, which is made up of procreation and the search for food. Most of these thoughts are already to be found in *Ancient Art and Ritual*. In this book, Harrison establishes early on the emotional basis for ritual. It is 'collectivity and emotional tension' (p. 36) which characterise a rite. The intense emotional desire for something to be done, either rain to fall or crops to prosper or a battle to be won, is enacted in the ritual.

Before going on to a further discussion of the *Epilegomena*, it is important here to situate Harrison within the discipline of Western anthropolgy. The enterprise of rediscovering and rereading Harrison with feminist eyes is indeed an exuberant one; it should nevertheless not blind us to the racism and ethnocentrism which mark her work and which still characterise a good deal of Western scholarship, not only in the fields of anthropology and folklore. Particularly in *Ancient Art and Ritual*, we find that the name of the subject of a seemingly disinterested discourse of investigation is the 'savage', whose face appears in varying forms, such as the Huichol and Omaha Native Americans, the Kikuyu, the Fijians.[13] Harrison studies the 'savage' in order better to understand her own culture. The working theoretical assumption is that the 'savage' is a simpler being, more emotional and devoid of the gift of abstract thinking. This is based on the belief in a chronological hierarchy of civilisation and thus allows Harrison to privilege the Greeks over the Egyptians, calling the Egyptians 'slower-witted than the Greeks', a 'stupid child' rather than an 'abnormally brilliant' one (p. 15). The care and concern of the scholar who says, 'Here, again, we have some modern prejudice and misunderstanding to overcome' (p. 30), must be considered in light of such statements as, 'The "beastly devices of the heathen" weary and disgust me' (*Reminiscences*, p. 83), and 'abstraction is foreign to his [the savage's] mental habit' (*Ancient Art and Ritual*, p. 71).

Although Woolf too should be situated within this tradition, she does occasionally break through this mould. *Between the Acts* shows her to believe in a primitive, originary state, but she does denounce colonialism, and devastatingly so. In Mr Budge, who acts the part of a Victorian constable directing the traffic of Her Majesty's Empire, Woolf succinctly and powerfully outlines the intersection of race, sex and class as they operate within colonialism. As Mr Budge describes his 'whole-time, white man's job' (*BA*, 1969, p. 163), brandishing his truncheon all the while, he touches upon the domestic and foreign controls, the rules governing manners and marriage, colonies, working conditions in the mines and the looms. As Budge says, 'That's the price of Empire; that's the white man's burden' (ibid.).

In returning to the *Epilegomena*, we can see that Harrison has begun to feel the influence of Freud and that that influence shows up later in *Between the Acts*. In her section on 'Totem, Tabu and Exogamy' in the first chapter, entitled 'Primitive Ritual', Harrison locates the beginning of society in the family and describes the 'primal family' as consisting of one male, several females and the children. The father–son competition that arises out of the possession of females results in exogamy. Harrison then makes a strong statement about sexual jealousy:

> The primal cardinal fact is that totemism consists in group distinction, that it functions through tabu and that it takes its rise in perhaps the strongest or at least the fiercest of human impulses in sex jealousy. Here, as so often elsewhere, the fabric of Church and State rests on a basis of savage animal impulse, crossed by the dawnings of a social impulse.[14]

*Between the Acts* begins and ends with sexual jealousy, competition, conquest and domination. In the first scene Mrs Haines is aware of the attraction between Isa and Rupert Haines and wishes violently to destroy the emotion that excluded her 'as a thrush pecks the wings off a butterfly' (*BA*, 1969, p.6). Both extra-marital attractions between Manresa and Giles and Isa and Haines begin at sporting-matches, cricket and tennis. Manresa, who attains a monstrous dimension each time Woolf calls her 'the Manresa', is clearly in the heterosexual market place, actiely and voraciously pursuing men. Woolf acknowledges female sexual competition when she says of Manresa that 'always when she spoke to women, she veiled her eyes, for they, being conspirators, saw through it' (p. 41). Isa remembers her first meeting with Giles while they were fishing: her line got tangled, she gave up, watched the masterful Giles and fell in love. Bart's childhood memory of his sister Lucy also centres around fishing. These reoccurring references underline the Isis–Osiris myth, upon which Woolf draws heavily. Evelyn Haller has discussed this at length in her important article.[15] Dodge's attraction to Giles is described in primal terms; it is 'the muscular, the hirsute, the virile' (p. 106) which distracts him from Isa. There is the newspaper account of a violent gang rape by military men that threads its way throughout the novel–play, reasserting itself in Isa's memory.[16] When Isa thinks of her physical attraction to Haines, she shores up the marital contract with Giles by repeating the cliché, as she calls it, that her husband is 'the father of my children'. Giles's killing of the toad-gorged snake is an act of violent bravado; the testament of this courage, the blood-stained tennis shoes, is seen alternately by Manresa as a sign of heroism and by Isa as the mark of a silly boy. In the Earlier Typescript *(PH)*, Woolf is explicit about Haines's sexual exploits, of which no mention is made in the final version: Haines has possibly impregnated the charwoman's daughter and is the father of William Dodge's child. The final scene of *Between the Acts* is the arena of domestic battle, love-making and procreation as Isa and Giles are compared to the dog fox and the vixen and are placed in a primal setting of cave-dwellers.

It is important to note that Woolf's presentation of sexual confrontation is intricately bound up in her syncretic use of mythical elements. As Evelyn Haller has correctly pointed out, 'I am arguing that for personal and political reasons – many of them anguished – Woolf chose early in life to become a woman of letters and in her craft to eschew male-dominated systems of thought for one informed by the oldest, most enduring, and most coherent female myth: that of Isis.'[17]

For Woolf, the uncovering of the underside of history, literature, myth and scholarship is not a smooth search ending in a positivistic reversal of 'male-dominated systems of thought', but more often than not, reveals a level of violence inherent in any contestative act. The violence embedded in 'A Society' and in Woolf's killing of 'the Angel in the House' in order to fight self-censorship are just two examples in Woolf's other writings. In *Between the Acts*, Woolf's use of syncresis obviates the positing of a conflict-free hegemonic ideal; instead, we have figures that are pieced together with different mythologies that are then seen through a twist of the lens as individuals situated in the personal and political spheres of Woolf's own time and place. This layering and fragmentation within the rubrics of sex, mythology and politics can be found in all the characters of Bart, Lucy, Isa, Giles, Manresa and William Dodge. Violence is an integral part of *Between the Acts*, not only within the relationships between characters, but as Woolf is careful to point out, within the very language itself.[18] As she says, 'Words this afternoon ceased to lie flat in the sentence. They rose, became menacing and shook their fists at you' (*BA*, 1969, p. 59).

It seems that, for Woolf, the painful and laborious act of creating language out of enforced silence in order to give voice to an oppositional vision against enculturated and institutionalised norms of knowledge always exacts a certain amount of blood. Thus, we have the figure of Isa, forged out of the elements of the Egyptian goddess and simultaneously marked by the reiteration of a rape, which has its foundation in Greek mythology and in a contemporary newspaper account that implicates the British military. This syncresis and violence are evident in perhaps the most gruesome incident in *Between the Acts*, in which Giles crushes the snake choked by a toad. As mentioned earlier, Giles is the king of the pageant as well as an Osiris figure. Harrison shows in *Ancient Art and Ritual* that the King of the May Day festivals has his roots in the figures of Adonis and Apollo. In this sense, we could view the mythological level of Giles's violent act as Apollo's killing of the python at Delphi and the possibility of 'an imagined transition from a matriarchal order to a patriarchal one'.[19] If we keep Woolf's syncretic methodology in mind, the kicking of the stone that leads Giles to the choked snake situates his action within an intersection of sex, myth and politics: 'The first kick was Manresa (lust). The second, Dodge (perversion). The third, himself (coward)' (*BA*, 1969, p. 99). Giles's bloody solution ('Action relieved him' – ibid.) firmly underscores Woolf's acknowledgement of violence in her own enterprise, as I see it in the writing of *Between the Acts*, of uncovering suppression and oppression within myth and sexuality.

The discussion above belongs in a broader and more careful analysis of Woolf's presentation of sexuality, heterosexual and homosexual, as it operates within the family, society, myth, religion and politics. Let us now turn to the possibility of community, as it occurs in the collective nature of the chorus.

## II   THE IMPORTANCE OF THE CHORUS

One of the most striking features of *Between the Acts* is the chorus. It is an amorphous group composed of villagers, who are also called pilgrims; this emphasises the religious aspect of the chorus as well as the possibility of some type of quest or search. The sacking they wear not only has religious overtones, but is a possible sign of poverty; the chorus sings the song of village labourers working in the fields. United by their lack of proper names, this group of villagers remains a strongly felt presence that performs a disturbing and occasionally disruptive background ritual procession, dance and song. When they reside in the background, their chant and song are marked by gaps that emphasise what phrases are lifted out of the sometimes inaudible, sometimes indistinguishable confusion of words. When the chorus appears in the foreground, it is joined by the actors; the group collectively recites or sings commentaries and counterpoints to the action within the play. The final scene with the mirrors is a joining of actors, chorus and spectators in a conflict of speculation and reflection that breaks down the barriers separating audience and actors. I believe it is this breakdown that constitutes Woolf's urgent call to her readers to take up their unacted parts, to take on the social responsibility of acting within the horrible arena of war, individually as well as within a group, by speaking out against the atrocities of nationally sanctioned murder and fascism.

In *Ancient Art and Ritual*, Harrison cites the chorus as the focal point for her study of the transition from ritual to art. It is primarily in the shift from worshippers–actors to spectators that this transition occurs. Harrison examines this transition in the fifth chapter, entitled 'The Transition from Ritual to Art: The *Dromenon* and the Drama'. She begins by stressing the strangeness of a Greek play for a modern viewer, saying, 'In many minds there will be left a feeling that, whether they have enjoyed the play or not, they are puzzled: there are odd effects, conventions, suggestions' (p. 119). Harrison could have been describing the spectator at the pageant who asks, 'And if we're left asking questions, isn't it a failure as a play?' (*BA*, 1969, p. 200). In *Between the Acts*, this unease with an impalpable, non-discrete meaning vibrates outward; the spectators of the pageant ask of La Trobe, 'But what does she mean?', and we, as readers of the novel-play, put the same question to Woolf.

If we look at Harrison's enumeration of those 'odd effects', we shall see how they might apply to *Between the Acts*. Harrison speaks of 'the main deed of the Tragedy' occurring off stage. The murder or suicide of heroine or hero is not seen, but rather reported in a messenger's speech. If we look at the pageant as the story of England in the last several centuries, as the nation is about to be plunged into the tragedy of war, we see that the most important agent in that history is indeed absent from the stage, much to Colonel Mayhew's chagrin. As he asks, 'Why leave out the British Army? What's history without the Army, eh?' (*BA*, 1969, p. 157). Instead, we are given hints of those exploits through the gramophone's chorus, 'Armed and valiant / Bold and blatant / Firm elatant.' Harrison mentions the end of a Greek drama, which finishes 'not with a "curtain", not with a great decisive moment, but with the appearance of a god who says a few lines of either exhortation or consolation or reconciliation' (*Ancient Art and Ritual*, p. 120). So also ends the pageant, with the 'loud-speaking affirmation' (*BA*, 1969, p. 186) of a voice. We might assume the voice is La Trobe's although Woolf describes it as an anonymous, megaphonic voice. Nevertheless, it rings omniscient and is indeed in the form of an exhortation, a call to 'calmly consider ourselves' (p. 187). Then Harrison speaks about the plot, which oftentimes is given in its entirety in the prologue, so that the modern viewer is robbed of her/his customary anticipatory excitement. Isa mentions that it is the emotion, not the plot, that matters; prologues are spoken and the programme oftentimes tells the viewer exactly what will happen, what has happened in the gap, or what must be imagined.

Harrison continues her discussion of the chorus, once again emphasising the strangeness of it all: 'At the back of our modern discontent there is lurking always this queer anomaly of the chorus' (*Ancient Art and Ritual*, p. 121). After stating that those 'odd effects' of prologues, messenger's speeches and choruses are ritual forms that have continued to survive in the drama, Harrison again speaks of the chorus in a passage that reminds us of Woolf's essay 'The Narrow Bridge of Art', and her hopes for what that as-yet-unnamed novel of the future will be able to achieve:

Suppose that these choral songs have been put into English that in any way represents the beauty of the Greek; then certainly there will be some among the spectators who get a thrill from the chorus quite unknown to any modern stage effect, a feeling of emotion heightened yet restrained, a sense of entering into higher places, filled with a larger and a purer air – a sense of beauty born clean out of conflict and disaster.   (*Ancient Art and Ritual*, p. 122)

In describing the physical set-up for the performance of Greek drama, Harrison says that 'the kernel and centre of the whole was the *orchestra*, the circular *dancing-place* of the chorus' (p. 123). The theatre was the place where the spectators sat and was made up of tiered stone seats; prior to that, the orchestra was placed next to a steep hill, which accommodated the viewers just as well. The scene, or skene, was a 'tent or hut in which the actors dressed' (p. 123).

As Harrison further describes the chorus, we can hear the echoes of 'digging and delving' reiterated by the chorus in *Between the Acts*: 'The chorus danced and sang that Dithyramb we know so well, and from the leaders of that Dithyramb we remember tragedy arose, and the chorus were at first, as an ancient writer tells us, just men and boys, tillers of the earth, who danced when they rested from sowing and ploughing' (*Ancient Art and Ritual*, p. 124).

In discussing the shift in the relationship between the orchestra and theatre Harrison continues,

If we want to realise the primitive Greek orchestra or dancing-place, we must think these stone seats away. Threshing-floors are used in Greece to-day as convenient dancing-places. The dance tends to be circular because it is round some sacred thing, at first a maypole, or the reaped corn, later the figure of a god or his altar. On this dancing-place the whole body of worshippers would gather, just as now-a-days the whole community will assemble on a village green. There is no division at first between actors and spectators; all are actors, all are doing the thing done, dancing the dance danced. . . . No one at this early stage thinks of building a *theatre*, a spectator place. It is in the common act, the common or collective emotion, that ritual starts.   (pp. 125–6)

So we see that there is an increasing distance set up between spectator and actor, so that the spectator becomes a viewer, no longer participating in the dance but involved in a removed process of abstraction.

What moves behind *Ancient Art and Ritual* is Harrison's steadfast belief that the morality of art lies in its social and collective aspects. As she continues in the fifth chapter to speak of the introduction of Homeric poetry and the heroic saga, she recognises the importance of its effect on Greek drama and further literature, but is clearly not drawn to a heroic age, with its emphasis on individual deeds based in war. As Harrison says, the scene of the heroic saga is the warrior's tent or ship, not the hearth; the individual is privileged over the group, which serves only as a background for the brilliant exploits of the hero.[20] This belief in the communal properties of art continue into Harrison's last chapter, 'Ritual, Art, and Life', in which she discusses modern art:

> There are not wanting signs that art, both in painting and sculpture, and in poetry and novel-writing, is beginning again to realize its social function, beginning to be impatient of mere indivdual emotion, beginning to aim at something bigger, more bound up with a feeling towards and for the common weal.   (pp. 245–6)

Literature written in the interest of social change must exact participation and involvement on the part of the consumer. La Trobe wants to 'draw blood' from her audience, to bind them in an emotionally jarring grip just as Woolf wants to jostle her readers out of acquiescence and apathy. Woolf attempts this by interchanging and blending the roles of spectator and chorus. The ever-present chorus occasionally acts as spectator when, for example, the group gathers round Queen Elizabeth's throne 'as if to form the audience at a play' (*BA*, 1969, p. 87). The spectators, on the other hand, have a choral function. Like the chorus of the pageant, they remain for the most part an amorphous group of villagers without proper names. Their comments on the pageant or on other topics can be seen as choral refrains given in passages of broken phrases that read like the choral texts within the pageant. The final reflective confrontation between actors/ audience does achieve a measure of unity and collective participation out of the dispersal and discord; for a moment, all are engaged: 'On different levels ourselves went forward; flower gathering some on the surface; others descending to wrestle with the meaning; but all comprehending; all enlisted' (p. 189).

*Between the Acts* is an urgent book. Virginia Woolf wrote her last novel amidst falling bombs. But the novel-play itself is set in June 1939, on a pastoral summer day overshadowed by bomb-laden planes; it is in the moment before Britian entered the war, a moment when voiced dissent should be heard. To call Woolf's work 'the longest suicide note in the English language', as Mitchell Leaska does, is to ignore the social import of the book. Leaska's publication and annotation of the Earlier and Later Typescripts of *Between the Acts* is indeed a valuable resource for anyone studying the novel. However, the Virginia Woolf given to us by Leaska in his Introduction and Afterword is moulded in the tradition of Quentin Bell, who also offers us a portrait of the brilliant artist controlled by the insanity of genius. This produces a criticism that is reduced to the psychology of the writer as egocentric individual and does little towards an understanding of *Between the Acts*. Copious and provocative footnotes, such as the ones detailing the Isis/Osiris references, could well lead to perceptive and helpful readings of the novel. The possibility of such readings unfortunately remains in the footnotes, since Leaska never incorporates that information in his Introduction or Afterword but remains caught within the preoccupations with Woolf's writing ego, as this passage indicates:

> For her, however, war did not carry just the ordinary meaning of devastation and loss of life. . . War meant to her something far less accessible to common understanding: it meant having no audience; no readers; no echo. And having no echo, she wrote, was 'part of one's death'. This may seem a little strange to those of us who do not rely on the public for private indemnity. But she did. And she knew better than anyone that art was the first thing to be jettisoned from the habits of daily life in a time of stress. . . No one knew better than she did that without the echo, there could be no Virginia Woolf. (*PH*, pp. 6–7).

What I hope to have shown through a reading of Harrison's work as a means of interpreting *Between the Acts* is that art has everything to do with times of stress. The crisis of war required Woolf as a pacifist to voice dissent in works such as *Three Guineas*,

*Between the Acts* and 'Thoughts on Peace in an Air Raid'. The echo is still there and the reverberations from these writings shake us even as we sit on the precipice of nuclear holocaust. In *Between the Acts* it is precisely through the process of art, in the creation of the novel-play, that Woolf passionately challenges her readers to cease being silent spectators and to take on the task of acting their unacted parts. As readers, spectators, artists and critics, we should do well to heed the challenge.

NOTES

1. For their help on information regarding Jane Harrison and Greek and Egyptian mythology, I am indebted to Jane Marcus, Kay Turner and Daniel Dawson.

2. Jane Ellen Harrison, *Ancient Art and Ritual* (London: Henry Holt, 1913) p. 218.

3. For further information on Woolf as an autodidact through reading, see Louise DeSalvo's '1897: Virginia Woolf at Fifteen: "the first really *lived* year of my life"', in *Virginia Woolf: A Feminist Slant*, ed. Jane Marcus (Lincoln, Nebr.: University of Nebraska Press, 1983); Brenda Silver's edn of *Virginia Woolf's Reading Notebooks* (Princeton, NJ: Princeton University Press, 1983); and Martine Stemerick's 'The Madonna's Clay Feet', in *Virginia Woolf: Centennial Essays*, ed. Elaine Ginsberg (Troy, NY: Whitston Press, 1983).

4. In a 1928 posthumous address on Jane Harrison, the then Regius Professor of Greek in the University of Oxford, Gilbert Murray, said this of Harrison's *Prolegomena to the Study of Greek Religion*: 'It is not too much to say that they [the first chapters] have transformed the whole approach to the study of Greek religion. No competent student writing after the *Prolegomena* operates with the same conceptions and problems in his mind as were almost universally accepted before the *Prolegomena*. It is a book which, in the current phrase, made an epoch.' – Gilbert Murray, *Jane Ellen Harrison: An Address*, delivered at Newnham College, 27 Oct 1928 (Cambridge: W. Heffer, 1928) pp. 11–12. It is in the light of this accolade that one should view Harrison's turning-away from Cambridge and the paucity of information available on her.

5. Jane Ellen Harrison, *Reminiscences of a Student's Life* (London: Hogarth Press, 1925) pp. 88–9. Further references appear in the text.

6. For an excellent discussion of the feminist politics in 'A Society', *Three Guineas* and *Between the Acts*, see Jane Marcus, 'Liberty, Sorority, Misogyny', in *The Representation of Women in Fiction*, ed. Carolyn G. Heilbrun and Margaret R. Higonnet, Selected Papers from the English Institute, 1981, n.s., no.7 (Baltimore: Johns Hopkins University Press, 1983).

7. See Jane Marcus, '*The Years* as Greek Drama, Domestic Novel, and Götterdämerung', *BNYPL*, LXXX, no.2 (Winter 1977) 276–301, and the continuation of this article, 'Pargeting *The Pargiters*: Notes of an Apprentice Plasterer', *BNYPL*, LXXX, no. 3 (Spring 1978) 416–35.

8. See Grace Radin's excellent book, *Virginia Woolf's 'The Years': The Evolution of a Novel* (Knoxville: University of Tennessee Press, 1981). Radin offers much helpful material from typescripts. This includes material edited out by Mitchell Leaska in his edn of *The Pargiters*; Radin's book reveals a much angrier, occasionally less than decorous Virginia Woolf.

9. To expand upon this would require another paper. But a brief enumeration of Brechtian elements might be as follows:

(a) Epic theatre relies on the retelling of a familiar historical event or fable; *Between the Acts* takes English history as its story. The exclusion of the British Army, in this context, is a strong commentary.

(b) The style of acting requires a self-consciousness on the actor's part that creates a distance between actor and part; the actors in *Between the Acts* are recognised as villagers with particular local identities and their costumes are made up of familiar household objects.

(c) The quotability of an actor's gestures is accomplished through programme notes, spectators' comments and the clergyman's speech. The novel-play form makes this a particularly rich area of investigation.

(d) The 'A-effect' (alienation effect or process of estrangement) is effected through the chorus and a combination of dramatic effects in the music and atmospheric interruptions. The mirror scene at the end is an ultimate example of recognition and estrangement, the making strange of what is familiar.

For more information, see Bertolt Brecht's 'A Short Organum for the Theatre' and Walter Benjamin's *A Study on Brecht*.

10. Virginia Woolf, 'The Narrow Bridge of Art', in *Granite and Rainbow* (New York: Harcourt, Brace and World, 1958). The essay was first published in the *New York Herald Tribune* on 14 Aug 1927. I should not have discovered this essay if it had not been for Jane Harrison's image of the ritual bridge between religion and art; it was because of that image that my eye was caught by the title of Woolf's essay. Page references are given in the text.

11. Poetry winds itself throughout *Between the Acts*. If we look at *PH*, Appendix D we find all the poems for *Between the Acts*. This might indicate that Woolf had questions about how to incorporate the poetry, if she did write it all in one lump and then scattered it throughout the novel.

12. Jane Ellen Harrison, *Epilegomena to the Study of Greek Religion* (Cambridge: Cambridge University Press, 1921). It might be worth mentioning that in a mere forty pages Harrison refers to several authors,

literary works and themes embedded in *Between the Acts*. They are the Hamlet saga compared to the Orestes saga, Don Juan and Keats.

13. Most of Harrison's anthropological examples are taken from Frazer's *The Golden Bough*, rather than any original field work.

14. Harrison, *Epilegomena*, p.9.

15. Evelyn Haller, 'Isis Unveiled', in *Virginia Woolf: A Feminist Slant* ed. Jane Marcus (Lincoln, Nebr.: University of Nebraska Press, 1983).

16. For a discussion of the rape as a rewrite of the Procne–Philomela myth, see Marcus, 'Liberty, Sorority, Misogyny', in *The Representation of Women in Fiction*.

17. Haller, 'Isis Unveiled', in *Virginia Woolf: A Feminist Slant* , p. 113.

18. For a discussion of language in the novel–play, see Sallie Sears, 'Theatre of War: Virginia Woolf's *Between the Acts*', ibid.

19. See Jane Marcus, 'A Wilderness of One's Own: Feminist Fantasy Novels of the Twenties: Rebecca West and Sylvia Townsend Warner', in *Women Writers and the City*, ed. Susan Squier (Knoxville: University of Tennessee Press, 1984).

20. Harrison shared with Woolf a dislike of the state, as this passage from the *Reminiscences* illustrates: 'I hate the Empire; it stands to me for all that is tedious and pernicious in thought; within it are always the seeds of war. I object to nearly all forms of patriotism' (p. 11).

# Index